D0838883

RED

RIGHT

RETURN

JOHN H. CUNNINGHAM

Red Right Return: A Buck Reilly Adventure

Published by Wheatmark®
1760 East River Road, Suite 145, Tucson, Arizona 85718 USA
www.wheatmark.com

ISBN: 978-1-60494-704-5
LCCN: 2011938646

The events and characters in this book are fictitious. Certain real locations and public figures are mentioned, but have been used fictitiously, and all other characters and events in the book have been invented.

www.jhcunningham.com

Acknowledgements: For their help with this book, the author is particularly grateful to Ross Browne, Renni Browne, Peter Gelfan and the entire team at The Editorial Department, Widgeon pilot and flight instructor Chester Lawson, fellow author Robert Gandt, my agent Steve Troha at Folio Literary Management, the Ortega family for such great memories, Chris, Bert and Jill for your encouragement, and special thanks to Holly, Bailey and Cortney.

Note: The Compleat Angler burned to the ground a couple years ago, so the scene herein pays homage to the historic watering hole…

This book is dedicated to my parents,
Cortlandt and Betty Cunningham

I miss you

Contents

Fair Winds and Past Sins

1

Fort Jefferson was visible in the distance, seventy miles from Key West, another outcast in the Florida straits. The Civil War fortress beckoned me, but I turned back to this morning's surprise, a beautiful, unscheduled one-way charter customer whose replies to my inquiries were met with hundred-dollar bills but no name.

My name's Buck Reilly, but don't bother to Google me. You won't find a thing. I used to go by my full name, it ended with "the third." Going broke forces you to change things, sometimes even your identity. Skills, however, can be recycled. Being a pilot taught me to travel light, a necessary talent in my new circumstances...

As we flew over the shimmering azure waters that morning, images of the past played out in my mind. Landing on a grass strip in the Andes, flying down narrow tributaries of the Rio Negro, a rough take off from a rock field outside Katmandu. And then there was the time I flew blind in a sand storm over Egypt, or taxiing over the flats near Porto Bello. I let out a long breath. I missed the adventure and excitement from my e-Antiquity days, but not much else.

Our destination appeared as a white spot on the horizon, and we closed the distance fast. We circled the boat once before landing in the light chop. A handful of men stared back from the transom, distorted by a thin mist of exhaust rising off the occasional boil from the captain's attempts to keep the craft straight in the press of the Gulf Stream. We taxied with the vent windows open, the sound of Betty's twin engines loud inside the cabin.

"Show me on the map where we are?"

I slowly unfolded the chart, pointed to the fort, then dragged my finger due west to our approximate location. Her eyes lingered on the eastern side.

"What's all that?" Numerous grid squares were crosshatched with pencil, pen, and magic marker. "Some kind of treasure map?"

I placed it back under my leg. "The company is Last Resort Charter and Salvage. You're a charter, that's salvage."

Calling Last Resort a company was a stretch. I take the occasional charter, if it interests me, but the salvage work is more diverse. Lost items to lost souls. When my first company, e-Antiquity, crashed I lost everything. Funny thing, it wasn't the money that mattered. Wealth only fueled the lust to acquire crap: cars, houses, toys, even relationships. The false Gods of Mercedes, Palm Beach, Wall Street, Gulfstream and Stock Portfolio had been a spiritual pursuit, but when the money was gone I needed a new place of worship. None of the *stuff* was left, but it was the flight of friends that hurt most. Success attracts, and failure repels. Especially in relationships.

We closed the distance, and my concern for the transfer was resolved when a lone man operating a rubber inflatable boat, Zodiac, or something similar was launched. With a tug on the throttles, Betty's propellers slowed immediately, and the green float under her port wing settled into the water.

"You have a welcoming committee," I said.

She flashed her white teeth. Part Latin, or maybe African-American and white—whatever her heritage, I found her exotic pale almond eyes hypnotic. Only the slight tang of perspiration belied her air of confidence.

Most pilots wouldn't accept an anonymous customer who paid in cash. It wasn't that I lacked ethics or good sense, or that I'd knowingly do something illegal, but times were tough and work was hard to come by. Besides, risk never bothered me, especially when my survival depended on it.

The Zodiac bounced towards us without altering its course to avoid the swells. The girl's sphinx-like smile returned as she watched the boat approach. I lifted the side hatch to a gust of thick salt air.

"This is it, Miss…"

Her eyes lit toward the hovering Zodiac. At the helm was a large black kid in a bright blue polo shirt. He gave my Grumman Widgeon flying boat a quick once-over and shook his head.

"You're crazy, girl!"

She slid from the edge of the hatch onto the boat's rubber bow and into the seat next to him. He looked more like he belonged on a football field than here in the gulf. Her "Thank you" blew like a kiss—my final reward.

I tucked her five hundred in my breast pocket and ducked back into the cockpit. The Zodiac retreated slowly to the mother ship, where the other men watched, unsmiling. Not the greeting you'd expect for a pretty woman. The boat was a good size, maybe fifty-five feet, with the lines of an old Bertram and a smart-looking red stripe along its side. As the girl pulled herself aboard, the name *Carnival* was legible above the water. She'd never said where she got my number, but now that she was safely delivered, my job was done. The bonus was that her drop point left me near the next open grid on the chart.

2

While I may not miss the money, much, I still crave
the hunt for treasure. My remaining assets from e-Antiquity were a handful of
commandeered ancient maps, letters and clues for the location of lost artifacts,
which if nothing more, provided me with a mental diversion from my own past.
The idea of actually finding something, however, terrified me, as I would be faced
with a concept I had sworn off - success.

I slid my finger over the squares already marked with X's. After eighteen
months of searching, the only result had been the occasional gratification of crossing off another section. With something like two hundred wrecks littering the
waters of the Dry Tortugas, finding an uncharted one required incredible luck,
cutting edge technology, and blind faith. With only the latter, the outcome was
no surprise. Treasure map, indeed.

My brother, Ben, once characterized any search for treasure as a fool's errand.
That's what he said when I started e-Antiquity, too. Until it made him rich. He
was always the conservative son, while I was out scouring the world. It's no wonder he thinks I'm irresponsible.

Mel Fisher of Treasure Salvors always said, "Today's the day," but it took
him thirteen years to find the half-billion-dollar wreck of the *La Nuestra Señora
de Atocha*. Aside from the fact that I lacked his patience and resources, sneaking
around national park waters forced discretion. Otherwise I could be towing the

improvised metal detector behind Betty instead of searching at a tenth the speed in my over-laden kayak.

The information from the 1933 letter from Ernest Hemingway to his editor describing a six-foot section of solid gold chain found wrapped around their anchor while fishing these waters was the hook, and to my knowledge, nobody else had ever taken the bait. Maybe—

The gray noise of emptiness that clattered in my headphones suddenly changed pitch. Most likely another false alarm, but the digital read-out pinged higher than most of the junk I'd found. Much higher. I paddled in a circle, methodically working to define the size of the anomaly. It was roughly twenty feet square.

The sky was clouded over, so I couldn't see into the water, but my anchor rope indicated the depth was nearly thirty feet. I secured the loose gear, donned mask, fins and the 19 p.s.i. pony tank that would give me twenty minutes of air at this depth, based on normal breathing. A last glance at the darkening sky made me hurry my pace.

I slid into the water and the whoosh of bubbles from my regulator brushed past my ears as I began to descend. A bulky coral head materialized in the gloom, surrounded by turtle grass, brain coral and a field of dead staghorn coral. How many times had I dove on similar formations, only to find garbage, old lobster pots or worthless wreckage? Isn't the definition of insanity the repeated attempts at a futile task with the same results? Or is that persistence?

The current increased with the depth and I swam against it to the far end of the mass so I could drift over the largest section. Once in position I let the flow carry me back. A quick shimmer caught my eye, right at the base of the up-current edge of the formation. The color was…I spun and kicked hard into the current, peering over the rocky edge until I saw it again. My heart thudded.

The water carried me back over the mass, but my mind was fixated on the three inch-square image I saw near the bottom. The color, brilliant and radiant, unaltered after how many years underwater? Or centuries?

3

Whether wishful thinking, or the result of having
read the patchwork history so many times, the recently discovered connections cut
a familiar groove in my mind. It was in 1621 when Governor Gíron of Cartagena
had sent a surprise wedding gift aboard the *Esmeralda*, a small, nondescript
galleon, to King Philip IV and Queen Elisabeth of Spain. Since it was a non-
official transport and thereby undocumented in Seville, no record of its journey
was ever noted in the royal archives. And since it never arrived, the king and
queen were oblivious to its existence.

The governor died shortly after the *Esmeralda* sailed, so the lack of recognition of his generosity never upset his renowned sensitivities. The existence of the
Esmeralda remained unknown for 350 years, until a Colombian biographer on
behalf of the University of Cartagena chronicled Gíron's reign, making note of the
gift referred to in the former governor's private diary.

I smiled. Thank God for the Spanish historians who challenged the work,
which splashed the news of the *Esmeralda's* existence onto headlines worldwide.
According to the limited information they cobbled together, the ship had a crew
and passengers of ninety people, and even though it didn't carry near the treasure
of the storied *Atocha*, the governor's journal entry summarized two dozen crates
of gold bars, fifty crates of silver bars, eight crates of emeralds, an unspecified
number of jewels, and a vast number of silver pieces of four and eight, not to

mention gold doubloons. A chill ran down my spine at the most recent estimates that valued the treasure in excess of twenty million dollars.

The fate of the *Esmeralda* may have remained a mystery, if it weren't for two eyewitness accounts from half-mad castaways found on an uninhabited island somewhere between Havana and Miami. They claimed to have been aboard a ship sanctioned by Gíron destined for Spain that was lost in a storm in 1621. How many times had I studied Spanish shipping routes of the time, the documented paths of galleons, the accounts of storms for the era, and cross-referenced them with the date the ship sailed from Havana, all of which led me to the area between the Marquesas to what today is Sugarloaf Key?

Until I found the obscure reference in a letter from Ernest Hemingway to his editor about the gold chain pulled up from the sea bottom on his anchor that led me to the Dry Tortugas.

And maybe, just maybe to the *Esmeralda?*

4

I fought back against the press of water, and even
in the sunless depths, the shimmer of gold sparkled briefly. I avoided a wall
of black sea urchins that threatened to perforate my palms and grabbed the
rough edge of a small coral fissure. I pulled myself toward the glistening
object, which was embedded in eons of sea growth. Using my dive knife,
I scraped at the coral, but the current was too strong to hold on with one
hand.

With the knife under my armpit and both hands on the lip of the crevice,
I drew myself closer. I tried to wedge my knee into the coral hole, but a sudden
sharp pain tore at my shin—I lost my grip. As the water carried me back, a fat
green moray eel darted halfway out of the hole and glared back at me.

There was no blood, so at least its sharp teeth hadn't punctured my skin. I
again swam up and drifted past the mound and wondered whether I could have
found the *Esmeralda*.

My pursuit of treasure used to be based on greed, a lust for recognition,
anticipation of more headlines and of e-Antiquity's stock skyrocketing yet again.
I sensed the familiar tingle in my hands, a numbness caused by excitement and
adrenalin. Those desires were foreign now, and the last thing I wanted.

I was alone, floating above a lump of ocean bottom that promised or threatened to reinstate my world to a life of material comfort and excess—

My rapid breathing came to a sudden halt—

The air gauge read zero!

I kicked hard toward the top, a growing fire aflame in my lungs. The distance seemed like a thousand feet until I burst through the surface.

I gasped for air and felt as if sweat was bursting from my head—not sweat, but rain, pounding rain. The storm that had been thrashing the southern straits most of the day was upon me. The kayak was anchored thirty yards away, into the current. Already exhausted, the effort it took to get there left my legs cramped. Thunder clapped as I climbed aboard and commenced to paddle into a black curtain of driving rain. Fort Jefferson was invisible in the reduced visibility, but my GPS showed that it was over half-mile away to—I stopped suddenly—the coral head! How would I find it again? I hit the 'mark' button on the GPS, then placed a quick 'x' on the soggy grid square where I thought the mound had been.

Hunched over in the six-foot sit-on-top kayak, I flogged the oars so hard my stomach muscles cramped like seized pistons. I ran ashore in front of the perfect hexagon of Fort Jefferson before I saw its brick walls, still cloaked in mist. Seeking shelter on-island would be smart, but the plane's anchorage would never hold under the force of this storm.

Whitecaps erupted in the shallows.

Green mangrove branches sagged under the driving rain, and their clotted mass of roots smelled of excrement. Cormorants and an egret hunched in the web of leaves as I sliced past. A flash of lightning lit the sky, followed closely by a roar of thunder that reverberated in my gut. The edge of the island was ahead, and a stiff headwind blew around the corner.

Betty was there, her bow-mounted anchor line pulled taut, her fuselage white against the black horizon. With no time for an orderly transfer of equipment I jumped into the waist-deep water, pushed in my gear, then the kayak and dove in. I scrambled into the left seat, stuffed the crosshatched chart into the waterproof pouch that bulged with several others, then jammed the packet into the makeshift slot under my seat.

Fool's errand?

Success, by most people's standards, had nothing to do with it. I've been driven to do what people tell me can't be done my entire life. Whether compulsion, or curse, I had a knack for the hunt. The pursuit of discovery sucked me in, even if my goals were different now. I was hooked on experience, excitement and challenge. Money was just a sideline—a necessary evil. If that lump back there was the *Esmeralda*, though, we'll see how those platitudes hold up.

The scene through the windshield cut short my reverie. I had to get out of here, and fast. I'd never completed my instrument rating and now I'd be taking on the storm with no pre-flight preparation whatsoever.

The sky and horizon had grown seamless, liquid, and were closing in fast.

I pulled anchor, fumbled with the fuel mixtures, primed the fuel pumps, and fired up the twin Lycoming engines. Jockeying the rudder with slippery toes, I maneuvered Betty toward the black wall of water and shoved the throttles halfway forward.

A loud cough sputtered from the port engine.

"Not now, Betty!"

Guilt pierced my heart for doubting the old girl, but she'd been built in 1946, and I couldn't help questioning her ability to muster the oomph to pull us out of the mess my failure to anticipate the storm had us in. It was like counting on your grandmother to carry you from a burning building.

The port engine caught and the hull jolted on course. Waves crashed over the windshield while I fought to hold Betty straight. Water detonated in all directions as we gained speed. I grappled with the controls to keep the nose high. Seconds passed at an excruciating pace. I stole a glance at the airspeed indicator and when I looked up, a waterspout was telescoping down from a leaden cloud directly ahead. Without fifteen more knots to escape the ocean's grasp, a collision with the liquid tornado would—

A sudden shout filled my headset. Words cascaded in, what, Spanish? The voice's urgency felt like a reprimand from God himself, but only one word registered: "Mayday!"

Something else sounded in the background—was it screaming?

We bounced onto a large wave and shot into the air. I nearly pushed the ceiling- mounted throttle through the roof, simultaneously stomping the left rudder to the floor, which spun Betty into a turn that almost forced her wing back into the same wave that had set us free. The waterspout reached out for Betty's starboard wing tip but we blew past and up into the black clouds.

The Mayday proved I wasn't the only idiot the storm had caught by surprise, but since the voice was in Spanish, finding their location would be hopeless. Any missed salvage opportunity irked me, but the hesitation in Betty's port engine threatened to turn us into one.

After acknowledging my approach into Key West airport, Donny, the air traffic controller, uncharacteristically broke the code of the airwaves.

"Jeez, Buck, looks here on the screen like you're coming out of the gates of hell. Called that one a little close, didn't you?"

I pictured the glistening glimmer on the coral head. "Closer than you think, Donny. Do me a favor and tell Ray Floyd to meet me on the tarmac. Betty's showing her age, again. Grumman one-seven-four-one-November out."

The old Widgeon banked around the corner of Key West, past the remains of Fort Zachary Taylor, the Southernmost Point, the Casa Marina, White Street pier, Smather's Beach, and down to land on runway 9 into the northeastern wind. The rain had yet to hit the island, and the sun lit its colors like an impressionist pallet. As I taxied to the end of the runway I looked down and saw my one-of-a-kind key out loose on the floor. It must have fallen from the pouch when I put the maps away. The same maps that I had liberated from e-Antiquity before the regulators shut us down.

By the time I'd finished with the post-flight checklist, Ray Floyd, resident aircraft mechanic and flower-clad philosophical guru, was there to greet me.

"How do you want it to read?" he said.

"What are you talking about?"

"Your obituary. 'Bankrupt entrepreneur cum charter pilot dies chasing dreams, antique plane now artificial reef.'"

"I'd rather die chasing dreams, than old and dreaming of the chase." I wanted to mention the gold, but knew I better not.

"Then we need to keep this old girl in the air."

"Speaking of which, Betty's port engine was backfiring, can you check it out?"

"I'm up to my elbows in airworthiness inspections—couple of days all right?"

"The sooner the better." I paused. "You hear the Mayday during that storm?"

"Nothing came through the tower. Should I check to see if any boats are missing?" On several occasions Ray and I had flown out together, with him returning by air and me at the helm of a repossessed or ailing boat. I hated repo work, but it had steadily been on the rise, and helped to keep me afloat.

"No point with Betty acting up," I said.

I wondered where this morning's mystery woman had been headed. She'd never said, but that had been hours ago.

Inside the Conch Flyer, Susie Pizzuti gave me two fingers of Barbancourt four-star rum and a lecture on not getting myself killed hunting wrecks. I bit my lip, fighting back the urge to tell her—anybody, for that matter—that I found gold. I felt like an alcoholic who had discovered a gigantic still. Desire was overwhelming, but the ramifications held me at bay. Plus, if word got out, every boat in Key West would light out with gold fever, whether they knew the location or not.

My imagination, of course, ran wild with scenarios.

5

Still soaked, I headed back to my sixth-floor
apartment at the La Concha Hotel in the heart of Old Town. The suite had been
an office when the hotel was built in 1927. I rented it on a month-to-month basis
and enjoyed the second tallest vantage point on the island. The only thing higher
was The Top, the rooftop lounge above me, and I had a private staircase right
to its balcony. What began as a temporary situation at one of the island's oldest
hotels had become my semi-permanent residence.

The picture on the dresser of me and my parents ringing the bell at the New
York Stock Exchange the day e-Antiquity went public bore no resemblance to me
now. Except for the blue eyes. Heather, my ex-wife, used to say my eyes made her
feel like I could look into her soul. If only I could have. It might have saved a lot
of heartache.

My old GQ image reminded me I was twice due for a haircut. Short and
slicked in the photo, my hair was now straw-colored and wild, hanging over my
shoulders like weeds. Armani suits had been replaced by shorts and flip-flops. The
world had broken and taken me down with it. And a whole lot of people who
trusted us, too. I didn't much like what I had been, and I damned sure didn't want
to repeat those mistakes, but if that was the *Esmeralda* out there off Garden Key,
the quiet world I had created may be blown wide open.

A flashing light caught my eye. Phone messages usually meant opportunity or trouble.

"Mr. Reilly? This is Willy Peebles here at Redeemer. I got your number from Lenny Jackson." *Conch Man?* "I have a serious problem, and I…or *we*, could use your help. Time's of the essence, so please, call me. God bless you."

The Church of the Redeemer. Why would Bahama Village's hard-case reformation center need me?

Betty's ailments and today's discovery put all of Last Resort's work on hold. After the day's near disaster I appreciated his blessing, and wondered why Conch Man was hanging out with the tough-love preacher. Instead of returning the good pastor's call, I dug out all the articles and loosely assembled facts about the *Esmeralda*, wondering again if it was her amidst the depths of the Dry Tortugas.

6

The storm that nearly finished me never reached
Key West, raging up through the gulf instead. A quick jaunt down the stairs led
me to the hotel lobby where the sound of my leather flip-flops slapped against the
terrazzo floor and raised nods from the familiar faces of the staff.

"Hey, flyboy?"

If the southern accent hadn't given her away, Karen Parks' nickname for me
would have. The hotel day manager's smile drew me to the mahogany and granite
reception counter.

"Have you given any thought to what I asked you?" She glanced quickly
toward my feet.

"Ah, sure, the Old Island Days festival. Nothing's come to me yet."

She'd signed on to be the festival's Chairman of Special Events, the latest in
an endless series of commitments her nurturing heart had driven her to make. Yet
another language I didn't speak: volunteerism.

"The festival's in two weeks and I'm starting to get desperate." She flashed
the smile again, pulling me closer. "I did have an idea you could help me with,
though."

"Nice to know you think of me when you're desperate."

"With your plane, flyboy." She pressed her lips together, stifling a smile. "By the way, Lenny Jackson was looking for you, said it's urgent. He seemed upset, no big smile and no flirting."

"That's a bad sign, Conch Man not flirting."

She batted her eyelashes. "About your plane?"

"She's in for service."

"For two weeks?" Her blond hair was tied up in a ponytail, which emphasized the long curve of her neck. She lifted a plastic clad newspaper. "Your *Wall Street Journal's* here—"

"Toss it—"

"…And your monthly FedEx envelope came."

Inside was the usual copy of a deposit slip. What's this? A note on Fox Run Farm stationary: *I haven't heard from you in months. This is it until I do. B.*

"Bad news?" Karen said.

My sigh must have been audible. "Something like that. I'll catch you later."

"You okay?" she called down the hall after me.

I waved without turning back. Once around the corner I stopped in front of an oil painting of a tropical courtyard to read the note again.

Shit! Why now, Ben? Our relationship had deteriorated, thanks to the ongoing investigation into our parent's deaths, and I really wasn't surprised he'd finally cut me off, but the timing couldn't have been worse.

Outside, I tripped over a chicken pecking at the asphalt. The hen was leashed to the bike rack and had a pink ribbon around its neck. The Chicken Rescue League was another of Karen's causes. She used colored ribbons to mark protected birds.

The smell of bougainvillea permeated tepid air, and unseasonable humidity quickly dampened my shirt. I unlocked my red bike, turned onto Fleming, and tried to remember what my plans were before getting the note. What started as a meandering path focused into a defined location. If my financial lifeline was being cut off, there was no choice but to point my bow into the waves. Opportunity was on the horizon, and I needed gas money to continue the hunt.

Several blocks later I arrived at Bahama Village,
the oldest settlement on the island. Known as Jungle Town when I first visited Key
West as a child in the late 70's, it was a calaloo of Cuban, African, Haitian, and
Bahamian ingredients that remained the historically black area. A chipped white
steeple pierced the palm canopy ahead. The neighborhood was normally quiet on
a Tuesday afternoon, and I was surprised at the number of people gathered by the
church. So many that they were spilling into the street.

I didn't bother locking my bike, less worried about these folks than the
drunken tourists at the opposite end of Duval Street. All conversation stopped at
my approach, and unfamiliar faces stared at me.

"Pastor Peebles around?"

Nothing.

A commotion stirred from inside the open door, and everyone turned to look.
"I'm talking an eye for an eye, Willy, nothing less!" someone yelled from inside.

I pushed my way to the door where a man in a tight black T-shirt spun on me.
His eyes were bloodshot, and something between concern and anger distorted his
handsome features.

"What are you, the press?"

His question wouldn't have surprised me more had he asked if I was here to
give a sermon.

"Buck, that you?" Lenny Jackson's short, muscular figure stepped forward from behind the small group.

"Lenny, who the hell's—"

He grabbed my arm, pulling me aside. "Real quick, man, I need to talk to you before you meet Willy."

An elderly light-skinned black man stepped out from behind him. He wore small round eyeglasses but was broad-shouldered and nearly as tall as me at six-two. Lenny stood frozen, uncharacteristically speechless. I extended my hand.

"Buck Reilly."

The man's grip was strong, his palm dry. He put a heavy hand on Lenny's shoulder and moved him aside.

"Sorry for the greeting." He glared at the guy in the black T-shirt. "But Manny here is...well, everyone's upset. I'm Willy Peebles. From everything I've heard I'm surprised we haven't met sooner."

"Willy?" Lenny was fidgeting like a child in need of the bathroom. "Can I talk to Buck before—"

"I'll see Mr. Reilly alone now, Lenny."

If he weren't black as the night sea I'd have sworn Lenny was turning red. It was the first time I'd ever seen Conch Man at a loss for words.

Pastor Peebles led me down the short aisle of the simple sanctuary. We left Lenny rubbing the sparse whiskers on his chin. The church had white walls, square windows, and a rough-hewn podium with a small cross of dark wood hanging behind it. We entered a dimly lit corridor that had three doors. He opened the middle one, which turned out to be his office. To my surprise, the guy in the black T-shirt—Manny—followed us in.

Inside, there was an old wood desk covered with neatly stacked piles of paper and a few folding chairs placed against walls covered with old black and white photographs, faces from an era gone by. None were smiling.

I had the distinct recollection of going to the principal's office as a kid.

Silence followed after we all sat. Pastor Peebles eyed me up and down, his gaze penetrating, his expression intense. He drew in a slow breath and held it. Was he having second thoughts?

"What do you know about the Church of the Redeemer, Mr. Reilly?"

"My father was *Mr.* Reilly, call me Buck."

"Your father's dead, right? Your mother too?" I swallowed and glanced at Manny, whose red eyes were simmering in their sockets.

I cleared my throat. "Redeemer's the oldest church on the island, isn't it? With a reputation for steering young troublemakers back onto the straight and narrow?"

"Adults, too." He raised his eyebrows. "We're old-island here, hanging on to the simpler times, before drunken money lined Key West's streets. We do what's needed to maintain a tranquil setting. Up until today."

Manny grunted and crossed his arms. His face had strong lines, a thin neat mustache, and golden skin that glowed like it was buffed.

Willy glanced at his telephone. "Tell me about yourself."

"Sounds as if you know my story."

"All I know is that you live in a hotel and run a low-budget charter service."

"Charter and salvage, I do—"

"I know all about you, Buck," Manny said. "Or should I call you, *King Charles?*"

What the hell?

"King Charles?" Willy said.

"Few years ago there was a picture on the cover of the *Wall Street Journal* of this guy sitting on top of a huge pile of Mayan treasure. Only back then his name wasn't Buck. The headline read, "King Charles hits the mother lode!" A real modern day pirate, our pilot."

"Those days are over," I said. "Besides, Buck's my middle name!"

"His company was a NASDAQ darling that plundered ancient artifacts and sold them on-line. Until the global economy cratered, and then, like any good pirate would, Buck turned and ran—"

"Who the *hell* are you?"

"Manny Gutierrez," he said. "MG International ring a bell? We bought and sold a lot of product through e-Antiquity before you went bankrupt, turned evidence against your partner to save your ass, then vanished. Figures you'd come to a place like Key West."

A long few seconds passed before I realized my mouth was hanging open.

"Your Chapter Seven cost me thirty grand, plus legal expenses trying to get the rest back." Manny said.

I turned back to Willy. "Didn't your message say you were in trouble?"

"That's right, but if what Manny says is true, I can't afford to deal with hustlers. It's against everything we…teach our youngsters."

An uncomfortable pause ensued. The pastor's response to Manny's exaggerated description of e-Antiquity didn't surprise me. Many people had opposed our efforts to find forgotten relics, even though we always worked closely with local museums to preserve the sites and create exhibits. We only kept a fraction of the finds, but it only took a small amount to stir up trouble. Success had made me numb to those accusations, but my skin wasn't as thick as it used to be.

I was about to stand up when Willy said, "But the situation leaves me no choice."

"What exactly *is* the situation?" I said.

"Our mission to Cuba. Three of our people left this morning for Havana by boat. A sudden storm hit and they called in a Mayday. We haven't been able to reach them since. The Coast Guard's been searching for hours, but still, nothing."

"Was this Mayday in Spanish?"

Willy nodded. "Word travels fast. The Coast Guard estimates our ship was halfway to Cuba when it disappeared."

"You're wasting your time with this guy," Manny said. "He can't be trusted."

"Maybe not, but we need all the help we can get," Willy said.

One of the reasons I came to Key West was because e-Antiquity had no clients here. Now, MG International…I vaguely remembered his account. We obviously left them hanging, like so many others. Guilt was a sensation I'd only recently begun to recognize.

"Any chance the boat only lost power?" I asked.

The pastor drew his hands together, interlocked his fingers, and squeezed them tight. "Just before the Mayday I got a cell call from Manuel Ortega, one of our people on board." He exhaled a long breath. "He sounded frantic, and the call kept breaking up before he finally got cut off. I couldn't make out a damn word he said. The Mayday followed a few minutes later over the ship's radio."

"The old guy was scared shitless about Santeria. Probably knew something we should have." Manny pointed his thumb at me. "I refuse to be associated with a cut and run type like Buck Reilly."

"He's got a seaplane, Manny. This isn't about you."

God, I hated being broke. "Why the mission to Cuba?"

The pastor stared at his finger tracing a deep gouge in the desk's scarred wood top. The tension and fear out front was palpable, as was Manny's anger in here, but Willy Peebles held his composure.

"Details don't matter, finding our people does. The Coast Guard's got a lot on their plate, that's why I want to charter your sea plane."

"This is a joke, the ocean's huge!" Manny said. "Believe me, I know."

Manny's attitude and knowledge of my past, along with Betty's symptoms this morning made me want to turn and run. A job that starts bad always ends bad. But the recollection of the golden shimmer in the Dry Tortugas, combined with Ben's note in the FedEx package left me no choice.

"Five hundred per day, minimum, plus expenses—"

Willy held his hands up. "Whatever."

"Tell me about the boat." I said.

"It's big, was loaded to the gills with supplies—along with our volunteers. The boat was an answer to our prayers, until this."

Manny rubbed his eyes and forehead. His fingernails glistened. Manicured.

"They gave their location to the Coast Guard, wait…" He dug into his pocket. "Here's the latitude and longitude, or GPS coordinates. I've lived on this island my whole life, but truth be told, I hate the damn water." He held out a piece of paper. If memory served, the boat was in the middle of the Florida straits.

The sky outside his small window had turned orange with sunset.

"This Ortega, he didn't say anything else?" I said.

Willy slowly shook his head. "Nothing that would help you find them."

My eyes locked onto a picture on the desk. It was at an angle, but—I grabbed it.

Uh-oh. "Who's this?" I turned the picture toward him. "This girl?"

"Shaniqua? She's my daughter. What about her?"

"And the name of the boat carrying the missionaries?"

A long pause. "*Carnival,* like the cruise line," he said finally. "Shaniqua wanted to go, thank God I didn't let her. You know her?" Willy stared at me, waiting, his eyes narrowing to a squint. Manny's stare remained hostile.

Crap!

The morning's nameless charter had come full circle. Figures…"My cardinal rule for salvage projects is that I won't do anything that could get me arrested." I nodded toward Manny. "So whatever he meant by an eye for an eye…"

"You mean arrested *again?*" Manny said.

"And, I stay out of the papers," I said.

"Don't worry," Manny said. "We don't want anyone to you're involved with us either."

I stood up. "What's your connection to Conch—ah, Lenny Jackson?"

"Better let him tell you that," Willy said.

I looked around his cluttered office one last time, getting a sense of the man who committed his life to making a difference in the lives of others, knowing his situation was poised to go from bad to terrible, thanks to me. Used to be I'd put my goals ahead of anything, no matter what. In this case, that meant ignoring Willy and the smell of gold. If nothing else, my failures had proven that the world didn't revolve around me, and whether it was my own form of penance, guilty conscience, or that I just didn't have anything all that important to do anymore, one of my credos now was to resolve any issues my actions have created before pursuing my own agenda.

There was no choice but to get Betty back in the air.

My mind wandered back out to the Dry Tortugas, where I'd seen the *Carnival* this morning, where I'd dropped Willy's daughter before the storm. A last glance at the photo now lying flat on the desk, her eyes staring up at me, mouth smiling that Cheshire-cat smile, and I walked out with Manny's recognition clinging to me like a curse.

So much for flying under the radar in Key West….

I could feel the stares drilling into my back as I
left the church. If Manny Gutierrez had a big mouth, my days of quiet living were
over, but with Ben cutting me off, Last Resort's revenues wouldn't be enough to
cover my costs anyway, much less a treasure hunting operation. As for Willy's
daughter, why should I feel guilty? I was just doing my job. I swallowed hard.

If that was the case, why didn't I say so?

I knew I had to find her, otherwise Manny Gutierrez's sentiment about me
will shortly become Gospel. I had a sort of damned if you do, damned if don't
moment. Ironic, considering my location.

Lenny was already gone, so I took my bike and left without turning back.
With my own near-Mayday coinciding with the *Carnival's*, the boat's sinking as
a result of that storm was not only plausible but likely. If the Coasties didn't find
them before morning, Betty would have to suck it up. My stomach churned, the
name of my business suddenly prophetic. Charter and salvage was never intended
to apply to the same client, all in one day.

The orange dusk had faded to black, leaving only car lights to illuminate my
way. Loud rap music shook the paint-peeled timbers of an old eyebrow house
on Thomas. Just one of the countless century-old dwellings that had survived
everything from hurricanes to fires. Most had been restored and converted into
seven-figure resort homes. The development sharks had bloodied the back streets

of Bahama Village, picking off holdouts one at a time, only to be foreclosed on when their mortgages went upside down.

At Blue Heaven I was greeted by the same dark wrinkled men that held vigil there every day. "Looky who's here, the Great White Hope," one said. Snickers followed, along with coughing from the geriatric group of wise-crackers I referred to as the Gargoyles.

"Shiiiit, you mean hope-less," another said.

"Evening, gentlemen."

The patio restaurant was crowded, and a jumbo-sized woman in a tropical print muumuu was perched under a tiny tiki hut rasping out a version of Jewel's "Who Will Save Your Soul?" The corner of the bar was open and Lenny was fresh on duty serving up drinks. His usual cadre of Bahama Village disciples was missing, relieving him of the need to pontificate about how locals could no longer afford the island, how thanks to cruise ships local government only cared about tourism dollars, and how he'd change things. His smile was missing too.

"Conch Man."

At the sound of my voice he dropped the glass he was polishing but made a quick save with his other hand.

"You get a call for a last-minute charter this morning? A girl?" he said.

"Hmm, let's see. You mean Shaniqua Peebles?"

He slumped at the waist. "Damn."

"Last Resort's not in the Yellow Pages," I said. "So you gave her my name?"

"She wanted to go on the mission, but her daddy wouldn't let her—"

"So you sent her my way, then had Willy call without warning me."

"I tried. Shit, I went to your damn hotel."

Lenny held firmly to the bar while I gave him the details of the drop in the Dry Tortugas. He grimaced, then licked his lips.

"Does Willy know?"

"*I* didn't even know until I saw her picture."

"Hard Case is going to kill me. You got to find her, man, all of them, but Shaniqua—"

"Did you give him the scouting report on me?"

"I've known Willy my whole life. Hell, the man was in the room when I was born. He asks me something, what am I 'sposed to do, lie? Boxing's been the shit here for seventy years." He nodded over to where they set up the ring next to the bar for boxing matches.

"I'm not talking about—"

"Lots of famous men spilt blood here. You just happen to be a not-so-famous fool got himself lined up to spill some too. I seen Bruiser Lewis knock out three men in one night. You had any sense, you'd leave town before Saturday night and never come back." He paused. "After you find Shaniqua, that is."

Jumbled lyrics from an old song my parents used to listen to tumbled through my mind. I hadn't thought of it for years, and even though it had been my personal anthem for my teenaged boxing matches, I couldn't remember it clearly. Something about a boxer standing alone, shamed, scarred by every glove that had cut him down, and no matter where he ran, he remained a boxer, a fighter to the end.

A chill took the wind out of me. I cleared my throat. "I wasn't talking about the fight." I leaned closer to him. "And you mean after *we* find her."

He stepped back quick as if dodging a punch. "Oh no, not me, I ain't going up in that relic, Bimbo Betty, man, no way, these people need me."

"Don't call my plane a bimbo. She may be old but she's got style."

"Style or not, you're not getting my black ass in that jalopy. Especially with those— what did Willy did tell you, anyway?"

"About what?"

"The mission and all the shit leading up to it." He pulled at the bottom stubble of his sorry attempt at a goatee.

"It's a Mayday, Lenny, the boat's missing. That's all that matters."

"Yeah, well, wasn't so popular with everyone, trust me on that."

"Is that what Manny meant about an eye for an eye?"

"Manny's a hot-headed Cuban, man. Showed up here on an inner tube, ten, fifteen years ago. Now he's a big shot art dealer."

"Whatever, Lenny, I have to find those people, and I—"

Interrupted by a waiter shouting a half-dozen drink orders, Lenny sprang into action. I watched him, not surprised at his reluctance to help. He'd given me excuses before when I invited him to go flying. At least he was finally honest about being afraid.

"Get Karen to help you, she's the type!" he yelled from the other side of the bar. "Plus, I think she's sweet on you."

"Perfect, just what I need."

"A woman? Damn straight. You haven't let anyone close since you been here."

"I can't afford to blow my deal at the La Concha, and I don't shit where I sleep."

"Un-hunh. And maybe she'd say no. Or worse, she says yes, you fall in love and she leaves you too, right?"

I didn't say anything, irritated by the memory Lenny had dredged up.

"Your ex must have really kicked your ass, brother, that's all I can say."

"Betty's my girl, now."

"Yeah, Betty. Antique bucket-o-bolts. She won't break your heart, right? Kill you, maybe, but she won't leave you—"

"Nice try, Lenny," I said. "Sunrise is at six-fifteen tomorrow. Meet me at the airport at six, by then every minute will count."

"You're blowing a great opportunity, man. Karen's fine inside and out. Rare combo."

"You got me into this shit then called me in cold to face her old man. Bottom line is I can't do it alone."

He shook his head. "Fine, I'll be there. Goddamn."

"What about the others on the boat? Who are they?"

"Rodney Claggett, Manuel Ortega, Jo Jo Jeffries. Bunch of bible thumpers."

"Which one's connected to Manny Gutierrez?"

"Nobody, man, he got the hots for Shaniqua. Him and everyone else on this rock who's laid eyes on her. He donated most of the food and crap they brought along, *and* threw 'em a going-away party last night at his gallery on White Street. Wait till he finds out she's on board."

I tapped my fingers on the wood bar. Could guilt be behind Manny's pissy attitude, or was it just because I was involved?

"If Gutierrez thought somebody was to blame, he'd be looking for revenge."

Another stream of abuse from the Gargoyles peppered my departure.

A full moon had risen above a stand of massive hibiscus trees across the street, and a chill had crept into the air. Lenny hadn't volunteered the nature of his relationship with Willy Peebles, but he was probably a past hard-case project, or romantically involved with Shaniqua, or who knows what. Why he'd keep that from me wasn't clear, but then we all have our secrets.

Mine, however, were at risk of becoming public. So, thanks to this mess, my salvage pursuits had to go on the back burner, and finding the missionaries was now priority one, *damnit*.

Back at the La Concha, I found Josh Bentley at the front desk. The night shift. Karen was never around after work. Not out on the town at night, either, at least the places I go. She lived here but vanished. I always thought it strange.

Lenny's idea about her helping would have been a good one, and this trip could have been a nice opportunity to spend some time together. What's the old adage, though? Once burned, twice chicken-shit? Romance was yet another luxury I could no longer afford.

9

The eastern horizon was aglow with dawn, no clouds were visible, and there was minimal wind. Betty's white skin reflected the early morning sun. The red float under the starboard wing and the green float under the port wing were dark in the shadows. The smell of Avgas 100 aviation fuel permeated the air. The plan to arrive early enough to get Ray Floyd to give Betty's port engine a quick once-over had been wishful thinking. I'd left him a message last night, but Ray was less than diligent about checking his answering machine.

The radio reported that the Coast Guard had found nothing during the night, and surviving twenty-four hours in the water was pressing it if the missionaries had capsized.

What's this?

A small newspaper article was taped to Betty's hatch. It was from the *Key West Citizen's* section called the "Tattler." I saw my name and groaned.

> "…Former entrepreneur Buck Reilly, who was the co-founder of e-Antiquity, the internet auction site specializing in rare coins, ancient pottery, jewels, paintings, sculpture, fine arts, antiques, collective memorabilia and other rare items, has appar-

ently been living in Key West's La Concha Hotel since filing for bankruptcy nearly two years ago.

Now operating Last Resort Charter and Salvage, Mr. Reilly's enterprise has dwindled in epic proportion since e-Antiquity's heyday as one of Wall Street's favorites. Sources speculate Reilly chose Key West based on clues of previously undiscovered sunken artifacts he learned of while at his former firm…"

I crumpled the article into a ball. Perfect, just perfect.

I stewed while I completed the pre-flight check and loaded the supplies. A shout from the terminal broke me out of the funk. Lenny came running with plastic bags in each hand. It occurred to me that today's rescue mission would either cement or ruin one of the few relationships I cared about in this town. Or had left, for that matter.

"Brought some sandwiches and shit." He spoke while scrutinizing Betty's port engine and three-blade Hartzell prop. His inspection continued down the fuselage. The dark wood cross from behind Redeemer's podium was around his neck. I sniffed the air, and wondered if he had a pocketful of garlic cloves too.

"You *have* been on a plane before, right?"

"I been on a jet, but never one of these prop jobs."

"Jets are like buses, Lenny. This is real flying."

"Nothing wrong with the bus, man."

Once on board, I fired up the port engine first. It coughed and sputtered before smoothing out.

"Why's that motor running so bad, spitting out blue smoke and all?" Lenny's voice sounded puny in my headset, like a child's.

"She's just a little cold. Sit back and enjoy the ride."

I taxied the plane to the end of the runway, was given clearance by the tower, and eased the throttles forward. A minute later we banked to the south, the morning's first plane out of Key West International Airport. Lenny had a two-handed death grip on the base of his seat. His nose was pressed against the side window as he watched the island disappear beneath us.

"It'll take about twenty minutes to reach the search area," I said. "Let me know if you're gonna puke or shit yourself."

He plucked ferociously at his chin.

The emerald water rushed past us as we ascended to 1,000 feet. Last night, while working on my flight plan, I'd run some calculations trying to figure out where the boat might be, extrapolating different speeds and distances along with the current and tides from the time I dropped Shaniqua. My models didn't match the Coast Guard's. The *Carnival* had twin screws, and based on a conservative cruising speed of fifteen knots, she'd have far overshot the location their Cutter was searching.

A tingle danced at the base of my brainstem with the decision to disregard the conclusions of the highly qualified branch of Homeland Security to pursue my own back-of-the-napkin analysis and wrecker's intuition. It made no sense to search the same patch of water as the Coast Guard. My former financial empire had been built on risk taking, and pursuing imperceptible paths toward my objectives. More recycled skills.

"Havana's dead ahead, ninety miles," I said.

"Don't get any fool ideas."

"Always wanted to fly there and buzz the Morro Castle."

"Too bad Uncle Sam's tight on giving permission slips. Took Willy forever to get his, even with things starting to open up. Probably was an omen."

"Come on, Lenny, where's your sense of adventure? One of America's last forbidden fruits, swaddled in mystery, history, fiery Latinas, famous cigars, and great rum—hell, I'd trade half my collection of Caribbean estate rums for a bottle of seven- year-old amber Havana Club."

"I'll buy you a case of that Haitian rotgut you drink, just keep me out of there. What's your interest in Cuba anyway, man? From being a Foreign Service brat, or another treasure hunt?"

The question made me pause. "Combination of things."

"Can't you ever just answer a damn question?" Surviving takeoff had done wonders for his confidence.

"My father was a maverick at State, Cuba was one of his hot buttons. He was never posted there but went on a couple occasions."

"How about you?"

"It's on my list." I smiled. "Our failed embargo kept me out when e-Antiquity was rocking, now I can't afford to go." I thought of the ancient maps below my seat, a couple of which were of Cuban waters. "Still one of the dreams I intend to pursue, though."

"Just keep this antique in the air so we don't wind up as a *wet* dream."

I checked my watch. "Fifteen more minutes."

Lenny let out a long yawn, then sat up straight.

"You know any of these missionaries?" I said.

"Rodney Claggett. We were tight when we were teenagers, man. Dude had a great jump shot. Then he started getting into some serious shit and we lost touch. Willy got a hold of him, and after a couple years he was totally different, all religious and shit." He shook his head. "Had to be a shock to his system, boy used to have more women than anyone I knew."

"What do you mean, Willy got hold of him?"

"Make boot camp look like Cub Scouts. Don't let Willy fool you, man, he'll kick your ass, trust me on that. We call him the Ruler."

I thought of the serious faces staring back from the transom of the *Carnival.*

"Willy had Rodney in charge, which was a good thing considering the others. Anyone help them survive, be my man Rod."

"And the others?"

"Bunch of lightweights, man. Ortega's an old loud-mouth, must be sixty—"

"A loud-mouth missionary?"

"Hates the Cuban government. Brother was a pilot who got himself shot down dropping water and shit to rafters. J-three's a skinny beanpole of a guy, and—"

"J-three?"

"Jo Jo Jeffries. Late thirties and real churchy, always quoting the bible."

"What about Shaniqua?"

Lenny sighed and shook his head. "Fine as wine, ain't she? Looks just like my Cuban aunt." He saw my expression and said, "Willy didn't tell you?"

"Now what?"

"Shaniqua's my cousin, man. She's all Willy's got left. Aunt Evelyn died of cancer last year."

"Willy's your—"

"Uncle. Little slow on the uptake this morning?"

Willy's wife was Cuban? The memory of Shaniqua's caramel skin stirred my increasingly uneasy mind. "I guess that explains it."

"What, why I'm here? Damn straight, man, Shaniqua's like my little sister."

"You never mentioned her before."

"Shit, boy, she's blood, you think I'd throw her to the wolves?"

The missionaries sounded anything but robust. Aside from Rodney, none of them might be capable of surviving if the boat had capsized. But sometimes the least likely people have a survival instinct that kicks in when they're faced with last call. I checked my watch, the heading indicator and chart.

"We're coming up on where the Coast Guard's searching."

"What you want me to do?"

"Sit tight for now, we're continuing on to the Cuban territorial line."

"But if the Coast Guard's—"

"They can search here. Unless the *Carnival* was trolling the whole way, my calculations have them damn close to Cuba when they called in that Mayday."

Another ten minutes elapsed, with nothing to see besides water, waves, and whitecaps. Finally I pushed the yoke forward and we began a slow descent.

We leveled off at 50 feet and dropped the airspeed down to 100.

"The hell you doing, man? Why we so low?"

"We need to be wave-top skimming to spot anything small in the water, like someone clutching a life ring. Unbuckle yourself, pull the plug on your headset, and reattach both in the back. You'll see better from the windows under the wings."

Lenny hesitated, then did what I'd told him to.

"Time to focus on search and rescue. With any luck, we'll find the *Carnival* floating with no power and your foxy cousin waving from the bow."

I didn't tell him if they got swamped in that storm, we'd be looking for bodies.

10

After flying in a grid pattern for three and a half hours, and exhausting six sheets of notepaper marking our coordinates on my kneeboard, I felt like I'd been in a whiteout during a blizzard. Like us, neither the Coast Guard cutter *Mohawk* nor their helicopter had found anything. The *Mohawk* and all its technological apparatus were scouring a twenty-square-mile grid but would only continue for another day unless they found something.

Lenny visibly vacillated between terrified and nauseous before stabilizing at bored. No matter how important the mission, the untrained eye can only concentrate on featureless water for so long. He tried drinking coffee, then Coke, then he ate his first sandwich, but his head moved around like a bobble doll with fluttering eyelids. The crystal-clear sky offered no distraction, and the seas were unusually calm for March, which is right in the middle of the windy season.

Boredom is contagious. On long flights I kept alert by calculating Betty's remaining fuel capacity, and diligently tracking course and heading. I didn't like to use autopilot in the cockpit, or in life. It's too easy for routine to take over, and days to fall like raindrops. I had exchanged working sixty-hour weeks with my entire focus on making money for living in the moment, but that was done in hindsight and as the result of many failures. But, holding on to the moment too tightly can also be destructive. I vowed to loosen my grip on the controls, later.

We started another search leg along a due easterly heading. Flying this low was exhausting because it left you with no margin for error—space out for a couple of seconds and you corkscrew into the drink, JFK, Jr.-style. I was good for maybe another hour but was starting to think we'd flown past the outside edge of where the current could have carried a powerless boat or anybody floating in a life jacket. I slid open my vent window.

Lenny was back to nodding off again. "We'll never find squat if you don't stay alert," I said. "Keep talking if that'll help."

"Where the hell are we, anyway?"

"Skirting the Cuban territorial line, roughly seventy miles south of Key West."

"Don't get any crazy ideas about buzzing that Moron Castle you were talking about." He sat up. "So how does a dude who went bankrupt still have his own plane and enough jack to live large?"

"I live in an old hotel, how's that living large?"

"This plane can't be cheap, even if it's ancient, and unless you discovered sunken treasure and never told nobody, you ain't found shit, least anything you could live off. You still getting some kind of corporate kick-back, or what?"

His question reminded me that I should be out in the Dry Tortugas, right now. "Let's concentrate on finding your cousin, okay?"

"We're just talking, right? To keep me *alert*. So, what about your look?"

"What look?"

"You got this whole grunge thing going, shaggy hair and that wild mustache? Ain't seen one of them since reruns of Starsky and Hutch on Nick at Nite."

"I've been told I look like Jimmy Buffett on the cover of *Havana Daydreamin'*."

"That's supposed to give me a picture? Last I saw, Buffett was bald." Lenny snorted. "That cracker's done as much damage as Hemingway around here. Damn island's turned into a white man's fountain of testosterone, everyone wanting to be big game fishermen, hunters, ladies' men. It's like a B-movie with him cackling the soundtrack. Between that and the damn cruise ships, no wonder locals can't afford shit."

"Not now, Lenny, we—"

"Thing is? Both those guys were tourists. Hemingway was hardly ever here, and Buffett was here just long enough to brand us Margaritaville. I mean, what kind of shit's that? My family's been here over a hundred years working our asses off rolling cigars, sponging, turtling, fishing, building freaking bridges, and every other damn thing to survive. This ain't no vacation spot for us, man, this is our home."

"Don't forget bartending and talking shit."

"Talking shit, huh? Be mayor of this town some day, trust me on that."

"Conch Man goes to City Hall?"

"If Captain Tony can get elected? Damn straight, man. In case you didn't notice, we got a brother in the White House now, and he ain't the butler, neither. Home grown black man'll be the ticket around here, you watch."

I'd heard all this before many times at Blue Heaven. "God bless you, Lenny, but my days in the spotlight are over. All I want now is to live a quiet life of adventure, fight for what I believe in, and maybe rescue a beautiful woman, or two."

"Adventure, huh? I know you're talking about treasure hunting. So you can be the next Mel Fisher, right? Least you're not an old drunk, yet. Then we going to see Buck Reilly plastered all over the damn place too, 'Buck Reilly drank here, Buck Reilly slept there'"— A laugh interrupted his tirade. "I can see it now, man, the Conch Tour Train going by Blue Heaven and the announcer says, 'And Buck Reilly got his ass kicked here by Bruiser Lewis.'"

My watch beeped and we began the turn south. When we leveled off I spotted a yellow object flash in the water. After a couple seconds' hesitation I spun the plane back around in a tight turn.

"The hell you doing?"

"Keep watch out the port window. I just saw something flash on the water. Something yellow."

Lenny fought gravity by clutching the handle above the window. We leveled off lower to the water. Where was that bit of yellow? Flotsam now dotted the rolling surface. A white plastic trash bag appeared, then another. The muscles in my neck tightened.

"Hey!" Lenny pointed. "What's that, off to the left? There!"

I banked hard to port while pulling the yoke back to keep Betty's nose up.

"Goddamn, Buck!"

The rhythmic pattern of waves made it hard to focus on the smaller pieces of trash. There! Something large rose on a wave and then dropped down. Was it a person?

I stabbed the "mark" button on the Garmin GPS, now Velcroed to the instrument panel. We flew for another minute before beginning a slow 180-degree turn, powering down, and adding ten degrees of flaps.

"The hell's going on?"

"It's called a water landing, Lenny."

He dove back into the right seat, ramming my shoulder as he went. He fumbled with the harness, glanced out the window, and let out an involuntary moan as his hands shot down to grab the edges of the seat frame.

The yellow figure again rose on the waves. I further decreased our airspeed and dropped the flaps to twenty degrees. We needed an angle free of debris, otherwise a crate of food could peel back Betty's hull like the lid of a sardine can. The only indication of wind was a slight spray off the low waves—perfect landing conditions. We would overshoot the mark, but we'd taxi back.

"I can't believe this shit!" Lenny's voice boomed as we splashed down.

Water shot up the sides of the flight deck windows, but the Widgeon was firm in the water without any bouncing or skipping. A sweeping turn led us back toward where I'd spotted the yellow. The concern for floating rubbish had me holding my breath.

Lenny fidgeted as the wings bounced precariously above the large red and green bulbous floats skimming atop the water. I studied the seas ahead, worked the rudder with my feet, checked the proximity to the mark, and eyed the compass while trying to keep the floats from getting buried and cart-wheeling us over.

Lenny unbuckled and peered up over the nose to get a better view.

"There! Over to the left, ten o'clock."

I looked where he was pointing. "I can't see anything, guide me."

"Straight ahead, fifty yards. You got it, Buck, just keep this bitch straight."

Betty bucked atop a wave and the nose dipped down hard.

"I didn't mean nothing, damnit," Lenny said.

The target appeared during the dip and I mentally prepared our rescue checklist. No need to scare Lenny, but opening the hatch on the ocean is not a wise maneuver. One rogue wave hits you broadside and you're toast, plus the flaps are inoperable with the hatch open, making you even more vulnerable.

"Here's how this is going to work," I said. "Go into the back and put on one of the life vests in the rear compartment, then lower the kayak. When I tell you to, open the hatch and latch it up halfway with a bungee cord."

"Then what?"

"Uncoil the rope ladder, leave the hatch open, and hang the ladder outside. You'll have to jump, get in the kayak and paddle over. You need to get out quick so I can keep Betty pointed into the waves. Whoever's out there will be weak and you'll probably have to push them onto the boat and drag them back. They might be unconscious or—"

"I get the picture."

Lenny was a good swimmer and should be able to pull this off, but damn if I'd let him get hurt out here. We took off our headsets and Lenny crouched back into the main compartment. He crashed from side to side on his way to the rear hatch, falling to his knees and crawling the rest of the way.

"Shut the storage hatch when you're done. The plane needs to be as watertight as possible if we get hit by a wave."

When I turned to see Lenny, our heading shifted and the plane suddenly moved hard to the left, which sent Lenny crashing into the kayak. The green float on the port wing was submerged—I reduced power, and it popped back up. I could hear his cussing over the whine of the twin six-cylinder engines.

"I've got to watch where we're going, yell out what you're doing," I said. Yellow again surfaced off the port side. "It's a man, face up."

"The boat's unhooked, you ready?" Lenny said.

I glanced through the side windows. "I'll run up past you, then swing back."

I could hear him struggling but didn't dare look back. Suddenly a whoosh of salt air blew my hair forward, and the sound of the engines roared through the cabin. The plane rocked under Lenny's shifting weight when he threw the kayak out the hatch.

"Don't leave my ass out here, man!"

11

The waves were gentle, maybe two-foot swells, which out this far was a blessing. Going broadside into the swells with an open hatch wasn't safe seaplane piloting, but failure wasn't an option. My heart rate had accelerated, my senses were pinging and I was on the edge of my seat. Being on the brink of danger and discovery always did that to me, and I was drawn to it like a hawk on a field mouse.

I radioed the Coast Guard and gave them our coordinates. They promised to redirect the *Mohawk* toward us.

Okay, Lenny, where are you?

Come on, Conch Man….

There! I could see Lenny wrestling with a man. There was nothing to do but overshoot them and make another pass. I powered to the left to keep the open hatch in the lee of the waves.

You can do it, Lenny, come on!

Water splashed in at the apex of the turn, but the float didn't catch, so I gunned the starboard engine and spun back into position. With a glance at the heading indicator and a minor adjustment to our course, I dodged another carton of floating food.

Seconds ticked off, and I couldn't find them. I scanned the surface. Then suddenly, through my side window, I saw the orange kayak bound over a wave with the yellow man lying on top of it and Lenny behind, pushing them toward Betty. I slowed the engines to the bare minimum, stalling until they disappeared under the wing. A second later, a jarring clunk made Betty lurch to port.

My eyes darted from the waves to the main cabin just in time to see a stream of water with a yellow mass dump into the fuselage to the sound of coughing and sputtering. Lenny fell in after but had the presence of mind to withdraw the ladder.

"Shut the hatch!"

I grabbed the throttles. We'd be in a much better position to attend to the yellow man flying in stable air than while getting thrown around on the ocean's surface. The waves ahead were steady, the wind direction good, and I imagined a runway. The familiar vibration of the hatch closing shook the plane.

"Hang on!" Betty rocked in the waves as we got up on plane, and after a 10-count the airspeed indicator touched 70. I hit the flaps, pulled back the stick, and we broke free of the water and into the air.

Lenny careened into my shoulder before collapsing into the co-pilot's seat.

"Good job," I said. "*Damn* good job. Now let's—" His expression looked anything but happy, and his skin tone was changing before my eyes. "You okay?"

He said something unintelligible through his fingers. I moved the headset away from my ear. "What?"

"I said—" A hiccup interrupted him. "He's dead."

12

Lenny's coal-black skin had a decidedly pale tinge.

"Open the sliding window!"

His chest heaved, and he slapped his hand over his mouth. I ripped off my seat belt, stretched across, and worked the handle on the window. Betty dove forward, then veered to the right while I fought with the latch, getting it open just in time for Lenny to empty his stomach all over the fuselage.

Our speed accelerated to 175, and it took all my strength to jerk back on the yoke to pull us out of the sharp descent. Lenny fell back into his seat, spittle-chinned and panting. He convulsed again but had hit empty. I thumbed back toward the yellow heap in the fuselage.

"Is it one of the missionaries?"

"J-three. Jo Jo." A waft of vomit-breath hung in the cabin. Lenny shuddered. Conch Man had put his life on the line and damn near drowned.

With food cartons, crates, and loose clothing bobbing all over the area, it wasn't certain how the boat had sunk. My arms suddenly felt like lead weights, and the emotional fatigue hit the way Bruiser Lewis likely would come Saturday.

"Kayak's history, man. I just didn't...couldn't..."

"How are we supposed to—"

BOOM!

The sound rocked us as Betty jerked hard to the left amidst deafening backfires that blasted one after the other. The port engine was sputtering badly, its tachometer needle bouncing back and forth like a heart monitor on a dying patient. I danced on the pedals, jockeyed the yoke, reduced power on both engines, and tried to keep the wings level.

"Wh..at th..e fu..ck is hap..pen..ing?" Betty's bouncing rattled Lenny's shout out like Morse code.

The altimeter read 1,250 feet above sea level but the needle was dropping fast, along with our airspeed. Adjustments to the fuel mixture and props did nothing, and the port engine continued to backfire and spew blue smoke. Something hit the back of my seat—the yellow-clad corpse.

Oh jeez.

"Lenny!" His eyes were wild. "Hook Jo Jo to the wall with one of the bungee cords before he makes us crash."

Lenny lit out of his seat like an alley cat, smashed into the bulkhead, and stumbled over the body. Jo Jo disappeared from my peripheral vision and the weight shifted back to an operable center of gravity. Another loud boom sounded, and again Betty veered to the left, sending Lenny into the side wall. Our airspeed deteriorated, and the yoke went limp as we began a stall there wasn't enough altitude to correct.

I fleetingly considered a water landing, but we'd never be able to take off with only one engine. The old girl bucked and rattled while I scanned the emergency checklist.

Lenny jumped back into the front seat. His eyes were no longer wild but determined. Something I'd seen in men facing inevitable death, financial ruin… or occasionally in the mirror.

"What's the deal, Buck, we gonna make it?"

Our altitude was now at 600 feet, and I tried to remember the ditch procedure. "Come *on,* Betty!"

I pointed the nose down to regain some speed. Lenny's eyes were shut tight and his knuckles white from clutching the seat frame. I killed the port engine, and the plane started to slide. I counted to four, hit the starter and the loudest backfire yet exploded with a huge puff of white smoke from the exhaust. The RPM's suddenly smoothed out and Betty leveled off and calmed down like an asthmatic after a coughing fit.

The altimeter indicated we were 60 feet above the ocean. Pulling back slowly on the yoke, I began a gradual climb, nervous at reactivating whatever ailment was lurking in the port engine. Moments passed in quiet. Lenny's breathing finally slowed. He slumped forward with both hands clutching the wooden cross.

"Get my ass home, man, before we add two more bodies to this mess."

I began a slow turn northeast. Only a fool would continue the search with

Betty's engine so unpredictable, but going home with one dead and three lost missionaries, not to mention three lost crew, could only be described as a failure.

And we had to face up to Willy.

Fifty miles out, I keyed the microphone and called Key West tower. A solemn Donny promised the authorities would be there to greet us.

13

The scene at the airport was pure bedlam. Within
fifteen minutes of our return there were representatives from KWPD, the Monroe
County sheriff's department, the county coroner, the Coast Guard, the marine
patrol, a reporter and photographer from the *Key West Citizen,* along with a
despondent pastor Willy Peebles. If that wasn't enough, an officer from the state
police was reportedly en route from Marathon. The cops were arguing about who
had jurisdiction. The Coast Guard wanted their investigative service, or CGIS, to
take the lead. The coroner wanted to take the body, the reporter from the *Citizen*
was yelling questions, the photographer was shooting Betty, and I just wanted to
crawl into a hole and disappear.

Pastor Peebles stared at me with gravedigger's eyes, and my chest ached,
knowing I was about to wreck his world.

After a brief examination, the coroner reported that the back of Jo Jo's head
was caved in, instantly shrouding his death in controversy. Had the boat exploded
and smashed his skull? The Coast Guard had already redirected the *Mohawk* and
a full contingent of three helicopters was headed their way. The sun was blister-
ing, the smell of aviation fuel had me nauseous, and my shoe was stuck on a piece
of bubblegum someone had spit out prior to boarding a commuter back to reality. The argument over jurisdiction climaxed when Trooper Ben Wallace arrived

and attempted to seize control. His six-five frame was a study in contours, with muscles stretching every stitch on his shirt.

I whispered in Lenny's ear. "You need to give a statement."

"The hell you talking about! Why me?"

"Just say I'm a rental pilot and you found Jo Jo."

A hush came over the bickering crowd when I called for quiet and pushed Lenny forward. He didn't like it one bit, but his political instincts kicked in.

"Listen up while I tell you all what happened."

Notepads and tape recorders materialized, and he recounted our day, even promising to give them copies of the coordinates we'd flown after "his pilot" duplicated the notes from his kneepad.

The photographer proclaimed himself an aviation buff and was visibly thrilled at seeing a Grumman Widgeon up close. He asked to see inside, but I declined. The coroner transferred Jo Jo into a black body bag and loaded him into his white unmarked van. Pastor Peebles sat with his hand on top of the sealed container. His white guayabara shirt was sweat-stained and he looked ten years older than when I'd met him yesterday.

The swarm of blue, white, and gray starched uniforms fired questions and took Lenny's name, number, and address. When they asked for mine, I explained I was just a pilot for hire and could be reached here at the airport. The last thing I wanted was to see my name on a police report or in the paper again.

The legal contingent drifted closer to the terminal while continuing the battle for dominance. A large crowd had gathered shoulder to shoulder, watching us from inside the building. Flights had been delayed while we stood in the middle of the tarmac, leaving angry travelers worried about connections and other inconveniences. They wouldn't spare a grunt for Jo Jo Jeffries, so they could rot in their Tommy Bahamas for all I cared.

Lenny's eyes were fixed on the van.

"You did a hell of a job out there," I said. "I don't know why Betty—"

"Bitch tried to kill us."

Pastor Peebles walked over, and Lenny closed his eyes when Willy pulled him in for a bear hug and then turned to me.

"Willy, I need to tell you something," I said.

The pastor looked into my eyes. His were dark, moist, and—hurt? "What you didn't tell me yesterday?" he said. "About my daughter?" His voice sounded more sad than mad. "Know all about it, Buck. You lied to me, or hid the truth, anyway."

"That's not—"

He glanced quickly at the police, then leaned in close, lowering his voice. "Neither of you says a word about Shaniqua being on that boat, you understand? I want her name kept out of it—we'll do our *own* investigation." His eyes bore into mine. "Now get the hell out of my face before I break my own rules."

Lenny grimaced as Willy took him by the arm and marched off.

What the hell? With the coroner suggesting Jo Jo had been a victim of foul play, Willy's reaction was...strange. Beyond strange.

I felt torn between saying "fuck it" and finding any means possible to continue the search. But with Betty on the fritz, what choice did I have?

Willy and Lenny power-walked toward the terminal, where, to my surprise, Manny Gutierrez stood just beyond the gaggle of police. They spoke for a moment before Willy pointed to me, then walked away. Manny's glower lingered a long minute more before he followed Willy.

There had been several former clients at our bankruptcy hearing, and they had been bitter and loud. Time had obviously not healed Manny's wound. Would I ever be free from my past? Did I deserve to be? Do I really give a shit?

I went to tie Betty down and found Ray Floyd in flip-flops, cargo shorts, and a tie-dyed T-shirt, inspecting her.

"Some day you guys had, huh? Brought out all the shit-fers."

Ray's choice of words was often bewildering. *Shit-fer?* Brains, got it.

"Betty nearly killed us out there, same symptoms as yesterday, times ten."

"Checked her records. Both engines and props are due for overhauls."

"How much would...never mind, I can't afford it. Can you just bandage her up? I need to get back out there."

"It's your ass," Ray said. "Don't these macho crew cuts epitomize the B/B ratio?"

"You'll have to explain that gem later, I'm beat."

After spraying Betty's fuselage down, mopping out the inside, checking to make sure everything was turned off, battened down, and screwed tight, I took my gear and headed for the terminal. I hesitated at the doors of the Conch Flyer. Susie was behind the bar, and I could have used a liquid Rx, but I didn't have the energy even for that. My old Series II Rover 88 carried me back to the La Concha, where a hot shower and room service awaited. What had begun as a one-day charter to search for a missing boat now felt like I'd lost a family member myself.

Failure ate at me like an illness, one that had metastasized through my life, once again resulting in an uncomfortable sense of urgency. Complacency invited capitulation, and the only hope for a cure was to succeed. Problem was, I didn't know how.

14

Freshly clean and wearing a towel, I answered the knock expecting a waiter with the hamburger I'd ordered but got a beautiful woman instead.

"I heard the news." Karen's eyes were fixed on the 380-year-old silver Spanish piece of eight hanging on my bare chest.

"Hold on." I went to my bedroom and returned in shorts and a *FOXY'S* T-shirt. She was opening a bottle of Cabernet from the rack on the counter and glancing around at the piles of books, articles, and old maps. As far as I knew, she'd never been inside my suite, and having her here now had my imagination going a mile a minute.

"You all right?"

"I was just the pilot—"

She rolled her eyes. "Cut the bullshit bravado, Buck. Are you okay?"

I shoved the pile of *Wall Street Journals*, still in their plastic wrappers, from the couch onto the floor and sat down. Karen was wearing shorts and a pink midriff tank top and looked as if she'd just come in from a run. Her musky scent combined with the concern in her eyes chipped away at the ice encasing my heart.

I took a mouthful of red wine.

"You'll feel better if you talk about it." She sat on the arm of the sofa next to me, and the day's events were suddenly a blur. "Search and rescue must be more draining than salvage—"

"Some rescue."

She put her hand on my shoulder, and an immediate sensation of warmth penetrated the cotton. She squeezed the muscles at the base of my neck, and it was as if she'd pressed a button. My eyes closed and my head slumped forward.

After a few moments Karen stood. "Better let you rest, you look exhausted."

Was there an alternative? She started for the door, then hesitated at the bookshelf.

"*The Wreckers*?" Her eyes lit up as she pulled the old book out. "Shipwrecks fascinate me, can I borrow this?" I nodded, and she turned back to the shelf. "Wouldn't have pegged you for all these art books. Impressionists, Italian Renaissance, Hudson River School, Latin. Must be a soft side underneath that tough guy persona."

My burger arrived. Karen said she'd leave me to it, then something on the shelf caught her attention and she moved some old bottles recovered from the ocean floor to reveal the small Lucite cube tucked among them. She scrutinized the small print, squinting at the engraving on the bottom.

"It says *e-Antiquity Corporation. Fifty-million-dollar initial public offering.*"

I paused, not sure what she knew of my past, or whether she had seen this mornings Tattler. "You're right, I'm exhausted."

"Too bad." She stared at me for a long moment. "If you feel like talking, I'll be downstairs." I let out a long sigh and turned to my burger. It was cold.

In many ways, Karen and I were complete opposites. She was the local activist fighting for causes as obscure as chicken's rights, raising money for the haphazard shelter that placed wild island birds up for adoption, and chairing the Special Events committee for the Old Island Days Festival. And here I was, exploiter of lost civilizations. What could she possibly see in a guy like me?

For all the guys sniffing around, I never saw Karen with any of them, or out at night anywhere. But whenever I did see her, I decided all over again that she was beautiful. A natural, soft beauty—she was too un-self-conscious to primp herself into the drop-dead gorgeous category, but still, I no longer trusted my choice in women. Although she *had* said wrecks fascinated her.

While I waited for the microwave to reheat my burger, the phone rang.

"I was just getting ready to leave and saw something weird." It was Ray.

"Stay away from the mirrors—"

"You leave Betty's hatch open?"

"What?" Thinking back, there was no doubt I'd locked her tight. "Not a chance."

"Because it's open, not wide but like a car door not closed all the way."

"Be right there."

"You want me to call the cops?"

"No, just keep an eye on Betty."

15

My sprint through the hotel and tear through the
back streets to the private aviation terminal passed in a blur. Ray was sitting in
a folding chair next to Betty, his head tilted back and his eyes closed, sunning
himself.

"Did you touch anything?"

He squinted up toward me. "I watch *CSI Miami*."

Sure enough, Betty's hatch was closed but not all the way, resting on its latch.
There was no evidence of tampering or scratches on the lock. I opened the hatch
slowly and craned my head inside. Everything looked normal. Ray peered over my
shoulder. We exchanged glances and crawled in. I scrutinized the interior. There
was an odd smell, almost like—

"All your craps in the back." Ray slammed the rear storage hatch shut.

"Everything looks norm—" Suddenly it hit me. A small square of naked Velcro was black on the dashboard.

"What is it?" Ray said.

"My GPS is gone."

I reached down below my seat, but my fingers touched only air.

No.

I reached deeper. Had the pouch slipped?

"What's wrong?"

On my knees, with my head wedged into the rudder pedals, all I saw were dusty springs and duct tape dangling. The waterproof pouch was gone.

"Shit!" I collapsed onto the floor.

"Are you okay? What was under there?"

"My whole future, my stash...everything."

"Stash? You keep money in here? *Drugs?*"

"My maps, damnit, the ledger, key...the GPS! How will I find the gold?" I felt as if the plane was in a sideways stall.

"Did you say gold?"

"In the Dry Tortugas, from yesterday—" In a heart-squeezing rush I realized my haughty declaration against returning to a life of material comfort was complete bullshit. But then again, it's easy to swear off addiction when there's no temptation. That epiphany aside, the only legacy I had retained from e-Antiquity, along with the key to my parent's Swiss bank account had vanished from the safest place I had known to hide them. I'm screwed, now. Totally screwed.

There was something else further under the seat. I reached under and—it was soft and furry. And the smell? I pulled it forward, along with a piece of paper. It was a bird, a white dove, but red and sticky. Ugh.

When I held it up, Ray jumped. He hit his head on the ceiling, and with a leap he was out of the plane.

"Ray!"

I hurried after him, still clutching the bird and paper. Ray held his hands up.

"Keep that thing away from me!"

It *was* grotesque, a bright red coating over the soft white feathers. But worse, its head was gone.

"What's it mean?" I said.

"The devil!"

Ray had always been the picture of calm, even when dispensing his own island philosophy. I had never seen him even a little bit scared, much less terrified.

"The devil?"

"Worse—Santeria, man, like voodoo! You've really done it now." He hustled away double-time into the hangar, leaving me holding the dead dove.

The paper turned out to be a note. "THIS BIRD NO FLY. LEAVE THE SPIRITS OF THE DEAD ALONE."

Bird no fly? Spirits? Dead?

Who had I pissed off now, and what had they done with my GPS and stash?

Dark
Skies
and Dead
Guys

16

Visions of the bloated Jo Jo Jeffries mixed with ax-wielding Santeria priests and images of undersea treasure just out of reach swirled through a long night of restless slumber. At sun-up I abandoned the sweat-strewn sheets and tore my room apart searching for the account identification that accompanied the irreplaceable key and maps stolen with my waterproof pouch. Thanks to the storm, without the GPS and chart I'd never find that coral head in the Dry Tortugas, but I could at least replace the Swiss bank key.

I spotted an envelope under my door. Inside was today's Tattler from the *Key West Citizen.* Now what?

"…Buck Reilly, aka Charles B. Reilly, III, formerly of e-Antiquity fame, now operating the shoestring operation Last Resort Charter and Salvage, has ties to the missing Church of Redeemer mission boat, *Carnival.* Word is that Reilly dropped Shaniqua Peebles off on the boat halfway to Cuba, just before it vanished.

Doing what the Coast Guard couldn't, Reilly found Jo Jo Jefferies' body yesterday, but all other crew and missionaries remain missing. Shaniqua's name has not appeared on the passenger list, and Reilly, although involved with the search, did not share the details of her drop with the authorities. Pastor Peebles refused to be interviewed. Word is Reilly's maintaining a low profile because he's poaching other treasure hunter's licensed dive sites while they're not around…"

Ever since I spotted that gold, everything had gone to shit. Betty breaking down, old e-Antiquity clients showing up, my name in the press, my maps, key and GPS stolen, even my fragile delusion of renewed integrity. The second I think my life has turned around, my feet get cut off. Hell, my calves and knees too, for that matter. Was the *Esmeralda* cursed? *Spirits of the dead*? Or had this all happened because of the girl?

I found my father's papers, read the account identification, and realized the letter inside the Swiss bank envelope was not an institutional memorandum at all. I read it again.

Swiss Bank
Geneva Switzerland

Contents: Records, files, documents, other materials

Account Key word: 'His boat'

The key is one of two, and each heir has one, but without both being presented simultaneously, the other is useless. If one is lost, the following five- character identification must be presented with the remaining key:

B C O D Y D C D E
H B L I W T W D M G R
O R Y H R I K L V O L I H

Five characters? How about 33? Key *word*?

My hands went cold. It wasn't an account number, it wasn't a five-character sequence, it was a word puzzle. A cipher. My father loved ciphers. He considered it diplomatic tradition to use them for important correspondence. Problem is I suck at ciphers. *Shit*!

Now even replacing the key was uncertain. I was left with no choice but to get my gear back.

If not for the dead dove I would have thought competing treasure hunters had stolen my maps. Ray said it was Santeria. Hadn't Manny mentioned that too? Could *spirits of the dead* mean Jo Jo? What else had Willy not told me? Why did he want Shaniqua's presence on the boat kept secret? The Tattler blew that wide open.

Who tipped the Tattler?

I pulled up a definition on the internet: "Santeria is one of the many syncrteic religions created in the New World. It is based on the West African religions brought by slaves imported to the Caribbean to work the sugar plantations. These slaves carried with them their own religious traditions, including a tradition of possession trance for communicating with the ancestors and deities, the use of animal sacrifice and the practice of sacred drumming and dance. Those slaves who landed in the Caribbean, Central and South America were nominally converted to Christianity. However, they were able to preserve some of their traditions by fusing together various Dahomean, baKongo (Congo) and Lukumi beliefs and rituals and by syncretizing these with elements from the surrounding Christian culture."

What did any of that have to do with me?

17

I took my backpack and made my way through the La Concha lobby and onto Duval Street. The fate of Betty's port engine still awaited this morning's inspection by Ray Floyd, mechanic, social critic, and island eccentric. I expected the worst.

Outside I found Karen tightening the laces on her roller-blades.

"You're up early," she said. "Feeling better?"

She was wearing spandex shorts and a tank top. Her figure left me momentarily speechless. "Sure."

She pointed to a backpack leaning against a potted plant. "Mind helping me with that?" The pack had a small, built-in cage that was empty. She caught my amused expression. "Morning's the best time to catch loose chickens," she said.

I couldn't help laughing. "Dr. Livingston, I presume?"

"Funny, flyboy."

She dug a heel in and bladed away, a fluid, graceful retreat. By far the best-looking chicken rescuer I'd ever seen.

Most days this was my favorite time to go for a run, since the tourists were out cold in alcohol-induced comas and the locals were preparing for another day working in paradise. Only fishermen, assorted town-dwelling rodents, loose chickens, and one foxy do-gooder were up and moving. Today, however, exercise was the last thing on my mind.

I went down Fleming, past the corner where B.O.'s Fish Wagon got its start, when "wagon" described the stand he operated like a hotdog vendor on the corner of what was then a gravel lot. I remembered lunching there as a kid, when my family stayed at the La Concha before we later rented what were then rustic Conch homes, now multi-million-dollar jewels. The sweet smell of moist flowers, bougainvillea, and hibiscus were made more fragrant by last night's rain.

I focused on the few existing facts about the missing boat. Nothing made sense. Since the theft of my stash had come after we found Jo Jo, whose death had been attributed to foul play, and since both had potential connections to Santeria, it was time to learn more about the *Carnival*.

The sun had not risen above the trees, but the coming glow of morning muted colors, details, and my depth perception. The path toward my objective led me into the city cemetery. The six square blocks that separated Old Town from the Meadows was the most peaceful patch of coral and concrete on the island. A series of gravel paths set in a grid made for simple navigation, locating loved ones, shortcutting, or a forced march to focus the mind.

It stirred the memory of my parent's dual burial in the Virginia countryside. They had been gone three years, and the circumstances contributing to and surrounding their deaths, why they had an account at a Swiss bank, and why my existence had changed so dramatically had all been stirred up by the theft of my stash.

What I had assumed to be their account identification but was actually a cipher was a major problem. How would I ever figure that out? Diplomatic codes? The vague remembrance that my father's favorite puzzle-making method included a sea of letters provided little comfort.

Surrounded by gravestones, *spirits of the dead* were everywhere. I wondered where Jo Jo would be interred. Would his widow curse him with a silly epitaph, damning him to become the butt of humor on the nightly cemetery tours? *I told you I was sick,* or *Good citizen for 65 of his 108 years?* Doubtful. Ray Floyd's wisecrack about my future epitaph now seemed portentous.

Questions about the *Carnival* quickened my pace, its point of departure a good place to start. A Harley with straight pipes accelerated down Eaton, and I followed it south before turning up William where a poster caught my attention. It advertised an art show at the San Carlos Institute scheduled for tomorrow night at 7:00 "m.p."

Across Caroline was B.O.'s Fish Wagon. No longer the hotdog stand, it was now a full-fledged shack tucked into the bowels of the Bight. Once the homeport for the island's shrimp fleet, turtle industry, and centuries of wreckers ignobly considered pirates, the Bight had evolved into a contemporary tourist-driven diamond. It was now fully equipped with countless water sports operations, restaurants, bars, and a multitude of transient boat traffic. And they called wreckers pirates.

Just past the Waterfront Market's parking area was the Port Operations and Administrative offices, where management of the sprawling twenty-acre seaport was handled. At this early hour their door was locked, but the sounds, smells, and activities of the harbor were not controlled by a time clock. I continued down the harbor walk toward Turtle Kraals.

18

Dockage at the bight was organized by zones, with the larger, deep-water commercial operators clustered around the "H" docks to the left and the live-aboards and ferry docks at the opposite end. The dockmaster's shack was at pier C, which also contained the Chevron fuel docks— and a scruffy fellow stooped in a plastic lawn chair, hovering over a coffee mug and clutching a cigarette. He looked to be at the end of an all-night shift, or just up from a booze binge, or maybe both.

"Morning," I said.

"Finally." His voice had the huskiness of a lifetime smoker.

"It's more quiet then when that mission boat set off yesterday, huh?"

He shrugged.

"Were you working then?"

The man's eyes shrunk to slits. He flicked the spent cigarette into the water, coughed, and lit another.

"You a cop?"

"I'm a friend of Pastor Peebles from Church of the Redeemer."

"Praise the Lord." He spit into the water.

"You remember the boat?"

"You kidding me? This place was a zoo, people everywheres, cameras, reporters. Got the hell out soon as my shift was over."

"Where does the *Carnival* berth?"

He hacked a phlegmy cough before spitting again. A pink bronchial clot lodged on his chin. A small boat zipped around the corner and was approaching the gas pump too fast. It had the words "RENT ME" painted on its hull.

"Slow down!"

The boat's starboard gunwale scraped loudly against the planking. "Use your damn bumpers! Didn't Billy tell you nothin? Damn fools come here, rent boats, and don't know their ass from a hole in the ground." He wiped his chin, collected the pink substance, flicked it into the water, and pointed with his thumb over his shoulder.

"They wasn't from here. Helped 'em tie up that morning other side of A dock there, near where the ferries come in." He laughed. "Ferry *boats*, that is."

"Didn't they have to clear customs before leaving for Cuba?"

He ran a hand through his oily hair. "Was a big truck here waiting for 'em, filled with all kinds of food and shit. The government boys had already picked it over. With all them people raising hell, you'd of thought they was carrying nuclear miss-iles."

"Raising hell? In celebration?"

"Picketers, boy, they not usually celebrators."

"Picketers? Could they have been Santeros?"

"San-*what*-os?"

"Religious people, kind of voodoo-like."

"Hell no, they was assholes, Cuban-like. Fanatics picketing the damn mission."

Why hadn't Willy mentioned this?

"Was there any violence?"

"Thought you was with the church."

"I missed the departure." His eyes remained squinted, and I held my hands up. "Somebody's got to work."

"I hear that. Yeah, there was some shoving. Big dude on the boat, he about kicked some loudmouth's ass for heckling this hot little *chica* on the dock."

"You said the boat wasn't from here. Was she from one of the other marinas? Garrison Bight, or maybe Oceanside?"

He tossed the cigarette into the water, coughed again, and checked his palm for fragments.

"Don't remember no port of call on the transom."

I thanked him and walked down the fuel dock past the Half Shell Raw Bar. Cuban-Americans had been picketing the departure? Could that have anything to do with Jo Jo getting his head smashed in? What about Santeria? I pictured the debris field where we'd found Jo Jo. Then it dawned on me. There was nothing from the boat itself afloat in the straits, only its cargo.

The realization clicked, but it left me feeling antsy instead of enlightened. If Willy didn't want my help, I'd have to tell the Coast Guard about this myself. I had to get back out to search for clues and figure out why what happened led to the theft of my GPS—

The coordinates where we found Jo Jo were saved on it too.

At least I still had notes on my kneeboard of where we found him.

19

My brain bounced information around like light off a disco ball. I walked down Caroline to the courthouse. The vehicle I sought in the parking lot wasn't there, so I meandered up Greene. My quarry's routine would eventually lead him my way.

The T-shirt shops that lined Duval flourished like remora clinging to the underbelly of a great whale shark, culling cruise ship cattle like plankton through its fine teeth. They competed by promoting vulgar statements on cotton placards in their windows. One caught my eye, displayed like a masterpiece: *TRUE LOVE IS A BLOWJOB AWAY.*

A purr of giggling whispered ahead, but every restaurant and saloon was locked tight. The sound seemed to emanate from the Bull, but it was closed until the 10:00 a.m. Bloody Mary hour began. The laughter grew louder. A sudden drop of rain hit my shoulder—not rain, but a gush of … beer?

The laughter overhead escalated. "Sorry, sweetie."

If I were anywhere else I'd have been shocked, but this being Key West I wasn't even surprised to see two topless women leaning over the railing of The Whistle, the upstairs dance club to the downstairs pool joint.

"Oh, you're a big one," the blonde said. "Wanna come up and party?" Her breasts cantilevered over the railing. The other woman had jet-black hair, and what she lacked in the mammary department she compensated for with exotic tattoos of dragons facing off on her pasty chest.

A rusted-out baby blue Cadillac Coupe d'Elegance, vintage 1980, lurched down Duval. I waved him over.

"Oyé, what'chu doing?" Currito Salazar peered through the half-open window.

"Curro, check this out."

He powered the window down and leaned out to behold the damsels in distress.

"Damn, cuz, they with you?"

"Uh, no."

"Look like future clients to me." He dug into the breast pocket of his stained *SOLDANO CONSTRUCTION* T-shirt. "Give 'em these, okay?" He handed over a couple business cards. *Conch Bail Bonds, Chartered and Certified.*

The ladies were back to giggling and spilling beer over the railing. "If the police give you any trouble, call my man Currito here." I put the cards in the crack of the door, then turned back to the caddie.

"Give me a ride?"

"The La Concha's two blocks away—"

"To the airport."

The passenger door swung open with a screech. I entered to wails of disparagement from the balcony. "Come on, honey, be our knight in shining latex!"

I pulled the door closed and the world dimmed behind the double-wrap of window tinting. The Cadillac edged onward, a wreck passing by the Wrecker's Museum. One of the oldest cars on the island, riding past the oldest home.

"I was looking for you," I said.

"Nothing happening at the courthouse yet, but if I drive up and down the strip long enough, someone always gets busted." It was the bail bondsman's version of ambulance chasing.

His nose twitched like a rabbit. "Damn, boy, you bathe in Aramis or what?"

I adjusted the backpack on my lap. "Didn't get a shower this morning."

A Parliament cigarette dangled from Currito's lips. There was a carpet of ash below the overstuffed ashtray and a gray smudge on his belly. A Michelob pony bottle stuck up between his legs. Short, old, and gray, Currito had as much charisma as anyone I'd met on this rock.

"By the way, cuz, you crazy?" he said.

"There's been speculation to that effect. Why—"

"Bruiser Lewis?"

I swallowed hard. "Too early in the morning to think about that."

"Any time's too early," he said. "That was some shit yesterday, finding J-*tres.*"

"Been better if we'd found him alive. Did you know the others?"

"Sure, boy, locals, all of 'em. Crazy fools." He hacked a laugh. "Plenty people die making that crossing. We found a raft one time, eleven people dead and one little baby crying." He waved the cigarette as he spoke. "You make that trip, you got to accept the risk."

I'd heard rumors about trips Currito made back in the '70's. Not to Cuba but to points further south, and not on cabin cruisers but shrimp boats, sans the shrimp. To the locals, though, he was good people. We drove slowly down Duval. At the La Concha I pressed my nose to the window to see my apartment six-floors up.

"Used to be a helluva disco there, called Fitzgerald's," Currito said. "My son was the disc jockey. Was the shit. Live bands came in from all over the country. And pussy? Damn, cuz, incredible." His extended fingers snapped together in a brisk whip of his wrist.

Now it was a chain hotel with a Starbucks where the disco had been. Progress.

"Where's your son now?"

"He left. Everybody left, one way or another. Jail, work, or dead. Hell, cuz, locals can't afford to live here any more. My house weren't paid for? Shit."

Like most cities, Key West had been stripped of its historic character, except for a veneer of city funded exhibits. The rest was engorged with mass-market franchises that left its only differentiation from the rest of the country climate, latitude and longitude. The homogenization of the planet may have been slowed by global economic failure, but human nature's inexorable lust for profit will once again surge like a fungus when conditions allow. Lenny was right, and his political instinct merited attention. We needed leaders willing to restore individuality to our communities.

"You mind telling me something, Curro?"

He glanced over the top of his glasses. "Depends."

"How did you feel about Redeemer's mission?"

"I could care less. But it lit the fuse, that's for damn sure."

"The arguing when the boat left?"

"Put it this way, my business indicators are up and I smell a bumper crop of activity about to pop."

"Bail bonding business?"

"No, bikini waxing, the hell you think? Of course bail bonding. Damn, cuz, Willy's people are sticking their heads in the wrong beehive."

An eye for an eye. "Santeria?"

"Don't even think of messing with those bastards. I've seen Chango do some shit.

Piss Santeros off, they'll fuck you up. One time, Bobby Delgado—you know him?"

How had I pissed them off? A headache began to fester behind my right eyeball.

"Can't say I do."

"His wife caught him nailing this girl from the high school, and Bobby had the *cojones* to kick *her* out of the house. Well, Theresa, that's Bobby's wife, her daddy was into that shit, and he got the Sancho on Stock Island to teach him some kind of curse. They sacrificed a goat or cat or something. Next thing you know, Bobby's busted for smuggling grass."

"Maybe it was a coincidence." I tried popping my ears.

"What, you think I'm making this up? Chango can't mess with you? Shit. That's what Willy Peebles thought. Why don't you ask him?"

A cringe curled my fingers.

"Cuz, trust me, Bobby's cousin was the chief of police. He'd never have got busted. It's the shit."

The car stopped and Currito nodded toward a building on Duval Street. Cardboard covered where the shop window had been.

"Exotica?"

"Shotgun blast in the middle of the night," he said.

"A sex toy shop?"

Currito turned sharply toward me, his faced bunched into a wrinkled scowl. "Sex toys? You crazy, boy? It's a *Botanica*. They sell shit for Santeria, candles, books, fucking goats for all I know. Game's on now, brother. Somebody from Redeemer lit the fuse, only on the wrong bomb. Now it's going to blow up in their faces."

"You mind stopping here a minute?"

He checked the rearview mirror. "Whatever."

Could Exotica have anything to do with Betty being broken into?

20

Cardboard was taped over the open window frame. After peeling its corner away, I could see bookracks, mounds of candles, clothing, and some small cages toward the back. It was too dark inside to see much detail. The store had the feel of those new-age mystical places specializing in crystals and incense, but Santeria had a much more ominous reputation.

The cardboard suddenly fell inside. Remnants of safety glass left an edgy border along the frame. It would be easy to crawl through—I glanced back at Curro, who was looking down the street. I reached in and brushed my fingers down the frame to the lock. Breaking and entering would be a new—

A sudden movement caught my attention.

A blur spun toward me to the sound of fluttering.

A shriek rang out as the blur sprang through the window right at me.

I swatted at it—

"*Bbaaa-kkkooookkk!*"

A fat hen crashed off my forearm and smashed into the side window, where it erupted into feathers and a shrill avian screech.

"Hey!" A voice shot out of the darkness inside, followed by the unmistakable sound of a shell being pumped into a shotgun. "Paulo! No! Paulo, be away!"

A gun barrel pushed through the broken glass. I dove back into the car, startling Currito from a trance induced by a female roller-blading up Duval.

"Let's go!"

He grabbed the wheel with both hands and hit that gas. I wondered if he could hear my heart pounding or if he'd seen me launch the chicken. I peered back over the seat. The roller-blader was Karen Parks, now bent over the scrawny hen on the sidewalk. She looked up and waved a fist at us. I hunkered lower in the seat and prayed she hadn't seen me.

"The hell's wrong with you?" Currito said.

"You sure Santeria isn't involved with the missing boat?"

"Willy didn't tell you about all the fuss?"

My eyelid twitched. "You mean the picketers?"

"That's the tip of the shitberg. This has Cuba's bloody fingerprints all over it. Now Poquito's coming unglued, screaming for action. I'm telling you, it's a different world today, cuz. We got a president trying to cover his ass for the last invasion. Starting another one might be the ticket."

Currito echoed what many news pundits warned. The administration might seek opportunities to divert public attention from the Mideast quagmire if an easy win could be achieved elsewhere. All under the guise of a pre-emptive doctrine, which was intended to make sure the first punch won. Iran's thumbing its nose at the United Nation's Security Council over their nuclear program didn't help matters.

"If the press jumps on this thing," I said, "they'll have it packaged and branded with theme music before the evening news."

For years my father, the statesman and puzzle freak, had been fearful that after the Soviet Union disintegrated and the Russians pulled out of Cuba, U.S. intervention there was inevitable. The thawing of relations had done nothing to change the hardliner's rhetoric, nor change the reality that the island was armed to the teeth, and the crevasse that separated political and military strategists on whether the eleven million Cuban people would welcome emancipation or fight out of nationalistic pride was wide. The proponents argued that it would be a short operation. Just as they had about Iraq.

"Who's *Poquito*?" I said.

"Mingie Posada. Local big mouth and coalition boss." Currito laughed. "The nickname goes back to high school, and it ain't because he's short. Yeah, the Cubans screwed the pooch this time, you watch. All that chicken blood, feathers, and burning candles at Redeemer's a lot of bullshit."

"Chicken blood and feathers?" I checked my forearm. Willy hadn't told me about that, either.

"I know some of those people. If you push 'em, they'll rain fire on your ass, but this ain't their style."

Great. Lenny had said much the same about Gutierrez. Did the police know of his calls for retaliation? Could that have anything to do with Exotica's shattered storefront? Or the bird in my plane? We passed the San Carlos Institute where more posters for the art show hung, all with the same "m.p." typo.

"Is that Manny's show?" I asked.

"You know him?"

"Not as well as I need to. You going?"

"Oh, yeah, me and Manny Gutierrez, we're tight. I gave him all my shit on consignment: Picasso, Renoir, Michael fucking Angelo. He's a *balsero* punk who hit it big. Now he's a *chulo*, a real playboy. Fancy cars, racing boats, he's an asshole. With any luck he'll flip defending his title at the offshore race next weekend." Currito's disdain reminded me of when I was on top of the world, thinking I had it all, before it all had me.

"Gutierrez is a piece of shit, stealing paintings from old women and peddling flea market crap in fancy frames. Now he's blaming the Santeros, which'll piss off his clients. Everyone else thinks it's the Cubans."

"He has guts to be the contrarian."

"Yeah, if that means asshole."

We turned right on Petronia, went past Blue Heaven and onto Thomas. The smell of decay intensified the deeper we drove into Bahama Village. Paint-chipped exteriors contrasted with the manicured world beyond Duval. The white steeple of Redeemer caught the sun above the dark foliage. The front door was open, and I could see people inside.

We cruised past, and an urge suddenly hit me. "Stop!"

Currito flinched and hit the brakes. "Damn, cuz, you scared the shit out of me."

"I'll get out here."

"Thought you were headed to the airport?" He took a slug off the Michelob as the door screeched shut.

The sun was casting long shadows onto the street. Willy's sentiment yesterday was clear, I wasn't welcome here. But with Betty broken into, there was more than guilt and a need for income driving me now. Especially if that coral head near Fort Jefferson was the *Esmeralda*. Plus, Currito was the second person surprised by something Willy hadn't told me. It was time to find out why.

I heard the sound of muted voices inside. When I stuck my head in the door, the conversation stopped. Several faces stared at me.

"You!"

21

"What the hell do you want?" Manny Gutierrez yelled.

A snaggle-toothed kid jumped up and came at me, followed by two others.

"Hey! Enough of that." Willy shouted from a center pew amidst a group that looked like a gathering of felons.

Manny's frown slowly turned to a smile. He stood and said something about people to see. As he walked past me he spoke in a voice only I could hear. "You can't keep your nose out of this, can you, Reilly."

"You mentioned Santeria before," I said. "Why would they have anything to do with the missing boat? Or Jo Jo's death? Could it be Cuba instead?"

I couldn't tell if he smiled or sneered. He sauntered out without another word. Willy pointed down the hall. A dozen lynch-hungry expressions quickened my pace.

Sunlight filtered through the wood blinds in his office, and shadows of foliage danced on the wall. Willy's eyes looked hard like black beans. The Ruler, as Lenny had called him.

"You tell the press about Shaniqua being on the boat?"

"Sure, along with all that flattering stuff about me. I came to Key West to forget about my past. Now I'm back to being fodder for the local rag. This keeps up I'll have to start over somewhere else."

"So, what do you want here?"

I swung the backpack off my shoulder, removed the lunch box, unzipped the lid, and dumped the dead dove onto his desk. Willy's eyes narrowed. "You ever seen something like this before?"

He held a steady poker face.

"Somebody left it in my plane. Why didn't you tell me your mission was opposed by Santeros and Cuban ex-pats?"

"I hired you for flying, not thinking."

"Believe it or not I can do both."

"That is till I found out you delivered my daughter to the damn boat."

"Not that it matters, but how did you know that?"

He picked up the dove, turned it over in his hands, squeezed it, and then parted the feathers on its belly. He held it up for closer inspection.

"I prefer them with bacon and water chestnuts," I said.

Willy popped something red out of the dove's chest. It landed on his desk.

"Cowry shell. Some kind of hex, or ritual, maybe."

"Don't I feel special."

I showed him the note, but Willy offered no opinion about its message.

"After Shaniqua didn't show up or return my calls, I went to her apartment and found a note. She apologized but said some fool had given her the number for Last Resort Charters and she was going to catch the boat."

"Charters *and* Salvage."

"I should have known she'd do something crazy. She was so damn fixated with seeing her mother's homeland. My wife was Cuban—"

"Did you tell the police that she was missing before it was in the paper?"

"Forget the police. Those boys out in the chapel are my investigators."

"You should at least tell the Coast Guard."

"Won't change how hard they're gonna search. And now everyone's blaming each other, hunting for Santero ghouls or Cuban provocateurs. I just want my daughter back." He pressed his lips together. "There, I said it, I just want my—" A tear made it onto the desk. He rubbed his eyes with bunched fists, but there was no other outward sign of emotion. His eyes quickly cleared.

"Why would anyone care about a church mission to Cuba?" I said.

"The area we targeted has a powerful Sancho. Maybe he didn't like the idea."

I lifted the dove, examined the cowry shell, and zipped both back in the box.

"Tell me about Santeria."

"Started in Africa," Willy said. "Then blossomed in Cuba nearly five hundred years ago because of the slave trade. People were dragged from the wilderness, but they brought their beliefs with them. Exploitation only made 'em stronger, blending African and Catholic traditions and it's growing bigger—"

"Catholic?"

"They disguise what they call 'Orishas' behind Catholic saints to avoid persecution."

"What's that have to do with Redeemer, or this bird?"

"Their Orishas are like Gods, and they number in the hundreds. Each of them has their own sort of specialty. Some of the more notable are Oggun, their god of war, and Chango, their god of thunder and lightning."

"Chango. Currito Salazar mentioned that name this morning."

"He's a warrior god," Willy said. "Encourages you to go take what you want. That dove's likely some kind of *ebó*, or sacrificial offering. They also use hens, roosters, and sometimes goats, but every Orisha has a preferred animal, foods, even colors and numbers used for worship."

"You take the competition seriously."

"I've got my reasons."

"So the mission was an attempt to thwart Santeria?"

"Wasn't really the plan." He leaned forward over his desk. "We were just trying to keep God's word alive amidst the paganism in the part of Havana where my wife grew up. Her family fled after the revolution, and well, it was her dream to have our church...." Willy suddenly sat down. He looked as if he hadn't slept at all.

"So Manny thinks Santeria's behind the boat's disappearance, and his rationale is... what, that if they sacrifice animals, why not humans?"

Willy nodded.

"What was behind the picketing at the *Carnival's* departure?"

"Manuel Ortega, the old Conch who called from the boat on his cell phone? His brother was one of the Brothers to the Rescue pilots dropping supplies to boat people several years back. A Cuban MiG shot him down." Willy didn't flinch as he threw the curve ball over the plate.

"So?"

"Now the CANC's involved. Cuban American National Coalition."

"I know who they are."

"They got a small, local chapter run by a guy who owns a restaurant."

"Mingie Posada?"

"Guess you can think and fly. Mingie bitched plenty about the mission, now he's rallied the heavyweights in Miami for some PR offensive."

The CANC was a highly effective political organization that had carried a presidential election a few years ago. The new détente had spurred them to action, and this situation would provide a golden opportunity to condemn the Cuban government. My father's hypothesis that Cuba was vulnerable to a U.S. attack synthesized with the media speculation that the administration was desperate for an easy win to take the public's mind off their Mideast nation-building blunders just took a big step forward. It was the kind of story the network news fear-pushers delighted in. A real rating's booster.

"Now everyone's giving up the search to gear up for a fight."

"Was Manny behind the attack on Exotica?" I said.

"He's rallying half the hotheads for a witch hunt, and the CANC's firing up the rest. Could have been anybody. Our people will be forgotten." Willy took a deep breath. "To make matters worse, when I got here this morning there was another surprise waiting." He pressed a button on the telephone.

After a couple of beeps, a deep voice began an eerie whisper. "Continue your mission and the stakes will escalate. Our reach is limitless."

"What did the police say about that?"

"Didn't tell 'em. I want them focused on search and rescue, not whodunit. My boys out there'll find out. Given enough ammo, both sides will use our people for their own purposes. Truth be told, I don't give a rat's ass about any of that. I just want my little girl back."

We sat quietly. I couldn't help thinking his daughter was likely dead. Now a vigilante war was breaking out on one front, and a well-connected political action committee was stirring the pot on another. Willy's simple mission to Cuba was in ruins, his people destined to become martyrs, and my world was dumped on its ear.

"We've got a memorial service planned for tomorrow afternoon." Willy said. "Jo Jo's getting buried at the cemetery. The *Citizen* covered the boat's departure. They have pictures of everyone who was on board. We're having some blown up for the service."

"What can you tell me about the boat?"

"Came from Miami—"

"Wait a minute, you said it was *our* boat?"

"It was carrying *our* people, so it was *our* boat. Man named Hector Perez was the captain. They were Cuban immigrants who read about our plans in the paper. Before that, we were going to fly commercial through the Bahamas, but with a boat we had a big food and clothing drive. You should've seen the mountain of stuff on board."

The flotsam in the straits.

The stereotype of Cuban expatriates from Miami wanting to help was in contradiction to the demonstration at the boat's departure. They rarely did anything that might help sustain the regime, indirectly or not.

"Can I use your phone?" I said.

He slid it toward me, and I dialed the airport. Once Ray answered his page, he reported no luck in finding the problem with the port engine. He planned to tear it down tomorrow.

"Ray, listen, this isn't one of our normal salvage projects. It can't wait."

"What about that dead bird?"

"Forget the damn bird," I said. "I can't afford a rebuild, just do what you can."

After I hung up, the silence in Willy's office was suffocating. From a pencil holder behind his desk, he removed an old wooden ruler and slapped it against his open palm. The ruler's wooden edges were dented and gnarled. The Ruler.

I told him about my realization of where we found Jo Jo. There had been no evidence of the boat itself, no charred wood, oil slicks, floating cushions, nothing. Optimism surfaced in his face, and he agreed to call the Coast Guard.

"You say the funeral's tomorrow?"

"Jo Jo's getting buried next to Reverend J. Van Duzer." I had no idea who that was but didn't show my ignorance. "We're offering a ten-thousand-dollar reward for each of our people recovered, alive," Willy said. "Sounds like you need money, so..."

"Each?"

"Shaniqua's still out there." He slapped the ruler against his palm. Willy had a reputation for fixing people others considered hopeless, but he probably knew that even the force of the Ruler might not be enough to solve this situation.

22

I left the church under a gauntlet of nasty stares,
but armed with a lot more information then I'd started with. Time to turn the
island over to find out why the *Carnival* was victim to foul play—and whether my
finding one of their bodies made me a target.

I considered stopping at Blue Heaven, but seeing the boxing ring might make
me nauseous. There was not enough time to prepare for my bout with Bruiser
Lewis, and the days were dropping fast. Basketball was my traditional conditioning routine, but my one game a week wouldn't do me much good. I jogged back
to the La Concha.

When I arrived at the parking lot I stopped to catch my breath. While brushing sweat off my forehead, I glanced at my Rover. What the—The back gate was
askew.

I remembered throwing my flight bag in yesterday.

I ran to the passenger door and peered in the window. Then to the driver's
side, then to the back.

My flight bag was gone.

I searched up and down the three rows of cars for any sign of my bag. Nothing. A few tourists next to the moped rental hut stared at me as if I were deranged.

"Zeke, you got a minute?" I said to the proprietor.

"Hey, Buck, hold on—you got to wear a helmet, dude."

"You seen anybody suspicious here in the lot?"

He glanced back over his shoulder and raised his eyebrows. There was a group of tank-topped, trunk-legged women in line.

"Kidding me, right?"

"Somebody broke into my truck."

"No shit, here? Hey, honey, no twofers, these scooter's have weight limits."

"How about anything strange or even just out of the ordinary this morning?" I waited through a short silence.

"You know, there was a dude earlier, kind of hanging around but behind the bushes, you know? I thought he was jerking off. I told him to beat it. I mean, not literally, but seemed kind of weird."

"Was he carrying anything?"

"Nah, I don't think so, but I got busy, so maybe he came back. Dude was wearing a blue ... what do you call those shirts the old Cubans wear?"

"Guayabara?"

"Yeah, and it stunk. You know how you get that smoky, boozy stink in bars?"

"You remember anything else? Was he old, young, fat, skinny?"

"Young, Latin-American-looking guy, good shape. That's it, Buck—sorry, man." He turned back to his customers. "Lady, listen, no insurance, you wreck it, you buy it."

Young Latino in a blue guayabara? Could that be the same guy who stole my stash?

I hustled inside the hotel.

"There you are!" Karen's yell nearly launched me out of my flip-flops. The customer she was helping stared me up and down. I stood, still in shock, while she called for back-up and then led me over to one of the rattan couches in the big lobby.

Please don't have seen me swat the chicken. I didn't mean to swat the chicken.

The fragrance of lilac emanated from her ponytail. I looked at her white teeth and pink lips and made myself think about the contents of the flight bag: my pilot's license, hand-held VHF radio, medical certificates, and kneeboard. Then she hits me with the soothing southern accent.

"I know this isn't the best timing, which is why it's perfect," she said. "You need a break, and I need your help, so I have another favor to ask."

"Ask away."

"Ownership wants to redecorate the lobby and public areas, and I have to go to an art show tomorrow night." She beamed a high-wattage smile to soften me up.

"You're actually going out at night? I didn't think—"

"Could you coach me on art a little first?"

Her request brought me squarely into the moment.

"You have all those art books… They want a Latin theme here—"

"The show at the San Carlos Institute?"

"How did you know?"

"Because I'm going too."

"Corporate introduced me to the dealer. He's been chasing me around ever since."

"Manny Gutierrez?"

"You know him?"

"Oh yeah, we go way back," I said.

"I'm not sure if he's interested in selling art or is just a flirt, but I don't know what I'm looking at anyway. Can you show me some of your art books?"

The scent of her hair tickled my senses. "Why don't we go to the show together? We could start with dinner."

The suggestion lit a tiny spark in her eyes, which put a glow in my heart.

"Sure you won't be too tired?"

"Seven Fish is right around the corner from…where I need to go first."

She cut a glance back to the reception desk. A short line had formed in her absence. "Perfect, we can also talk about how you're going to help me with the festival. I'm striking out on the special events front."

"Still desperate?"

She smiled. "I have an idea how you could help launch the entire event. We can talk about it at dinner." The excitement in her voice was contagious.

"So, great," she said. "Seven Fish. The shows at—"

"Seven o'clock m.p." Her eyes narrowed. "Posters all over town have that typo. Let's meet at five-thirty."

"I'd never have figured you for an art connoisseur," she said.

"Speaking of the festival, I'd bet Manny can come up with some ideas."

"You think?" She sat up straight, a new light in her eyes.

"He's a big shot philanthropist who donated the food for Redeemer's mission."

On my way upstairs I had a flashback. In my days at e-Antiquity, manipulation was part of my job. Among other things I had to entice museums to sponsor our archaeological pursuits. Then there was pimping the boys on Wall Street in order to inflate share price and liquidity. Is that what this date with Karen was about? Was I taking advantage of her request for help to further my own interests?

The art show would be the perfect opportunity to investigate what the people hostile toward the missionaries had against me. With Karen on my arm, Manny would have to talk to me, so the answer was unavoidably, yes.

But it was her smile at the proposition that had my heart pumping in overdrive, not the show.

23

Once inside my apartment the first thing I saw was my flight bag on the table.

How did—

Two men dressed in black jumpsuits rushed out of my bedroom. One, wearing a Bill Clinton Halloween mask, was pointing a pistol at me. The other's mask was George W. Bush.

"Sit in the chair," Bush said.

I didn't hesitate, given the gun in Clinton's hand.

"Fantasy Fest is six months away, you boys are little early," I said.

"Shut up and listen," Bush said. I detected a slight Latin accent. He reached into a bag and pulled out something that caused me to grip the arms of the chair. My waterproof pouch. Clinton held the gun up, no doubt reading my expression.

"The charts aren't inside the satchel, so don't get any stupid ideas. I wanted you to understand that if you ignore me, there will be severe ramifications."

I concentrated on breathing. That, and Clinton's pistol.

"What do you want?" I said.

"For you to butt out of the search for the boat."

"So this is about Redeemer?"

"Discontinue your search, or the contents of this satchel go to the police."

My heart sank.

"Why would the police care about my business expenses?"

Bush laughed. "The payments Ben Reilly has been making to Mrs. Dodson—isn't that your brother and former partner's wife? Given your bankruptcy and Dodson's incarceration, I suspect the police would be very interested in these payments. Two hundred grand over the past two years, plus another hundred grand to you."

I slumped back into the seat.

"I say we boil him," Clinton said. He had a much thicker accent. Cuban?

"What's the big deal about the missing boat?" I said.

"No more questions! Butt out, or your documents go to the police, and the articles in the *Citizen* will get much more explicit. They're dying for more. Even in Key West the public loves stories of fallen tycoons."

I swallowed hard. "Can I at least have my GPS back?"

"Boil him!" Clinton shoved the gun in my face.

Bush laughed again. "I'm going to compare the GPS points you saved to the notations on the nautical charts, see what you were up to."

With that Bush picked up the bag containing my waterproof pouch and walked to the door. Clinton followed after, but when he passed by me, he bent down and whispered: "You don't butt out, I boil you."

"Don't leave your room for thirty minutes," Bush said. "Remember, your bird no fly, and leave the spirits of the dead alone."

"What the hell's that mean?"

The door slammed shut. At least they had returned my flight bag.

When I picked it up, it was noticeably heavier than usual. Standing still for a long few seconds, I listened but heard nothing. I unzipped the bag, peered in—and dropped it.

There was a dead chicken inside, decapitated with a wash of blood coating everything. Underneath the bird was a small clay figurine of a man with nails protruding from his body. The chest cavity was hollow, and inside it was the finger from a leather glove. I recognized the frayed seam on its tip. It was the index finger from the work gloves in my truck.

Everything else was there, except…my kneeboard was gone.

I watched from my window but never saw them on Duval Street.

Now, in addition to all my charts and my GPS being gone, which included the location of the gold, the notes from where I found Jo Jo were gone too. The thieves hadn't mentioned the Swiss bank key, but they were going to compare the GPS points against those marked on the chart. It would lead them to the gold.

If I continued the search for the *Carnival,* all the payments Ben had been making to keep Dodson quiet would be exposed.

Crap.

24

Pastor Willy Peebles led an emotional service at
Redeemer aimed at calming the growing cries for blood. He never mentioned his
missing daughter. Jo Jo Jeffries's wife gave a heart-rending eulogy, which although
brief didn't leave a dry eye in the sanctuary. All the raw emotion rekindled mine
from my parent's funeral. After everything I'd been through, their deaths were the
straw that really broke me and led me to abandon the real world for Key West.

Pain will either paralyze or inspire most people. For me it erased a decade of
success-- along with any semblance of family. I had been squeezed, twisted, bent
in half, crumpled, crushed and discarded, and somewhere along the line, I just
stopped caring. The pain in Willy's eyes reawakened me, though. And the theft of
my stash was a kick in the ass.

Willy helped the widow Jeffries down, then returned to the pulpit.

"Now's not the time to cast stones." His voice was low but clear. "Now's not
the time to assign blame or seek retribution. It's time to mourn, to heal, and to
continue searching for our missing loved ones."

At the end of his sermon he asked for people to share "words of memoriam"
about Jo Jo. Several stood next to his pewter urn upon the altar and gave testimony, blinking away tears. A quiet calm followed. After a respectful pause, Willy
returned to the podium. Then another man stood up in the middle of the pews.

It was Manny Gutierrez.

"Are we going to let the Santeria swine get away with murder?"

Every head spun toward him, and Willy's mouth fell open. Manny smashed a fist into his palm. "One of them left a threatening message at my gallery this morning, warning me to butt out, or else!" A wave of commotion erupted.

Did he say, *butt out?*

A short, bald man suddenly jumped up and stabbed a finger toward Manny. He began to shout in Spanish. I couldn't understand him, but it had to be Mingie Posada, the local CANC boss. A half dozen others leapt to their feet, also screamed in Spanish, and lifted signs with pictures of Shaniqua, and "REVENGE" boldly above her smiling face.

The room exploded. The sudden anger reignited the cries for retribution, which continued outside the church, where Manny and Posada squared off.

"Santeria's nothing but a tool used by the Cubans! Don't be a fool," Poquito said.

Younger and more fit, Manny could drop Poquito with a backhand, but he maintained his poise.

"Mingie, you can't blame everything that happens on the Cuban government."

Willy burst out the door ready for battle but was restrained by Lenny and a couple of the other rough-cut young men who'd been at the church yesterday. The tension was thick during the procession to the cemetery, where Jo Jo's powdered remains were lowered into the coral tomb. Willy's fears that the missionaries' deaths would be manipulated to advance other agendas had become a self-fulfilling prophecy.

25

I stood under a broad gumbo-limbo tree, back from the crowd. The threats from the blackmailing thieves had worked. Renewed problems with the law, not only for me but my brother, snuffed my ability to search for either the gold or the girl.

A fresh concrete crypt had been poured next to a corner grave belonging to Reverend J. Van Duzer, which for some reason was a big deal. Nearly the entire population of Bahama Village was in attendance, in addition to a smattering of old Conches paying their last respects, not only to Jo Jo but to those still missing at sea. His widow was a skinny woman with a build similar to Jo Jo's, and his two daughters were both thin to the point of frail. They all had dark black skin, nearly blue in pigment and were all struggling to remain composed.

From my spot under the tree I saw that Lenny was still shaken. He stood near Willy and looked like a pillar of the community. Maybe Conch Man's political ambitions weren't so far-fetched after all.

No results from Jo Jo's autopsy had been made public, but considering the coroner's initial assessment of foul play, could any of these people be something other than concerned friends? Were the goons here now? Bush and Clinton? If so, were they keeping an eye on me? Had they left the message on Manny's machine?

Currito Salazar edged up next to me.

"Some shit, huh? What you get for sticking your neck out," he said.

Was he referring to me or Jo Jo? I aimed my chin at the neighboring plot. "Who's J. Van Duzer?"

"Ah, the Reverend. First missionary to Cuba. Killed by the Spanish."

"Listen, Curro, yesterday you said you knew a Sancho." His eyes narrowed, and he nodded toward Willy like a kid worried he might get scolded by his teacher. "Can you introduce me to him?" I said.

He waved me off and pressed into the crowd.

A rumble sounded from the group. Willy had bent down to close the lid on Jo Jo's crypt, sending a shudder through the mass of people as if they were a single, living, breathing body. A wail made me wince—had to be one of the daughters. The sobs continued, gradually augmented by others. The sobbing grew louder until the entire crowd was gushing. I felt a hot streak down my cheek.

I watched the widow Jeffries and recalled Jo Jo bungee-corded in place of the lost kayak. A chill made me shiver. Why did the thieves want me off the *Carnival's* trail? Had Jo Jo died a hero or a victim? Or a coward?

Afterwards, Willy came up behind me and caught my arm. "The Coast Guard hasn't found squat. Your plane ready yet?" Dark bags bulged under his eyes.

"I don't think so," I said.

Behind him the crowd was in retreat, the placards with Shaniqua's photo again on display. The anti-Santeros and the anti-Cubans were back to arguing. For Willy, mourning would be impossible. He'd be forced instead to try and keep peace while the authorities investigated. Anger and helplessness pulled at his face.

The six enlarged photographs from the memorial service stood on easels next to Jo Jo's grave. Four of the pictures were clear and of good quality. One was a strong-looking young black man, Rodney, the Polo-clad Zodiac captain. Another was an old Cuban American, Ortega. Next was a shot of Jo Jo with one of the posters of Shaniqua sharing its easel. The other three pictures were grainy and had the feel of surveillance shots. Pictures of the three crewmen taken when the *Key West Citizen* covered the *Carnival's* departure. I was struck by the realization that not a soul had appeared on their behalf at the memorial service.

I leaned in closer to study their faces. One man was older with a serious expression and had the air of a captain. The picture of the next man was poor, his face turned away, but he was muscular and young, maybe in his late twenties. The final picture took my breath away. The man stared straight into the camera lens. He had matching scars on his cheeks, broad slashes running from his ears down to his chin. Young, under thirty, but with an old emotion chiseled on his face: hate.

He was the only black man on the crew. I tripped over a broken headstone.

J.E.A. Van Duzer
M.E. Church, South
First Missionary to the Cubans

Died
June 7, 1875
22 Years
Don't give up the Cuban Mission
His last words.

I did a double take and read it again. The words hit me like a kick in the shin. A moment later, Willy, who was leaving with Jo Jo's widow, hurried back over to me.

"Can you come by Redeemer in the morning?"

"I don't think so—"

"But make it early, I'm meeting with Jo Jo's widow and kids at nine o'clock."

I took a deep breath. "I can't make it, sorry."

"Okay, then come after lunch, I have—"

"Not at all, Willy. I'm off the case."

His forehead wrinkled, his eyes narrowed. "Off the case? This is my daughter we're talking about. You're the only one who can help find the boat."

I had the sensation of shrinking and wished I could vanish all together. Willy's expression soured from surprise to what, disgust?

"Something's come up…I, ah, need to lay low."

"Lay low, huh?" He spat on the grass. "I guess Manny Gutierrez was right about you. Can't be counted on or trusted." He stared at me for a long second and then returned to the widow Jefferies. He put his arm around her trembling shoulders and continued down the path followed by her two young daughters.

Not one to duck a fight, capitulating to the blackmailers had me swallowing back bile. Willy's reaction made it even worse. I'd caused my share of misery over the years, and it doesn't feel good. But cowering to blackmailers, and destroying Willy's hopes to find his daughter was a new low. I was on a roll.

The long-awaited date with Karen could not have fallen on a worse evening. I tried to press Redeemer's situation into a distant recess of gray matter. Even though she'd only asked for some art advice, we'd been building up to something for months. There had been so much riding on the art show when I first suggested it, but now I wished I could call it off.

Van Duzer's epitaph again flashed in my mind's eye, its message haunting: *Don't give up the Cuban mission.*

26

Aside from a couple of waiters, Seven Fish was empty. I sat at a table in the corner overlooking Elizabeth Street and awaited a Captain Morgan and ginger. My thoughts turned to the assault and my flight bag cum chicken casket in my apartment. After removing my gear, I'd stuffed the flight bag into the La Concha dumpster, chicken and all. Karen would be appalled. The right-hand glove had indeed been missing from my Rover, the significance of the severed index finger was yet another mystery. If Clinton had his way, though, I was destined to be boiled, whatever that meant.

To the thieves, the value of my stash seemed secondary to forcing me off the *Carnival's* scent. An unplanned bonus for them, a kick in the nuts for me. They had known enough about my past to deduce the ledger entries and also the potential of the maps and letters. But if they figured out that the key led to a Swiss bank account, it could produce worse problems. The chicken delivery, statue, and their meaning were unclear, and even though their accents sounded Cuban, because Cuba was also ground zero for Santeria, that provided no insight into their identity.

The waitress brought my drink, and I savored its sweet taste. Karen and I had never spoken much about our pasts, and her reaction to the e-Antiquity IPO memento on my bookshelf left me unsure what she knew about me. Anxiety hit, and I took another gulp. Karen had come to Key West to manage the La Concha. She worked hard at the hotel, but her volunteer work ate up days off and weekends, and at night she vanished.

A back view of a woman in a tight black miniskirt outside the window caught my attention. She was tall, with long wavy blond hair. I scanned her from the three-inch spike heels, up her tanned and perfectly formed legs, past her shapely derriere and graceful arms. Now *that* was a piece of art. When she turned to the restaurant's entrance and revealed her profile, I choked on my ice. Karen.

When she spotted me, her smile lit the entry. I felt underdressed in linen pants and a silk shirt. Her outfit warranted a handmade Italian suit.

"Don't look so shocked. What did you expect, my La Concha uniform?" Her smile was radiant and genuine.

"A Chicken Rescue League T-shirt, maybe." She smelled of lilac, and the halogen light lit the honey streaks in her wheat-colored hair. I pulled out the chair and she slid in, after a quick glance at my feet.

Was Karen dressed to the nines for Manny or me? I bit my lip. The waiter brought me another drink and took Karen's order for cold chardonnay.

"And you abandoned your flip flops, I'm honored," she said. Her interest in shoes was legendary around the La Concha. I teased her about it, called it her fetish, but she refrained from naming the brand I was wearing, so I let it pass.

"How was the funeral?" she said.

"It turned into a—did I tell you I was going there?"

She laughed. "It was in the paper. Made sense you'd be going. I saw the posters with the girl's face on them."

Out of nowhere came one of those moments when you imagine your own funeral and wonder who would come. If I died tomorrow, I could only think of a handful of friends who'd show. Karen probably thought of me as a loner or maybe even anti-social and arrogant, but the walls I'd constructed were for survival. The equation added up to loneliness, which hadn't bothered me much until right now.

"Are you always so observant?"

"It passes the time, studying people, things that happen," she said.

"Speaking of time, how come I never see you around town after work?"

A look of dismay passed slowly over her face before the smile returned. "What makes you think I'm ever *off* work?"

"Is that the same bullshit bravado you accused me of?"

"I'm chairing a critical part of Old Island Days, and my work with the Rescue League—"

"Nights, Karen. Chickens sleep. How about Old Island *nights*?"

She bit her lip. It was clearly a subject she didn't want to discuss, which only made me more curious. Maybe she was into something I didn't—

"Okay, but I don't want everyone to know. I'm a writer, at least trying to be."

"Writer? Like books?"

"What, you don't think I'm capable? That I should stick to hotel management?"

She went on to explain that she was writing a mystery-thriller, her first, and that she had a friend who was a former editor at a major publishing house reading it now to offer advice. She had originally come to Key West for inspiration and was using the town for her setting.

"The protagonist is an amateur detective. An adrenaline junkie of questionable repute."

"But he turns out okay in the end?"

"Too soon to say." She leaned forward. "Want to read it? I'm normally reluctant to show it to anybody since it's not finished, but, well, if you do read it, you'll understand."

I leaned back in my chair. The news that she was a writer, along with her coming to Key West for inspiration, cast a new light on her. All the volunteer work showed she had a big heart, but writing added…what? Another dimension I found intriguing.

We took our time-sharing appetizers, and when the plates were cleared I told the waiter not to rush the main course. We had an hour before the show, and I was in no hurry to get there. I told her about the recent chicken sacrifices, and she was shocked but mostly mad. She promised to check with her associates for ideas on possible culprits. I was tempted to tell her how my life had been turned upside down in the past forty-eight hours, but didn't want to scare her. Plus, the way my luck had been going, she'd probably have to evict me for importing so much trouble into the hotel.

"Charter, salvage, *and* detective work?" she said. "You'll have a big business before long."

"I don't think so."

"Not compared to e-Antiquity maybe," she said. "But for Key West, it's not bad."

"So you know about that?"

"Anybody who follows the news, past and present, knows about your former company. Besides, I had access to your social security number through the hotel. Anybody can Google the public records. But your subscription to the *Wall Street Journal* that you never read? And the FedEx letter you get every month, from that farm in Virginia? That's what I'm curious about. It comes and you pay the rent the next day, in cash. Is Fox Run Farm yours?"

I was momentarily tongue-tied. "No, it's not my farm—"

"Your ex-wife's?"

"I don't even get hate mail from her."

She leaned closer. "What about the—"

"Fox Run Farm's my brother, Ben's place." I held up my empty glass to the passing waiter. "How about some more rum over here?"

"And the paper?"

"I think of it as a *memento mori.*"

She looked puzzled.

"Consider this your first art lesson. It means a reminder of death, or that we're all mortal. The paper reminds me of the death of my company, and how greed is the root of so many evils. It's been a common element in several centuries of paintings, too."

Her eyes were steady, and a little smile pressed dimples in her cheeks. "Let's talk about how you can help me with the festival. I've been having trouble coming up with unique events."

"What do you have so far?" I was relieved to discuss anything besides my past.

"Bed races down Duval, a rum runner bust at Mallory Square, a grunt fry—"

"Grunts? Not exactly *haute cuisine.*"

"That's what the Conches subsisted on during the Great Depression, and given our economy these days, it might come back in vogue. But you're right, I'm digging deep. If you can't help me, I may resort to bungee jumping off the top of the La Concha to start the ceremonies." We both laughed.

"What do you have in mind?" I said.

She leaned closer. "The offshore races start the same weekend as the festival. I was hoping you could fly me over the starting line to drop a checkered flag, and then we could buzz over to Duval. I could have my cell phone dialed into a P.A. system to announce the commencement—"

"There are restrictions on altitude, Karen. We can't just *buzz* Duval Street." The sag in her smile cut me short. "But, sure, if my plane gets fixed, I'll help you."

"I knew you would!"

"Here's a thought for you. Manny Gutierrez is the reigning offshore champ. Maybe he could do something to help."

Her expression turned serious. "If he wants to sell art to the hotel, there may need to be some quid pro quo."

Poor Manny didn't know what he was up against. Her teeth sparkled in the candlelight, and I found myself imagining us—

"What about you, the salvage business enough to hold your interest, or do you see yourself back in the corporate world someday?"

Her question stopped me cold. "I got sick of life's routine. The alarm rings, you go to work, the clock hits six, you go home, the alarm rings, you go to work, the clock hits six, you go home. Hamsters on a wheel, that's all we are. By twenty-eight I was eaten up and spat out by corporate America, so I checked out."

"Your fall from grace continues to be well documented, but from all I've read, the last chapter hasn't been finished." Her eyes bore into mine. "You still have skeletons in your closet, flyboy?"

"I don't know about a whole skeleton. A couple ribs and a femur, maybe."

The moment passed, and my blood suddenly felt carbonated. Getting the past behind me was a liberating sensation. If she knew about the worst parts, at least she had the decency not to mention them.

Dinner was served. We exchanged bites of blackened grouper and baked yellowtail. "I've never flown on a sea plane." Her eyes twinkled. "I'm really excited you're going to help, and I promise not to make you break any rules."

The rum had loosened my tongue. "There are only three things I want out of life now. An adventure to live—"

"That explains the airplane." She held up her index finger.

"A battle to fight—"

"Your salvage missions?" She held up a second finger, and her connecting my dots made me pause. I balked on the third part, suddenly not wanting to share the last of my desires: a beauty to rescue.

"I'm still working on the last one."

The laser focus returned. "A treasure to find, maybe?"

It dawned on me that Lenny had the same response. I didn't take it as a compliment. "Yeah, well, used to be."

"With e-Antiquity and your divorce, at least I understand you better now. I wasn't sure if you were a loner or on the other team."

My jaw fell open.

"This *is* Key West, after all." She checked her watch.

"I haven't made that many friends here," I said. "By choice, I guess, but it suddenly feels lonely."

She reached forward with both of her soft, French-manicured hands, stopping my heart by wrapping them around mine. She leaned over and the smell of lilac swirled between us. Her eyes were half-lidded, and I couldn't break free of them to watch her full lips as they parted.

"You're not alone, Buck Reilly, you're not alone."

27

If Karen's arm weren't wrapped through mine, my feet would have been floating above the ground as we walked the few short blocks to Duval Street. My heart felt lighter then it had in ages. The sidewalks were crowded, but my world had shrunk to a five-foot sphere around us. Until the familiar roar of twin in-line engines screamed over our heads.

Betty streaked past at an altitude that would get most pilots' licenses revoked, unless they were Ray Floyd. Her engines sounded strong and in perfect cadence.

"That's my girl," I said.

"So much for those flight rules you were worried about."

We watched Ray bank over the La Concha.

"What's with the Christmas bulbs under the wings?" Karen said.

"They're floats. The colors represent channel markers. Green's on your right when you're leaving port, and red's always on your right when returning home."

"The right one's red, does that mean you're home?"

"Too soon to say."

Seeing Betty brought all my problems crashing back in an inescapable reality check. Dinner with Karen and discovering her secret passion to write was great but I'd originally planned to come to the art show for answers. Presidential politics changed that. Clinton and Bush in particular. I'd never felt so impotent, but if

I wanted to stay in Key West to try and learn their identities and the whereabouts of my GPS and stash, I needed to keep a low profile.

We were nearly at the San Carlos Institute, and under different circumstances I would have felt wined and dined, emotionally charged, and on the brink of romantic discovery. But romance was just another luxury I couldn't afford. Instead, I wondered how Manny would balance his accusations against the Santeros, since his patrons largely believed in a Cuban conspiracy.

A fight on the sidewalk bled onto Duval Street. A crowd of people had circled, but as we approached, something was missing. There was none of the typical cheering and shoving associated with the street fights of my past. The scent of beer and a cigar filled the air. The elegant façade of the San Carlos Institute rose above the melee of what turned out to be the mob of attendees jockeying for entry into the art show.

Karen scanned the crowd ahead. She stopped to check her makeup in a small mirror from her purse. "The mayor and half the city council are in line," she said.

Local politicos, heavy hitters, and self-proclaimed big shots, as expected. Karen was drawn to them like an electron to a nucleus. She immediately stepped into her role of Old Island Days Festival promoter.

Down Duval loomed the dark windows of my corner apartment at the La Concha. The image of Betty turning a wing over The Top made me smile. Ray must have managed to avoid a total rebuild of the port engine, thank God.

"I'm Karen Parks, manager of the La Concha," Karen said to someone in front of us. Standing behind her, I couldn't see who it was until she stepped aside and pointed to me. "And this is—"

"Buck Reilly! What a surprise." Rosalie Peña, the director of the San Carlos Institute gave me a bear hug and a wet kiss on the cheek. Over Rosalie's shoulder I could see Karen's mouth hanging open.

"My landlady here asked me for some art advice." I didn't wink, I didn't smirk, I just looked at Karen. Her mouth closed.

"Come right in, Buck, and I'm sorry, what was your name again?"

"Karen Parks."

Rosalie had already turned toward the door and was pulling me by the hand. I grabbed Karen's arm, and we passed by the others waiting to get in. The lobby was packed. There was a steady flow of people moving up and down the ornate stairway, but what caught my eye were the missing missionaries' faces emblazoned on posters hanging on the walls between the paintings. A three-piece ensemble provided a classical background to the cacophony of blended languages.

"You've got to meet Manny Gutierrez, the dealer putting on the show? He's fabulous." She lowered her voice to a gravelly hush. "And gorgeous, too."

A big smile bent Karen's lips. "I'm redecorating—"

"Manny has some wonderful Portocarrero's and even a Botero, Buck," Rosalie said. "Are you here to add to your parents'…" She paused. "Did you get their collection?"

"My brother did."

If what Rosalie said was accurate, then Currito's description of Manny's material was way off. By her account, he was at the pinnacle of the Latin art scene.

Karen explained her involvement in Old Island Days to Rosalie and asked if the San Carlos might be available for an event.

"The Institute is about heritage," Rosalie said. "Not tourism."

I pointed to one of the posters. "There's a lot more than art being pushed tonight. I thought Gutierrez didn't believe that Cuba—"

There was a sudden shout for silence. Everyone turned toward the center of the room where Mingie Posada stood with his arms raised. The mayor was by his side.

"The Cuban government must not get away with murder. Again!"

A murmur of support rippled through the crowd.

"Oh, God, not *that* jerk," Karen said.

"Mayor Schwartz has graciously granted the Cuban American National Coalition's request for a demonstration tomorrow, coinciding with others in Miami, Washington, D.C, and Paramus, condemning this terrorist act against freedom!"

The murmur grew to loud applause. *Uh-oh.* The CANC had rallied to use this opportunity to denounce the Cuban government. I leaned into Rosalie.

"What does the CANC hope—"

The words froze in my mouth. There was a blue guayabara in the middle of… then another. A quick count found three. Could they be the blackmailers?

A loud clatter echoed through the room, and Manny Gutierrez descended the steps with the speed of a wide receiver.

"Mingie, Mingie, please," Gutierrez said. "My guests are here for a night of festivity. I allowed the posters, but spare us the rhetoric."

Posada smiled and took a bow to the loud applause that encircled him. Gutierrez maintained a diplomatic expression. Dressed in white linen, he looked ready for a GQ cover shoot. Every female eye in the room was focused on him, including Karen's.

Rosalie rushed into the breech, visibly thrilled at the drama playing out at her party.

"You know Posada?" I asked.

"We've gone toe-to-toe a number of times," Karen said. "The sick bastard's notorious for butchering island chickens and serving them at his restaurant. We've pressed the police to raid him, but my guess is he pays them off."

"Quite the collection of Key West big shots, isn't it?"

"They have good taste, for the most part," Karen said.

"Shoes?"

Karen puckered her lips, and then smiled. "Your friend Rosalie's wearing Manolo Blanik, a woman over there has on Valentino." She nodded toward a tanned man speaking with the mayor. "He has on a nice Santoni loafer, and Manny's wearing Ferragamo's."

"How about Posada?"

She frowned. "Wal-Mart."

The crowd was boisterous after Mingie's speech. How would the CANC's pressure play out? Would the press seize the opportunity and dial-up the paranoia-promotion? Would the president consider Cuba a logical target for their pre-emptive doctrine to get the country's eyes off the Middle East? Regardless of the recent thaw, Cuba had been a fifty-year embarrassment to American foreign policy, so it surely could, which would be the worst case for Willy. Not to mention me finding my stash.

I snatched two glasses of champagne off a passing tuxedoed waiter's tray, handed one to Karen, and held mine up.

"To the chickens."

"So how do you know Key West's top socialite?" she said.

"Old friend of the family."

"Friend, huh? She practically licked your face."

Rosalie was the fifty-something widow of one of the top ophthalmologists in the country, a Cuban émigré who'd dropped dead five years ago, leaving her a small fortune. She was lovely, well connected, and the queen of local entertaining. The San Carlos Institute was the perfect vehicle for her reign.

Karen rubbed lipstick off my cheek, then led me to begin touring the art. A path opened, and it took me a second to realize that everyone was staring at us—at Karen, actually. She *was* stunning and with her high heels not only taller than any woman in the room but half the men. She was also oblivious to admiring and envious eyes.

"This your idea of laying low?" I turned to find Willy Peebles in a tight-fitting sport jacket and tie. "Wrecker, boxer, and patron of the arts? I might have thought you some kind of New Age Renaissance man, had you not quit on me."

"Boxer?" Karen said.

"Buck's supposed to fight Bruiser Lewis this weekend, but now the odds are that he won't show. Too bad. The Village was thrilled, since most opponents are shipped in from up north. Bruiser's already worked through the southern part of the state, and nobody's wanted a re-match."

"Why on earth would you—"

"Blue Heaven pays $1,000 for every round anyone survives Bruiser, and $5,000 if they make all three, but boxings anything but laying low." Willy curled his lip at me.

"You're full of surprises, flyboy," Karen said.

"That your plane that flew over tonight?" Willy said.

I didn't answer.

"Stop by Redeemer in the morning," he said. "I have a surprise for you."

"I can't—"

"Relax, nobody's going to kidnap you."

"What do you think about the demonstration?" Karen said.

"They're predicting a thousand people. Like I figured. My daughter, all of them are more useful to these people dead than alive."

Willy was right. They were now being used as a means to an end.

"These jerks and their political lapdogs won't let history repeat itself, especially if they can rally an invasion," Willy said.

Willy was then engulfed by fiery-eyed consolationsists. I excused myself under the premise of searching for the champagne tray but really wanted to locate Gutierrez. Another old man in a blue guayabara walked past me. Could the blackmailers be connected to the CANC?

The swarm was thick in the lobby. I searched the crowd for Gutierrez and looked at the paintings as I went. Most of the artists were unfamiliar, but there was an impressive amount of pre-and post-Revolutionary Cuban art, including works by the cubist René Portocarrero. No sign of a Botero, but I didn't doubt Rosalie, I'm sure it was there.

With two new glasses of champagne, I circled back to find Karen. She had vanished, no doubt pitching Old Island Days' ideas. Maybe Poquito could arrange to hang a Castro replica in effigy for a public flogging.

There was a commotion by the stairs. I spotted Karen pointing a finger at Posada. Gutierrez stepped between them. He said something that made Posada laugh and spin away. The mayor put an arm around Karen.

I navigated through the crowd with the drinks held to my chest. As I reached the stairs, the mayor's wife swung her arms in the midst of a story and knocked both glasses onto my shirt. Oblivious to what she had done, she offered no apology or recognition, not that it would have changed the fact that I was now soaking wet. Karen saw me and tried not to smile.

Gutierrez was nestled up to her side. Art looked to be the last thing on his mind. He sized me up from head to toe, and once again I felt underdressed.

"Buck, what happened?" Karen said.

"Champagne front blew through. I was bringing you a fresh glass."

"Oh, Manny took care of me." I detected a slight slur in her voice.

I held out my hand. "Nice show."

Gutierrez took my hand just short of my palm and squeezed my fingers in a strong grip that pressed my knuckles together.

"King Charles," he said. "The newspaper reported that you took Shaniqua Peebles out to the *Carnival*."

A quick study of the expectant faces around us led me to conclude that Gutierrez was either trying to humiliate me, adroit at sarcasm or a ham for information.

"What are your thoughts about the local Santeria community," I said.

"Not another Mingie Posada. Please, tonight's show is to help the San Carlos Institute. At the moment I'm helping the lovely Ms. Parks consider major improvements for the hotel."

"Buck lives at the La Concha."

"Then perhaps he should go home so he doesn't catch cold walking around all wet." Gutierrez nodded toward my soaked shirt. "While we continue discussing your ideas for the Old Island Days and I show you my suggestions for the hotel."

I bit my tongue.

Gutierrez leaned closer to me and whispered: "Enrique Jiminez is the Sancho on Stock Island. Come by my gallery tomorrow and we'll talk." He paused. "Better make it in the afternoon, this could run late." He smiled and stepped back to Karen.

"Wait." Karen took me by the arm. "Are you all right?"

"Not particularly, you ready to get out of here?"

She hesitated. "I can't leave, Buck. My general manager's expecting me to buy art. Plus Manny's got an idea how he can help with the races."

Our eyes locked for a long second. "Good luck, then."

She frowned, looked from me to Gutierrez, and then stepped reluctantly back toward him. They started up the marble steps. His hand was planted in the center of her back, and as they turned the corner, it dropped to her waist. Was the giggle that echoed down the stucco wall hers?

In the second I stood stewing, Rosalie descended the steps. "I see your friend already knows Manny."

"So she said."

"He took her to see his Botero."

"I'm sure. Are there any other works up there?"

"Dozens, darling, don't worry, lots of admirers, too. What would she want with Manny anyway?" She laughed after she spoke, as if she could think of a few things. "Anyway, she'd be a fool to squander a catch like you for an *art dealer*. He's hoping to become rich, and you—"

"Used to be."

"Freeze!" a voice shouted from behind me. A sharp hoot sounded. Rosalie jumped, and her hand shot down to her rear end. Mingie Posada cozied up next to her, and she introduced us as a photographer stepped in and lowered his camera. She put an arm around Posada and pulled me into the photo. I ducked away as the flash pulsed.

"Buck? Wait!" Rosalie shouted after me as I hurried into the crowd.

Damn it! The last thing I needed after the articles in the *Citizen* was my face published in the society pages. Might as well send a press release to *The Wall Street Journal*: Bankrupt King Charles Reilly Living the High Life in Key West.

If the blackmailers were here, I couldn't risk talking to Gutierrez or Posada. I was an art show washout. Just what I deserved for revealing my inner secrets, fears, and desires to the first woman I'd been interested in for two years. Cloud Nine had turned into a microburst. I left the show soaked and alone.

At least Gutierrez had given me the name of the Stock Island Sancho and suggested we talk tomorrow.

28

There were no presidents hiding in my room, and once changed, I tried to recollect details of my father's interest in encryption, an art he proclaimed essential for diplomats. A memory stirred that led to an internet search. My father used to refer to the *original* American diplomat in a bad French accent as his philosophical mentor, but who was that?

Word searches on codes and ciphers produced a staggering list of different types: transposition, homophones, monoalphabetic, polyalphabetic, digraphs, bigrams, polygrams, nomenclators, none of which rang familiar, and collectively they weakened the likelihood of my ever solving the account identifications or learning the five-character code to the missing key. I concluded that my time would be better spent finding out who the blackmailers were and getting my possessions back.

For the next hour I sat with the lights out, watching the traffic down Duval Street. Shortly after ten o'clock, the balance of the crowd trickled out of the San Carlos. There was no sign of Gutierrez, or Karen.

I took a sip of warm rum and finally saw movement. Gutierrez filled my binocular lenses. Karen was by his side. She pointed to the La Concha. He was talking, gesturing. Finally he put his arm around her waist, and they turned the opposite direction down Duval.

Damn.

29

A glorious dawn spread a wash of reds and oranges
over the island. From my sixth-floor window I could see the beacon at Key West International airport flash on the horizon. Ray Floyd had doctored Betty, so if it weren't for the blackmailers I'd be back on the offensive.

Real blackmail for money would at least give me an excuse to call my brother, but this was extortion. I had to find out who Bush and Clinton were, which meant I needed to stay close to Willy, whether I was helping him or not. He said he had something for me, so at least he hadn't totally written me off, not that I would have blamed him.

Anxious to leave early, I didn't want to bump into Karen. That is, if she was even home yet. How far had the need for Old Island Days ideas pushed her last night? Was the chemistry we shared at dinner my imagination, or just to convince me to give her a plane ride? Part of me was angry, and part was embarrassed, but I had to listen to my heart. The fact that it had been insulated in scar tissue for twenty-four months increased my margin for erring on the side of self-protection, but you can't get hurt if you don't get too close. Dead men don't bleed.

My Rover was tucked in next to the moped rental kiosk behind the hotel. The streets were quiet, and I turned down Catherine looking for El Aljibe—oh jeez! I jammed on the brake. The street—the whole neighborhood—was packed a block before the restaurant, and teemed like an engorged anthill. The demonstration. The minute I got out of the Rover someone grabbed my arm.

"Can you hand out these signs?" Placards with not only Shaniqua's face, but each of the missionaries were emblazoned with aggressive slogans: "Revenge," "Remember the *Carnival*," and even: "War Now!"

A loudspeaker pierced the air. Posada's bald cranium glistened above the swirl of activity. The more I slogged through the human mass, the denser it became.

"Watch out!" A squat, mole-chinned woman hissed when I brushed past her.

Posada stood at the small podium, shouting instructions into the microphone. White spittle was caked in the corners of his mouth, and his demeanor reminded me of newsreel footage of Mussolini. The CANC was preparing to launch their assault onto the Isle of Bones, and Posada was poised to capitalize on Redeemer's suffering.

"Mingie?" My voice failed to carry over the din. By the third try, I was nearly screaming. Posada stopped mid-rant and looked down on me. "We met last night at San Carlos? Rosalie Peña introduced us?"

He squinted momentarily, then continued his tirade.

"Are you certain that Cubans instead of Santeros attacked the boat?"

My question inadvertently blasted out over the loud speaker. Posada looked at me as if I'd flung dog crap on his straining guayabara.

"Certain? They plant human garbage with their boat lifts, criminals and spies in our midst, they're brewing biochemical weapons, they've killed and imprisoned dissidents and refugees, and now this?"

He dismissed me with a broad wave. Currito's nickname for him fit: *Poquito*. Crouched like a linebacker shedding blockers, I forced my way toward the restaurant.

"Have you signed the petition?" A wrinkled man with a watery smile and ill-fitting dentures pressed a clipboard in my face. "Mingie says everyone must sign."

I finally made it to the front door. The interior of the restaurant was deserted.

Pictures of old buildings with Spanish architecture adorned the walls. A cathedral, the Morro Castle, along with other sappy mementoes of Cuba. The dining area was totally open except for a small room next to the kitchen.

After a glance out the grease-smeared window, I entered the office. Stacks of invoices formed a glacial heap on Posada's desk. The walls were filled with pictures of Mingie with a wide variety of others, all of whom wore strained smiles. In the center was a letter from President George W. Bush expressing gratitude for Posada's help with his first election.

Not knowing what to look for, I hoped to get a measure of the man but found only clutter. On a packed shelf above the desk was more junk, including a dusty highball glass filled with…pink and blue ribbons.

A dozen, at least, of the same ribbons Karen used to mark her "rescued" birds.

Nothing else here beside confirmation that Posada was politically wired. I turned to leave and hesitated again at the photos. A face caught my eye. I thought back to Jo Jo's funeral, and the pictures on the easels.

The snapshot was of Manuel Ortega standing shoulder to shoulder with Posada at some black tie event. It was the only picture on the wall where people were laughing. Ortega was the missionary embittered from the loss of his brother to a Cuban MiG—

"What are you doing in here?"

I spun to find a woman with her hands on her hips. Mid-twenties, and a knockout.

"Looking for the restroom."

She gave me a once-over. "You're not here for the rally, are you?"

"Breakfast, actually."

"Can't you see we're closed?"

"Seemed like there was a party going on."

As I squeezed through the crowd, I watched the girl make a beeline toward Posada. Every time she glanced over at me, I pressed harder, careening into surprised people until I disappeared into the mass. If she had the chance to point me out, Posada would recognize me, but if he was behind the blackmail, he already new my identity.

Was the photo of him and the missionary a coincidence, or more?

Nearly back to the Rover, I came upon a sedan with government tags. There was a man inside studying the crowd. His presence triggered alarms in my head. If the Feds were monitoring the Key West demonstration, they were either taking the situation seriously or knew something I didn't about Posada. Government agents made me nervous, especially after my name had appeared in the Tattler a couple times. I took a deep breath. They're here watching Posada, not me.

30

I drove down A1A past Smather's Beach, where morning walkers meandered along the thin sand spit, no doubt dodging bottle caps, cigarette butts, broken glass and used condoms. Smather's was a multipurpose facility and its lack of hygiene symbolic of the island's sanitary standards. Superficially tidy, with rubbish peeking out from under each burrow. The scene was tranquil, quite a contrast to the shit storm brewing a mile away.

I walked through the private terminal and out onto the taxiway. Ray Floyd materialized, rubbing his hands on a red rag.

"This was a first for me," he said.

"Why do I feel like you're going to ask me to cough?"

"Flying fish smooshed into the filter of the air intake, cooked through and through. Tasted like chicken."

I held up my hand for a high-five. "That's a relief, I was afraid—"

"Not so fast. She still needs to be rebuilt, flying fish or not." My shoulders sagged. "Even at cost, that's nearly ten grand," Ray said.

"Ten—"

"Per engine."

"Was I hallucinating, or did I see you fly over the La Concha last night?"

"She's got about a hundred hours left in her, max."

"That's it?"

"I'm an environmentalist. I keep guys like you from polluting the ocean with old tin cans." He thumbed toward Betty. "Maybe it was bad luck to change her name."

"I didn't change it, I gave her one. *Lady of the Waters* was more of a description."

"I still remember Buffett's face when he showed up here and saw her parked under the palm tree. He practically shit."

"So Betty's okay to fly?"

"Gassed up, de-boned, and ready for treasure hunting."

"That reminds me, what's Floyd's Law?"

"'Without balls to drive brains, underachievers wear chains. Without brains to rein balls, overachievers hit walls.' Floyd's Law, a.k.a. the Balls/Brains or B/B ratio."

The world was closing in on Key West, but Ray Floyd was comfortably tucked away in his own private conch shell.

"The anti-Cubans may be goose-stepping through Old Town today, but have you heard about the religious crusaders' latest casualty?" he asked. "Some poor slob got his leg broken and was tossed into the shark tank at the Aquarium last night."

"What's that have to do with 'religious crusaders,' as you call them?"

"He was a local Santero guy. Said a huge black dude with barbed wire around his bicep did the nasty and left him as a snack for Bobby the bull shark. A worker found him clinging to a piling this morning, in shock."

"Keep an eye on Betty. Someone broke into my Rover yesterday, swiped the knee board from my flight bag, and left a dead chicken in its place." Ray wouldn't handle the news well that I was being strong-armed, especially if it was by Santeros.

"First a dove and now a chicken? What's next, an albatross? Speaking of that, did you find your stash, or whatever it was that freaked you out so bad?"

"Still trying to figure out where to start."

"A fallow mind is a field of discontent."

Crossings

31

I left the airport full of Ray Floydisms and drove
up along Sears Town, and past Garrison Bight. Where would the demonstration
route be? Would it be idiotic to try and talk to the local Sancho? Enrique Jiminez
was the name Gutierrez mentioned.

The road north up the Keys was already packed. Locals fleeing the Cuban
American deluge before the Overseas highway became too congested to negotiate. I thought back to when I first came down here as a kid, before all the modern
bridges were built in the early eighties. The old ones, constructed by relief workers
in the thirties and forties, were narrow as hell by contemporary standards. There
were no SUV's, and eighteen-wheelers were a lot smaller back then. When you
drove over those bridges you really got acquainted with the oncoming traffic.
My mother's shrieking voice as we approached a tractor-trailer halfway across
the seven-mile bridge, only to clear by fractions of an inch, had left an indelible
impression that these islands were remote and inaccessible. Once the new bridges
were finished, the floodgates opened, and the Keys have never been the same.

Orange cones blocked off the island's main drag at Truman and Duval.
Posada had positioned his crusade for maximum visibility. It paid to own friends
in high places.

The lighthouse marked my entrance into Bahama Village. I parked the Rover
in front of the church, and two burly young men stepped up to meet me. I noted

bulges wedged into their waistbands. Guns? They patted me down before nodding me onward.

"Hello?" A muffled response to my call came from deep within.

Willy rushed down the hall. "Buck, I'm glad you came."

I told him about the scene at El Aljibe but didn't mention the picture of Ortega in Posada's office. I nodded toward the door.

"New security?"

Willy's eyes narrowed. "We had an uninvited visitor last night. Tried to burn the church down. Threw a Coke bottle filled with gasoline and a burning rag in the back window. Lucky I was here."

Why was the intimidation escalating?

"Based on what I saw last night, Gutierrez has a successful gallery," I said.

"Real raft-to-riches story. Started with a frame shop on White Street, then made some contacts in Miami and became a high-end art broker overnight."

I remembered admiring his contrarian position, but it now seemed foolish. Why would he buck success by alienating his clientele?

"Anyway, like I said, I've got something for you. Lenny?" Willy said.

My surprise must have been obvious, because Willy laughed when Conch Man carried a new green Kayak out from the back hall.

"Sorry about the last one, man."

"You didn't have to do that." It was even more compact then my old one.

"Don't get all sentimental," Lenny said. "You needed another one to keep the search going. So Betty's fixed?"

"Just had a little indigestion, but I can't—"

"Remember I thought Shaniqua was still alive?" Willy said. "An FBI agent showed up last night to find out why we hadn't reported her missing. Told him I didn't know for sure she was on board. *Got* it?"

"You say so," I said.

"Thing is, they had some amazing news. Turns out they dialed her cell number, and someone answered."

"*What?*"

"I must have tried it a hundred times with no luck, but when they called, a man picked up talking Spanish. They asked for Shaniqua and the guy hung up."

"Why did the FBI tell you all this?" I said.

"Played me the tape, wanted to see if I recognized the voice."

"And?"

"Wasn't any of my people." Willy said.

"Was there anything else in the recording that might help?"

"Pretty damn sure we heard engines, whistles, a loudspeaker," Lenny said. "Marina sounds. I've called every damn boatyard from Key West to Fort Lauderdale."

"Could have been picked up by a Cuban patrol, or sunk, but either way her cell phone's still working. Now we're at the mercy of the FBI."

Could that have been an FBI agent in front of El Aljibe? A sudden shiver made me cringe.

"Follow me back here a minute," Willy said.

Inside Willy's office he held up a letter. The logo on top caught my attention.

"The hell's this?" I said.

"A golden opportunity," Willy said. "I got permission from the government to send four more missionaries to Cuba, and you're one of them."

"But I can't, Willy."

"Buck, I don't know why you quit, but I need your help. I don't know whether the Cubans or Santeros killed Jo Jo, but if I can get my men inside Cuba, with you as ready transportation home, I think maybe we'll find out. It's my only hope."

The blackmailers were specific – 'butt out,' or my ledger goes to the police, along with an explanation. So not only had I lost my stash and the coordinates where I found the gold, my ass was on the line too, possibly even jail for fraud, just like my former partner Jack Dodson. Why was I so intent on fixing the messes I caused for others before attending to my own? It was all a real noble idea, until it became a royal pain in the ass—like now. I'm no Don Quixote, or a knight-errant, I have no white horse, or black mask with pointy ears, I'm just…just…aw hell.

Willy's eyes were locked onto mine.

"What about you, Lenny?" I said.

"Willy won't let me go."

"Lenny's already on parole. He gets nailed again he can forget about politics."

"Some people got their house repossessed by the bank," Lenny said. "Couldn't make the mortgage. I helped 'em get some of their stuff out, and the bank that foreclosed on it had me busted. Petty theft bullshit, trust me on that."

"You need to keep your nose clean, boy, in case your political career catches up to your mouth." Willy turned to me. "That Sancho in Havana? One that was bitching about our mission? His name is Salvo. I've got just the man to talk to him. But only if you take them."

Could I risk the blackmailers finding out? I needed to find the thieves, but what if I could learn something that would help? Like I have anything left to lose?

I took a deep breath. "Okay."

Willy pumped a fist in the air.

I was concerned that with today's demonstrations, we might not get in if we wait, so we agreed to leave at 1:00. Cuba might also provide the opportunity to figure out the code for my missing key, provided my father's reference to "HIS BOAT" meant Hemingway's. Last night's research on the different types of encoding systems had reacquainted me with his word puzzles, and I recalled a pattern to his selecting key words. Hemingway's home outside Havana, a place I thought I would never see, was now a beacon of hope.

"Is that reward still being offered?" I said.

"Bet your ass. $10,000 for each of our people recovered. Alive, that is." Willy picked up the framed picture of his daughter. "You're my only hope, Buck."

"This has to be on the super down-low, Willy. Nobody can know I'm involved."

OUTSIDE, LENNY HELPED tie the kayak to the Rover's roll bar. "I can't believe Willy won't let me go, man, maybe I should stow away."

"I don't think so, Mayor Conch Man. Plus, nobody can know I went, so you need to cover for me. Tell people I'm out poaching someone's salvage project." Neither of us smiled. "Also, keep tabs on Gutierrez. I want to know if he's behind the reprisals on the Santeros."

He wished me luck, and I was back out on the road. My world had turned to two scoops of shit, and even though I was finally going to Cuba, it was under the worst possible circumstances. At least I'd be away from Key West. Things couldn't get worse if I'm not here.

32

I packed light, not sure how long I'd be gone.
Havana was a gamble, but three new missionaries / investigators might flush out
or learn something about those opposed to Redeemer's mission, and indirectly
help get me information about the blackmailers.

Karen had still not appeared by the time I returned from Bahama Village.
Several days in Cuba would put some distance between us, and when I saw her
next, the disappointment should have subsided. Just as well, it was time to focus,
again.

The roar six floors below hit like a tsunami. From my window I saw a sea
of people marching up Duval that extended all the way down to Truman. Signs
waved and voices repeated unintelligible chants. The estimate of a thousand
seemed way low. Camera teams scurried ahead of the throng, and as the leading edge neared the La Concha, I could see Posada goose-stepping out front.
The CANC had pounced on the terrorism paranoia, pounded into the public by
political and media pushers who used fear as a drug. Their excitement over the
potential aggression against Cuba was palpable on every news channel, as would
be their fervor to condemn the very same response.

If the Cuban authorities had attacked the *Carnival*, then how would they
respond to a private American plane coming out of the eye of the storm in Key
West? We needed to get there fast, but could we beat the news? Defying the black-

mailers made me smile. It was reminiscent of my decision to flee the corporate world. No more 10-K's, 10-Q's, kissing ass or fuck yous. It was back to adventure and a battle to fight. With Willy's needs ahead of mine, the adrenalin rush coursing through me was no longer driven by the smell of profit. It was an interesting feeling.

With a duffel and backpack-cum-flight bag in hand, I left my apartment and stopped cold in front of the open elevator. It would deposit me in the back of the lobby, right next to the reception desk. I took my private staircase to The Top and caught the elevator into the front lobby. I didn't want to bump into Karen.

I cut through Starbucks and outside stood Karen thirty feet away on the corner holding a sign: SAVE KEY WEST'S CHICKENS. She spotted me staring at her with bags in my hands. Her eyebrows lifted and she stepped my way before I could flee.

"Off on another salvage mission?"

"You buy some art last night?"

"I'm not sure, but my head's killing me." She rubbed her temples.

"Gutierrez take advantage of you? I mean, since I left you hanging?"

"He's a closer, all right. I used your suggestion about the offshore races. He said he has a great idea—oh, hey, you were going to be my next stop." She reached into her knapsack and pulled out a large envelope. "I just got back from seeing my editor friend I told you about. I made you a copy." She held the envelope to her chest.

"Your book?"

"You said you'd read it, and well, the story's kind of up your alley." She squeezed it closer. "But just remember, it's a work in progress. And even though the protagonist is kind of…" She paused, took a deep breath, and held the package out to me. "You'll understand, just come see me when you're done."

"I'll be gone a few days, at least."

She glanced at my bag. "The life of adventure?"

"And a battle to fight."

Our eyes held, then last night's memory of Gutierrez steering her the opposite way down Duval ruined what could have been an altogether different goodbye.

I cut through the demonstrators across Duval. I stumbled between old men, stern-faced women, and laughing kids before being squirted out the other side. I looked back toward Karen but she was gone. Seems my lousy track record in romance had been recycled too.

33

My first stop was the library. I entered the building
and saw Walter Wagner, the librarian, talking to an elderly blue-haired woman.
He peered over his round glasses and smiled when he saw me. He pointed the lady
toward the romance novels.

"Buck, long time no see."

"I'm in a hurry, Walter. I've got a charter—"

"Always in a hurry, rush, rush, rush. When are you going to learn that Key
West's about relaxing and taking time to enjoy life?" A devilish grin bent his thin
lips. "And experimenting with alternative lifestyles."

"Austerity's my alternative lifestyle. What do you have on Havana and Santeria?"

"Santeria, huh? That's been a popular subject."

"Popular?"

"Fads come and go, that's been my hot topic lately," he said. "You look like
you saw a ghost."

"You caught me off guard. I've been helping Willy Peebles at—"

"He's one of them."

"One of what?"

"I suppose it's not very discreet of me, but hey, I'm a librarian, not a shrink.
The Ruler, he's checked several books out on Santeria, bless his soul. What a

shame about his girl, so gorgeous. You'd never guess *she* was a minister's daughter."
His giggle was followed by a long sigh.

"What are you talking about?"

"Shaniqua Peebles, silly."

"I know that, what about her?"

"Oh, she's read all our books on Santeria." He scanned the room. "And party?
My, my, my that girl could dance, oh Lordy, and what I wouldn't give for that
body—"

"Slow down, Walter. Did Willy know she was interested in Santeria?"

The smile on his face changed to a pedantic scowl. "Either he knew or was
curious himself, because he read all the same books. Here's your list of what's in."

I stumbled down the aisles trying to figure out the significance of Walter's
revelation. Shaniqua was interested in Santeria? And Willy too? Why would he
keep that to himself? I stopped in my tracks. Could that be why he wanted her
presence on the *Carnival* kept secret?

I found a book on Havana that contained several good maps. Those on Santeria were split between religion and witchcraft. One in particular boasted insight
into the religion, the faith, the rites, and the magic.

Walter peered over my shoulder. "I saw the article about you taking Shaniqua
to the boat." He hesitated. "And the one about your past...."

"That reminds me, do you have any books on codes or ciphers?"

"Quite the contrast of subjects, Buck. One might conclude you were up to
something."

He directed me to a fat book on the history of codes and secret writing that
contained many examples. Back in the Rover I turned down White and dodged
some pedestrians running toward Duval to take part in Posada's crusade. The
news of Shaniqua and Willy gnawed at me. Was he reading the books to study the
competition or to see what she was doing? Is that why he hadn't wanted her to go,
or why she did? Lot's of questions, no answers.

I pulled up to José's Cantina hoping for some discreet advice on Havana but
learned that José was off marching with Poquito. The skeleton crew was taking
phone calls and cheering reports from the front. Maybe Posada was right and
history was being made. Every news station in the country would be preparing
sound bytes to tout the tension. Information alchemy at its best.

José's wife, who everyone called Abuela, was surprised to learn I was taking
a charter to Cuba. I didn't mention Redeemer. After an awkward pause she said
she had a favor to ask, ordered the waitress to make me a Super-Cuban, and
disappeared into the back room. I inhaled the sandwich, fried plantains and a
Hatuey beer. Abuela returned and explained that even though the United States
had ceased restrictions on how much money they could send their relatives, her
grandson in Havana was living in poverty. She pulled an envelope out of her

apron and asked if I could give it to him. His name was Ivan Machado and he worked at the Ambos Mundos Hotel. I agreed and swore her to secrecy about my going. Her request gave me an idea.

Back in the Rover, I rolled slowly down White Street reading merchants' signs. Gutierrez had said he thought his show might run late and for me to come by in the afternoon. I'd been too self-absorbed to realize that was because he intended to make a move on Karen.

I drove past a mortuary, a dry cleaner, and at the corner with Truman found a KWPD squad car with its lights flashing in front of MG International. Gutierrez was pointing toward the charred, glassless frame of his front door. On the ground lay a burned carcass of what looked like a cat, covered with broken glass. Had Manny received the same treatment I had? Or had Posada's rivalry taken on solid form? I realized that both the church and Gutierrez's gallery had been threatened by phone calls yesterday, then hit within twenty-four hours. At least they got warnings.

Gutierrez was yelling at the cop. As much as I wanted to take him up on the offer to discuss Santeria, it would have to wait until I got back.

I spotted a large painting in the window that was vaguely familiar.

As I pulled away, I noticed a black convertible Mercedes SL 500 roadster in Gutierrez's driveway. The art business must be thriving.

The philanthropic efforts to help Redeemer's mission, along with his calls for revenge, had made Gutierrez a target. Seeing his land shark sparked a dull memory, and for the first time in nearly two years, a fleeting homesickness for the fast lane smoldered in my heart. I didn't pine for long, because Betty and I were headed for Cuba.

Unmet dreams come true in the future, not the past.

34

The road ended at Atlantic Boulevard, and White
Street Pier was dead ahead. Fishermen cast lines, roller-bladers scissored toward the horizon, and a group of teenagers sat on bicycles smoking cigarettes or some other combustible substance. Once at the airport I grabbed the forty-pound kayak along with my gear and dropped it all at the fence gate.

I filed my flight plan, checked the weather reports, and verified communication procedures for Havana Center. Out on the tarmac Ray was working on a Cessna 172. He waved to me from behind the raised engine cowling.

"That don't look like fishing gear," he said.

"Grab that green kayak on the other side of the gate and lock it to my tree, will you? I'm heading out for a few days."

He shrugged. "No more than a hundred-hour round trip, I hope."

"Shouldn't take but an hour each way. Keep it quiet, but I'm delivering a new load of missionaries to Cuba."

"You just dropped down to seventy-thirty."

"Ah, the Balls/Brains Ratio. I'm surprised you pegged me that high."

"After all that stuff in the paper, maybe you're right."

I shrugged.

"So why are you doing this, the gold or the girl?"

"Now you're giving me shit?"

"If that gold you found was in National Park waters, you'll go to jail if you take anything."

Ray's gaze shifted toward the terminal, and his eyes opened wider. Pastor Willy Peebles was leading three men out toward us. They were rougher around the edges than the pictures of the last group.

"Speak of the devil," Ray said.

I arrived at Betty ahead of them, wanting to stow my bags and get the pre-flight check started. A candle burned on the ground beneath Betty's port engine. It stopped me cold. My bags fell to the runway. Did the blackmailers know I was headed to Cuba? Their intrusion into my world had robbed me of more than my frail sense of financial optimism. They had pierced my courage and hurled me back into the ring. This time, to fight against my own demons—the ones that divided me between self and selflessness. Alone stands the boxer, trying to punch out his own shadow. Again.

Willy and his people were approaching, so I scooped up the candle and scurried back to the hatch. Melted wax burned my palm. My mind raced with questions. What was the significance of the damn candle? Would the blackmailers send my files to the police?

Willy introduced me to his three men, but I didn't catch a single name. Once inside the cockpit, I studied the candle closely. There were no markings of any kind.

What did I expect, chicken prints?

35

Willy was huddled up with his three volunteers,
who on closer inspection looked more like Hell's Angels than missionaries. My
scrutiny of the plane's exterior was twice that of a normal pre-flight check. I
reached into both engine's air intakes, half-expecting to find goat chunks, but
they were clean. So were the all the various moving parts vulnerable to hexes and
voodoo curses.

Ray silently followed me around while I did the inspection. Willy and his
men were still in discussion, with maps and documents being circulated between
them.

"You leave her unguarded, she'll be converted to car parts before you finish
your first Cuba Libre," Ray said.

"Don't you have some spark plugs to change?"

Willy finished calling his plays, and they broke their huddle, the only thing
missing was the clap of hands and a resounding "Break!" The smallest of the
three men was the only one inspecting the plane with fear in his eyes. They were
all in their mid to late twenties, and with the exception of the nervous one, they
were thick-bodied, muscular, and wore serious expressions. The pastor removed
a cell phone and some brown, letter-sized envelopes, each presumably stuffed
thick with cash. Cuba was 100% cash and carry because of the U.S. government's
prohibition of credit transactions on the island. I brought a few hundred of my

last reserves too. I hadn't been allowed a credit card in two years anyway, so it was nothing new to me.

Willy handed me an envelope. "This is for the other day and an advance for Cuba."

Did Gutierrez know about Willy and his daughter's interest in Santeria? Was there more to the religious feud than local hegemony? How could I ask without pissing him off? Should I bag the trip because of the candle? I took a deep breath. Screw it. Aside from helping Willy, I needed to find out what "HIS BOAT" meant.

A tattoo of barbed wire around the bicep of one of the men peeked out just below his shirtsleeve. Was it Christ's crown or an indication of the man's nature? I did a double take. Large, black, and with a barbed wire tattoo? He matched the description given by the shark tank survivor of his attacker.

My mind spun, but I managed to complete the balance of the pre-flight inspection. The plane sunk as the threesome stepped on. Barbed wire squeezed into the right seat next to me. His size was even more impressive up close. Ray shut the hatch and ushered Willy away from the engines.

"You can wear that headset," I said.

After powering up the magnetos and fuel pumps, I started the port engine and held my breath. I checked the hour gauge and noted what the total would be after another 100 hours. Barbed Wire studied my every move.

"I'm sorry, what's your name again?" I asked.

"Truck." His voice was commanding, even in the headset. "Truck Lewis."

The starboard engine kicked in just after I heard his name. "Lewis, like Bruiser Lewis?"

"That's right, he's my little brother." Truck's short square teeth appeared in a smile, incongruous with his eyes, which were ominous. I had completely forgotten about my fight with Bruiser tomorrow night.

"You skipping town, then?"

"Not exactly—"

"Uh-huh." He rolled his eyes.

I let out a long exhale and eased the throttles forward. We taxied with the wind to the end of the runway and awaited clearance to take off. Out of habit I reached down below my seat to touch the corner of my waterproof pouch, forgetting for a moment it was gone.

Miami Center's signal came. I added power and Betty started down the runway, pivoting unsteadily on her tail wheel before lifting heavily into the air.

Before we banked south, I saw a monstrous cruise ship heading in from the west. I wouldn't miss today's inrush of Americana descending upon Old Town to imbibe a thousand gallons of booze, smoke a hundred acres of tobacco, and collide head-on with the Cuban American welcoming committee.

"I didn't see you at Jo Jo's funeral," I said.

"Had to see a man about a fish."

I swallowed. "What are your plans in Havana?"

His eyes were expressionless. "Keep an eye on you and kick some ass."

Perfect. Now I was transporting a probable felon out for revenge. The shit pile I'd stepped into was up to my waist and rising fast.

36

The Cuban air traffic controller vectored us toward Havana in precise English. So far, so good.

"Why are you keeping an eye on me?" I asked Truck.

"You're the asshole got me into this shit, right? By taking Shaniqua to the boat?"

"From what I hear you needed to get out of town anyway."

A sudden laugh rocked his large frame.

"They arrest first and ask questions later in this country," I said. "Way later."

I let Betty drift west, and before long the Cuban land mass gained clarity. We were instructed to divert east and line up behind a Yak 42, an aircraft of Russian origin under the flag of Air Cubana, but I held course. "Up ahead is the Marina Hemingway, where the *Carnival* was headed."

"You might be all right after all," Truck said.

Havana Control reiterated their instructions, but I waited, taking a chance on a quick survey of the marina.

"It's huge," Truck said. He was right, we'd never be able to see much of anything in a single pass, and doing more would be too obvious.

I turned east and began our descent to José Martí Airport.

"Grumman one-seven-four-one-November, this is Key West Tower, over."

My grip tightened on the wheel. Why would Key West Tower be interrupting Havana Control's guidance?

"Roger, Tower, what's up?"

"Change to frequency 118.3, Grumman." It was Donny, his call highly irregular. Truck could hear the radio traffic over his headset, but his attention remained focused out the side window.

I made the change in frequency. "What's up, Donny?"

"I've been asked to relay a message."

Truck turned toward me.

"10-4, Tower. What's the deal?"

"The Coast Guard found another body, out where you found Jo Jo. Big difference though. This one had half his head blown off. Bullet wound, close range."

Truck flew back in his seat as if struck with a cattle prod. He began shouting, and nearly put his fist through the microphone button on the dash.

"Who'd they find? You hear me, who was it?"

"Someone else is on this freq—"

"That's my co-pilot, Tower." I held my hand up to Truck, and then pointed to my chest. "Has the body been identified?"

"Affirmative. Rodney Claggett, I repeat, Rodney Claggett."

Truck and I exchanged glances. Fury blazed in his eyes.

"Pastor Peebles wants you to return to Key West, pronto. He said the FBI blew a gasket when they found out you guys were headed to Havana. Plus, today's demonstrations were on the national news. Things are getting ugly. You got that, Buck?"

Truck's face was bunched into a tight scowl. After a moment's pause he shook his head and pointed a rigid finger toward the Cuban jetliner. He pumped his hand toward the plane. He didn't need to push the mike's button, I could read his lips.

No fucking way.

"Negative, Tower. Tell Willy his men want to continue."

Havana Control was pissed when we returned to the proper frequency. Truck held his index finger to his lips and thumbed back toward the others.

That's your business, Bubba.

My hands felt slippery on the stick. Rubber hit asphalt and we floated a hundred yards before the tail wheel touched runway 23. The concrete terminal had planes from a wide array of international carriers lined up like hogs at the trough. The Cuban flag fluttered in the breeze, but my rapture was dashed upon seeing tears on Truck's cheek. You don't think a man of his size and rugged appearance has feelings, but even barbed wire will rust.

We were directed toward the end of the terminal where several small jets, one-

and two-engined planes, and an odd array of antique aircraft were parked. Betty would feel right at home.

An armed customs officer appeared outside the plane to escort us into the terminal. Willy's envelope contained $2,000, which I'd placed in my money belt with the few bills already there.

The news about Rodney sank in. I pictured him in the Polo shirt aboard the Zodiac. The odds had just plummeted for anyone else still being alive. Everything considered, the theft of my gear was nothing in comparison, but all of it, including the blackmail and vandalism suggested that whatever had happened was far from over.

Leave the spirits of the dead alone. The calls for revenge in Key West would intensify, along with the media pressure that could enable the president to follow the CANC's lead and escalate the situation into a diplomatic crisis.

Customs seemed blessedly unaware of current events in Key West. Outside, the heat was oppressive. I had no idea where Truck and his men were going or how they'd get there, but I had a hotel in mind.

"We got somebody supposed to pick us up," Truck said. He removed the cell phone Willy had given him, dialed a number, and handed it to the nervous one of the three, who said something in Spanish.

After he hung up, I had a sudden urge. "Can I borrow that thing for a minute?"

Truck hesitated, then handed it over.

"Hotel La Concha." Josh Bentley answered.

"Hey, Josh, it's Buck. Is Karen there?"

After a brief delay, Karen's voice sounded. "Buck, I'm glad you called," she said. "About my book, maybe it would be bad luck for you to read it..." The phone suddenly crackled with static.

"Karen? Can you hear me?"

"Buck?"

"I called to say I'll check out any of Gutierrez's paintings you're interested in, if you still want my help—" The phone cut out.

An old blue and primer Ford pulled up to the curb. A man leaned over to peer through the passenger window. "Redeemer?"

Truck nodded, and the driver jumped out and grabbed the luggage.

"We've got a place in central Havana, in Cayo Hueso." Truck nodded to the skinny guy who'd made the phone call. "Chucky here, he's our guide. Me and Jimbo are going hunting."

I finally knew their names, thrown off earlier by the mysterious candle under Betty's wing. *Shit*, I'd forgotten about that.

"Can you give me a lift to the Ambos Mundos Hotel in Havana Vieja?"

Truck nodded without asking the driver. The ride into the heart of Havana was surreal. We passed the Presidential Palace, where once Fidel, and now Raul Castro kept his office, Revolutionary Square, where countless emotionally-charged America-bashing speeches had occurred, and across from that a large building that looked like a cheap hotel on which hung a massive mural of Che Guevara's face.

"What's that over there with the mural?" I asked.

"MININT's offices, State Security," the driver said. "The phrase underneath it says: *Hasta Victoria la Siempre*, or Always Toward Victory." He shrugged. "More like poverty."

We turned onto a seaside boulevard with antiquated buildings on our right side, their façades paint-chipped and crumbling, contrasting with the brilliant absinthe water on the left. It was the Malecon. The Morro Castle appeared in the distance across Havana harbor. We continued to the end of the Malecon, past dilapidated buildings dating back to the 1500's, then wound through narrower streets until the car's brakes screeched us to a stop.

"Ambos Mundos," the driver said.

I grabbed Truck's bicep and gave it a squeeze. "Don't do anything crazy."

He grunted. He'd be looking *for* trouble, not hiding from it.

"If you talk to your brother, tell him we're still on when I get back."

It was his first smile since the news about Rodney.

"Right."

37

After checking into the hotel I went to the bar and asked for Ivan Machado but was told he wouldn't be on duty until dinner. I checked my map and arranged for a cab to take me to San Francisco de Paula, a suburb fifteen miles outside the city.

The clue to the key word in the packet of Swiss bank ciphers stolen from my plane was "HIS BOAT." A serious Hemingway buff, my father's affinity had rubbed off on me, so my hope was that he used key words I would recognize. When in Cuba ten or twelve years ago on State Department business, he'd visited the writer's *Finca Vigia*, or Lookout Farm.

In order to replace the missing key, a verbal password that contained five blanks had to be recited. But the clue contained thirty-three letters. I had no idea what kind of cipher Dad had used, but if I was right, the key word to decode it might be at the *Finca*. And if I was really lucky, I might learn something about my treasure hunt out at Fort Jefferson, because if I don't recover my stash before the thieves compare the saved points to the X's on the chart, they'll get there first. Ray's warning about it being in Park waters ate at me. He was right, as usual.

Had I been here under different circumstances, seeing the house exactly as Papa left it, with shoes piled up, typewriter atop his bookcase, a lizard in a jar of alcohol, and a year's worth of cryptic notes of his daily weight penciled on the bathroom wall would have been a real thrill. But my thoughts were focused on studying every obscure detail, hoping a five-letter word would jump out at me.

After I jotted down two pages of notes, my thoughts shifted to the fate of the *Carnival* and the situation in Key West. I felt a sense of lingering guilt for ignoring Willy's order to return home, but learning something in Havana was critical.

"HIS BOAT," the *Pilar,* was at the back of the property and also proved to be thought- provoking. I stood on its stern rubbing my fingers along the scarred wood of the gunwales. Was the letter true that Hemingway wrote to his editor, Max Perkins, in 1933? Was all my time searching in the Dry Tortugas—what's this?

My finger traced a six-sided shape. Just like Fort Jefferson. Then I found an *X*—

"*Oye!*" The maid, a.k.a. caretaker, a.k.a. security guard stood below the boat, pointing to her wristwatch. "*Vamanos!*"

It was a half-hour past closing time, and she was kicking me out. I took a picture of the map carved into the wood. When I climbed down, something else under the name on the transom caught my eye: *Key West,* its port-of-call.

The dockmaster at the Bight had said the *Carnival's* port-of-call was not painted on the boat. Another idea gave me pause. It took another rebuke from the caretaker to bring me back to the present. I filed the thought away until back in Key West.

I pocketed the notes, amazed at finding possible evidence of the gold Hemingway referenced to Max Perkins but no closer to solving the five-space key word for the missing cipher. Ivan Machado should be on duty by now. I just hoped his grandmother's surprise gift would be a sufficient inducement for him to help me.

38

During the cab ride back to Havana Vieja, I mulled over some bothersome questions. Could Ortega's connection with the Brothers to the Rescue be more than just familial? Could he have been Poquito's operative against the Cuban regime? Could they have been captured by a Cuban patrol that then scuttled the *Carnival* and killed its passengers with an opportunistic crewman keeping Shaniqua's phone? Would Willy ever confess Shaniqua's interest in Santeria? Or his own?

The description of the occult religion in my library book included no mention of assault, blackmail or murder as standard operating procedures. Animal sacrifices and incantations to influence the future were far removed from blowing someone's head off and tossing them into the ocean.

Back at the hotel, I found a note under my door. "Mr. Reilly, Jimbo called to say your truck is missing in Cayo Hueso. Please call."

My truck is missing? Truck Lewis?

I dug their cell number from my pocket. Surprisingly, the room phone worked. Jimbo answered with a shaky voice.

"Truck went to that dude's place, the Sancho in Cayo Hueso? Said he'd be back in an hour. That was over four hours ago. Something ain't right, man." Truck had wasted no time going to confront Salvo but had made Jimbo stay behind to watch Chucky.

"Rodney getting killed has him crazy," Jimbo said.

"You guys stay put. I'll go to Cayo Hueso and check it out."

"That's just what Truck said."

Pacing around the room led me to an idea. It was almost dinnertime. Downstairs, I found the same bartender from earlier. Yes, Ivan was here, he said before disappearing into the kitchen. I tapped my fingers on the bar until a man appeared at my side.

"*Yo soy* Ivan."

Older than I expected, he was skinny and balding. There was no resemblance to the fat, white-haired José in Key West.

Once I told him who I was and discreetly passed him the envelope, his droopy eyes lit up. He didn't open the envelope, but like me he must have calculated it to be something substantial. I tried to appear relaxed, but my heart was pounding double.

"Are you a chef?"

"No. But how you call it? I bust the tables. Dinner people come soon."

I pulled the corner of a hundred-dollar bill halfway out of my pocket and asked if he could get the night off. The note, equivalent to a week's pay, sent him running into the kitchen, pulling his apron off as he went.

My confidence grew at the prospect of a translator. I mentally thanked Abuela for sending me to her grandson. He nearly skipped back into the room holding a key aloft. A man in a dirty white apron followed him out and yelled something at Ivan, who saluted and then waved me onward.

"Gregorio's the chef." He held the key up again. "I rent his car."

The stern-faced cook watched us leave.

A '54 Chevy Bel Air two-door was parked behind the hotel amidst potholes the size of artillery craters. I sat on the edge of the threadbare passenger seat, trying to decide what to tell Ivan. When he started the engine a plume of blue smoke enveloped a small *bodega* behind us. The smoke hanging in the air reminded me of Betty's problems during our rescue mission. Maybe Ivan should check the air cleaner for stray fish.

"You interested in tourist places or *jinteras*?" he said.

"Neither. You know Cayo Hueso?"

He turned to look at me. "Key West?"

"Isn't there a suburb here called Cayo Hueso?"

"Oh, in Centro?"

"Right. There's a man there, a Sancho named Salvo—"

"The crazy-painted walls?" He spun his arm in a wide circle.

"I don't—"

"Murals, all the buildings are painted with bright colors and pictures. Salvo paints them. The priest, he's famous." Stale nicotine permeated his breath.

"Santero priest?"

"*Sí*. Santeria."

"Do you know where Salvo lives?"

"Of course, in Cayo Hueso." He eased the fragile transmission into gear. The car lurched forward and the interior immediately filled with a stench of burnt oil.

Salvo was famous?

If Truck was missing, was Abuela's connecting me to Ivan good luck, fate, destiny, or an Orisha's spell drawing me into the enemy's lair? It didn't matter, I had to find him.

My head ached from fatigue. We passed through a maze of streets where four- and five-story buildings loomed close to the curb. Paint-chipped plaster façades were crumbling, succumbing to decades of neglect. Ivan told me the government provided free housing, jobs, subsidized food, medicine, and education, but the trade-off was maintenance and abundance. He had the ho-hum indifference of a man resigned to having no control over his life. The regime was lucky that Cuban people are proud, nationalistic, and patient, otherwise rafts would extend to Florida like stepping-stones.

"People say the U.S. will invade Cuba. You think that's true?"

"What does Cuba have that America needs?" I said.

He hesitated. "Cigars?"

"Raw materials and religion drive invasions, not Cohibas."

I pointed to an old sign for Havana Club Rum dangling above the dark windows of an abandoned bar named Sloppy Joe's. The saloon was sister to the one in Key West, and dated back to the 1930's. Ivan offered to pick me up a bottle before I returned. Considering the circumstances, a shot of rum sounded like a good idea right about now.

Colorful murals began to appear intermittently on buildings. Ivan took a right, and the walls burst to life with strange organic shapes in myriad hues. The murals went down the block as far as I could see. How had Salvo gained permission for such a comprehensive tableau? The car slowed to a loud, brake-squealing stop.

"*Bienvenido a* Cayo Hueso."

"Where can I find Salvo?"

He rolled his hand out toward the front of the car like a game show host gesturing toward a prize on stage. Through the windshield were bizarre crystal-shaped metallic sculptures in front of a two-story building. Every surface was painted in vivid colors and geometric symbols.

"I'll wait up the block," he said.

I held my breath from the shower of exhaust as he beat a hasty trail down the road, leaving me alone in a Klee-like world completely devoid of people on the streets. I turned in a full circle and saw no living creature. Not even a bird was flying by these buildings.

39

Was Truck really missing, drunk in some bar, or pursuing a lead he might have found here? If he'd barged in on Salvo, who knows what might have happened, especially if the Cayo Hueso Sancho did have something to do with the *Carnival*.

Amidst the strange architectural sculpture by the entry was a white candle burning. Romantic dinners would never be the same. A steady rhythmic drumbeat reverberated from inside, along with the smell of incense.

I glanced around once more, and then peeked inside the door. A young woman was seated on the floor with her back to me. She faced a cluttered altar in one of the room's corners. More candles, glasses with clear and amber liquid, a banana, and some photographs were scattered in a random pile. The sound of a phone rang somewhere within, but the woman didn't seem to hear it. Her body swayed in cadence with each drumbeat, the sound coming from a tape recorder on the floor next to her.

The incessant ringing of the phone finally stopped. Maybe nobody else was here. I spotted a staircase on the opposite wall from the entranced woman.

I can't believe I'm doing this....

The stairway was dark. It led to a landing lit by a naked bulb. I couldn't hear anything beyond the drumbeat downstairs, and my pounding heart. The sun had descended below the buildings, and twilight struggled through a dusty window. I walked cautiously down the long corridor and into a larger room.

If I was expecting a place of worship, I couldn't have been more wrong. The room was a large art studio, with sketches and partially completed paintings spread everywhere in a haphazard fashion. The palette and organic figures matched those outside.

Salvo's work?

A roach scuttled across my foot. I flinched and took a calming breath. There was a small altar over the paint-splattered workbench. Similar contents to the one downstairs, but this one included a carved white bird with its wings spread in flight.

The room was filled with dusty furniture, easels, and half-finished canvasses. There was no sign that a struggle had taken place. If Truck had come here, maybe he'd found the place empty and left.

Santeria was supposed to be a peaceful religion. People feared their followers because they used spells and incantations in an attempt to influence events. The library book compared those same activities to Christian prayer. Seemed like apples and orangutans to me.

"Salvo?" A woman shouted up the stairs.

My heart seized.

"Salvo?"

Nothing. The drumbeat continued.

I took a deep breath and tiptoed over to where a burgundy curtain hung on the wall. I slowly peeled the corner back—and found a room as large as the studio, but dark. A group of wood crates piled one on top the other emerged in the darkness. On top was a large flat one with an address stenciled on its side.

#1 Obrapia - Florida

I felt as if my feet were sinking, then realized the room had a dirt floor. On the second level? A flicker of light in the far corner caught my eye. I tiptoed over and found a small fire burning beneath a huge bubbling cauldron. Sticks lined its interior. A larger altar surrounded the pot. There were nail-encrusted figurines similar to the one in my flight bag, along with paintings, a large horn from either a steer or ram, and several unlit candles placed haphazardly on shelves.

And then I looked inside the pot.

A human skull and other bones stuck out of the boiling water. I jumped back.

The thief with the Clinton mask kept threatening to boil me. Is this what he meant?

"*Truck?*"

I caught a sudden movement out of the corner of my eye. A dark figure darted through the shadows, and vanished through the burgundy curtain. Was that a man? Had he seen me? Was it Salvo? Or Quasimodo tending his master's business?

A scratching sound started from the darkness in the opposite corner. My feet felt sunken in the dirt floor. The sound continued with greater urgency. I followed the noise until I saw a large lump in the darkness. It was... a seated man?

"Truck?"

It was him! Gagged and bound to a chair. His eyes bulged with menace. I untied the rag from around his mouth.

"Get me the fuck out of here!"

"What the hell happened?"

"Untie me, man!"

While I worked on the knots, he explained what had happened. "Salvo denied everything, said he could care less about some silly mission."

"Then why are you—"

"I didn't believe him, so I started to get a little rough, tried to get him to fess up. Somebody cracked me over the head from behind. Cheap shot, man. I woke up in this freaking dungeon."

I untied the rope on his ankles. When he tried to stand, he stumbled. "Can't feel my feet."

"We've got to get out of here."

The drumbeat from downstairs suddenly stopped.

"Uh-oh," I said.

I helped Truck past the giant pot with human remains and into the studio. The sound of voices downstairs came up through the floor. Male voices. Although they spoke in Spanish, there was no mistaking their concern.

"The hell we gonna do now?" Truck said.

There were three windows in the room. I ran up to the closest one and tried it, but it wouldn't budge. Plus it was a sheer drop, two stories down into an alley. The voices stopped.

There was only one set of stairs. We were trapped. Truck grabbed a wooden chair, limped over next to the door, and held it over his head. There had to be something—

Standing next to the altar by the workbench, I spotted what I had thought was the carved bird but now realized wasn't a bird at all. It was a crudely carved white plane with one green wheel and one red one. My plane!

"Buck, try that window." Truck pointed to the one in the hall toward the staircase. As I ran over, I heard the sound of feet on the stairs below.

The window opened. A steep roof angled below it toward the ground.

"Come on!"

Just as Truck reached me, two men peered around the corner. They shouted in Spanish.

"Go!"

Truck dropped the chair and climbed through the opening, immediately sliding down the roof. The men ran toward me. The one in front wore a white robe and had a sharply pointed goatee, which gave him the look of a crazed conquistador. I took Truck's chair, threw it at them, and dove through the window. I landed on the metal roof and tumbled down and over—

Everything spun as I dropped into darkness. My fall was broken by the shriek of metal collapsing, accompanied by a loud grunt.

"Damn!"

It was Truck. We collapsed onto the roof of a car, then bounced to the ground. We had crushed in the roof of a Russian Lada. "You all right?"

"Freaking great," Truck said.

More shouting sounded above us. We took off down the road. Ivan should be waiting right around—

"I'm going this way!" Truck pointed down a side street. "Our apartments down there. Jimbo and Chucky gotta be freaking out."

Someone dropped off the roof behind us. Without waiting for my response, Truck lit out down the road and disappeared quickly in the shadows. I ran into the night, surrounded by surreal paintings and images, their colors aglow in the darkness. Ivan was parked two blocks down. My lungs felt ready to explode by the time I reached him, but I didn't see anyone behind me. Once I was in the car, Ivan stomped on the gas pedal.

Truck had been captured by Salvo. Was it because of his accusing the Sancho of attacking the missionaries, or in self-defense? And who was that darting through the shadows in the back room? What freaked me out the most, though, was finding the rudimentary version of Betty on Salvo's altar.

How had he known I was coming? Or what my plane looked like?

40

The smell of coffee wafted up through the open window in my fifth-floor room. Another restless night with vivid dreams of fleeing from adversaries cloaked in darkness had me up early. I'd had dreams of being chased my entire life. I've been told they were connected to my drive to pursue impossible tasks, together forming some kind of psychological ying and yang, a daisy chain of fear and aggression. The hunter being hunted, predator and prey wrapped into one. Psychobabble. But to some PhD the dissection of my life would make a compelling case study.

I checked my watch, then tried the phone. Truck answered his cell.

"Ghetto don't describe this shithole."

Spoken like a true missionary. "Havana in general, or—"

"The apartment we're in? It's ready to collapse. Overloaded with smelly people, everyone smoking shit and playing music all night long. My head's killing me."

"You could have been stew by now." *Boiled.*

We rehashed what happened at Salvo's studio. Truck couldn't remember anything definitive that would link Salvo to the *Carnival*. I told him I'd read about the repetitive drumbeat in the book and that its purpose was to propel followers into trances so their gods could possess them.

"You saved my ass last night, bro."

"We'll laugh about it back in Key West."

"What's your stake in all this, Buck? Bounty hunting?"

"Willy hired me for search and rescue, but I've got my own reasons. Plus, the news about Rodney made it clear that whoever's behind this is playing for keeps."

"Be hell to pay when we find the bastards. We're going out to that Marina Hemingway to look for the boat. Want to come?"

"I've got another idea to hunt down, but that's a good plan. Let's circle back later and compare notes." Truck's likely involvement with the shark tank assault came to mind. "Try a little diplomacy around the marina, okay?"

He told me that he was the captain of the *Sea Lion*, a century-old sailing ship now used for sunset cruises in Key West, and was used to being diplomatic with idiots. Hard as I tried, I couldn't imagine him sucking up to the rum-punch crowd.

"Our driver's waiting," he said. "We'll talk later."

"One question first. Was Shaniqua Peebles into Santeria?"

His laugh was without mirth. "She's a freak, man, but if I find the mother-fucker who answered her phone? Take a lot more than poultry to protect their ass."

"Is that a yes?"

He hung up, leaving me to ponder his non-response.

41

After last night's escape from Cayo Hueso, Ivan
had reluctantly agreed to meet me this morning. With time to kill I made a list
of five-letter anagrams from the *Finca Vigía* out of the thirty-three-letter cipher
in my father's note.

Then, I took Karen's manuscript from my backpack. Bad luck, huh? A handwritten note fell from the typed pages:

> "K, Love it. The first thirty pages establish a ruthless pro-
> tagonist, and the idea of a down and out salvage hunter who ex-
> ploits Key West's many potential victims is brilliant. You might
> soften some of his rough edges, but great so far..."

Ruthless salvage hunter?

After thirty minutes I had read enough. The story was about a renegade who
used a boat rather than a plane, had black hair instead of blond, and was generally
a cold-hearted loner. A handsome yet insensitive man, who although resourceful
and well intentioned, was unwilling or unable to show his feelings, and when
faced to make moral choices always defaulted to greed. He'd come to Key West in
the wake of his failed marriage, and while Karen painted him as compelling, he
was also his own worst enemy.

Had she been talking to my ex-wife?

The writing was quite good, her prose crisp and commanding. Had I not known otherwise, I might even have mistaken it for Elmore Leonard. The story would have been enjoyable were it not for the mirror-effect of seeing myself through Karen's eyes, which was as flattering as being recognized in a police line-up. If her opinion of me was this bad, the moment I thought we'd shared at Seven Fish was pure fantasy.

I paced the room like a tethered dog while I awaited the rendezvous with Ivan. The book on codes offered the only distraction. Most of the examples contained letters and numbers, and others had circular, wheel, and disk ciphers that were far more sophisticated then what my father had used. I struggled to conjure an image of him constructing his word puzzles. All I could remember was a sea of letters.

Some ciphers used geometric symbols, some only numbers, and fewer still contained "nulls," which was often an ampersand utilized to confuse code breakers. Most, though, were made up simply of letters.

My father felt the use of ciphers was the tradition of great diplomats, or secretaries of state, which he had yearned to become. That memory gave me an idea. I scanned the book's index. A name jumped out at me: Franklin, Ben.

Franklin's shuttle diplomacy with England and France before, during, and after the Revolutionary War was legendary. My father had several volumes of biographies on…another memory clicked. The French accent Dad tortured us with. "The language of diplomacy," he called it. Was Franklin America's first diplomat to France?

The book chronicled Franklin as a secret emissary to France in 1781. He'd assigned consecutive numbers to each of 682 letters in a long French passage, whereby he concocted a homophonic substitute cipher. The passage used an example, but his use of numbers diluted my adrenalin. Dad stuck to letters. The connection to Franklin, France, and diplomacy had struck a chord. Memories of my father's passion for cryptology were still embedded in my mind, but could they be recovered?

My stomach rumbled like plate tectonics. Last night's liquid dinner of daiquiris in the lobby bar with Ivan calmed my nerves but did little for my hunger. We had debated both sides of why either his government or Santeros would care about the missionaries. Due to his obvious fear of Santeria, I didn't mention the huge cauldron and its contents, or my rescue of Truck.

I still had yet to find a rationale, political or otherwise, for killing seven people and risking an international incident or holy war. There had to be something more, but damn if I knew what.

I filled my backpack with the camera, note pad, and the book on Havana. I hesitated, looked at the one on Santeria, then stuffed it in too. There had been no mention of giant pots, cannibalism, or kidnapping in the book. The elevator carried me to the rooftop bar, where the view of Havana Vieja was incredible. I could see all the way to the harbor in the East.

Hemingway had used the Ambos Mundos as his base of operation on extended fishing trips with Joe Russell in the thirties, long before he bought the *Finca* outside Havana. The hotel took credit for his writing *For Whom the Bells Toll* there and charged a dollar to visit his room on the fifth floor. He kept the *Pilar* in walking distance for his daily fishing adventures in pursuit of marlin and sailfish. It was sad that the same boat was now parked on a tennis court ten miles inland. Could the answer to the missing cipher be here? *Ambos?* I added that to my notebook.

The sun was bright, no clouds cluttered the sky, and a light wind blew napkins off outdoor tables. The lounge was empty. I walked the perimeter of the roof and studied the city below. One block over was Obrapia. I traced it with my eyes until it blurred into the city on one end, then back to where it terminated at Havana harbor.

#1 Obrapia must be located down by the water. Willy had described marina sounds in the background of the FBI's recording of the cell call. The waterfront had boats docked intermittently along its length.

The elevator opened and Ivan stepped onto the terrace.

He looked all around before acknowledging me. For a Cuban, guiding an American in town to investigate a crime potentially committed by their repressive government was a dangerous task, a hundred dollars a day or not.

Once on the street we turned toward the harbor, and took Papa's path to where the *Pilar* and Gregorio Fuentes, his Cuban captain, had launched their daily hunt. The taste of salt was in the air. I gave Ivan the address from Salvo's crate, and he led me over a block onto Obrapia. Sure enough, the addresses descended toward the water.

After a fifteen-minute walk we stood next to an ancient brick warehouse that faced the muddy harbor. Boats were randomly tied up to haphazard docks, and a smattering of small fishing craft were anchored off shore. The warehouse blocked our path. Its walls were pressed flush to the sea wall, ten feet above the water, and a barbed wire fence prevented access onto the dock. I stared through the fence. Suddenly, a door slammed out of sight.

"Sorry!" The loud shout followed the slam.

A second passed before I realized the voice was in English. I waited, listening, then caught a whiff of a freshly lit cigarette. Smoke blew into my face, and a man stepped up to the edge of the dock just a few feet away though still hidden by the wall.

Why had he spoken in English?

Still uncertain of the address, I set off for the front of the building. The cobblestone alley led past a loading dock, stacks of wooden pallets, broken bottles, and a landscape of trash. I glanced back, and Ivan was gone. I hesitated before continuing around the corner. The front of the building was pressed up against the street. I walked toward the door, and opted to play the dumb tourist.

A sleepy-eyed guard was slouched in a chair. When he saw me approach, he jumped up and waved me away.

There was a faded number "1" painted above the door. I kept my distance but continued around the building. The parking area narrowed to an alley that funneled toward the water. A walkway led along the sea wall beyond the warehouse's dock.

A wood dory sputtered toward the shore, where pelicans stood on pilings. I heard the sounds of horns and a scratchy loudspeaker in the distance. Marina sounds.

From my position it was impossible to see into the dock, so I stepped out to the walkway where there was a clear view into the loading area that had been invisible from the other side. This side was fenced too. Four pallets sat in the middle of the wharf, each piled with wood crates.

They were the same types of crates as those in Salvo's studio.

It was too far to see what was printed on them. Official-looking signs written in Spanish were attached to the fence, their messages meaningless to me.

Whoever had yelled "Sorry!" upon the slam of the door must have finished his cigarette and gone back inside. I removed the camera from my backpack. Through the telephoto lens I studied the loading area.

Suddenly, behind me, I heard a shrill sound, along with feet stomping against asphalt. I glanced around and saw the guard from the front of the building running in my direction, waving his arms and blowing his whistle.

Uh oh!

I spun on my heels and sprinted down the harbor walk. Maybe thirty yards along, a gray-shirted cop, known locally as a PNR, jumped out from the bushes and crouched with a gun pointed at my chest.

I skidded to a stop.

What the hell happened to Ivan?

42

Inside the warehouse, chain link separated the open room into quarters, low-watt bulbs hung from cords strung along the rusted roof joist lit a pair of decrepit chairs by the door, and there was a distinct smell of urine in the air. I checked to make sure it wasn't coming from me.

Two guards stood between me and the door, one antiquated handgun between them. Neither spoke English. The gray-shirted PNR had radioed somebody. The other man, who wore a different uniform, rummaged through my backpack, and removed my camera, books, passport and wallet. At least my money belt, filled with Willy's two grand, had not been discovered.

"Why are you holding me?" The tenth time I asked this brought the same no-response. A persistent twitch flourished in my right eyelid.

When they first grabbed me, I'd said I had done nothing wrong, vehemently—which earned me a billy club to the stomach. It was pointless to argue. Whether they had reason to hold me or not didn't matter. This was a Communist country, and like all nearly extinct species, their actions were driven out of a manic desperation to survive.

What had happened to Ivan? Couldn't he just say I was a guest at his hotel? Did he think I was dumb enough to reveal the gift from his grandmother?

Each warehouse quadrant contained stacked wood crates. Some were long and skinny, others more rectangular. None were stenciled with FLORIDA, but they were similar to the ones in Salvo's studio.

The PNR kicked my calf. He barked something in Spanish and pointed to the warehouse.

I got the message.

Brakes squealed outside. The gray-shirted guard stepped out, leaving the PNR to keep watch over me. Voices indicated several people but settled into one monologue, most likely a description of me wandering around the warehouse like an idiot, only to be intercepted and wrestled into submission by this crack security team. The guard returned, followed by three other men. Two wore uniforms similar to his, but they stood aside for the third man, who was dressed in plain clothes.

His eyes locked onto mine. "Why did you try to enter a restricted area?"

"I was looking to rent a fishing boat—"

"You were taking pictures of a secured facility. Who do you work for? The CIA?"

"I'm a tourist."

"Here illegally, then."

"I have a license from the United States Treasury Department."

"Since when are they granting permission to tourists? Maybe they ended their embargo and haven't told us?" Plain Clothes was maybe forty-five years old, solid-looking, and had a piercing glint of conviction in his eyes.

"I'm a missionary with the Church of the—"

"Missionary!" He laughed. "Fishing missionaries trespassing at a secure installation, that's a good one." He stopped and ripped my passport out of the PNR's grasp. "Charles B. Reilly III, Washington, D.C."

"The passport was issued there. I live in Key West. I got here yesterday and—"

"I wasn't aware that the Ambos Mundos had become a mission."

"The mission's in Cayo Hueso."

He made a quick statement in Spanish, his eyes never leaving mine. One of the uniformed men gathered up my possessions and walked outside.

"You're under arrest for espionage against the Cuban government."

The PNR saluted and stepped aside. Each of the remaining two uniformed men took one of my arms and pulled me up. I was too stunned to resist.

A beat-up, white, unmarked van was outside. They shoved me into the middle of the back bench seat, and a guard sat on either side of me. Plain Clothes sat up front. We lurched away, with no siren or flashing lights to mark our departure.

I remembered the Mayday in Spanish the day I was nearly broadsided by the waterspout. It had seemed a condemnation from God, but it occurred to me now that it might have been a warning. My cardinal rule of avoiding arrest was shattered, again, and my worries escalated from Betty being confiscated to my being dumped in a Cuban jail and tried for espionage.

As we pulled away, something caught my attention. *What?*

Ivan was talking to the PNR guard who'd arrested me. He pointed to the van. I sucked in a sharp breath. Was he a rat or just trying to find out why I'd been arrested?

The driver angled his head toward Plain Clothes. "*Combinado del Este?*"

"No." He extended his arm toward the front of the van and flung his wrist.

Combinado del Este was a notorious cesspool of a prison on the outskirts of Havana. Contingency plans swirled through my head, along with wild theories as to why I'd been arrested. I flashed back to last night's daiquiri-debate: could the Cubans and Santeros be one and the same?

Plain Clothes lit a cigarette. Its smoke slightly improved the city smell—decay and rot from a half-century of neglect.

The José Martí tower appeared above the rooftops. We drove past the Plaza de la Revolución. The immense area of crumbled asphalt made me think of an abandoned stadium's parking lot decades after its last big game. Che Guevara's face stared down at me. The black metal sculpture was omnipresent, and Oz-like. MININT, the State Security apparatus' headquarters, grew before us as we entered their driveway, passed through several security checkpoints, and descended beneath the building. Before I knew it Che had swallowed us whole, and I was in the bowels of State Security's hotel-no-tell, where they held people indefinitely without reason or cause. Just yesterday I'd thought the building looked like an aged hotel, but I never expected to be getting a room.

The van's brakes announced our arrival. Plain Clothes marched ahead, his stature within MININT evident with every nervous face we passed. The uniformed guards urged me onward, poking me in the back with billy clubs. Remarkably, my confidence grew despite the gravity of the situation. It was the same feeling I'd had when my partners and I went on our road show, meeting with Wall Street analysts and market makers when we took e-Antiquity public. My free-fall into the abyss of bankruptcy taught me that terror is best diluted with confidence, feigned or not.

From a maze of poorly lit corridors, I was unceremoniously dumped in a windowless, furnitureless, and toiletless cube of a room that stank of piss, vomit, sweat, and fear. Plain Clothes would be checking my passport, custom's information, port of entry, and any other data he could find about me.

Did he have access to the internet? How deep they would dig?

Given the chance, would I contact the U.S. Interests Section here in Havana? In another time I would have had a wealth of diplomatic connections rush to my rescue, but those died with my parents, soured by the accusations that surrounded their deaths. Cuban State Security could easily accomplish what the U.S. Courts had failed to do, and my freedom was in danger of expiring. Plain Clothes stated that I was arrested for spying, a powerful charge in a society where spies are hung and even citizens whose sole desire is to emigrate can be jailed indefinitely.

My personal effects had been confiscated. Plain Clothes himself removed my belt, and his eyes bulged at the twenty-two hundred-dollar bills inside. That alone would be reason enough for me to disappear. They also took my watch, so I could only guess at the time passing.

Would Truck realize I'd been captured? My money would be on his hunting me down, only I didn't have any money left. If only I'd never met Shaniqua Peebles, my destiny would have been completely different. I'd have been back out in the Dry Tortugas by now, maybe even have found the *Esmeralda*. But Ray's warning echoed in my head. If I tried to covertly salvage treasure from Park waters it would be a criminal offense. But, if I found it and then got the Park Service involved, it could right the foundering course my life had taken these past few years. Archeology for history's sake, instead of profit. What a concept.

That's what I'll do, if I could just get out of here. I promise to tell the Park Service about the gold and Hemingway's letter. I'll help them find it, I'll—The single bulb that dangled from the ceiling suddenly went off.

I drifted in and out of sleep as the hours passed. A vision of flying in Betty above distant cays, spotting schools of bonefish, reading wind, waves, currents, and searching for suitable landing spots played like a silent film. Creamy green seas beckoned…Betty's hull wet in Caribbean waters…taxiing on the step toward a lone dock that extended from a tiki hut on a talcum powder beach. A tall woman sauntered slowly down the narrow dock and gave a single languid wave of her arm, my yellow, waterproof pouch in her hand.

Closer now, I could see her golden hair tied back, her tanned skin, her bikini top a matching green to her eyes. A warm smile welcomed me. I licked my lips in anticipation of her kiss.

"You're not alone, Buck Reilly, you're not alone."

43

My cell door suddenly opened and my sweaty body jerked awake. The light was blinding. New guards shoved me down the hall.

Plain Clothes awaited me in a small interrogation room. Two chairs, a table with my camera, the books, my watch, and wallet on it. No sign of the money belt. My heart sank at the sight of my duffel bag from the hotel on the floor. "Sit." He waved the guards out. "You've been charged with spying, Señor Reilly."

"Is this my trial?"

"That's tomorrow." He smiled, "Due process, Cuban style."

I took a deep breath. "I never caught your name."

His eyebrows arched momentarily. "Detective Raul Dumbas. Now, Officer Fernandez, the PNR who arrested you, caught you photographing a restricted area."

"I was using the camera like binoculars, searching for a fishing boat."

"How long have you worked for the CIA?"

"I told you—"

He reached into my duffel, removing… *oh, shit*. "And this?"

"It's called a book."

"On codes and ciphers? Strange reading for a missionary. Perhaps you're de-coding the Bible? Tell me about the so-called mission."

"Redeemer's?"

"What were you taking pictures of?"

"Develop the ones in my camera, they're of Heming—"

"Who are you working for?"

"I want to speak to the U.S. Interests Section."

"That's who you work for?"

"So they can get me out of here."

"Why were you interested in that boat?"

"*What* boat?"

He paused. "Yes, Señor Reilly, what boat indeed." Dumbas stood and said something in Spanish.

"I don't speak—"

The door opened. The two guards who'd escorted me here flanked another man dressed in a suit, but of a higher quality. He was older, had silver hair and a matching tightly cropped beard. His eyes, a piercing blue, zeroed in on mine like a double-barreled shotgun.

"This is Director Sanchez," Dumbas said.

Why would the Director of State Security be interested in me?

"I want to speak to the U.S. Interests—"

One of the guards swung a baton down across my back, knocking me to the floor. Pain shot up my spine. My instinct was to spring up and fight back, but this wasn't a boxing match. I stayed down and took the ten-count.

"Why were you taking pictures of the warehouse?" Sanchez asked.

"I wasn't. I wanted a fishing boat, I like to—"

"Then why did you struggle with the security guards?"

"They surprised me, I hadn't done anything."

His blue eyes stared through me. "That's a nice airplane you came in. Yours?"

Damn. "What about it?"

"Having an airplane that lands on the water would be quite useful."

"I want the U.S. Interests Section. This'll be an international incident—"

A guard held up a black rubber hose, but Sanchez raised his hand.

"Your father's State Department associates are of no use to you any longer, are they?" I swallowed hard. "Tell me, why would a successful capitalist like yourself fly missionaries around?"

They had been digging. Dumbas and his goons must be tied into cyberspace after all. Just because they wouldn't let the Cuban people access it didn't mean they wouldn't.

"It's called philanthropy."

"How generous, King Charles, but from what I can tell, you don't have much left to give. If it were not for the code book, I may have thought you came seeking asylum."

He had *really* been digging. An involuntary frown bent my lip and he laughed. Yeah, you hit a nerve asshole, congratulations.

"This man's nothing but an amateur detective. He's too incompetent to be a spy." Sanchez said something in Spanish, and then switched back to English. "But he's no missionary either. Neither are Lewis, Stackelborough or Roberts."

Uh-oh.

Sanchez laughed again. "Did you really think they could spread their religious poison in Cayo Hueso? You've been there, are they mad?"

"Always Toward Victory."

Sanchez jumped back as if I'd spit in his face. He shouted something and the black hose landed an instant later, knocking me to the floor. Another blow hit my thigh. I curled up in a self-protective ball. Several more strikes landed, each in different locations and all inflicting serious pain. My body convulsed in spasms even after the guard stopped beating me.

"The U.S. Interests Section," I said. "I want to talk—"

"We've arrested your accomplices," Sanchez said. "They too are being questioned. Your stories will be compared."

Sanchez continued in Spanish, and Dumbas's expression turned to surprise. He left with the guards. I slowly uncoiled myself and saw black shoes next to me. Handmade Italian. Karen would know the designer. I pulled myself onto the chair, nearly incapacitated from the pain. Sanchez looked at me as if he were an angry dog owner whose puppy had crapped on the foyer carpet.

"You should have stayed in the internet business, Mr. Reilly."

"I didn't do anything wrong."

"You have a knack for putting your nose in places where it can get broken." He held up my book on Santeria. "Breaking into a Tata's studio, violating his prenda, photographing a government facility—"

"*Tata?*"

His eyes narrowed. "Cuban worms are digging at old scabs in America. If your government is foolish enough to allow media exaggeration to dictate their foreign policy, they'll be in for a big surprise. Our influence goes far beyond our waters."

"Surprise?"

His teeth appeared. They reminded me of a barracuda. "Let's say the result would make 9/11 feel like a stubbed toe."

I balled my fists. *Bring it on, asshole.*

"Your U.N. Ambassador Boltnek made a statement today. America is demanding an inquiry into the CANC's accusations about a missing boat."

Prior to the president's attempts to open dialogue with Havana, Allen Boltnek, the U.S. Ambassador to the United Nations, was a strong advocate for increasing sanctions against Cuba. And worse, he was a ham for the cameras. He and Posada were made for each other.

Sanchez suddenly laughed. "Perhaps you will be the key, Señor Reilly."

The key?

Sanchez knew of all my activities here, including rescuing Truck from Salvo's. I was either followed, Ivan was an agent, or one of the others had broken under questioning. He walked out and left me alone with my throbbing back and limbs, and wondering if when an American screams in Cuba, could anyone hear it.

44

How did Sanchez know my father was a diplomat?
A sudden thought hit me. Diplomat. Again I heard Dad's voice, in his best French accent: "The original diplomat, a Virginian."

His inspiration couldn't have been Franklin. He was a diplomat, yes, but not a Virginian, and was never Secretary of State.

I sat up straight. That job was first held by Thomas Jefferson, a Virginian.

Was Jefferson into codes? The original diplomat, a Virginian—it must be! A shriek down the hall interrupted my thought process, which was irrelevant to my present situation. I sank back down the cell wall.

More bottom-numbing time elapsed before I was handcuffed and wedged between two brawny guards in the van that brought me here. Detective Dumbas was in front, along with my two bookends. My inquiries about our destination were ignored, as was my request to speak with the U.S. Interests Section. The *Combinado del Este* prison was the inevitable destination.

Sanchez's joke about my seeking asylum was an all-time low. That and his statement about my being the key bothered me. If he meant my abduction along with the three other missionaries being the key to trigger U.S. aggression, he could be right. Posada would use us as his next rallying cry, and the administration would be pushed closer to using the pre-emptive doctrine. I vowed that if I ever got out, somebody was going to pay, Sanchez, Salvo, Ivan, somebody.

Our course took us southeast of Havana, through neighborhoods that seemed familiar. But every building outside the tourist center of Havana Vieja was crumbled in condemnable disrepair. A French jetliner descended slowly through humid air.

We were close to the airport.

Betty.

Had she been pillaged down to her airframe? Would she become Sanchez's personal plane? The van swerved down a narrow lane and stopped at a guarded gate. Security was minimal, less than what I'd expected for a prison. I absorbed the details, because the first chance I got I would try to escape.

The sound of an engine raced up behind us. I blinked once, and then again, not believing what I saw. A van prominently marked with a red CNN on its side. How did they know?

Dumbas saw them in the side mirror and rolled down his window. Time to—

The bookends pushed in on me like a vise.

I heard the sound of a door open behind us. Dumbas shouted something in Spanish, and the security guard opened the gate. My body felt like a coiled spring. If I didn't do something now—

"CNN! Help!"

Dumbas swung around fast. "Stop that! Not another word!"

Our driver stepped on the gas, and we shot down the serpentine lane through a scrubby pine forest. God bless 'em, the CNN van hung on our tail. Come on, guys, keep up!

We came to another gate, and what I saw next caught me off guard. Airplane hangars. Were they flying me to some remote prison? Dumbas looked over his shoulder, then past me to the van. He was smiling.

We rounded a squat building, and there, surrounded by single-engine antique planes, and a couple of modern ones, was Betty. The CNN van raced up, their side door flew open, and a camera crew jumped out.

"Say nothing, or you will be sorry. Extremely sorry," Dumbas said.

The van door slid open, and one of the guards pushed me outside. Dumbas grabbed the chains on my handcuffs, which sent shock waves through my bruised body. The CNN crew pointed their camera back and forth from me to Betty.

Dumbas ran a palm through his oily hair and cleared his throat as the camera crew rushed over.

"Buck Reilly," Dumbas said, "You're being expelled from the Republic of Cuba for espionage...."

All I heard was "expelled." The reporter pressed the microphone in my face.

"What were you doing at the government installation where you were arrested? Our Washington bureau has been covering live debate in Congress discussing possible action against Cuba. Are you CIA?"

"I—" Dumbas squeezed my arm, cutting me off. "What about the others?"

"Expelled with you." He nodded toward Betty, then unlocked my handcuffs. "Your entire spy network is to leave immediately."

The reporter stood to the side and turned to the camera. "This man, along with three other CIA operatives, has been expelled from Cuba in a gesture by the Cuban government to counter accusations being made in the United States about a missing boat carrying missionaries."

Dumbas was barely able to contain his smile. These bastards were using me in a game of global misinformation. *The key!*

One of the guards dropped my duffel on the tarmac. I placed my hand on Betty's fuselage, then jerked it back at the sound of a muffled noise inside. I listened closely, tuning out the newsman's hype.

"Open the goddamn hatch!"

I popped the side door to find Truck, Jimbo, and Chucky inside, soaked with sweat. "Get us out of this shithole!"

Dumbas stood next to me and faced the camera. "The allegations about Cuba and the missionaries are false. In the face of the U.S. threats of aggression, our release of these covert operatives is a goodwill gesture. We desire peace in the hemisphere."

It was all I could do not to deck the bureaucrat.

I stuck my head inside the plane. "Open the front windows to get some air circulating. I'm going to check her closely, make sure these jackals haven't stolen anything"

I felt a hand on my back. Dumbas.

"Priority passage has been arranged with air traffic control. You're to fly at fifty-five hundred feet. Leave now."

"Not before I inspect—"

"*Now.*"

Pain shot through my back as I climbed the ladder. I had come to Cuba hoping to solve my father's cipher and maybe learn who was behind the theft of my pouch and the murder of the innocent missionaries, and possibly earn a $30,000 reward. I was going home a pawn in an international game of chicken that had been going on a half-century. The other guard came from the van with my bag in his hand. He placed it inside the hatch, and I heard the unmistakable sound of glass against glass. Glass?

Dumbas winked at me. I slammed the door in his face. What I found inside the duffle made me want to throw up.

"Rum?" Truck said.

"Get up front."

I contorted my bruised limbs and torso into the left seat. Truck rubbed his knuckles, which showed fresh abrasions and raw skin. Whoever had the assignment to roust him out of Cayo Hueso must be missing a few teeth.

"Get us out of here before they change their minds," he said.

Prevented from checking the exterior of the plane, I ran through a quick review of the basic systems, concluding that Betty was as I'd left her. We had half a tank of fuel, her hours hadn't changed, and the batteries were charged. Out of habit I reached down to touch my stash, only to feel my heart trip yet again.

The port engine turned over and a loud backfire sounded. Dumbas, vamping in front of the camera crew, dove to the ground and covered his head with his arms. My laughter stopped when I saw Truck's terrified eyes.

I remembered the human stew and carved plane in Salvo's studio. Was that carving now in ashes on his altar?

This bird no fly. Leave the spirits of the dead alone.

I'd rather swim back to Key West then be stuck on this surreal rock any longer, but with CNN broadcasting my involvement here, and with Dumbas' statement associating me with the missing missionaries, my plan for out of sight, out of mind was shot to hell.

So much for lying low. Despite my good intentions, I was back in the public eye. Who was I kidding anyway? I had tried to help Willy when I discovered it was his daughter I'd taken to the *Carnival.* I guess it's like they say, no good deed goes unpunished. The press, of course, would see it differently.

45

Havana control guided me through a series of taxiways until we finally stopped at the end of runway 4. I clicked the internal mike and turned to Truck.

"You ready?"

"Pedal to the metal, Bro."

The others were strapped in and sweating profusely. The television crew and European passenger jets were lined up in wait while Betty roared down the runway. When we lifted into the sky there was a collective cheer from all on board. The tower vectored us east of the city and echoed Dumbas's instructions to climb to 5,500 once out to sea. We gradually increased altitude, and I peered through my side window. The brown ribbon of Havana harbor spread out below us, extending like a ditch of sewage toward the green waters of the Gulf Stream.

It hit me that Dumbas hadn't returned my money belt. Willy's advance of $2,000 was history. An uncontrollable urge came over me. I broke off from Havana Control's instructions and followed the ribbon of dark water along the city's western shore. My altimeter read three thousand feet. The voice from the tower grew anxious.

I keyed the internal mike. "Hang on, partner."

Confusion twisted Truck's features. I gave the other two guys the circled okay sign with my index finger and thumb. Havana Control again repeated instructions for me to vector east. I cleared my throat.

"Havana Control, we're having engine problems. We can't maintain altitude."

Truck's eyes narrowed. I pressed the yoke forward. Betty began a steady descent toward the harbor. I scanned the coast until I could see the warehouse where I'd been arrested. Something Dumbas asked me resonated in my head, and I had to check it out. Little boats, smacks, a container ship….

No.

A big white fishing boat with red stripes on its bow-flare was moored at the warehouse. Could it be?

Betty rocketed toward #1 Obrapia like a Japanese Zero of similar vintage. A pallet of wooden crates sat on the dock. Just as I started to pull us out of the dive, some people ran out of the boat's salon onto its back deck. One, two, three men, and…a woman?

Truck elbowed my bicep, inadvertently hitting one of the welts from the rubber hose. I pulled back on the yoke and barely cleared the *Carnival's* tuna tower.

"You fucking crazy, man?"

"Did you see—"

"All I saw was you trying to kill us!"

The interrogation began to make sense. Why Dumbas was asking about the boat, along with Sanchez's concerns.

The air traffic controller's voice went apoplectic. I maintained that our engine problems were persisting. Our altitude had increased to six hundred feet, and between us and open water another target emerged. Truck's mouth formed a perfect circle as we bore down on the towers of the Morro Castle, perched high atop the hill at the mouth of Havana harbor. Alarm bells would be ringing all over José Martí airport, radar screens at the closest military base, and even surface to air missile batteries hidden within the city.

I blocked out the screaming air traffic controller along with Truck from the seat next to me and pushed the yoke down even further, aiming Betty at the ancient Spanish fortress. The startled tourists' eyes stared up as we spun on the port wing a hundred feet above them, dodged the domed lighthouse, then banked hard to starboard. The top of the sea wall was above us as we lit out over the Gulf Stream.

"*Adios*, assholes!"

Havana Control had gone silent. Truck had paled like coffee diluted with cream.

"Come in, tower, I'm trying to get the problem under control."

"*Y coño*. Roger that, Grumman. Maybe you should return to José Martí."

Truck turned to me with Bela Lugosi eyes.

"Negative, tower, we're going to try and make it across." He repeated our flight instructions, reiterating that we were to climb to 5,500 feet as soon as possible, but I'd already tuned him out. "Paybacks are hell, Bubba."

Truck hadn't seen the boat, and if I told him now, I wasn't sure how he would react, but air piracy wouldn't be out of character. I knew there had been something about that warehouse. It was controlled by the government, but the crate in Salvo's back room had its address. Did the *Carnival* tie them all together? And if so, how? To what end? And why would they threaten me to 'butt out' in Key West, and then let me go when they had me in Havana?

Betty skimmed the azure sea. Cannonballs and MiGs be damned. They'd have to find us kissing wave crests to get even for the stunt over the Morro Castle, because my flight plan had us in stealth-mode. I was done kowtowing to Havana Control, or anyone else from the Cuban government. They wanted me at 5,500 feet? Betty's altimeter read 55.

Once we were clear of the Cuban territorial limit I radioed the Coast Guard to report sighting the *Carnival.* Truck turned toward me so fast I thought he'd hurt his neck. *Dejá vú* set in when they promised to dispatch the Coast Guard Investigative Service to meet us at the airport. All things considered, seeing that boat had at least added some value to this trip, but at what price? Were the blackmailers the type to watch CNN? Willy's response to the news would help explain his behavior about Shaniqua and the secrecy about Santeria.

After the Mayday and two dead bodies, the news of the *Carnival* afloat in Cuba would launch the media frenzy into overdrive and add validity to the voices demanding a government reprisal. Were the three men on board the original crew? And the woman, could it have been Shaniqua? There had to be answers in Key West. I just hoped finding them would be easier than solving my old man's riddles.

Truck watched my every move like a prison guard. "You bother with those gauges, man?"

"They help, but mostly I fly by these." I pointed to my eyes. "VFR."

"Hell's that?"

"View From Roof."

"No shit, like a two-story Conch house."

Had the authorities connected him to the attempted feeding of Bobby the bull shark at the Aquarium? I imagined him at the helm of the tourist-packed Sea Lion and shook my head, pitying any mouthy drunks.

Something else struck me about when I dropped Shaniqua at the *Carnival.* Her interest in my chart. "Looks like a treasure map," she'd said.

"What does Shaniqua do for work?"

"You mean what *did* she do?" His expression hardened. "Something at the Treasure Salvors store. Sales or tours, I don't know."

Oh no.

The out-islands around Key West began to emerge as faint smudges on the horizon. Thunderheads rose above them. It looked like we were in a race to reach the airport before a storm hit. Having never succumbed to the dull addiction of golf, the term *par for the course* still felt appropriate. I aimed Betty straight into the darkening skies. Neither hell nor high water was going to keep this bird away from its base of operation.

Adrift, Alone, Alive

46

"Charles B. Reilly the third. Why am I not surprised
to find you in the middle of this?" My legs faltered at the sound of my full name
off the lips of an FBI agent with wild eyes. And worse, I recognized him but
couldn't place from where.

"Who the hell do you think you are, interfering with a federal investigation?"

"I wasn't—"

"You jeopardized our entire operation with that hair-brained frontal assault in
Havana. CNN, for God's sake!"

"I didn't—"

"I ought to throw your ass in jail for obstruction of justice, on top of the other
investigations pending against you."

Truck glanced over at me. We were in the Conch Flyer, which had been
closed for our interrogation. I'd been getting my ass chewed by Special Agent T.
Edward Booth of the Federal Bureau of Investigation. He waited until I finished
explaining what happened in Cuba before he blew my mind.

"It's been what, two years since you were allowed to leave Virginia? Now
you're mixed up in this Cuban mess."

Truck pulled his sleeve down over the barbed wire tattoo. Booth had a badge
in the belt of his khakis, and his blue blazer might be concealing a 9mm Glock,
but he'd never have the chance to reach for it if he didn't back off.

"Hell's the FBI messing with us for?" Truck asked.

"Agent Booth was in town investigating a smuggling operation. The state's attorney asked for his help after Jeffries's body was found," Lieutenant Killelea from the Coast Guard Investigative Service said.

"We went to Cuba on a religious mission," I said. "We didn't know jack about any operation, we didn't even know Rodney was murdered until we got there, and I certainly didn't expect to get my ass pummeled by Cuban state security, or to find the *Carnival*."

The door flew open and Willy filled the frame. His face was taut. Gutierrez peered over his shoulder.

"Not a word about the boat, any of you." Booth's voice was a low hiss.

Huh?

Willy pushed his way past the two KWPD patrolmen. "These are my people, damnit, my mission." The officers let him in but closed the door in Manny's face.

"Mission?" Booth laughed before turning serious. "Is that it, Reilly? Guilty conscience turned you from an inside trader and suspected murderer to an evangelist?"

Every eye turned my way.

"That's libel, Booth, I could—"

"The Swiss authorities don't think so, their case is still open."

"They've never once tried to—"

"Murder?" Willy said.

"It's bullshit—"

"Buck and his partners cooked their books and went bankrupt. There's no solid evidence, yet, but he's also a suspect for murder. His partner's doing time for insider trading and fraudulent conveyance of assets."

"What's that got to do—" Willy's forehead bunched together.

"Did you know his parents cashed-out with millions, just before e-Antiquity crashed? They bolted to Europe on an extended holiday, which turned permanent."

All the depositions, interrogatories, and accusations flooded back. I had taken the fifth but was forced to testify against Jack Dodson, my partner. A year of my life, all my money, and worse, because of—

"Mom and Dad never got to enjoy their fortune, though" Booth continued. "They were killed in a car wreck outside Geneva, just after Bucky's bankruptcy case was finalized. But that didn't work out so well, did it? You make the money for your family, and they left it all to your brother. That's the basis of the Swiss case. Did your parents think you were still a fat cat, or had they cut you off so you iced them?"

I clenched my fists. "The judge—"

"I've got your judge." Booth patted the bulge under his jacket and took a step toward me. Truck jumped up and Lieutenant Killelea dove in between us. My body was battered, I hadn't eaten in twenty-four hours, and instead of being welcomed home with what should have been an earth-shattering revelation, this bureaucrat with slicked-back hair finished the hatchet job Gutierrez started in front of Willy days ago.

"All right, that's it for now, gentlemen," Killelea said. "I'm sure we'll have more questions for you, and maybe some pictures to look at in the next few days."

Booth's eyes burned holes in mine. "I don't want to hear one word about your escapades. Not in the *Key West Citizen*, not in *The Miami Herald*, not in Sloppy stinking Joe's. Nowhere, got it? This is a national security issue of the highest priority. You, hotshot, can crawl back in your hole. Don't leave town, any of you."

Booth stormed out of the restaurant. Lieutenant Killelea shrugged then followed. Still numb, I considered climbing back inside Betty and finding a cozy banana republic to call home. Costa Rica, Belize, just get lost once and for all. Forget my stash, forget the gold, forget everything. Only problem was, I was broke.

Willy glared at us while rocking back and forth on the toes of his Nikes.

"Congratulations, boys. You managed to ruin our chance to learn anything in Cuba. Now all hells breaking loose."

"Wait a minute, Willy, these guys—"

He spun on me. "None of this would have happened if you'd come home when I told you to! My people have been murdered, and my own daughter's missing!"

"Hold on, pastor," Truck said.

Willy jammed his finger in Truck's chest. "Zip it, Clarence."

Clarence?

"I made him keep going," Truck said.

"You should have known better, Buck. I knew how these boys would react to the news about Rodney. I was counting on you to be the cool head. I was counting on you to turn your plane around and bring 'em back until we could regroup. But after all that?" He waved toward the door. "Even Redeemer can't help you."

"I can explain—"

"Arrested and expelled from the country, and for what? *Spying*?" Willy's eyes bore into Truck's, Jimbo's, then mine.

"Silence? All I get's silence? Every television network in the country has a news team holed up here pushing this 'War on Cuba' crap like it's a done deal." He lowered his voice. "We buried Rodney today, and I should be with his family right now, but I had to find out what in God's name happened. And all I get's *silence*?"

"Booth told us not to talk about it," I said.

"Fine, let's go, you three. We'll see about not talking about it when we get back to Redeemer." He took a fast step toward the door.

"Hold on, Willy, let me tell you—"

He spun back to face me. "That money I gave you better cover your cost, 'cause we're done."

Chucky and Jimbo followed Willy out the door. Truck put his big paw on my back. I winced, the black hose treatment still fresh.

"Guess we both had reasons to be out of town, huh?"

My mind reeled from the escalating deterioration of an already fragile existence. Truck thumped me again on the back and left me alone in the Conch Flyer. First the FBI, now Willy Peebles. Hell, that didn't even include the blackmailers or the goons in Cuba. Why was Booth so familiar with my background? A banana republic would be the ticket, if I could only scrounge up gas money to get there.

So much for confronting Willy about Shaniqua's interest in Santeria, or her role at Treasure Salvors.

47

The sound of a commuter airline's Dash-8 roaring
down the runway couldn't shake me out of the funk. My days as a Conch Republic
recluse were over, but too much was riding on this mess to bail-out now, Willy
firing me or not.

Ray Floyd was washing Betty down. "That dead dove was bad luck."

"I'm starting to think a dead dove is my astrological sign."

"And you're back in the news. Maybe that will boost Last Resort's business."

"Right. Charters, salvage, piracy and espionage. Unique niche," I said.

"Been like D-Day around here. Bay of Pigs II is coming down the pike."

Our conversations had turned from sunken ships, airplanes, and philosophy
to the bizarre war playing out at the Last Resort. I reached into the brown bag
Dumbas had stuck inside my duffle and pulled out one of the two bottles.

"Havana Club, *siete años* rum. Thousand bucks a bottle."

Ray's nose curled up after he took a shot. "I can't believe Betty made it back
in one piece. I figured I'd seen the last of her."

The carved wood plane with red and green wheels on Salvo's altar came to
mind. "Do me a favor? Check her out, will you? She felt fine coming back, but
make sure nobody swiped anything."

With that I gathered my gear, locked Betty, and walked out to my old Rover.

The La Concha appeared like Mecca ahead on Duval. Tourists lined both sides of the street, and the sound of steel drums emanated from Margaritaville.

A block down was a van with a satellite dish on its roof, parked illegally in front of the hotel. There was another one behind it, and then another. Three television vans straddled the curb, their occupants milling around outside, holding lights and microphones.

Here to pick up where CNN left off? The exiled spy from Cuba? No way the blackmailers would miss this.

Roger Dixon, the assistant manager, was outside speaking to them and pointing toward the door.

I parked out back, and half-expected federal agents to jump out of the croton bushes. There was no sign of the press back here. Zeke waved from the moped rental stand where a line of dangerous-looking newbies stood ready to assault the streets on single-cylinder knee breakers. I shouldered my bags and braced myself for the onslaught of press and the inevitable face-to-face with Karen.

The lobby was crowded but miraculously clear of news teams. God bless Roger Dixon. Something intangible felt different. Bruce, the concierge, was handing out fun-tickets to smiling tourists, but Karen was missing behind the counter.

"Hey, Buck," Josh Bentley said. "You see the welcoming committee?"

"Anybody sticks a mike in my face, you better call an emergency proctologist."

"That's why we kicked them out."

"Karen back there?" I pointed my chin toward the small office.

"Took the day off."

"That's a first."

"Old Island Days has her running crazy. You okay?"

"Every day's a holiday, every meal's a feast."

At the elevator I realized what was different. New paintings of decidedly Cuban subjects hung in place of the former fruit-juice-colored canvasses of local scenes. I stepped back and surveyed the large room. Eight new paintings adorned the walls.

Karen obviously hadn't needed my advice.

The ride up the elevator may have been my loneliest minute ever.

The apartment felt empty, or I did in it. The bruises on my biceps, thighs, and back were already yellow and purple, my only souvenirs from Cuba except for the bottle of Havana Club rum. The pictures on my camera had been erased. The shots from Hemingway's *Finca Vigia* I hoped to use to crack my father's code, and find the *Esmeralda* were gone forever.

After a hot shower, I sat on the couch with a sandwich and a cold beer, only to find my book on Latin art still on the table. Tempted to throw it through the window, I paged through it instead. I wondered if Gutierrez had sold Karen anything of value. But I was more curious about whether Manny had enjoyed any other success with Karen.

The Cuban art sparked an idea. From my duffel I removed the book on codes. One way or the other, I had to find my stash.

Bingo! In the index there were several mentions of Thomas Jefferson—who as it turned out, was heavily into ciphers. I read on and learned that he required them from his diplomatic corps. Jefferson could easily have been my father's role model.

The last couple of days had produced a number of ideas. Given today's events, the need for answers urged my aching body off the couch. Would the press still be hovering? Worse, would Clinton and Bush be readying their retribution?

I pulled on my *FEAR NADA* T-shirt, flush with skull and crossbones, jumped into my flip-flops, and took the stairs down two at a time. I rushed outside and took a couple deep breaths. The air had cooled, and the storms that were on the horizon during my approach into Key West had stalled in the Gulf. There was still an hour of light left in what had been one of the longest days of my life.

48

At first stiff, I found that riding my bike gradually
helped loosen my limbs. At the end of Whitehead was the Treasure Salvor's museum
and gift shop. Inside were select artifacts on display, a fraction of the thousands of
emeralds, gold and silver bars, countless gold doubloons, silver pieces of four and
eight like the one around my neck— all from the Spanish wreck of the *Atocha* that
sank off the coast of Key West on September 5, 1620. She was the holy grail of
shipwrecks, with a bounty approaching a half-billion dollars. Although the *Wall
Street Journal* deemed me to be the heir apparent, the find had made Mel Fisher
the king of all treasure hunters. Treasure Salvors continued to harvest the wreck
today, some twenty years after its discovery…and I live in a hotel.

If Treasure Salvors discovered the letter Hemingway wrote to his editor about
the nine-foot gold chain that came up with the *Pilar's* anchor off Fort Jefferson,
or if they had my chart, their capabilities to pursue that wreck would far exceed
mine.

I entered the gift shop and asked for Danny Pogue, the manager and former
e-Antiquity client who had previously expressed curiosity about my low-budget
salvage efforts. Danny's eyes got big when he saw me.

"Buck, here to trade up for that gold doubloon you always wanted?"

"Still plan on finding my own." I said. "What did Shaniqua Peebles do here?"

"She's one of our top sales people. So damn pretty, people can never say no.

Sure hope the Coast Guard finds her." His expression was sincere. "I heard you flew her out."

"Thanks to the *Citizen.*"

"No, she called me, Buck. Must have been right after you dropped her off. Said you had a chart of the Dry Tortugas all marked up that I should talk to you about." His candor caught me off guard. "Is that why you're here?"

"I didn't realize she worked for you."

Danny had a solid reputation, but treasure hunters inherently break rules in pursuit of gold and glory.

"I heard you were hunting treasure, and I've wanted to talk to you about it, but not if it's in Park waters. Life's too short to go to jail."

Acid reflux bubbled in my throat. "Is anyone around here into Santeria?" I said.

Danny laughed. A mid-western boy, pale and pudgy, he never looked the part of a treasure hunter, much less the follower of an occult religion.

"Not as far as I know. Why you ask?"

"Someone broke into my plane after I found that dead missionary, stole some stuff, and left some Santeria crap behind."

"I don't know nothing about witches or voodoo." He licked his lips. "They take the map she called about?"

"You think I'm stupid enough to leave valuables on my plane, Danny?"

He reiterated Treasure Salvors' interest in helping with my efforts—for the lion's share, of course, and provided the site was in open waters. Yet another warning about jail, but the maps and GPS were gone, anyway. He also wanted to stay abreast of any news about Shaniqua. My gut said he didn't know anything, but she *had* called him. The question was did she call anyone else?

Back on my bike, I rode past the cemetery and wondered where Rodney had been buried. Had there been more placards? Rodney's face along with Shaniqua's? The irony hit me that the poster girl might still be alive. Was she being used to advance the goals of others, or in pursuit of her own?

49

I stopped at José's Cantina. José and Abuela had
some explaining to do about dear Ivan, but their door was locked. It was Monday,
their night off. Was there something more in Abuela's letter to Ivan than cash? A
description of what was happening in Key West? Could she have known I was
taking Willy's investigators to Havana? Had Ivan turned me in or just jumped on
the bandwagon when I was grabbed?

A flyer written both in Spanish and English was taped to the door. It was
for a missing dog. There was a picture of the cute mutt, black with a white circle
around one of its eyes. A reward was offered. I made the mental note to avoid
Chinese restaurants for a few days.

I rode past Seven Fish. Karen's and my table was empty.

My hands were numb on the handlebars. I'd spilled my guts, prattled on
about my failed marriage and business, but I'd also discovered her secret ambition
to write and some ways in which we were really alike. Plus I had the feel of my
hands in hers, her saying I wasn't alone, and the halo of lilac still etched in my
mind.

And, damnit, her strikingly familiar protagonist. The ruthless salvage hunter.

I pushed off the curb and continued down Elizabeth, feeling worse than
when I'd set out. My stomach screamed for attention, so Blue Heaven became
my default location. Lenny would fill me in on Rodney, Gutierrez, the latest on

Santeria aggression, the political reaction to the media coverage, and the pulse of Willy Peebles.

The glass and charred timbers around MG International Gallery's front doors were already repaired, and the black land shark was gone. Enrique Jiminez was the name Gutierrez had mentioned as the Stock Island Sancho. Considering everything else that had happened, that put him next on my list. After checking with Lenny.

I found Truman bumper to bumper, so I pedaled down side streets and stopped at a red light on Simonton. I could hear the steady rhythmic beat of Cuban salsa before the source came into sight, and when the black Mercedes appeared before me, top down and turning my way, a raindrop would have knocked me from the bike. Manny Gutierrez, with his hair slicked back, his eyes hidden by gold-framed dark glasses, and Karen seated next to him with a restrained smile on her face.

I sat frozen as they whizzed past. Did she notice me sitting there with my heart dripping off my sleeve? He flew down the street and swerved rather than braked as a kid came out of a driveway on a scooter. Manny Gutierrez had been the beneficiary of Karen's rare day off from work. Why him?

"You're not alone, Karen Parks, you're not alone."

The rest of my ride was a blur. Karen with Gutierrez was the proverbial straw that broke my resolve. I found myself at Blue Heaven thirsting for a belly full of rum.

"Well, well, well, look who's finally showing his face."

Shit. The Gargoyles.

"Couple days late there, Bubba. Chickened out, huh?"

"Damn lucky, son. I'd of hated to see Bruiser whoop yo' ass."

I stood and took their abuse, trying to conjure a worthy reply. The past few days had taken their toll, but the past ten minutes was the *coup de grâce*.

"This isn't Saturday night?" I said. "And I was ready to go. Son-of-a bitch."

"Heh! Listen to that fool!"

The Gargoyles were now armed for an evening of laughter at my expense, but I didn't care any more. I had hit bottom, again. I found my corner of the bar amidst Lenny's usual disciples gathered to hear him expound on the future of Key West. He brought over a tall Barbancourt on the rocks.

"Welcome home."

"No two words could feel less appropriate."

"Heard you had your hands full, man." He plucked at his chin.

Truck must have ignored Booth's warning. "A grand time was had by all."

Lenny's sympathetic smile helped to mend my wounds, visible and not. He reported that Willy felt horrible at the tongue-lashing he'd given me, then filled me in on the national news and the goings-on around Key West.

Darkness hit like a hammer, as did the Haitian rum. Before I knew it, the need for cash flow had caused me to challenge Bruiser Lewis all over again. The Gargoyles howled their excitement, and pretty much everyone else hooted and hollered at the prospect of bloodshed for entertainment. The ring was reserved for next Saturday night, and Lenny promised to advise Bruiser of the new schedule.

The storm that had threatened Key West all afternoon finally hit, killing the electricity all over the island. Chango, the Orisha of lightning, had flexed his muscles. The open-air restaurant closed in a hurry, and after refusing several offers for nearby shelter, I foolishly chose to ride my bike instead. My motor skills had run off with my common sense, and the only good news was that my hose-beaten body was numb to its bruises, thanks to the anesthetic properties of rum. I wobbled through blinding rain, dodged lake-sized puddles, and managed to crash only once.

What's a bloody kneecap when your whole body looks like a week-old banana?

I arrived at the Church of the Redeemer. A fool's errand to confront Willy about his daughter. No longer on his payroll, all I cared about now was finding my waterproof pouch and GPS. If I didn't head off the blackmailers they'd trash what was left of my reputation, and beat me to the gold.

The chapel's front door was ajar.

I stopped suddenly. What must have been a hundred white candles burned inside. My hands instantly went cold. It looked just like Salvo's studio only days ago.

50

I stared at the panorama of candles inside.
Chango's revenge or another altar to the Orishas? My heart pounded at a rate my alcohol-impaired mind could not keep pace with. I pushed the door open, and the drawn-out squeak of the hinges tore at the silence.

A dark figure jumped from the middle of the pews into the main aisle. He had a sawed-off shotgun in his hands, pointed straight at my chest.

"Who the hell's that?"

Staring down the shotgun barrels, I was unable to respond.

"Buck, that you?"

Willy lowered the twelve-gauge welcoming committee and sniffed me like a dog. "You reek like a backwater still. You know it's past midnight?"

A sense of nausea spread over me. I slumped into the nearest pew. "I saw the candles, and figured…."

"The powers out, Buck." Willy smiled. "Thought there was foul play, huh?"

"I need a drink of water."

Willy disappeared into the darkness and returned with a pitcher and glasses. "I put some coffee on, too. Listen, I'm sorry about blowing up at the airport, I had no idea what you'd been through."

"I wanted to tell you. Booth'll be pissed at Truck."

"You think that pencil-necked suit's gonna harass Truck Lewis?"

"Clarence," I said. "Why are you sleeping in here with a shotgun?"

"While you were gone we had another delivery of chicken parts and more threatening messages. When I catch those sons-of—"

"You need to tell me the truth about Shaniqua."

He stood up quickly. "The hell's that supposed to mean?"

"Start with her interest in Santeria. Was that why you—"

"Watch your mouth, boy. My daughter's a good girl." Willy loomed over me.

"What about the library books?"

A long exhale slumped him forward. "The damn mission got her interested. That and wanting to see where her mumma came from. Cayo Hueso, that is."

"Did Truck tell you he met Salvo?"

"He told me you saved his ass. You've got guts, son, brains I don't know."

"My B/B ratio's gone to hell."

"Say what?"

I waved his question off. Willy poured coffee and hung on every detail of the trip, and my interrogation at State Security by the director himself.

"Tell me about the boat. Was there any sign of Shaniqua, or Manuel?"

"There were two, maybe three men…" I paused. Why Willy tried to keep Shaniqua's presence on the boat a secret had still not been answered. Was he just being protective? Had they both studied Santeria to prepare for the mission? During my hesitation, his eyebrows settled from arched to flat.

He said, "I've tried her phone a thousand times. Nobody else has answered."

"There was a woman, too."

A sudden intake of breath sat him down. "Was it her?"

"Couldn't tell, happened too fast."

"You tell all that to Booth?" Willy asked.

"Only about the boat. The fool didn't give a damn. He said I was interfering with a federal investigation."

"Booth couldn't find his butt with both hands."

"He found me—" I slapped my hand over my mouth.

"Knew a lot about you, didn't he?"

I rubbed my eyes, tired of avoiding my past, tired of lying. My emotional dam burst, and I spilled my guts in one long vomit of a confession. Everything. My failed marriage, my success turned to ashes, my partner in jail for fraudulently hiding assets, warning my parents of e-Antiquity's impending crash, and worst of all, the details of my on-going hell.

"My parents were our original venture capitalists. They bet their entire life savings. I couldn't let them get hurt. I didn't know we were going to get wiped out."

Pastor Hard Case stared me in the eye, waiting. I swallowed hard and told him about the Swiss police's investigation into my parent's death.

"You get charged?"

"They accused me of plotting their deaths and tried to get me to crack. I already had, they just hadn't realized it. The FBI vowed to keep digging." I drank some water. "My parents never anticipated I'd go bankrupt, so they left everything to my brother. The Feds couldn't touch his inheritance, and it drove them nuts."

"Pain's a part of life, Buck, makes you—"

"Don't say it, Willy. It's only gotten worse. My brother doesn't even believe me any more. He's been reluctantly lending me money to survive, money I'm supposed to pay back from a joint trust we have in Geneva."

"Switzerland? You got one a them numbered accounts?"

"We don't know what's in it, and now my key's gone, I'm flat broke, and I'll never be able to repay—"

"Slow down, boy."

"It's all in my pouch. That and the key, copies of my treasure maps and a ledger that could put my brother in jail too."

"The package that was stolen from your plane? *Treasure maps?*"

"Copies of ones I bought on behalf of e-Antiquity to auction but kept instead. I gave the originals to my parents. My father's diplomatic career was ruined. Then they died trying to avoid the shit storm I created."

Willy put an arm around my shoulder. I cursed the rum for bringing me here. He gave me a pep talk I would have normally considered idealistic platitudes, but tonight it worked like acupuncture needles in my soul. A deep breath pushed the past away. I stood up, wavered, and reached out to steady myself.

"Tomorrow I'm going to find the local connection to Cuba," I said.

"You're not going anywhere like this." He led me back to a tiny room where a day bed was made up.

Thunder and rain reverberated in the heavens. The sound of water hammered the tin roof and led me into the deepest sleep I'd had in a week.

51

First light was like a finger in my eye. In the half-
minute between sleep and consciousness, my mind spun like a slot machine with
images of my childhood bedroom, Clinton and Bush, the Cuban jail, the La
Concha, and Karen in Manny Gutierrez's car that flickered until I realized I was
at the church. My lips were stuck shut, and my tongue was dry-sealed to the roof
of my mouth. Dressed in yesterday's clothes, I stank of the bar at Blue Heaven.

A quiver of dread shook my body. The confluence of the last week's experiences had melted me to a puddle at Willy's feet. When I swung my legs off the
single bed, pain shot through my thighs. Trying to stand sent it tearing through
my back, shoulders and biceps. Was it just yesterday that Sanchez's goons had
pummeled me for a wisecrack? Mono-color bruises covered my limbs like prison
tattoos. I ventured cautiously into Redeemer's sanctuary. Last night's candles were
gone, along with Willy and his shotgun.

When I tried to climb aboard my bike I lost my balance and almost fell over.
I walked it a block, awaiting the return of circulation. I swerved and wobbled my
way past Hemingway's house, which reminded me of the *Finca Vigia*. The *Pilar*
had not only revealed a potential clue to my Fort Jefferson hunt and contained
some hidden clue about my father's cipher, it had also given me an idea about the
Carnival.

The majority of the town was asleep, but where I was headed they never rested. After being broadcast worldwide as a spy, I couldn't afford to rest either. The blackmailers certainly wouldn't.

Inside the nondescript building that housed the U.S. Customs office, I put my disheveled appearance out of mind and ignored the once-over from the button-cute brunette receptionist. After introducing myself as connected to the Church of the Redeemer, it occurred to me that she may have seen me on CNN too. There was no recognition in her eyes, which fluttered.

"What can I do for you?"

"Our missionary boat that left—"

"Yes, the *Carnival*. I'm so sorry, it's just awful." Her voice sounded like she'd just taken a helium hit.

"The reason I'm here's a little embarrassing, but lost with the boat was our documentation about all the donated provisions."

Her head cocked sideways. "What does that have—"

"Everything considered, it sounds petty, but it's our responsibility to, well, the donors, we need to verify all the cargo for tax purposes. Charitable contributions, you know."

"I see."

"Tax time comes faster than any of us likes." I held my breath, while the spontaneous lie floated with the grace of the Hindenburg.

"Right, well, we have the records, of course—ah, what was your name again?"

"Reilly, Buck Reilly."

"Do you have any church identification?"

A slow smile tugged at my lips. "We don't exactly carry business cards, but you can call our pastor, Willy Peebles, if that would help."

She hesitated a couple of seconds. "That won't be necessary, hold on."

The woman disappeared down the hall. Good thing I came in early. A crowd might have laughed me out of the place. She returned with a couple of warm sheets of paper.

"The FBI made a copy of this yesterday. Hopefully they'll learn something, I mean, who hurts missionaries?"

The standardized form contained a long list of items brought aboard the *Carnival*, but it was the information on top that caught me by surprise.

"The boat was registered in the Bahamas?"

"Everything okay?" she squeaked.

"Fine, fine." I cleared my throat. "Hard to believe how generous people can be."

The sunlight outside made me shield my eyes. I read the information again and shook my head. Maybe my B/B ratio was finally on the rise, but I wasn't sure which B was dominant.

Back on the scent, I set out to find Currito Salazar, bail bondsman, native Conch, and my connection to the local underworld.

52

I hit a dry hole at the phone booth. Currito Salazar was not home, so I left a message on his machine. I quit toting a cell phone around when I came to Key West. The fact that I was no longer on anybody's speed dial was another revelation on the road out of Hermitville.

I cut behind Sears Town and arrived at the *Key West Citizen's* office. It was a well maintained yellow building shaded with jacaranda trees. The blast of air conditioning made the big open room feel like a walk-in freezer. A woman hurried to the counter. Her tortoise-shell glasses and red Lacoste shirt gave her a dated, preppy air.

"I'm looking for one of your staff photographers," I said.

"We only have three, which one do you want?"

"Who was at the airport when the first of Redeemer's missionaries was recovered?"

Crow's feet appeared at her temples. "Doug Friedland wrote the story, so Bobby Barrett probably took the pictures. You have something to add?"

I felt like the hen that crashed the fox den. "I was the pilot—"

Her eyes bugged out as if she'd won the lottery. "Hey, aren't you the guy from Cuba?"

I pointed to my hair. "Do I look like a spy?"

Her smile faded. "Will you comment on the other stories we've run about you?"

"Sure, and you can quote me, they're bullshit. As for what happened in Cuba, all I did was fly a charter to and from Havana."

Her smile returned. "Sounds like that's going to be a popular route for the military. Look at this place," she swung her arms around. "The shit's hitting the fan."

"How so?"

"The CANC's getting what they wanted. At least, that's the word on the wire. We won't know for sure until the president's speech."

I bit my lip. "When's he speaking?"

"Tonight. It was scheduled to cover foreign policy, but the buzz is he's giving the Cubans an ultimatum. Either admit sinking the boat, or else."

Sunk? Booth knows I saw the boat in Havana, so the president should too. Something wasn't right.

"A few missionaries merits an 'or else'?"

"It's a fuse. Ambassador Boltnek issued a statement yesterday noting that Cuba has the second largest biotech program in the Americas. Ten thousand researchers and their government has spent three billion dollars developing products since 1986."

"Pharmaceuticals, thanks to the embargo."

"They have a biochem pact with Iran that the administration's comparing to their former nuclear relationship with Russia. They could produce more WMDs than Saddam Hussein ever dreamed of."

"Biochem pact, is that new?"

"It's been around awhile, but with Iran's growing nuclear program, there's genuine fear they could work with Cuba on bio-warfare."

A fuse was right. The Middle East and Cuba all wrapped into one. The ambassador to the United Nations didn't release statements like that without it being a coordinated event. Would invading Cuba really be that easy? More shock and awe-shucks?

Cuba's director of Secret Police had joked that the American press set foreign policy through exaggerated headlines. Would tonight's speech prove that correct? What if Cuba's bio-capabilities really were a major threat? I remembered the wooden crates on the Havana harbor dock. Could they have contained offensive weapons? Sanchez had warned that 9/11 would seem like a stubbed toe if America invaded them.

"Any idea where I can find Barrett? He was interested in my plane. I want him to take some pictures for me."

"Bobby's a wannabe pilot, it's all he talks about. He's in the back, hang on."

I counted eleven people shouting on phones and stabbing frenetically at their keyboards. Spring break statistics, fishing summaries, and obituaries had morphed into stories on demonstrations, invasion speculation, and anticipation over a presidential speech. Key West had turned on its ear.

A man rushed around the corner. His tall, beanpole stature seemed familiar. "I couldn't believe it when I saw you and your plane on CNN yesterday," he said.

The preppyish woman was now tapping her fingers on the counter.

"Anywhere we could speak in private?" I said.

He led me into a small conference room.

"What year's your Widgeon?"

The rundown on Betty turned his eyes glassy. I'd seen that expression before. Flying boat lovers get that faraway look when encountering one of the old Grumman fleet: Widgeon, Goose, Mallard or Albatross. With less than two hundred Widgeons still in operation, they're an increasingly rare sight.

"You shot the story about Jo Jo, so, how about the missionaries' departure?"

"Burned two rolls that morning," Barrett said.

"You don't use digital?"

"I develop all my own prints, always have. My editor tolerates my passion for celluloid. It's not like I've ever sold anything outside of Key West, at least until now."

"You still have the other pictures?"

"Sure. I have a bunch of the picketers."

"Have there been any breakthroughs not reported yet?"

"Not as far as I know. The Santeros deny involvement, and Redeemer won't comment on the reprisals, but the owner of Exotica, Carlos Jiminez, claimed he was being persecuted. Manny Gutierrez is adamant that the Cuban angle is a ruse to throw the police off the real culprits."

"Did you say Jiminez?" I said.

"Yeah, the guy whose store window got smashed in."

It was the same last name as the Sancho on Stock Island. "Have the police looked at your pictures from the boat's departure?"

"Nope."

Willy was right. Booth couldn't find his ass with both hands.

"Do you have them here?"

His freckled forehead wrinkled. "No way, there's no conditioned storage here. My images are my livelihood. I don't take care of them, I've got nothing for follow up pieces."

The whole office felt like conditioned storage to me. Barrett told me he kept his negatives at home but hesitated when I asked to see them.

"How about a ride in the Widgeon?" he said.

"When can I see the pictures?"

"I was going to split and get lunch in a while. Why don't I make up a set and meet you at the airport?" We agreed upon the Conch Flyer at one o'clock.

Outside was a sauna compared to the meat locker inside. A head rush hit me when I climbed on the bike. Hangover residue. My discovery at customs had sidetracked my plan to pursue the Stock Island Sancho but had also led me to learn that the owner of Exotica had the same last name. Based on the speculation about the president's speech, my discoveries in Havana must not have made it to the White House. Unless they were playing possum, which meant I could still leverage the information. Provided I wanted to take on the FBI and the executive branch of the government.

53

The streets were filled with late risers. My mind
spun like the bike's wheels until I arrived at the gate of the Coast Guard station on
Trumbo Road. When I asked to speak with a senior officer from the *Mohawk* the
sentry curled his lip. I gave him my name—no recognition. But at the mention of
Havana, and finally CNN, his eyes got wide.

"Are you—"

"Under orders, can't talk about it."

He retreated into the security shack. I could see him on the phone, gesturing
and glancing back at me. When he returned, he stood very straight and spoke
clearly. "Ensign Frank Nardi's the Officer of the Deck on the *Mohawk*. He's in a
briefing now but asked for you to call him at this number after fourteen hundred
hours."

I restrained the urge to salute. The sentry stared after me, undoubtedly wondering if he'd just met a bona fide CIA operative. Back at the La Concha I locked
my bike to the rack and was reminded of the chicken that had been leashed there
a few days ago. Then I thought of the jar in Poquito's office. And then Karen.

She was at the front desk, and the image of her in the black mini-dress the
other night was still fresh. She was helping a customer but caught my eyes as I
dug into my backpack. She nodded toward one of the new paintings next to the
counter and winked.

Nice of her to rub it in.

The customer left as I pulled her manuscript from my pack.

"Reads like a bestseller, except your main character's a real jerk," I said.

Her face soured. "You don't understand, the protagonist needs to show growth—"

"Save it, Karen. Your opinion of me was pretty clear."

She yanked the pages out of my hand. Her cheeks flushed beet red.

"I should have never—I told you not to read it…oh, never mind." In two long strides she was in the small office. She closed the door fast, but held it from slamming.

54

"No man is an island." These words begin
Hemingway's *For Whom the Bells Toll*, but they weren't his. John Donne penned
them in 1674 after being imprisoned for marrying an "improper" woman, was
released, was twice a member of England's parliament, was financially ruined,
widowed, and ultimately ordained. It was the book where the heroine Pilar was
immortalized, but I could find no clues related to HIS BOAT or Pilar in my
father's cipher.

The week had been an eye-opening, cocoon-tearing and seclusion-ending
experience. Unable to reach Currito, it was time to find the Stock Island Sancho
myself. Would my crashing Enrique Jiminez go the same way it had for Truck
with Salvo? I had to find answers. I started by reading the *Key West Citizen's*
website, catching up on the stories Barrett had mentioned. Then another idea
overcame me.

I Googled Thomas Jefferson.

As a president, author of the Declaration of Independence, and the first Secretary of State, his name produced millions of hits. I added "codes" to the search
string, which narrowed the field. His passion for encryption was well documented.
Jefferson had invented something called a wheel cipher, used to protect foreign
policy dispatches. It was a device that used a cylindrical bar, six inches long, with

twenty-six disks, each containing all the letters of the alphabet. The wheel cipher was much more complicated then my father's system.

Jefferson was another dead end.

Damn! The connection had seemed certain. Diplomacy and a Virginian. We used to laugh at Dad's French accent. "*Le premiere Virginiare.*" I scrolled down the list from the last search, then hit 'back,' and scanned down again.

Something caught my attention. It was a word in italics. *Vigenère?*

Was it *Virginia* misspelled? The word surfed my brain waves. *Le premiere Vigenère* began as a haunting whisper and built to a steady beat in my head.

The article said Jefferson had selected the Vigenère cipher to protect communications with the Lewis and Clark expedition.

What I found next made my heart skip…a sea of letters.

	A	B	C	D	E	F	G	H	I	J	K	L	M	N	O	P	Q	R	S	T	U	V	W	X	Y	Z
A	A	B	C	D	E	F	G	H	I	J	K	L	M	N	O	P	Q	R	S	T	U	V	W	X	Y	Z
B	B	C	D	E	F	G	H	I	J	K	L	M	N	O	P	Q	R	S	T	U	V	W	X	Y	Z	A
C	C	D	E	F	G	H	I	J	K	L	M	N	O	P	Q	R	S	T	U	V	W	X	Y	Z	A	B
D	D	E	F	G	H	I	J	K	L	M	N	O	P	Q	R	S	T	U	V	W	X	Y	Z	A	B	C
E	E	F	G	H	I	J	K	L	M	N	O	P	Q	R	S	T	U	V	W	X	Y	Z	A	B	C	D
F	F	G	H	I	J	K	L	M	N	O	P	Q	R	S	T	U	V	W	X	Y	Z	A	B	C	D	E
G	G	H	I	J	K	L	M	N	O	P	Q	R	S	T	U	V	W	X	Y	Z	A	B	C	D	E	F
H	H	I	J	K	L	M	N	O	P	Q	R	S	T	U	V	W	Q	Y	Z	A	B	C	D	E	F	G
I	I	J	K	L	M	N	O	P	Q	R	S	T	U	V	W	X	Y	Z	A	B	C	D	E	F	G	H
J	J	K	L	M	N	O	P	Q	R	S	T	U	V	W	X	Y	Z	A	B	C	D	E	F	G	H	I
K	K	L	M	N	O	P	Q	R	S	T	U	V	W	X	Y	Z	A	B	C	D	E	F	G	H	I	J
L	L	M	N	O	P	Q	R	S	T	U	V	W	X	Y	Z	A	B	C	D	E	F	G	H	I	J	K
M	M	N	O	P	Q	R	S	T	U	V	W	X	Y	Z	A	B	C	D	E	F	G	H	I	J	K	L
N	N	O	P	Q	R	S	T	U	V	W	X	Y	Z	A	B	C	D	E	F	G	H	I	J	K	L	M
O	O	P	Q	R	S	T	U	V	W	X	Y	Z	A	B	C	D	E	F	G	H	I	J	K	L	M	N
P	P	Q	R	S	T	U	V	W	X	Y	Z	A	B	C	D	E	F	G	H	I	J	K	L	M	N	O
Q	Q	R	S	T	U	V	W	X	Y	Z	A	B	C	D	E	F	G	H	I	J	K	L	M	N	O	P
R	R	S	T	U	V	W	X	Y	Z	A	B	C	D	E	F	G	H	I	J	K	L	M	N	O	P	Q
S	S	T	U	V	W	X	Y	Z	A	B	C	D	E	F	G	H	I	J	K	L	M	N	O	P	Q	R
T	T	U	V	W	X	Y	Z	A	B	C	D	E	F	G	H	I	J	K	L	M	N	O	P	Q	R	S
U	U	V	W	X	Y	Z	A	B	C	D	E	F	G	H	I	J	K	L	M	N	O	P	Q	R	S	T
V	V	W	X	Y	Z	A	B	C	D	E	F	G	H	I	J	K	L	M	N	O	P	Q	R	S	T	U
W	W	X	Y	Z	A	B	C	D	E	F	G	H	I	J	K	L	M	N	O	P	Q	R	S	T	U	V
X	X	Y	Z	A	B	C	E	D	F	G	H	I	J	K	L	M	N	O	P	Q	R	S	T	U	V	W
Y	Y	Z	A	B	C	D	E	F	G	H	I	J	K	L	M	N	O	P	Q	R	S	T	U	V	W	X
Z	Z	A	B	C	D	E	F	G	H	I	J	K	L	M	N	O	P	Q	R	S	T	U	V	W	X	Y

When the phone rang I jumped.

I expected it to be Currito Salazar, or the blackmailers, and was surprised to hear Ray Floyd's voice panting on the other end.

"Buck, you won't believe this—I can't believe—hold on." He pulled the phone away from his mouth, and I could hear yelling in the distance.

"Call the police, not the FBI!" Ray's sharp voice made me flinch. I sat down. "You need to get over here! This is seriously fucked up."

"What are you talking about?"

"Betty, man, *Betty*!"

I sucked in a shallow breath. "What's wrong with—"

"Remember when you asked me to look her over, after you got back from Cuba?"

"Yeah, so?"

"I was giving her a rundown, started with the starboard engine, fuel tank, magneto—"

I bit my knuckle. "Ray! What the hell's wrong?"

"I'm looking around, and everything seems fine, and then I get on top of the wing, and what I see freaks me out—I mean, I fell right off the damn plane."

"Get to the point!"

"There's a bomb on cylinder four of Betty's port engine!"

I jumped to my feet. "Did you say *bomb*?"

"A grenade, rigged to some sort of balloon-looking thing—hold on." He held the phone away, but I heard him yell: "Get the SWAT team, or bomb squad, or whatever the hell they have on this island."

I imagined pandemonium at the airport.

"Ray, I'll be right there. Ray?"

I ran around the apartment looking for my keys.

A bomb on my port engine?

Could it have been planted in—*Sanchez*! That bastard! Or, what about Salvo, or Quasimodo?

Betty's port engine had been a magnet for flying fish, hoodoo candles, and now a grenade. Why hadn't it exploded? And why did someone want me dead? The phone rang, and I realized the message light was blinking. I feared Ray was calling back to say Betty was toast.

"*What!?*"

"Fuck you too."

"Who's this?"

"You ready or what?" Currito Salazar.

"Listen—"

"He's willing to see you, but it's got to be right now. I'm parked illegally on Duval, so hurry up."

"I can't, Curro, not now."

"You what? Listen, cuz, this guy don't exactly grant audiences every day, you know what I'm saying? Especially with all this shit going down. You don't post now, forget about it."

Shit! "All right, I'm coming."

He hung up, pissed. The police probably wouldn't let me near Betty anyway. I stared at the phone and saw the message light blinking. After a couple of charter inquiries came an icy voice that stopped me cold.

"You should have listened to us. Now you'll be sorry." The strong Cuban accent led me to conclude it was Clinton. Did they plant the bomb? Or was my ledger on the way to the police? Or was I going to be boiled?

I flew down the stairs three at a time, my flip-flops slapped loudly on the landings. I flung the door open and sprinted through the lobby spreading a wake of people jumping out of my way.

Currito's blue Caddie was visible through the glass door, along with a cop on a bicycle pointing to a no parking sign. I dove in the passenger door and surprised them both. Currito hit the gas and left the patrolman standing in the road with his mouth open.

"Go hassle a drunk, cracker!" Currito yelled at his rear-view mirror.

I rubbed the sweat off my face with the front of my shirt.

"Damn, cuz, you don't look too good, eh?"

"You wouldn't believe it if I told you," I said.

"Well, pull yourself together, this guy don't mess around. If he thinks you're a flake we'll be out the door."

With the air fouled by two decades of Parliament cigarettes, the antiquated air conditioner labored to keep the interior cool if not fresh. Bubbles in the window tinting made the view surreal, distorting reality with a hallucinogenic twist.

"Or if he thinks you're a threat—"

"There's a freaking bomb on my plane!"

"What?" The car swerved, nearly sending a moped through a T-shirt shop window. "Damn, cuz." Currito's rheumy-eyes peered above his sunglasses as he flung his hand, its thumb and fingers slapping resoundingly together. "You CIA, or what?"

His question released a sudden laugh that took all my wits not to melt into hysterics. The harder I shook, the more serious Currito's expression became. He pulled off North Roosevelt into the Publix parking lot and sat there staring at me until I got myself under control.

"You all right, Bubba?"

"Is this it?"

"We ain't going anywhere until you pull your shit together."

I held up my hand. "I'm fine, Curro, don't worry, I won't embarrass you."

"Shit, boy, take a breath." He pushed his sunglasses up the bridge of his nose. I stifled another fit of hysterics, and worried that maybe I *was* coming apart at the seams.

We left Key West heading north on A1A. Cars sped past us, and Currito cruised steadily at 40 miles per hour in a 55 zone. We passed the first wave of Stock Island's shabby retail strips and turned right, but my mind was centered on what would be happening at the airport.

We turned onto a dark street. Dirty trailers pressed close to the curb, and dried, brown palm fronds hung over them. I tried to refocus my brain onto the present when Currito pulled into a gravel drive where an ancient Ford Bronco was nestled amongst the bushes.

"All right, cuz, you ready?"

Two dark men emerged from the shadows. Each of them held machetes.

"You owe me, brother." Currito rolled down his window. "He's expecting us."

One of the men waved his machete toward the trailer. The gravity of the meeting hit me. What if Enrique was Bush or Clinton?

We got out and walked to the cinderblock steps that led up to the front door. Volkswagen-sized palmetto bugs scurried away like sentries guarding the castle. There was an intricate painting of a black eyeball amidst swirling red and orange paint on the aluminum wall next to the door. A shiver passed through me. The door opened. I couldn't see anyone but heard a low, steady drumbeat.

It was the exact the same rhythm I'd heard in Salvo's studio in Cayo Hueso.

55

I couldn't keep my eyes off the colorful paintings that covered the walls of Enrique's doublewide. Whimsical figures floated on brilliant backgrounds that gave life to the otherwise dark interior. I flashed back to Cayo Hueso, outside Salvo's studio, and recalled his all-encompassing murals. In the corner of the trailer was an altar that contained wooden animals, a glass of amber liquid, a Snickers bar, and what appeared to be plastic doll limbs.

A muted television showing a lusty soap opera scene drew our host's eyes from us to the screen. If this was the nerve center for the Santero assaults, then their battlefield commander sought guidance from even stranger sources than his occult religion. Somehow, Currito had negotiated the visitation smack in the middle of The Young and the Restless.

My second visit to a Sancho could not have been more different then the first. There was no cloaked figure darting around the shadows, no entranced woman gyrating on the floor, no replicas of my airplane foreshadowing my demise. The drumbeat, however, thumped steadily from a stereo in the corner.

"So you're the dude got thrown out of Cuba?" Enrique said.

"For being outside a government warehouse," I said. "And for rescuing a friend from Salvo's studio."

His eyes remained fixed on a silent argument on the screen. "Lucky you got out."

Currito sat next to me on the nappy, lime-colored love seat. The Stock Island Sancho was reclined spread-eagle on a faded green Barcalounger. The man was huge, not in height but girth: three hundred pounds packed onto a 5'9"ish frame, tucked miraculously into yellow polyester coaching shorts. He was much larger than the two blackmailers. The soles of his feet were bright pink, in contrast with his asphalt black skin. Empty liter bottles of Dr. Pepper surrounded his chair.

"The Bondsman says you're connected to Redeemer. What do you want?"

"To know why the hell I've been targeted."

He held up his remote control, snuffed the television, and swung the recliner forward in one swift motion. He landed with a trailer-rattling thud. Surprise pushed me into the back of the loveseat against Currito.

"Come on."

Currito and I exchanged glances, then followed him into the next room. My impression of Enrique changed once there. Soap operas and spent junk food containers were replaced with shelves of books, a more serious altar, several larger paintings, and enough white candles to light Duval Street.

"Redeemer needs to back off," Enrique said.

I checked the ground. "Carpet—"

"Messing with my people, throwing them to the sharks and shit."

"Where's your big—"

"You listening to me? We're not going to sit around and get our asses kicked, especially by a jack-off like Manny Gutierrez."

"Gutierrez thinks it's all your doing."

"He's pissed off 'cause I wouldn't hook him up with a brother who has some Santero art, a sweet Wilfredo Lam."

"Willy and I have been bombarded with chickens, and what about doves?"

"Why would we do that? Willy Peebles don't bother me, least up till now. He wants to send people to Cuba, that's his business. And before those newspaper articles and CNN, I'd never heard of you."

"Then why the intimidation?" I said. "Someone threw a Molotov cocktail in Redeemer's window, I've been robbed, threatened, people are dead, and all because of Willy's little mission?"

"I don't give a shit about their mission! And Santeria may dominate in Cuba, but it don't explain everything they do. Until you fuck with them, then anything goes."

"Would Salvo think Willy's mission was a threat?"

"A handful of do-gooders are mice nuts to him."

"What would Salvo be sending to a government warehouse? Portraits of Orishas? Biological weapons?"

"Oh, yeah, right. Maybe a nuke or two." Enrique looked at Currito as if to question whether I was crazy. Currito lifted his shoulders, unsure.

I pointed to Enrique's altar. "Why do you put that stuff on there? The Snickers bar, that drink...?" *My airplane?*

"Offerings to the Orishas."

"Like candles in a Catholic church, or is one of them going to eat that candy bar?"

"They're symbols. Sometimes people place pictures there, or things they're worried about for consideration."

"Symbols, huh? Like a blood-coated dove or a fricasseed cat?"

Enrique pressed his lips tight and leaned in my direction. "Ebó's used to heal sickness or help solve a problem. An animal sacrificed to gain strength is eaten by the worshipper, unless it was to fight illness."

"All those good chickens go to waste?"

"Would you eat cancer cut out of your body? No. Why? It's infected flesh. The animals are taken wherever the Orisha directs."

"Like the front steps of a church, or stuffed into my flight bag?"

Currito groaned next to me.

"*He who takes fire into their hands, cannot wait.*"

"What's that, a riddle? Another code I'm supposed to figure out?"

"Believe it or not, our religion's peaceful. We don't cast spells, hex people or make sacrifices to hurt others. And we don't perform *ebó* on cats and dogs."

"Unless someone fucks with you, right? Then all bets are off?" I reached into my backpack. "I assume this isn't a good luck charm?" The sight of the clay figurine with protruding nails caused Enrique's eyes to widen.

"Where's your big cauldron?" I said. "Salvo's had a human skull—"

"*Endoki!*" He sat heavily into the chair. "Was there dirt on the floor?"

"Fresh from Transylvania," I said.

"That explains it, Palo Mayombe, black magic."

"Oh, shit," Curro said.

"What are you, Glenda the Good Witch?"

"Did you see any sticks nearby?"

The image of Salvo's back room returned. After I described its contents, Enrique let out a deep sigh.

"*Brujerea.* Witchcraft. Salvo must be a Palero. What you found was his prenda."

Prenda? Hadn't Sanchez used that word? "Sorry, I didn't bring my English / Mumbo-Jumbo dictionary."

"Palero's a Palo priest. Prenda is what you called the cauldron, and the dirt on the floor was from a cemetery. What about his Nikisi—that's their form of Orishas—did you see any other symbols or items on the altar?"

I tried to picture the dark room. "There were some animal horns."

Enrique bit his lip. "Siete Rayos."

"Oh shit. He's like Chango," Currito said.

"Of course, Mr. Happy," I said.

"Not exactly Chango, but close. Palo is—"

"Palo, Prenda, Nikisi, it's all gobbledygook, Santeria double-talk I don't—"

"No! Palo is *not* Santeria. It's different, but combined with Santeria, or used by a Santero, it can only be endoki. That statue means you've been hexed."

"Gosh, and things were going so well," I said.

"Dark spirits." Currito shivered.

"When Santeros are desperate they sometimes use a Palero. Their methods are more direct," Enrique said.

"Maybe I should find one. I'm sure as hell getting nowhere on my own." I turned to Currito. "Dark spirits?"

"The skull and Siete Rayos, they're for the spirits of the dead."

A lightning bolt crashed inside my head. *Leave the spirits of the dead alone.* "When my plane was broken into, a package was taken. Know anything about it?"

Enrique's eyes didn't waver. "I already told you, I don't even know who the hell you are—aside from being CIA, that is."

"Right, and you're the Pope."

A sharp laugh. "You're an asshole, but I like you." He rubbed his chin. "There was an *Abererinkula* on the missionary boat."

"What the hell's that?"

"Uninitiated person, a rookie. Guy had broad scars on his cheeks."

A tingle ran up my spine. "I've seen his picture."

"He came here last week and asked me to perform a rite called *Asheogún Otá*. It's a prayer for victory over your enemies. I didn't know him, and, well, he had a crazy look in his eyes, so I refused."

The sound of an airplane sent my heart into overdrive. The bomb. I needed to get out of here, but I sensed Enrique knew more than he was saying.

"This guy with the scars, you catch his name?"

Enrique guzzled Dr. Pepper and swiped his mouth with a broad forearm. "Dude had some kind of accent. But isn't he dead? Killed by pirates, or whatever shit was in the paper?"

"Cuban?"

"I'm no expert, Russian for all I know."

"No name?"

Enrique paused and shifted his gaze back to the altar. He reached for a small leather cup, shook it once, and tossed a half-dozen small brownish bones onto the table like they were dice. He touched them tenderly as the scent of decaying marrow reached my nostrils.

"His name was Jackson Rolle."

"Yahtzee." I said.

"That's it. I've got things to do." Enrique looked back toward the television. "First the FBI, now the CIA."

"FBI?"

"Some asshole was here a couple hours ago, asking the same kind of questions."

"Guy named Booth?" Enrique's expression didn't change. "Did you tell him about Rolle?"

"He was only interested in my connections to Cuba." He herded us to the door.

"One last question," I said. "Was Shaniqua Peebles into Santeria?"

Currito took a step back. "You crazy, cuz?"

Enrique's smirk said otherwise.

"One fine honey there."

"Any chance she knew Rolle, or could be mixed up in something illegal?"

"That girl's always mixed up in something."

I waited but all I got was a steady grin.

"Did she call you from the boat? Tell you anything about me?"

"Your friend has an ego, Curro." He sighed. "You want to leave that statue, I'll see what I can find out."

56

We hurried from the trailer under the scrutiny of Enrique's machete-wielding bodyguards. Back in the dilapidated Cadillac, we headed toward the airport. Currito lit a Parliament and exhaled a blue lungful toward the windshield.

"At least you got a name, eh?"

"Jackson Rolle." Booth may have been one step ahead of me, but he hadn't gotten the information that mattered. That was comforting with respect to my own situation.

"I'm glad that's over, cuz, Enrique gives me the heebie jeebies."

"Does he have a real job, or does being a Sancho pay his bills?" I said.

"He's my postman."

We drove past the old houseboat row in silence. Picturing Enrique as a postman was too much for my fatigued imagination.

"Do you think the Cubans sent spies over in the boat lifts?" I asked.

"Are you kidding, cuz? Castro was the original opportunist."

"Is that opinion or fact?"

"Boy, you never believe shit without questions, do you? Hell, I nearly bonded one out once. Had it all set up before he spilled his guts trying to negotiate asylum."

That word caused me to squirm, another reminder of Sanchez. "What happened?"

"Kid came over from Mariel, started acting funny, got into a fight trying to recruit another *balsero*. He was supposed to weasel his way into the Cuban American community to keep watch for any crazy plans. Fidel was always worried about another Bay of Pigs, you know?"

"Sounds more like a mole than a spy."

"A fucking rat's more like it. He fingered a guy in Miami who bankrolled Castro's network here. It was a big deal. Kid bragged that he was going to be Cuba's ears in South Florida."

"Or a terrorist, maybe?"

Currito shot me a quick glance. "You're watching too much CNN." He grinned. "Sorry."

What Sanchez said now made sense. Of course Cuba had planted moles in the million-plus people who had emigrated here. They could easily number in the thousands, which gave some weight to his brash statement that 9/11 would be a stubbed toe compared to what they could do. My cotton mouth returned with a vengeance.

Cause and effect, action and reaction. 50 years of animosity with Cuba had produced a generation of negative consequences. In my travels to Latin America I had been cornered several times on the failed embargo and the hypocrisy it represented. America sought to punish Cuba for its human rights record by preventing the Cuban people access to food, medicine, modern convenience and trading partners. I'm far from political, but any moron can see that after 10 presidents and five decades of failed policy, it'd be time to change course. Let common sense guide the rudder and you'll find the rhum line.

57

The same news vans that were at the La Concha
were now parked in front of the airport. I hit the ground running but didn't make
it far before being stopped by a Key West police officer. I explained who I was,
which ignited the lurking news hounds. They screamed and pushed to get at me,
but were restrained by another cop.

The terminal was packed with grounded travelers, camera crews, and a variety
of suits. Ray Floyd was talking to Jess Waters, the airport administrator. Jess and
I had never gotten along. He didn't like amphibious aircraft using his airport,
convinced they weren't safe. I'm sure he was thrilled that mine was now equipped
with a bomb.

"Buck!" Ray said.

"What's happening?"

"Bomb squad's out there now. Agent Booth's on his way in. He said for you
to wait here." Ray was still pale.

Booth came back through security and came toward me with a maniacal glint
in his eyes. Through the window I could see two men in space suit-like outfits
moving away from Betty in slow motion toward a white Chevy Tahoe with a huge
steel vault that looked something like a concrete mixer.

I suddenly realized where I recognized Booth from. He was the guy in the
government car by Posada's restaurant the day of CANC's rally.

"You've got a lot of explaining to do, mister," Booth said.

"What was it?"

"Russian grenade, wired with some sort of balloon-rigged trigger mechanism. Pressure related."

"We came back from Cuba on the deck, never higher than three thousand feet." I tried to remember our altitude on the trip to Cuba, maybe a thousand feet higher. Booth's analysis sank in and my thoughts shifted to my release at José Martí airport and Dumbas's sudden joviality.

"*You've been given priority clearance....*" His and Havana Control's instructions were to fly at 5,500 feet. Would rescuing Truck from Salvo make them want to get rid of me? Or seeing the crates at the warehouse? A vision struck. When Betty's port engine backfired, Dumbas dove to the ground as if expecting an explosion. *Son-of-a bitch.*

"Can these guys tell what altitude it was set to ignite?"

"What's your point?"

"I'm trying to figure out how close I came to being shark bait."

"You better start worrying about being jail bait, Reilly. Interfering with this investigation has rekindled your own."

"How's the investigation going so far, Booth? Any big discoveries?"

"As a matter of fact, a little birdy left me a message about you. Something about some spreadsheets? Said they'd be sending them over. Any idea what that means?"

The blood drained from my head.

Booth's mouth twisted into a nasty grin. "And we're impounding your plane as evidence, hot shot. They'll strip it down to—"

Something snapped, and I leapt at him with a haymaker. Wide-eyed, he ducked impact. Two uniformed police officers grabbed me from behind.

"That's your ass, Reilly! I'll nail you on obstruction, assaulting a law enforcement officer, and—"

"Touch my plane and I'll have *your* ass!"

"You men are my witnesses, Buck Reilly just threatened me. Bring his sorry butt downtown. I want to know why someone thought him worthy of blowing up."

Ray Floyd rushed up. "Hey! What are you guys doing? He wouldn't blow up his own plane!"

Booth's thin lips lifted to reveal his caffeine-yellowed teeth. He leaned in. "Just another satisfied e-Antiquity investor."

A kick to the balls wouldn't have surprised me more. I stood open-mouthed, staring at him as he strutted away. Reporters and cameramen swarmed Booth like flies on dog shit. One broke away from the crowd and walked toward me. It was the lanky, freckled photographer from the *Citizen.*

"Guess we can forget about that ride, huh?"

My eyes were still boring holes into Booth. "Looks that way."

He exhaled loudly, then reached into his pocket. "Here are the pictures, anyway. Maybe you'll get the plane back."

The thick envelope snapped me out of the funk. Inside were at least thirty pictures of—they were ripped from my grasp.

Booth.

"Let's go, hot shot."

"You've got no right to take those!"

"Shut your yap and march."

Led away by two officers, my guess was we were headed to the KWPD offices on Simonton. I was becoming much too familiar with law enforcement facilities.

The name of the boat's Santero crewmen and Barrett's wad of pictures gave me a couple of Get Out of Jail Free cards in case Booth planned on taking Betty away as some sort of crazy revenge for speculating on the stock market, or if the blackmailers sent him my ledger, but first I had to get the pictures back.

High-powered lights outside the terminal suddenly blinded me. The press pushed in, and I shielded my face. If the mention in the Citizen was enough to run me out of Key West, the national networks could propel my flight to a banana republic. In the past two days I'd gone from accused inside trader and suspected murderer to CIA spy and in the middle of a potential war with Cuba. They were going to have a field day at my expense.

58

"Your brother paid a half-million dollars for that junk airplane, and he doesn't have a pilot's license. Rough bankruptcy, Reilly."

"I don't even own a house."

"I see right through the slight-of-hand bullshit you boys have pulled. I guess that's why you're down here under an assumed name."

"Buck's my middle—"

"One day you're worth millions, now a once lucky has-been who bailed out to this shit rock. You want to know what real ambition looks like, Reilly?" He pointed to his chin. "And you're my ticket. Know what else? Your old partner's getting tired of his jail cell. Dodson's making hints about a deal."

The Key West police officer in the room squinted at me. Sweat broke out on my forehead. My deal with Jack Dodson was detailed in the ledger stolen from Betty. If the blackmailer's threat was true, then Booth may have all he needs before the day was out.

Booth bent down, his face inches from mine. "I own you, boy, you got that? You may not have any accounts left for me to freeze, but I've got your plane, and hell, I could rip that Middleburg farm out from under your brother's ass, understand?"

"I told you what happened in Cuba, why—"

"Right, the head of State Security tried to kill you. That fits your mammoth ego—"

"It's got nothing to do with my ego. It was the whole chain of events around finding—" Booth suddenly shoved his palm over my mouth. I slapped it away.

He turned to the police officer. "Leave us alone, Klausner."

When the door closed, Booth turned back to me. "Open your mouth about that boat, I'll bury you in a federal safe house. You hear me?"

How Booth got to be a special agent in the Federal Bureau of Investigation was beyond me. "Why are you sticking your neck out, Reilly? Your charter for Redeemer's long over. As far as we're concerned, the case of the missionaries is closed."

"What do you mean closed? Based on what?"

"Your evidence, hot shot." Booth's crooked teeth shone dully in the fluorescent light. "When you saw the *Carnival* at a government installation, that was all we needed."

"That's crazy, there's no—"

"Back off, butt out, and keep your mouth shut—"

"Did you say butt out?"

"The information's classified as national security until the president says otherwise. If you were the only one that saw the damn boat I'd put you under a rug, but with those so-called missionaries…You say one word, or leave town, your other problems will seem like jay-walking."

"The boat's being at the warehouse doesn't prove it was the Cuban government. And I met the Stock Island Sancho, Enrique Jiminez, to discuss calming things down—"

"Heh! You humiliate your old man, and now you're the family diplomat? Statesman for the Conch Republic?"

"Jiminez is a federal employee, just like you."

"That whacked-out stamp-licker on Stock Island?" His shrill laugh made me cringe. "I suggest you focus on your own problems."

"How do you explain the bomb, then, Booth?"

"Like you said, the big, bad Cubans wanted to blow you up for finding the warehouse. It's a fit, congratulations." I balled my fists at his self-satisfied grin. "And now I get to go to Washington and present the facts to the director."

"You'll start a war if you push this, Booth."

"And finally be an assistant director."

"Am I under arrest?"

"Not yet, at least until I see what this mysterious tip is all about. Don't get any ideas about stepping foot off this god-awful island. Consider your plane grounded as evidence."

I had provided the fuel for this opportunist's obsessive ambition. And worse, my past was just an indictment away, and the hard evidence that would bury me was about to fall into Booth's lap.

"Remember, I own your ass." Booth pulled Barrett's envelope from his pocket and dropped it at the floor by my feet without looking inside. "Now get out of here."

59

A rain squall was blowing, so I took off running
up the street. I stopped under Key West Island Bookstore's awning. As I stood there, breathing heavily, I peeled open the envelope. The only way to prevent Betty from being mothballed by crazed government officials was to beat Booth at his own game.

I fanned through the pictures. All the same faces as the ones from the easel. One of Rodney stopped me. The blue Polo shirt. Then Scar. Even at the small scale, his evil grimace gave me a chill.

The next picture was of the crowd. People waved to the boat as Scar threw a line toward a piling. Mingie Posada was standing in the back of the crowd, dead pan, with picketers behind him. Next to him was a guy in a blue shirt. I held it closer....

I took off through the rain across Duval and lit into the La Concha's lobby with the same speed I'd left only hours ago. The difference was, I'd left full of anticipation and adrenalin, and was returning soaked to the skin, the eyewitness to substantiate Cuban aggression, grounded indefinitely with the scabs freshly picked off my legal woes, and Booth's new bitch to top it off. The squeak of my flip-flops on the terrazzo floor announced my approach.

Karen was at the reception desk, eyebrows raised.

"Not looking so good, flyboy."

"Really? I feel marvelous."

"I've been hearing a lot of stories about you lately."

"The ruthless treasure salvor, the stuff novels are made of...."

"Fiction can't keep up with your life."

A puddle formed under me. "There's something I've been meaning to tell you. Don't ask why, but I was in Posada's office at El Aljibe, and I found a glass full of pink and blue ribbons on his shelf, like souvenirs."

Her face darkened. "That bastard."

Even when she was angry, her green eyes were beautiful—and calculating. She was wearing a tight black T-shirt, shorts, and her hair was down.

"Where's the business as usual uniform?"

"I'm off this afternoon." She paused, "Listen, I know you're upset about my book, and yes, the protagonist is a renegade, but I intend to soften his edges by the end." She smiled faintly. "I appreciate the dirt on Posada, but don't worry about helping me with Old Island Days any more."

She turned her head slightly to check behind me. A horn sounded and her eyes spooked. "Josh?" Karen shouted inside the office door. "I'll see you tomorrow."

The black land shark had pulled into the alley next to the hotel. "Gutierrez, huh? You two've become quite the item." The horn pierced the air again. "Classy guy."

"Manny invited me on his boat for the offshore races this weekend. I'll have an open mike that will broadcast on the radio. It's a killer event to kick-off the Festival. We're going to practice now. "

I felt my shoulders sag. My sixty-something airplane was trumped by a championship-defending thrill ride in a water rocket. Karen's hunger for festival excitement had paid off. Gutierrez rolled his window down as we approached.

"Any more assaults on your gallery?" I said.

"You know what they say about the best defense...."

"I met Enrique Jiminez today. I don't think he has anything to do with the boat's disappearance."

His smile vanished. "Isn't that how you got Willy's people extradited? Sticking your nose where it doesn't belong?"

It dawned on me that Gutierrez had never been interested in my help. "The Cuban government and the Santeros are connected, don't ask me how—"

He shoved his cell phone in my face. "Quick, better call CNN with your hot lead. I'm sure they're over the embarrassment about you being a spy."

I held my fists so tight my fingers went numb. First Booth rips my head off, now Gutierrez shits down my throat. The rain started again. As I stood in the deluge, his anger turned to a smile.

"All right, boys, take it easy." Karen bunched her lips for my eyes only.

"You might as well lay off Enrique until after the president's speech tonight. Based on Cuba's relationship with Iran, the government has other ideas." I wanted to shout that the *Carnival* was still afloat with a girl that might be Shaniqua on board, that the CANC had trounced him in the accusation department, and that Palo Mayombe made Santeria look like Baptists, but Gutierrez had sunk to last in line of the people I would confide in.

"Do yourself a favor, Reilly, leave diplomacy and intelligence to the experts."

The sound of his revving twelve-cylinder engine annoyed me as I slid into the lobby and nearly busted my ass on the slick terrazzo. Manny had blown past me with Karen while I was off chasing shadows.

Cuban scenes pressed in on me from both sides down the back hall. I again walked out into the rain. Zeke waved from the moped rental booth.

"You didn't get much out of that," Zeke said.

"What?"

"Your fifteen minutes of fame. CIA agent?" He laughed.

I pulled Barrett's pictures out. "Do you recognize the guy from the day my Rover was broken into?"

He shuffled the pictures like a deck of cards. I watched his expression while he worked through them. A lustful grunt for Shaniqua, a cringe at Scar, and then about half-way through he stopped. Without hesitation he stabbed the photo with his finger.

"That's the guy. Same shirt and all."

"You're sure?"

"No doubt, man. I can almost smell him. Like a bar, you know?"

The photo was from the embarkation. Picketers, Scar tossing the line, Posada stone-faced, and the guy under Zeke's finger was in a blue guayabara.

"You calling the cops?"

I suddenly realized my Rover was missing from its usual spot. A numbness crept up my legs as I tried to recall where I'd left her.

Whitehead on a meter. *Damn.*

A ticket was plastered to the wet windshield. As I searched for the dollar amount of the penalty, a stench smacked me in the face.

"What the...?"

I looked all around, and finally peered in the back window. A tribe of Orishas trampled my soul. There was a dead animal splayed out in the Rover's bed. Its throat was slit, and caked blood had dried into a burgundy collar.

I swung the gate open and a rush of fetid air doused me. My gag reflex kicked in, and if my stomach weren't empty I'd have barfed it clean. Black fur mixed with white—it was the remains of a dog. The same dog from the poster at José's Cantina. So much for Chinese restaurants.

Enrique said they didn't sacrifice dogs or cats. But did Paleros? Explanations were secondary to exorcising the rotten carcass from my vehicle. Doves, candles, bombs, blackmailers, hexes, sacrificed canines, Cuban Secret Police, the FBI, pissy art dealers…I was on a roll.

"*Our reach extends further than you think.*" Sanchez's warning again ran through my head. If I called the police, it would only fuel Booth's agenda. My Rover would be threatened with confiscation just like Betty.

"What the hell's that?" Zeke peered over the chest-high croton hedge.

"Santero trick or treat. Got a trash bag in your hut?"

Zeke's eyes cut from me to the dog and back. "I'll check."

He returned with a green plastic bag and reluctantly held it open.

"Oh, man, that's disgusting." Zeke's sickly look was at odds with his burly physique, long ponytail, and indecipherable blue tattoos.

I tied the top of the bag into a knot, and lugged the foul load toward the hotel's dumpster. First my flight bag, now this.

My plan to confront Posada was shot. The evening would now be spent mucking out my vehicle. A quick wash of my hands with the gardener's hose, and I was back at the Rover. What's this on the floorboard? Red wax was melted into a puddle, but also a piece of—I dove forward, hitting my head on the steering wheel.

It was a copy of the first page of my missing ledger.

I scraped off the wax. There was a note written below the financial entries my brother had paid out on my behalf. "*The original went to Special Agent Booth. The rest will too, along with the key, if you don't butt out.*"

I stared at the page, breathing fast. I felt no fear, hesitation, or doubt. Anger had replaced all that, combined with a healthy dose of determination. If my growing number of adversaries hadn't stopped me, dead dogs and blackmailers wouldn't.

60

Mingie Posada's name played in my head like a Santero's drumbeat, but the hour it took to clean the stench from the Rover helped me to think more analytically. A frontal assault on Posada would be risky. My nature urged me to action, but the result was too often failure. Strategy took time, which I had in abundance, but I was short on patience. That's why I liked boxing. It's a kind of physical debate that requires poise, but dooms hesitation. Life, unfortunately, wasn't so simple.

Upstairs, the message light was blinking next to my phone. Just what I needed, another threat, more bad news, or someone else looking for help.

The sense that my life had veered into an uncontrollable vortex had me jumpy. I'd never won a fight clinging to the ropes, but with the bad guys cloaked in fog, I didn't know where to strike. It was oddly comforting that my stash was being used piecemeal against me. At least I knew it was still here.

The Vigenère cipher sat on my coffee table.

	A	B	C	D	E	F	G	H	I	J	K	L	M	N	O	P	Q	R	S	T	U	V	W	X	Y	Z
A	A	B	C	D	E	F	G	H	I	J	K	L	M	N	O	P	Q	R	S	T	U	V	W	X	Y	Z
B	B	C	D	E	F	G	H	I	J	K	L	M	N	O	P	Q	R	S	T	U	V	W	X	Y	Z	A
C	C	D	E	F	G	H	I	J	K	L	M	N	O	P	Q	R	S	T	U	V	W	X	Y	Z	A	B
D	D	E	F	G	H	I	J	K	L	M	N	O	P	Q	R	S	T	U	V	W	X	Y	Z	A	B	C
E	E	F	G	H	I	J	K	L	M	N	O	P	Q	R	S	T	U	V	W	X	Y	Z	A	B	C	D
F	F	G	H	I	J	K	L	M	N	O	P	Q	R	S	T	U	V	W	X	Y	Z	A	B	C	D	E
G	G	H	I	J	K	L	M	N	O	P	Q	R	S	T	U	V	W	X	Y	Z	A	B	C	D	E	F
H	H	I	J	K	L	M	N	O	P	Q	R	S	T	U	V	W	Q	Y	Z	A	B	C	D	E	F	G
I	I	J	K	L	M	N	O	P	Q	R	S	T	U	V	W	X	Y	Z	A	B	C	D	E	F	G	H
J	J	K	L	M	N	O	P	Q	R	S	T	U	V	W	X	Y	Z	A	B	C	D	E	F	G	H	I
K	K	L	M	N	O	P	Q	R	S	T	U	V	W	X	Y	Z	A	B	C	D	E	F	G	H	I	J
L	L	M	N	O	P	Q	R	S	T	U	V	W	X	Y	Z	A	B	C	D	E	F	G	H	I	J	K
M	M	N	O	P	Q	R	S	T	U	V	W	X	Y	Z	A	B	C	D	E	F	G	H	I	J	K	L
N	N	O	P	Q	R	S	T	U	V	W	X	Y	Z	A	B	C	D	E	F	G	H	I	J	K	L	M
O	O	P	Q	R	S	T	U	V	W	X	Y	Z	A	B	C	D	E	F	G	H	I	J	K	L	M	N
P	P	Q	R	S	T	U	V	W	X	Y	Z	A	B	C	D	E	F	G	H	I	J	K	L	M	N	O
Q	Q	R	S	T	U	V	W	X	Y	Z	A	B	C	D	E	F	G	H	I	J	K	L	M	N	O	P
R	R	S	T	U	V	W	X	Y	Z	A	B	C	D	E	F	G	H	I	J	K	L	M	N	O	P	Q
S	S	T	U	V	W	X	Y	Z	A	B	C	D	E	F	G	H	I	J	K	L	M	N	O	P	Q	R
T	T	U	V	W	X	Y	Z	A	B	C	D	E	F	G	H	I	J	K	L	M	N	O	P	Q	R	S
U	U	V	W	X	Y	Z	A	B	C	D	E	F	G	H	I	J	K	L	M	N	O	P	Q	R	S	T
V	V	W	X	Y	Z	A	B	C	D	E	F	G	H	I	J	K	L	M	N	O	P	Q	R	S	T	U
W	W	X	Y	Z	A	B	C	D	E	F	G	H	I	J	K	L	M	N	O	P	Q	R	S	T	U	V
X	X	Y	Z	A	B	C	E	D	F	G	H	I	J	K	L	M	N	O	P	Q	R	S	T	U	V	W
Y	Y	Z	A	B	C	D	E	F	G	H	I	J	K	L	M	N	O	P	Q	R	S	T	U	V	W	X
Z	Z	A	B	C	D	E	F	G	H	I	J	K	L	M	N	O	P	Q	R	S	T	U	V	W	X	Y

The directions spelled out in the book had me write PILAR continuously above the first passage:

P	I	L	A	R	P	I	L	A
B	C	O	D	Z	D	C	D	E

I traced down the Vigenère's column that began with a P until I came to B. Then back across the row to the left where I found M, the first letter of the cipher. The first three letters spelled MUD. The completed cipher read:

P	I	L	A	R	P	I	L	A
B	C	O	D	Z	D	C	D	E
M	U	D	D	H	O	U	S	E

MUDDHOUSE? What did … another cipher? Crap.

The second string of encoded letters, HBLIWTWDMGR, produced nonsense when matched with MUDDHOUSE. After another half-hour, so did PI-LAR and several key word variations. MUDDHOUSE was yet another word puzzle, or clue, like HIS BOAT. An hour of puzzle torture led to another dead end. I was no closer to getting the code needed to replace the key, or to finding the blackmailers.

An idea hit and I powered up my laptop. I found Ron Zilke's phone number. Could I really call him? As e-Antiquity's technical director, Ronnie had lost a ton during the crash. But he was a researcher extraordinaire who could find answers a hell of a lot faster than I could. My role in the company had been sales and acquisitions. Jack Dodson and Ronnie were the technical wizards.

Ronnie had been implicated in the case against Dodson too, and although he was ultimately cleared, the strain of those accusations along with the ones against me fractured our friendship. The question was, had it healed? I took a deep breath and dialed the number.

"King Charles? I thought you were dead."

"I just didn't bounce back as fast as you did."

"Who said I bounced back? I'm in debt up to my ass and working as an MIS schmuck in a fifty-person company. Thanks to you and Jack. Do me a favor, lose my number." A dial tone followed.

So much for healing.

The ensuing internet searches produced nothing on Jackson Rolle, Mingie Posada, *Carnival*, or MUDDHOUSE, but from it another idea emerged.

This trip was made on foot. My mind was back to orbiting Posada like a satellite. Given the hour, the odds were poor, but I found the door open with Rosalie Peña inside the San Carlos Institute pouring over a stack of bills.

"Buck!" She pressed her hand to her chest. "My God, you scared me."

I held up the picture.

"Why do you have a picture of Mingie Posada?" she asked.

"It's from when the *Carnival* left."

"Ah, yes, the signs," she said.

I laid the photo on her desk. "Who's that with Posada, in the blue shirt?"

"Him?" She pointed to the man. "I don't know his name, but—"

"You recognize him?"

"Why, sure. He's one of the waiters at El Aljibe."

61

From my sixth-floor window the morning appeared
quiet on Duval Street. After last night's veiled threats by the *real* president toward
the Cubans about their connections with Iran and their "murderous attack" on
helpless missionaries, it felt like the calm before the storm troopers. The stage was
set for an escalated response if his demand for a confession, apology, and return of
the remaining two bodies wasn't met within forty-eight hours.

As usual, for every frenzied media action, there was an equal or greater political reaction. No mention was made of the boat's being sighted in Havana harbor,
but the names of the dead and missing were piled up like face cards in a poker
game, and I was their ace in the hole. How far would the bluff go, and what would
happen if I busted the flush?

Sometime during the night it occurred to me that Posada might be a Santero,
with Blue Guayabara boy his henchman. Another person suddenly came to mind.
A man who had been integral to my former business.

What the hell.

After several rings I was about to hang up when a sudden spate of heavy
breathing was followed by, "Harry Greenbaum."

I hoped he wasn't still having heart problems. "Harry, it's Buck Reilly." A long
silence followed. "Harry?"

"I'm trying to decide what to say." His New York/British flavored-with-Yiddish accent was as distinctive as ever.

"How about 'nice to hear from you'?"

"How about you owe me twenty million dollars?"

I winced. "Venture capital's risky business…."

"So is fraud, my boy."

As our largest venture capitalist, Harry lost more than anyone, but it was all on paper. He'd cashed out a healthy multiple of his investment while e-Antiquity was still riding the crest of financial fantasy.

"I'm not calling for money, Harry, I just need some information."

"Truth be known, Buck, I'm happy to hear from you. I don't think we've spoken since your parent's funeral."

"That's when I dropped out."

"Disappearing made it look worse."

We caught up, and he admitted that treasure hunting in Key West sounded more fun then grinding it out in another start-up company.

"I swore off life's hamster wheel," I said.

"That's why I own the wheel." He laughed. "I always liked your swagger, young man, and if some information will help get you back on your feet, perhaps you'll be in a position to reduce our marker. What is it you need?"

"Do you still have access to hard-to-find information?"

"Owning positions in sixty-eight companies does augment one's resources."

I rattled off my list of names.

"You finally surface from oblivion only to ask for information on an FBI agent?"

"That one's just for curiosity. The others are critical. If you get anything on them it may lead to more questions. I'll save the explanation until then."

We hung up, and I felt a high I hadn't enjoyed in a long time. Harry had been one of the key people in my company's success, and it was exhilarating to have him once again go to bat for me.

The random dots needed to be connected before it was too late, because if Booth figured out the significance of my ledger, he could impound more than Betty, and if the president's threats materialized, the missionaries would be forgotten. Plus, my feeble code breaking skills were a stretch to replace the Swiss bank key. MUDDHOUSE? Could the five-character code be *adobe*?

Breakfast beckoned. Not for food, but information. Booth never said not to continue my salvage efforts, so I set out to check the island's storm signals. No decomposing animals were affixed to my bike, it being the least identifiable thing I owned, so with my backpack strapped to the handlebars I pedaled toward the light of discovery. Breakfast could be my best cover yet. Health-nut tourists were out speed walking, jogging, standing tall at smoothie stands, and in general giving Key West a false appearance of health-consciousness.

The sound of cutlery against porcelain rose above the low wood fence that surrounded El Aljibe's outdoor dining area. Laughter pierced the hum of conversation. I spotted something—no, someone outside the dining patio.

Karen. She was crouched amidst a small copse of pygmy palm trees. I swallowed a smile. Our motivation might be different, but we both sought the truth. A thought struck me. Chickens. If Posada was serving up island chickens, could he also be using them as offensive weapons?

Karen saw me. She stepped out from her cover with bunched fists on her hips and stared me down as I entered the patio. Poquito hovered over a petite Latina in a bulging tank top who greeted my entry with a harried smile. It was the same girl who'd caught me in El Aljibe's office the day of the rally.

"Just one?" she asked.

"Mingie?" He turned my way with a forced smile. "Buck Reilly."

The fake smile went flat. "Right. Willy Peebles's pilot. The CNN spy."

"Never ate here, so I thought I'd come by."

The Latina hostess led me to a table in the rear corner of the crowded patio. Before my rear end hit the seat, a waiter in a blue guayabara popped out of the kitchen. My heart leapt until I saw he had twenty years on the guy from the picture.

Deep breathing did little to calm my pounding temples. Could this be it? Poquito? His restaurant had been ground zero for the anti-Cuban fanatics, but could it also be a hotbed of Santeria? Or Palo? The chicken launch pad? La Casa Blanca for Bush and Clinton? Could my ledger, maps, GPS and key be buried in his office with Karen's ribbons?

I looked at the picture and committed the younger man's face to memory. Observation, I'm just here for—

Another man came out of the kitchen wearing a blue guayabara—it was him. He sauntered up to the podium and whispered in the ear of the Latina. She elbowed him and tried to suppress a giggle. Posada flicked his palm and nodded toward the patio.

Breathe deep, breathe…deeper. Was it my imagination, or did his smile fade as he approached?"

"Decided what you want?" His thick Cuban accent rung familiar.

His expression morphed from the arrogant boredom of a person too exalted to be taking orders to…what? Recognition? I held onto the seat of my chair with both hands.

"Any chicken specialties?"

A croak of air intake preceded his step backwards. Blue Guayabara Boy turned and dashed into the kitchen.

The restaurant became a blur as I raced after him. The Latina dropped a handful of menus, and Posada's round face inflated as I shot past. Spanish shouts followed like small arms fire. I flew into the kitchen, where a half-dozen blue guayabaras skidded me to a stop. The room was eerily quiet, with all eyes on me and only the hiss of frying eggs audible above my heavy breathing.

He wasn't there. The back door was askew, and I ran toward it. More Spanish erupted, and a cook jumped in my path. I kept running, and knocked him into the pot rack. The resulting cacophony was deafening. I yanked the door open to find an alley ahead. I ran out, surprised to see Karen at the end of the alley.

She waved her hands at me as I ran past the dumpster.

I was aware of a flash over my shoulder a split second before pain shot into a supernova. Then everything turned bright white....

62

"He's awake!" a voice shouted.

A sea of blue shirts hovered over me amidst the smell of garbage. EMT's? Posada's face appeared in the middle of them. I tried to coil up, ready to fight back, but my limbs would not respond.

"The hell you doing?" Poquito said. "Running crazy, chasing Emilio? You attacked my cook. Come on, get up!"

The blue shirts were guayabaras. "I…he…."

"Another jealous boyfriend," one of the guayabaras said. The others giggled.

"Where is he?" I asked.

Posada turned to the others and loosed a burst of Spanish that scattered them into retreat. He then redirected his scowl toward Karen.

"And what're *you* doing here?"

I probed the welt on the side of my head.

"You ran through here, tripped, and crashed into the dumpster." Poquito said. He studied my eyes, his own unsure.

"That's not what happened," Karen said. "One of those waiters smashed you over the head with a two-by-four."

I turned to Posada. "Was that Chango's lightning or Siete Rayos'?"

His eyes widened, he crossed himself and muttered something in Spanish. "Don't come here again, I don't care whose friend you are. You come back, I'll call the police. And you, Ribbon Lady—" He waved his arm toward Karen as if shooing away an animal. "Get off my property!"

I stood up in a daze. I must have only been out a minute or two. "Where's the guy you called Emilio? And what's his last name?"

"History." Posada stormed off. So much for observation.

"What happened?" Karen asked. "Did you find more of my ribbons?"

"The guy who whacked me stole some stuff from my Rover and left a dead chicken in my flight bag." He had to be either Clinton or Bush.

"That sick bastard! Why would he do something so, so disgusting?"

My quick summary of the other incidents involving Santeria and Palo Mayombe left her appalled. She looked ready to go back inside to kick some ass.

"I read something about that in the paper, but there were no details. It's called *ebó*? Animal sacrifices?" She shuddered. "I'll check with the Rescue League. Maybe they've had issues with Santeria before."

"Good idea."

"Let me help you home."

"Thanks, but I've got to return some overdue books." I nodded toward my backpack. She looked at me as if she thought I was delirious.

A knot the size of a ping-pong ball had ballooned on my hairline. Way to go, dumb ass. If the blackmailers hadn't already sent my ledger to Booth, they would now.

63

Blue Guayabara boy's name was Emilio, and he
worked for Posada. But Posada...*genuflected*?

I sat in the shade next to a laundromat a half-block up the street, hoping for Emilio to emerge from El Aljibe. I waited twenty minutes, he never appeared.

My old red bike carried me past hundred-year-old houses and down streets whose names were lost on my tunnel-visioned eyes. I coasted past the cemetery and tried to spot the gumbo-limbo tree above the small arch belonging to Reverend J. Van Duzer.

What had Jo Jo and Rodney seen? Why had they been murdered? The lump on the back of my head throbbed. Maybe Karen would turn something up through her connections.

I entered the library anxious to lighten my load. Walter smiled upon seeing me. "Well, if it isn't Bomb Reilly, Key West's newest national celebrity."

I cringed. "Do you have anything on Palo Mayombe?"

"*Pollo*, isn't that chicken?"

"P – A – L – O. It's like Santeria, but worse."

"Worse? That's hard to believe." He turned to the computer and after a moment looked up. "Nothing on Palo. Isn't it ironic that Willy launched a mission opposed by Santeria, his daughter stowed away only to disappear, and Santeria might be to blame? Maybe that's why Manny's so torqued."

"Gutierrez? Why do you say that?"

"He introduced Shaniqua to the occult in the first place."

It felt as if another hammer came down on my head.

"How do you know that?"

"That's what she told me. He had the books out before she did, and she was curious what had him so interested."

"Manny Gutierrez is into Santeria?"

"I don't know about that, he just borrowed the books. But I could tell Shaniqua was fascinated by it, so who knows? These books have made the rounds, though, that's for sure." He glanced quickly around the room and leaned onto the counter. "An FBI agent came in to review our records on a series of subjects, including Santeria."

"Records?"

"As in who checked out what books. He ran his finger down the list, stopped, and read your name out loud."

Great! "What did he say?"

"He wasn't smiling."

I stumbled out of the library, bumped into a woman, and knocked her books to the ground. First Emilio, now Gutierrez and Booth. I pedaled hard into town.

Answers, I needed answers!

Blue Heaven was quiet. The Gargoyles were absent, and there was no sign of Lenny. Next stop the Church of the Redeemer. As I approached, I saw that the front door was ajar and tried to peer inside as I rode past.

A white truck suddenly swerved at me. I reflexively veered away, hit the curb, flew over the handlebars, and landed palms first on the concrete sidewalk where my bike crashed down on top of me. The truck screeched to a stop.

What now? Santero goons? Emilio? Or maybe Booth to haul me in?

Willy leaned through the window. "Sorry about that, Buck. You all right?"

Oh jeez. I peeled pebbles from the jellied abrasions on my palms. "Yeah, great."

He jumped out and lifted the bike off me. "I was coming looking for you, and I guess when I saw you, well…."

The bike's front wheel was bent beyond repair, the angle of the curb pressed into its aluminum frame. My palms burned, *sans* a layer of skin.

"I was on my way to see you, too," I said.

"Hop in." Willy lifted the bike into the back of his truck.

"How well do you know Mingie Posada?"

"Not very well, he attends a different church," he said.

"Could he be into Santeria?"

Willy cut me a quick glance. "He's a deacon in the Catholic church."

"You know a guy who works for him named Emilio?" I handed the picture over. Willy held it atop the steering wheel as he drove.

"There's Posada," he said.

"Emilio's the guy next to him, in the blue shirt."

"Don't think I've ever seen him, why?"

I rubbed the skull lump and shuffled photos until I found the one of Scar. I handed it over. "This is Jackson Rolle."

"That's a Bahamian name," Willy said. "Remember the actress, Esther Rolle? She was Bahamian."

"That fits." I dug into my backpack and retrieved the customs form. "The *Carnival* was registered in the Bahamas, but this doesn't say which island. Did you ever talk to Rolle?"

"Only Perez, the captain. Bahamas? Does the FBI know this?"

"I don't think so, at least not all of it. Booth's still investigating, though, case closed or not."

We turned onto Duval. The lunchtime revelers were in full swing. Girls of all sizes roamed the road, with bikini tops and shorts the predominant fashion. Crowds from Sloppy Joe's and Hog's Breath poured into the street. Heavy metal music throbbed from one, hip hop from the other.

"From what the president said last night, we're running out of time." Willy swallowed a couple times. "I wanted to keep your seeing Shaniqua quiet because I was afraid, maybe she was involved."

We pulled over in front of Fast Buck Freddy's.

"When Booth played me that phone recording, I knew she could be alive."

"Considering her fascination with Santeria and the call she made to Treasure Salvors from the boat, you need to prepare yourself that she might be involved with whatever the hell's going on," I said.

"Treasure Salvors? Where she works? What's that got to do with anything?"

"The stuff stolen from my plane included some old treasure maps. She saw them and called her boss from the *Carnival*."

He rubbed his eyes with both hands. "*Treasure*? Those people were her friends, Rodney adored her, she wouldn't have done anything to harm them. Over treasure? Or Santeria?" He hesitated, then said, "I thought she was just curious. But she's been friends with Enrique her whole life."

"I met him yesterday. He was a cool character. Too cool to tell if he knew anything but he claims they've got nothing to do with the boat, or the murders." I decided against mentioning Palo Mayombe, just yet.

"Maybe it's time we tell CGIS about your seeing Shaniqua." Willy said.

"Not yet. In the Fed's zeal to condemn Cuba, she'll be guilty until proven innocent."

Willy slapped the steering wheel. "What the hell do we do, then?"

"Give me another twenty-four hours, and if I don't make any progress, I'll go to CGIS."

He turned onto Petronia and stopped in front of Blue Heaven. "Remember I said I was looking for you?"

My oozing palms throbbed.

"Lenny's got something important to tell you."

I looked toward the restaurant. "Like what?"

"Let's go."

The Gargoyles were back on duty. "Looky who's coming!"

"Enough of that," Willy said.

The old guy's mouth clamped shut like a mousetrap, but he winked as I passed.

Lenny was stacking glasses behind the bar. "About time," he said.

"What's up?"

"Your fruitcake friend out at the airport? He was in here looking for you. Said the shit was going down with your plane, man."

The welt on my head throbbed. "Not another bomb?"

"Worse." Lenny lifted the phone onto the bar. "You better call him. Now."

64

"Booth got a court order," Ray said.

"For what?"

"To impound your plane, what else?"

I slumped onto a barstool.

"An FBI pilot'll be here in the morning to take Betty to Miami."

"Did you talk to him?"

"Her. She wanted to make sure the fuel was topped off."

"I'll bet that made that prick, Booth's day."

"You got an attorney that can block a court order?"

"Oh sure, I keep three on retainer." Blue Heaven suddenly began to spin around me. "What time are you leaving?"

"Five o'clock sharp, why?"

"Can you stick around until I call you back? I've got to think—"

"One other thing. Betty's ex showed up in his Falcon a couple hours ago."

"Buffett?"

"He's doing a Party for Peace concert at Margaritaville tonight. He walked around the perimeter of yellow tape the cops left around her. He was pretty freaked."

"Join the club."

I hung up. Lenny was pulling fiercely at his sparse chin hairs. Willy held his hands up wanting to know what was wrong.

"Booth's taking my plane."

"What the hell for?" Lenny asked.

"Evidence, but that's just an excuse. He's got it in for me. It's a long story." Or, maybe he got the ledger from the blackmailers.

"Just like that? He can—"

"If he takes your plane, how we going to find my daughter?"

Lenny slapped a palm against the bar. "I say we kick Booth's ass!"

Willy grabbed my bicep. "If that boat makes a move, you've got to find it. No matter what, I want Shaniqua back in the U.S."

Our eyes held for a long second, and then I headed for the door. The Gargoyles lit into me about Saturday's fight with Bruiser Lewis, but I breezed past them. Outside, my bike still lay crumpled in the bed of Willy's truck, so I ran.

Stay off the Ropes

65

Inside my apartment the first thing I saw was the
message light blinking by the phone. The number five was illuminated in the LED.
Would Booth have called to gloat? I was surprised to hear Harry Greenbaum's
wheezy voice leave his office, cell, and home phone numbers.

Karen had left the second message. "I heard about the bomb on your plane.
I'm worried about you. I need to talk to you about something." The details of my
latest fiasco for her yarn, no doubt.

The third call was someone who'd phoned earlier about a charter, an income-
producing opportunity I needed to—

The next voice startled me. "Get your butt over here, *now*." Enrique Jiminez.
Must be about the figurine.

The machine beeped again. "Reilly, you there? Pick up...." The voice was
familiar, but—"I just got to the airport and saw *Lady* wrapped up like a burn
victim, only in yellow police-line tape. What the hell's going on? Meet me at
Margaritaville. Come by and ask for Sunshine." The line went dead.

"Not this time, Bubba."

I stared out the window, as a sense of loneliness started to grab me around
the throat. I had no place to turn for help. Finally, I silently spoke to my father,
seeking help, direction, wisdom, the answer to the damn word puzzles and to the
riddle of why I was being attacked from all quarters. Even the brief attempt to

reinvigorate my love life had been thwarted by a hostile art peddler. The media's paranoia promotion was dialed up to high with speculation that the hemisphere would soon be at war. Based on the president's speech, it was clear that he was toying with the idea.

And I was caught in the middle.

I had wracked my brain, going back to when I first found Jo Jo, but nothing added up. The pressure had intensified, not diminished, so I must be Helen Kellering my way toward some sort of epiphany.

Tired of getting my ass kicked against the ropes, it was time to start swinging. All I could think of was Betty exiled to an indefinite fate in a federal hangar in Miami. If Booth's taking my plane, odds are he'll be coming for me too.

Of the four messages, only one warranted a return call.

"Yes?"

"It's Buck."

"I'm late for a board meeting, so we must be quick. A fellow named T. Edward Booth purchased twenty-five thousand dollars' worth of e-Antiquity stock a year before the decline."

"Right at the peak."

"He sold it for twenty-five hundred just before you filed chapter seven."

"Mazaltov, chump. How about Jackson Rolle?"

"We found three Jackson Rolles in the U.S. One's a dentist in Manhattan, one's a mechanic in San Diego, and the other's a third grader in Petoskey, Michigan."

Rats. "Probably an assumed name—"

"There was a case of a Cuban immigrant arrested for spying in Miami who died in jail awaiting his trial after boasting about being Castro's financial distributor to cells in South Florida."

"Some sort of spymaster?" I said.

"They never found out. Only that he was planted in the Cuban émigré community to keep his ears open for any plans against Fidel."

"No doubt replaced on the next raft out of Havana." I shivered, and felt as if a spider had run up my back. If the Cuban government believed the media hype, and if there were Cuban moles in the U.S., would they be readying their plans for retribution?

"Without more information there's no way to triangulate in on Rolle, or the bloody boat, and I'm sorry, dear boy, but I must run."

"Wait, Harry? Any idea what MUDDHOUSE might mean?"

"As in adobe?"

"Tried that."

"You've lost me now. I have no idea, and I really must go."

I paced the apartment like a caged hyena, only I wasn't laughing. The customs form said the *Carnival* was Bahamian, and Rolle's a Bahamian name, but there are eight hundred islands in the Bahamas.

I dialed another number from memory.

"Who is it?"

"Buck Reilly."

"Shit, cuz, I thought I'd hear from you sooner or later. You in jail?"

"If the court wants to impound a vehicle, do they have to give you notice?"

"If they've got your ass locked up or if they say you bought it with funny money they don't."

"How about as evidence in an investigation?"

"Your plane, eh?"

I grunted.

"Shit, boy, it had a bomb on it, right? They damn sure could take it."

"Crap." My palms were oozing. A mixture of sweat and bodily fluid from the scrapes.

"That it?"

I hesitated. "If they told me to stay on the island, and, well, if I heard they were coming to impound my plane, and—"

"You're kidding me, right?"

"Okay, stupid question. Next time I call you, it *will* be to get my ass out of jail."

"That's what I do," Currito said.

I sat staring at a blank wall. Harry's results were a disappointment. My fingers rubbed the lump on the back of my head. The swelling was down but the spot was still tender. How was the *Carnival* tied to Blue Guayabara Boy? If I could catch him, the truth would come out, that's for damn sure.

66

Nassau and Freeport were the two most populated
Bahamian cities, and the two most likely places the boat came from. Another
name popped into my head, and the realization that I had forgotten to call him
launched me off the couch. I jammed both hands into my pockets and threw
everything on the table. Where was it? Here.

I punched the buttons and desperately tried to conjure up a convincing story.
A woman answered. "Ensign Frank Nardi, please," I said.

A clipped answer was followed by silence. No Muzak for the U.S. Coast
Guard. How did they find somebody on a giant ship like the *Mohawk*?

"Nardi."

"This is Buck Reilly, I stopped by—"

"You were supposed to call back at fourteen hundred hours, *yesterday*."

"I got stuck in a meeting with the FBI. About the *Carnival*."

"This the same Buck Reilly from Douglas Community Center?"

"Douglas—"

"Basketball on Tuesdays? You weren't there this week, but after seeing the
news, you've got a good excuse."

An image of a tall guy with short dark hair and a tattoo on his bicep came to
mind.

"Franko?"

"That's right." He laughed.

"You never said you were Coast Guard."

"We're not supposed to talk about it. If what they said on CNN's true, you can understand that."

"I, ah, don't talk about my...listen, damn, I still can't believe—anyway, I wanted to brief you on Cuba. I'd come over, but I'm kind of pressed for time."

"This is a secure line."

"Mine too." I imagined the La Concha operator listening in. "The *Carnival's* still afloat. I saw it tied up at a government warehouse in Havana harbor. # 1 Obrapia." I held my breath.

"That explains why Lieutenant Killelea from CGIS is on his way here to brief us. We've been scrambled out on patrol."

Killelea was the guy with Booth at the airport. He'll freak when Nardi tells him I called. I bit the nail on my thumb.

"Customs tells us that the *Carnival* was from the Bahamas."

"Right, registered to San Alejandro."

San *what*? "Is that near Nassau?"

He paused. "The ownership entity, San Alejandro, LLC, registered in... Don't you have this briefing? It came from intelligence."

I froze.

"Reilly, you there?"

"Ah, yeah, I'm getting an urgent e-mail. I have to run, Franko, but where did you say San Alejandro was registered?"

"I didn't. Maybe you should come meet with me and CGIS at 5:00."

"Got to run, but keep this confidential, Killelea might be upset that I shared the information before he could." I wiped the sweat off my forehead. Frank Nardi was not going to be happy if I ever saw him at Douglas Community Center again.

Now I was lying to the Coast Guard. More incentive for Booth to grab me. A phrase popped into my head that dated back to my boxing days: *stay off the ropes*. I sprang to my feet, dashed into my room, and pulled the duffle bag from under my bed.

Could the Feds have learned something about #1 Obrapia? If spotting the boat in Havana was the only hard evidence, along with the bomb on Betty, and we both disappeared, what would happen to their case?

Going public about the boat's being afloat would throw a wrench into whatever angle Booth was working. But it would be a Go Directly to Jail and Don't Pass Go move, especially if the Feds were using this as the rationale, with the real concern being the Cuban biochem pact with Iran. Breaking the law or disobeying an FBI agent was unfortunately not new to me. My Cardinal Rule of not getting arrested was going the way of the Great White Buffalo.

The digital clock read 4:50. I grabbed my last seven hundred bucks from the back of my underwear drawer. I felt a deranged glee at the sound of the front door closing behind me. Booth would shit bricks when he found out I'd vanished, and being forced to tell Washington that their case against Cuba had flown the coop would wipe that shit-eating grin off the face of ambition.

67

On the elevator ride down, I thought about what to tell Karen. Our evening at Seven Fish, and her staking out El Aljibe looking for captive chickens were etched in my mind. So was seeing her with Gutierrez.

The elevator door opened, and Karen was standing in front of me.

"There you are!" Her voice was an urgent whisper. "You didn't answer your phone, I knew you were here—"

"You spying on me too?" I stepped off the elevator.

"Special Agent Booth from the FBI's in the lobby. I wouldn't—"

"Here? Now?" Was this it? Am I getting arrested? I peeked around the corner. Booth was standing next to the concierge desk looking at tourist brochures. He was alone.

"How's your head?" She reached up and touched the lump, then her eyes flashed to my duffel. "Where are you going?"

"Listen, Karen, I need your help." I pushed my bag toward her. "Can you take this stuff and—"

"Whoa, flyboy, mind telling me what's going on?"

"You read about the bomb on my plane, right? Special Agent Booth wants to impound it as evidence, in which case I may never see it again. Not only that, but I've got a lead on the missing missionary boat, and—"

She held up her hands. "Follow me."

She pressed the button and the elevator doors reopened. Once inside, she pressed another button and the doors in the back opened into the bowels of the hotel.

"You weren't kidding about a life of adventure, were you?"

"Or a beauty to rescue," I said.

"What?"

I forgot that I had hedged on that third goal at our dinner.

"Buck, I need to talk to you about something."

"I promise I'll give you every detail for your novel."

"That's what you think this is about?" Her face contorted into an expression I'd never seen in her. "Is that all you think I care about?"

"I can't talk now, Karen. Can you meet me at Margaritaville in an hour?"

"You're hiding at Margaritaville?"

"Buffett's in town for a surprise show—"

"You're going to—"

"No, he called me about Betty, and—"

"You *know* Jimmy Buffett?" Her face twisted more with each question.

"I really need to run, but will you meet me?"

"The festival starts in two days, we have a director's meeting in a couple of hours. You're not going to jail, are you, Buck Reilly?"

That was the question of the day.

"My rent's paid in advance."

She didn't smile.

"I'm just going…fishing."

Her eyes welled up and my heart somersaulted in my chest. I dropped the backpack and took her shoulders in my hands.

"Will you meet me?"

She nodded, her face so close to mine. The urge to kiss her was overwhelming, but she eased out of my grip and looked from my bags to me.

"Margaritaville in an hour. Go, leave through the back hall."

"If I do that Booth will get suspicious."

"Leave your gear, then."

She shooed me back through the elevator. This was a huge gamble. I strolled into the lobby, whistling. Booth turned and I stopped, my tune cut short.

"What are you doing here?" I held my breath.

"Keeping my eye on you, Reilly, making sure you don't bug-out like you did at e-Antiquity."

I exhaled. "Jimmy Buffett's in town for a show at Margaritaville. Even *you* might enjoy that."

He frowned and I walked out the side door before he could muster his typical scathing response. For once, the high road worked. I just hoped it wasn't a dead-end with a cliff. Nardi had almost blurted out where the boat was registered, but I'd blown it. With eight hundred Bahamian islands, it didn't make sense to go searching until I narrowed the field.

The FBI pilot would arrive at dawn, so time was short, and getting shorter. My guess was that Booth intended a simultaneous raid to arrest me then too. I couldn't return to the La Concha, and my options were dwindling fast. Answers were no longer enough, I needed results.

The dead dog stench in the rover forced my head
out the window. I parked on Thomas and hustled into Blue Heaven. Thankfully
the usual welcoming committee was absent. Lenny watched me as I scanned the
restaurant for anybody who might be staking out my haunts.

"You rob a bank, or something?" he said.

"Booth was waiting in the La Concha lobby. My guess is he's trying to figure
out if I know they're impounding Betty. Smug bastard must think tomorrow's
his next big step up the ladder, boosted off my back." I withheld my other fears.

"I still say we stomp him."

"Let me have your phone."

Lenny lifted the old black rotary phone onto the counter. I dialed the airport.

"I'm sorry, sir, Mr. Floyd isn't here," the operator said.

My watch showed 5:20. "Did you see him leave?"

"Ray leaves every day at five—"

"Can you check, please, he was waiting for my call?"

Her icy reply indicated omnipotent knowledge, but the next voice was Ray's.
"Yo, Buck?"

"Can you do me a favor and stick my fishing gear and kayak inside the plane?"

"Why?"

"And pull down the police-line tape?"

Silence followed on the line. "What the hell you thinking?"

"I'll owe you, Ray." My list of IOU's was growing like Jack's beanstalk.

Lenny handed me a highball glass of amber liquid on the rocks. "Liquid courage, man." The rum burned my throat. "Word is Gutierrez has something heavy coming down on Enrique," Lenny said.

"I haven't been able to connect Enrique to this mess." I took a gulp of the rum. "Time to get off the ropes."

"The hell's that supposed to mean?"

"Flying by the seat of my pants, brother." I drained the glass, a no-no before what I had planned. "One last thing? Tell everyone you know that Buffett's doing a show at Margaritaville tonight."

"That cracker's in town? Another shitty night at Blue Heaven."

I checked the sky, then spotted the antique boxing gloves that hung from a nail. *Shit!* Tomorrow was my date with Bruiser Lewis.

69

Lightheaded from the rum, I felt my confidence
mounting. Flagler led me to A1A and Stock Island. On the southern side of the
highway was a hodgepodge of tradesmen's shops, third-tier retail, late night bars,
mini-marts, decrepit marinas, remnants of the shrimp fleet, and a maze of trailer
homes. I drove fast through the labyrinth of hurricane bait, and had to brake
for some kids on bikes before I spotted the rusted Bronco nestled in overgrown
bushes.

The funky painted eyeball on the side of the trailer stared me down.

Enrique's voice had been insistent on the machine. It was time to find out
what he really knew about the double-crossing and manipulation. His door
opened before I knocked. Enrique's mass filled the narrow space. He stood aside
while two men with machetes patted me down.

"You stink, man."

"Somebody butchered a dog and stuck it in my Rover, complete with red
candles and a love note. You know anything about it?"

"Was it black?"

"Mostly."

"That fits with all the other shit that's happened. I was going to say someone's
using Santeria as the fall guy, but they use black dogs in Palo Mayombe rituals
when they're out for blood."

"Didn't Rolle ask you to perform some sort of ritual?"

"Yeah, but he's just a pawn."

I pulled Barrett's photos out of my breast pocket. "You know any of these guys?"

Enrique fanned through them and shook his head. "Nope." He stopped on the close-up of Shaniqua and made a guttural sound in his throat. "Except her."

"You never answered my question about her."

His attention lingered on the picture. "Wild thing? She's a player."

"Why won't anyone give me a straight answer about Shaniqua?"

"There *is* no straight answer."

"Freak, wild thing, fine as wine, player—"

"And a whole lot more."

"How about victim? Criminal? Conspirator?"

"That's not what I meant. She's just a free spirit. Funny, crazy, but not that other shit. She's the kind of lady make anybody feel good, know what I mean?"

"Not exactly, but that's more than anyone else has said." I dug through the pictures until I found the one I wanted and put it in front of him. "How about these men?"

He held the picture at arm's length and squinted. "That guy has a restaurant, doesn't he? Cuban one?"

"How about the one in the blue shirt?"

Enrique's gaze was steady as he shook his head. "Don't recall."

I bit my lip. "What about Gutierrez, is he into Santeria?"

His laugh held no amusement. "Gutierrez is into cash, and that's it. He came around a few times pretending to be interested in our religion, but he really wanted me to hook him up with some Santero artists. Then I heard he was talking shit about me, calling me a chicken-worshipper."

"What do you know about the stuff stolen from my plane?"

He ignored me and continued through the pictures before stopping on a shot of Scar. He held it up to a candle. "Hmm."

"What?"

Enrique inhaled half the air in the trailer, held it, then blasted me with Dr. Pepper breath. "That's the guy who was here. See his necklace?" I hadn't noticed it before, but Rolle was wearing a small, beaded necklace. "Both Chango's and Siete Rayos's colors are red and white. But if this has a pendant with a two-headed axe, then it's Chango's weapon of choice. If it's a ram's head or has a horn, then it's Siete Rayos'."

I was over the hocus-pocus mystique of the Orishas, but the expression in Enrique's eyes showed he thought it significant.

"So?"

"Rolle's a bad dude, that's all. Stoned on the power of the sword. He won't let anything get in the way of whatever he's after."

I took the pictures back. An uncomfortable silence spread between us.

"You called me," I said. "Did you find something out about that statue?"

Enrique sauntered into the TV room, the empty Dr. Pepper bottles were now gone and the soap operas turned off. He lowered himself into the Barcalounger and began to rub his temples.

"Yeah, but that's not why I called." He hesitated. "We're not supposed to turn against our own, but Rolle's a nut, and based on all the bullshit fake *ebó* going down along with Gutierrez's threats and the invasion crap, I need you to figure this out. And if there's any chance Shaniqua Peebles is alive, well...."

I bit my rum-laced tongue while he appeared to wrestle with his conscience.

"I've prayed to Olodumare, my shells were cast and showed harmony, so..."

"What's the deal?"

"The *Carnival* left Cuba a couple hours ago."

"How do you—"

"I made some calls after you and the bondsman were here. This afternoon I got word the boat had just left."

"You know where's it going?"

He turned toward the back room, where he threw the bones down last time. "Only that it won't be going back to Cuba."

"How about their cargo, or who was on board?"

"All I know is that it left, that's it."

When I checked my watch, I realized my hands were shaking. "You did the right thing calling me."

"As for this..." He pulled the nail-spiked clay figurine off his shelf. "It's a doctor, judge, and priest, all mixed into one. They're supposed to settle disputes. Where'd you find it?"

"In my flight bag."

"Between the dove and this, I'd say someone wants to make your airplane crash."

"Don't forget the Russian grenade. Does Siete Rayos use them too?"

"That would be a secular approach."

I shook his hand and felt sweat on my own. "By the way, watch your ass, there's a rumor that Gutierrez is planning something big against you."

Enrique's eyes narrowed. "Be a shame for his gallery to burn down."

I ran from the tin can leaving Enrique stewing. The first time I met him I knew he was concerned about protecting the integrity of his religion. Assuming Santeros were a bunch of voodoo nuts was a natural conclusion based on my Anglo Saxon upbringing, but it seemed like he was trying to help. Or trying to shift the spotlight off Santeria.

The *Carnival* had left Cuba. Would it come to Florida, and if so, where? I needed more information. Nardi was out in the Gulf, so if they came directly north, the *Mohawk* would nail their ass, but if not….

Impervious to the lingering stench in my truck, I hauled ass through the dark streets and made my way back to A1A. Could the Cubans be sending the *Carnival* out to be scuttled, getting rid of Shaniqua and all ties to their involvement? They could have planted drugs or human cargo on board, blamed the entire mess on a misunderstanding, and accused the U.S. for unwarranted threats of aggression. Unless Enrique was lying and the boat was a cutout, a feint to distract everyone.

Darkness had nearly set in, which grounded me for the night. Since I wasn't rated for Instrument Flight Rules, IFR would translate to Idiot Flying Rescue if I left to search now, especially with the nail figurine blessing my plane. I idled down Catherine Street, parked, then hopscotched my way through the shadows until the patio was visible. I edged closer until I was hiding in the same pygmy palms where I'd spotted Karen.

Four different blue guayabaras circulated around tables, but there was no sign of Emilio. Posada alternated from hugging arriving customers to yelling commands at his staff. Twenty minutes later, I left for the Rover. My lust to find the waiter and combine retribution with discovery was denied. Posada had either fired Emilio or had him hidden.

There was still one avenue to try. Duval Street was swollen with a mob of Parrotheads partying pre-concert style near Margaritaville. For the die-hards it would be a night dreams were made of. The pilgrimage to Key West, and Jimmy performing at the restaurant that bore the name of their Nirvana, even if it was a politically charged Party for Peace.

Unlike last night, the front door of the San Carlos Institute was bolted tight. *Damn.* I continued toward the crowd, a moth drawn to the flame-thrower.

70

Scott Washington, Buffett's 6'8" full-time bodyguard, was helping Drew the doorman handle the crowd. "The show won't start for two more hours, people." He spotted me and said, "Hey, Buck, why you so early?"

Washington nodded to me, apparently remembering our few brief encounters.

"Bubba asked me to meet him here."

Drew ushered me inside. *PARTY AT THE END OF THE WORLD* blared over the speakers, all but drowned out by the boisterous crowd. Karen waved from a booth in the back. I squirmed through the compressed bodies and dropped onto the bench like a sardine squirted from a can. Karen's expression was serious. I slid in close.

"Your stuff's in the kitchen."

"You okay?"

"That FBI agent cornered me and asked a bunch of questions. He wanted to know if you'd said anything about leaving town, so I lied. I told him you'd prepaid six months of rent. That guy's got the eyes of a rat." She glanced around the room as she spoke. I regretted putting her in the middle of my mess, but... she lied for me?

"Hey, stranger."

Garrett, Margaritaville's manager, stood over us. We shook hands and he had the worried expression of someone whose boss was making a surprise visit.

"Is Bubba upstairs?" I nodded toward the office over the stage.

"Naw, he's having dinner at Louie's. He'll be here in about an hour."

"Do me a favor? Tell him I stopped by, and everything's fine."

"Will do."

"I still can't believe you know Jimmy Buffett," Karen said.

"Long story."

"You're full of long stories."

Cerebral lightning struck out of the blue. "MUDDHOUSE! The doctor who set John Wilkes Booth's leg was Samuel Mudd!"

"You've got lunatics clubbing you over the head, the FBI staking out the hotel, and you're doing crossword puzzles?"

"Dr. Mudd was imprisoned here in the Keys—at Fort Jefferson."

"Isn't that where you've been hunting for a sunken ship?"

"MUDDHOUSE must mean Fort Jefferson."

"You've lost it, Buck." But she looked curious, not alarmed.

"Look, I can't stay but I appreciate your bringing my bag—and for helping me." I slid toward the end of the booth.

She grabbed my arm. "I'm sorry I haven't been around for you."

My mind was already running through my next move, but her touch and statement stopped me cold. I scooted back over.

"What do you mean?"

"Ever since we went out that night, I've been—"

"I left *you* at the art show. I thought you were pissed at me."

"I was, at first, but you planted the thought in my head about Manny helping me with the festival, and well, the ideas started flowing."

"I figured I'd blown it when I saw you leave with him after the show."

"You were spying on me?"

"Great view from the corner of the sixth floor."

She shrugged. "We went back to his gallery to get the contract for the paintings.

He had more on his mind, but once I picked up the contract, it was bye-bye." Her face softened in response to my reaction. "You look surprised."

"I don't know what to...what about the day off? I saw you cruising in the land shark—Gutierrez's Mercedes."

"He insisted on a celebration dinner. It was a big sale, and, well, he tried taking me to Seven Fish. I couldn't do it."

So much for my intuition.

"He doesn't seem the type to take rejection well," I said.

"Tell me about it, he's got anger issues. When we went out to practice on his boat—"

"That's tomorrow, isn't it, the races? The start of the Old Island Days Festival?"

She nodded. "He drives like a lunatic. I asked him to slow down and he was furious. I'm not sure I can make it through the race, killer special event or not."

"Has he said anything about Santeria? Or Enrique Jiminez?"

"Not that I can think of. But what I wanted to tell you is that Manny's always asking about you. It's like he's obsessed for some reason. He knew your parents were dead, he knew the details about your partner at e-Antiquity being in jail, he knew you were helping Willy." She paused. "He called me this afternoon. He heard you got clubbed at El Aljibe. He said you deserved it."

"How did—"

"He thinks he knows who did it."

A tingle passed through me. Adrenalin or appreciation, I wasn't sure, but Karen's concern felt like a ray of warmth. Gutierrez could identify Emilio?

"Since Emilio worked for Posada, I'll bet Gutierrez would love to finger him," I said.

"Manny asked if I could describe him, but all I saw was a blur."

"I don't know what to say, Karen. I thought you and Gutierrez..." My heart had inflated like a helium balloon. "Listen, about your book—" She started to respond but I held my hand up. "You've obviously picked up on some of my flaws, better than I have for that matter, but the thing is, the more I think about your novel, I found the character, well, compelling."

She leaned over and kissed me. Her lips pressed hard against mine, launching a thousand electrical impulses between my brain and heart.

"Ah, Buck? Sorry to interrupt, man, but some suit's asking about you." Garrett hovered above us with concern on his face. Booth appeared over his shoulder. Karen was right, he did have rat's eyes.

"Here to Party for Peace, Booth?"

"Don't you two look cozy?"

"There are some great gay bars down the street, if you'd rather—"

"Just remember what I told you, hot shot. National security. You don't want to be classified an enemy combatant on top of everything else." Booth held two fingers to his forehead and saluted before pushing his way back through the crowd. A grimace in a sea of smiles.

I expected Karen to be concerned, but her expression said otherwise.

"What the hell's his problem?"

"Mr. Ambition? You don't want to know." I kissed her forehead. "I need to go."

"You said you weren't leaving?"

"I'll be back."

Garrett reappeared. "Boss called to check in. He said to do what ever I could to help."

"Karen dropped my bag in the kitchen, mind if I slip out the back?"

"Follow me."

Karen squeezed my hand. "I expect a complete summary of your adventures. Maybe you can help me come up with some material for my protagonist's sensitive side."

"If you stay close to Gutierrez, and see if he can find the guy who clubbed me."

Her green eyes were the last thing I saw before the crowd engulfed me. Nobody noticed my hasty departure amidst the blizzard of activity in the kitchen. Outside, next to the dumpster, immense palmetto bugs eyed me like raw meat.

The night was clear, and the brightest stars peered through the reflection of city lights. Where was a full moon when I needed one?

71

Sparse clouds hung low in the night sky. At first
light I'd be flying among them, but for now I handled the Rover with the careful
attention of a teenager seated next to his driving instructor. The FBI pilot would be
here in the morning, so I had to be ready by sun-up, which meant camping in Betty.

Smather's Beach was quiet. Silhouettes of rental kiosks, palm trees, and the
naked masts of day sailors blotted out the water. Karen's lilac scent was on my
hands. The recollection of our kiss distracted me, and I nearly missed the pair of
police cars parked in front of the airport terminal. I chose a parking spot on the
back corner of the lot, close to the private aviation building. The Rover had been
my parent's farm vehicle in Virginia, and abandoning it here felt the emotional
equivalent to walking out on them.

A string of taxis patiently awaited the trickle of new arrivals. I carried my duffel over one shoulder, the backpack over the other, and walked toward the dark
windows of the private terminal. The patrol cars were empty. Why was KWPD
here? I needed to get on board Betty before anyone thought to look for me. Ray
Floyd was long gone, but his assistance enabled my covert departure. I placed my
key in the door's lock.

I kept the lights off and allowed my eyes to adjust. It made me think of celes-
tial navigation. Had my flight instructor not advised against an instrument rating,
I could have snuck out under the cloak of darkness.

"*All you'll do is kill yourself.*" He had actually laughed at the idea.

I shuffled toward the locker room, where inside the windowless void I turned on the light. I stopped and pulled the chrome handle.

What the hell?

My Sage fly rod and back-up flight bag were still crammed in the narrow space.

Ray hadn't put the gear on Betty.

With the aluminum rod tube under my arm, the flight bag and backpack over my shoulder, I swerved awkwardly toward the door that led to the flight deck. Two trips to the plane would be easier, but it wasn't a night to press my luck. After a few clearing breaths, I turned the handle and pushed the door open. Once outside, I studied the main terminal.

The engines of a Dash 8 kicked over, and a ramp girl signaled an "all clear" to the pilot with her red-tipped flashlight. I took the message to heart and shuffled toward the far corner of the tarmac. A Stinson bi-plane blocked my path, and past that was a large private jet. Buffett's. As I veered around his Falcon, the rod tube under my right arm started to slip. When I spotted Betty, I dropped all my gear in a loud clatter.

The plane was still mummified with police-line tape. I peeked back around the jet's wheel to see if my fumble had alerted the police, but all remained clear. What the hell had happened to Ray? Was it a sign? Was I being ambushed?

Damn!

I piled my gear under Bubba's plane, checked the main terminal for activity, then chanced my way out to Betty. There was enough tape wrapped around her to stretch from Cuba to Key West's Southernmost Point. The green kayak was still chained to the palm tree behind the plane. I put my hand on Betty's fuselage. It felt cold in the darkness.

"Sorry, old girl, but come morning I'm getting you out of here."

I ran my palm up her port side and spotted a note taped on the hatch.

Attention, FBI.

I peeled it off and scurried behind the plane where a blue runway beacon offered scant illumination. Inside was a handwritten note.

"*Dear FBI Pilot,*

I was going to clear the tape off for you, but Special Agent Booth said not to. Since you're arriving <u>BEFORE SUNRISE</u>, he wanted it left on for security purposes. She's fueled and ready to go, so sorry about not having her cleaned up. Best of luck."

The letter was unsigned, but Ray's scrawl needed no signature.

Double-damn!

I peeked over Betty's tail section and didn't see anyone outside the terminal, but several shadowed areas existed where guards could hide. A cool drop of sweat ran down my spine.

Now what?

72

The airport would be a hive of Feds before the sun was up, all swarming to supervise the extraction of my plane. I unlocked the hatch and peeled enough tape off to open it. I retrieved my gear from under Buffett's jet, hauled it to Betty, pushed it inside, climbed aboard, and closed the door. Options ticked off in my head as I leaned against my worldly possessions on the teak floor. I was a stowaway in my own plane.

The blue runway lights provided some operating visibility, so I opened the storage door and dug through my junk box. I scraped my knuckle on the anchor before finding the duct tape. I covered the windows in case any night watchmen peered inside with flashlights.

How had my life had come to this? I rehashed all the facts, loose ends, and people involved in this nightmare, which somehow led me to think of my brother. I could blame him for the letter that left me no choice but to go see Willy, but at this point it didn't matter. Opening the Swiss bank box required both our keys. If I didn't retrieve the stash or crack the code, we were both out of luck.

The epiphany that MUDDHOUSE must mean Fort Jefferson caused me to dig the book on codes out of my backpack. Using the Vigenère table, I drew a graph. The number of letters didn't match. Fort Jefferson had two more letters than MUDDHOUSE.

Abbreviation? Worth a check. The empty spaces took shape.

F	T	J	E	F	F	E	R	S	O	N
H	B	L	I	W	T	W	D	M	G	R
C	I	C	E	R	O	S	M	U	S	E

CICEROSMUSE?

I laid out another graph for O R Y H R I K L V O L I H, but when combined with CICEROSMUSE the remaining thirteen-letter clue produced only garble. Cicero was familiar, but my computer was at the La Concha.

Locked inside the dark plane, I felt like I was in a barrel floating toward the peak of Niagara Falls, ready to drop into the deepest abyss of my life. Karen's concern for me and the thought of our kiss stirred a sudden loneliness that reminded me of the emptiness of losing my parents and the speculation that I killed them for inheritance. And now I had yet another word puzzle. That thought ricocheted through my brain and clicked on a cell that sat me up straight.

From the cockpit I studied the airport buildings, main and private terminals, gas shed, private hangar. Nothing was moving. Adrenalin flooded my system. I jumped from the hatch onto the tarmac and checked the sky. Red taillights of military jets descended like fireflies toward Boca Chica Airbase to the north.

I dug into my pocket. The sound of change clicked through the payphone on the private terminal wall.

"Any idea who Cicero's muse might have been?" I asked Harry Greenbaum.

"The Roman? Are you referring to muse in the creative sense?"

"Hell if I know. Maybe inspiration? Anyway, you said you needed more information to triangulate Rolle and the *Carnival,* so see what you can do with this."

After reciting the information from customs and the Coast Guard, I paced like a defendant awaiting his jury's verdict while Harry roused his source of technical wizardry from one of his sixty-plus companies. An eternity passed, and convinced Harry had fallen asleep, I was ready to give up when a sudden sound caused me to jump.

"Dear God, my boy, next time keep your inquiries within the United States."

"Any luck?" My voice sounded breathless.

"Afraid not, at least with Rolle."

My shoulders dropped.

"However, we may have solidified a connection between the *Carnival* and San Alejandro."

"May?"

"It's ten o'clock at night, dear boy. We found an address of what I presume to be an attorney's office for San Alejandro, LLC."

"And?"

"The address is in the Bahamas."

A loud bang caught my attention, but I couldn't see where it came from. "Which island?"

"701 King's Highway, Alice Town, on an island called—"

"Bimini?"

"Well done."

I would have never—Bimini's not much more than a sand spit in the overall chain.

"By the way," Harry said. "Julius Caesar."

I looked at the phone. "Grover Cleveland."

"Cicero's muse. He and Caesar, although politically divergent, maintained a secret dialogue."

"Secret, as in with codes?"

"Precisely."

Thank you's, IOUs and promises for explanations preceded my abrupt farewell.

The sky was a featureless void.

I would be a complete moron to try flying in darkness.

Ray's note indicated the FBI would arrive *before* sunrise.

73

I rubbed my palms together and began pulling
the tape from Betty's fuselage. My stomach felt more twisted by the second. There
was an endless amount of the thick yellow marker, which I rolled steadily into
a ball as I ran around examining the flaps, rudder, pitot tube, tires, and engine
cowlings. When I finished, I flipped the basketball-sized wad inside the hatch.

Two points for the home team.

After running to the palm tree behind Betty, I returned with the new kayak
over my shoulder. The skiff fit easily through the hatch.

Once the door was secure and the gear was bungyed down, I shimmied into
the left seat. No flight plan and no radio communication would mark tonight's
voyage. I was joining the ranks of dope smugglers who sweated out low altitude
missions to avoid detection. I switched on the batteries and sped through the
start-up procedure. The starboard engine kicked over and sputtered out some
white smoke before it settled into a steady hum.

I cracked my knuckles before reaching for the port ignition. Flying fish,
voodoo hexes, Santeria candles, and Cuban bombs had plagued that engine,
and cranking her now felt like preparing for a duel in a spaghetti western. She
coughed, spat some smoke, and grumbled in mechanical misery.

"Come on, baby."

With a fast glance at the terminal and silence in my headset, I shoved the throttles forward, cut a glimpse at the faint silhouette of the windsock, and nearly broke the land speed record getting to the head of the runway. Once there I pressed the throttles down and launched Betty into the black abyss. The tail wheel swung wildly, and the aft section shook back and forth until the rushing air met the critical point where natural equations and forces ignited to lift our 5,000 pounds off the earth. The airspeed indicator showed 85 mph as Betty climbed into the troposphere. I prayed we would clear God and man-made impediments. We banked to the southeast, and I pressed the stick forward. The sound of the wheels in the wells did little to ease my churning stomach, and the sight of F-18s over Boca Chica only made it worse.

According to my altimeter, "flying boat" was an accurate description as we roared thirty feet over the dark water. The image of Booth drooling on a hotel pillow at the Holiday Inn with twisted dreams of revenge dancing through his mind made me smile.

"The early bird gets the Widgeon."

I steered Betty on an evasive seventy-degree heading. Radio traffic was minimal. I alternated between Miami Center, Key West tower, weather, and traffic advisories. Betty ran with spirit like a stall-bound horse set free, even if her jockey was flying blind.

How would the FBI's discovery that Betty and I were missing manifest itself? If I was going to survive the crossing and reach Bimini, I needed to stay focused. I compared my chart with the heading indicator under the glow of the instrument panel and cross-referenced it with the information displayed on the new GPS unit. I calculated my airspeed to time our bank north into the heart of the Bahamas as if I had a clue what I was doing. A steady course and fixed vectoring points were the result of equating fuel consumption with airspeed to gauge distance. I'd read about these practices before giving up on the IFR rating. I didn't remember enough to be dangerous to others but was fool enough to be fatal to myself.

After flying east for an hour I turned north. Our course should have taken us south of Andros, the largest Bahamian island. Was that the long dark silhouette that now filled the westerly horizon? I cross-checked the chart with the GPS and decided we were pointed toward Nassau. From there I'd bear west toward the Berry Islands, then head up to Bimini.

Betty had climbed to two thousand feet, the highest we'd been all night. A waning gibbous moon had risen, and what were clear turquoise waters by day now shimmered silver below us. Tiny spits of mangrove, coral, and sand were black holes, randomly dotting the ocean's surface. Nassau was a distant glow of casinos on the eastern horizon. At the northern end of the dark landmass, I vectored west.

The stars were brilliant. One was especially bright, and it appeared to be moving. Satellite?

It wouldn't be long before I'd have to initiate radio contact with—

An ear-splitting roar penetrated the solitude of my headset. The star *was* moving, its bright light blinding—Betty suddenly dropped as if cut from a rope.

I pulled on the stick and stomped on the pedals, but nothing happened. The silhouette of a 737 blew over us like a hawk over its prey. Jet wash!

Betty began to spin in an uncontrollable stall.

I pressed the stick forward, and the nose dipped sluggishly. Our angle of attack was askew and the altimeter needle was dropping.

Inertia tipped us hard to starboard, the nose fell, and a gradual sense of pressure returned to the controls. Velocity led us to clean air, I got Betty back under control, and the nose slowly began to lift.

The veins on my hands throbbed. I loosened my grip. Blind in the night, I had steered us into the Nassau approach, nearly colliding with a commercial airliner on its descent. My first night flight was nearly my last. My blood ran cold at the thought of the imminent water landing. Stay focused, Galileo.

The boomerang shapes of North and South Bimini materialized ahead, where a small cluster of lights identified Alice Town. I steered for their crotch, where the seaplane ramp was located. The lights of a large marina along with small settlements began to appear. I circled the harbor, amazed to have made it this far.

The first time I came here was aboard a Chalks Mallard, a larger version of Betty that seats seventeen. The short flight from Fort Lauderdale unleashed the fantasy of having an amphibious aircraft, which made tonight's journey a sort of homecoming. The landing area was free of boat lights, so I added flaps, reduced power, and swung from the base leg onto final approach. Crab pots or channel markers might finish the job the jet wash had started, but at this point there was no choice.

Fuel mixtures were set to full rich, the tail wheel was raised, both tachs showed 2,500 RPM's, airspeed was 80 mph, and Betty descended into the deep blackness with unwitting grace. We hovered, as did the needle kissing zero, until the sense of anticipation became unbearable. I edged the wheel forward a hair, and the bow hit the surface before the fuselage.

We bounced hard.

The rapid deceleration launched me taut into the four-point harness as the fuselage slapped over and over.

A staccato sound erupted within the cabin as if the ancient rivets were ripping loose while the plane convulsed and recoiled with a dangerous force. I couldn't move—negative g-forces pressed my arms against my chest. The blind porpoising felt like we were in the grip of an earthquake.

I wrestled the yoke steady and shoved the throttles forward to increase RPM's while we struggled to regain the proper attitude and trim angle. We finally burst off the surface and leveled out above the water. Oxygenated by several deep breaths, the blood returned to my arms. I repeated the landing process, more patiently this time, and was rewarded with the uniform sense of touching down properly. A long, slow exhale blew my cheeks into balloons. My first IFR experience had been one long disaster.

A bright light penetrated my vent window, and I shielded my eyes. Not another—

"Grumman one-seven-four-one-November, come in."

How did air traffic control know—

The agent waved a spotlight from the shore, close enough to read my tail numbers. I asked permission to come up the ramp, lowered my landing gear on the approach, and wonder of wonders we emerged from the sea onto dry land. I taxied to an open corner, turned Betty to face the water, and cut power.

A dark-skinned official in a light blue shirt with red and yellow epaulettes stood outside waiting for me to deplane. Based on reciprocal consular agreements, the countdown on the Fed's learning my location had just begun. I got out of the hatch and set my feet on Bahamian soil, an official fugitive from American justice.

"The airport's closed. What on earth are you thinking?"

I gave him an animated story about engine troubles, along with my documents, then followed him into the sun-bleached hut that served as terminal, customs office, and flight services center. With my presence in Bimini officially established, I crawled back into my plane, where exhaustion overtook me.

The wildest of dreams could not suppress what the reality of my life had become. And, having risked my freedom in a gambit to learn the origin of the *Carnival*, I had defied the largest law enforcement agency of the most powerful nation on earth. Not the best odds I'd ever taken on.

74

I awoke to the sense of being ingested in some
great esophageal tube. The air was thick inside the plane, and why I was there hit
like an electric jolt. I held my breath and listened outside. Nothing but the sound
of boats in the distance.

My watch read 7:50. Last night's precarious flight had repeated itself like a
broken record in my nightmares. I hoped the gamble of finding San Alejandro,
LLC, would prove a worthwhile trade for becoming a renegade.

I set off on foot toward Alice Town. In the out-islands of the Bahamas, far
away from resorts, time stands still. Silhouetted people stood idle under the long
reach of casuarina trees, no doubt seeking respite from the growing heat. Modest
dwellings lined the road, painted in juice-colored hues and set back at staggered
distances. Gauzy curtains fluttered in open windows.

A series of squat buildings lay ahead, across from the broad marina and hotel
complex known as the Bimini Big Game Club. Randomly marked numbers led
me to 701 King's Highway, a pink two-story wooden structure with light blue
shutters. On its door was a sign for *Liquor and Cuban Cigars*. If the attorney was
a local big shot, the threat of being connected to multiple murders should provide
the leverage I needed. Inside I found a large woman in a colorful wrap who coolly
eyed me from behind the cash register.

"I'm looking for an attorney's office on the second floor?"

"Attorney?" She cocked her head at an angle. The local accent, developed over generations of British rule and undiluted with independence, made the word sound like 'A-tah-ney.'

"I'm buying a boat registered to this address."

"Ah, Sidney Jamison." A smile followed. "He ain't no attorney. He calls himself a holding agent, or some such thing."

"Is he upstairs?"

Her face wrinkled around her broad brown nose. With a nod of her head she directed my attention out a small window.

A man lay crumpled in the fetal position under an immense pine tree.

Equipped with a cold bottle of Kalik beer, I stood staring over the inert body snoring amidst the ants and pine needle carpet. A tap on his foot lifted his head off the ground. His eyes opened slowly. Confusion turned to distrust, then anger.

"Mr. Jamison? I'm interested in buying a boat."

One eye squinted open and blinked rapidly. He grunted something unintelligible, the word "boat" bracketed in heavily accented expletives and garble.

"You thirsty?"

The eye cracked open again. He sat up slowly. Pine needles clung to him like leeches, and a spittle trail was caked in his shaggy salt and pepper beard. Another grunt marked the acceptance of the beer, and he swallowed a long slug.

I knelt next to him. "You're the holding agent on a boat I'm buying."

"Ain't got no boat." I estimated more gaps than teeth on his gums. He guzzled the beer as if I'd take it back.

"It's a fifty foot fishing boat called *Carnival*, registered to your address."

A vague sense of recognition widened his eyes. "What about it?"

"I'm interested in buying it."

He held up the now empty beer and smacked his lips. "I don't know, I'm still...." I pulled a half-pint of Bacardi rum from my back pocket. "Thirsty," he said.

"You *are* the holding agent for the *Carnival*, aren't you?"

His sudden laugh surprised me. "Sure, that's me. I'm an *agent*." He laughed again, his eyes on the rum. "Who be selling you that boat?"

The question caught me off guard. He squinted up at me, waiting, and I handed him the rum instead of answering. The cap was off with a flourish. He sniffed the contents before taking a small drink.

"It belongs to San Alejandro, LLC."

"Good, good. I'll be around, if'n you and Mr. Salendro, ah, San, ah....need me to sign anything. My fee's $100 for signing papers. I've got a postal box number." Sidney Jamison winked at me, then took a longer pull on the rum. I stood up.

"I know where to find you." My body suddenly felt hollow. I'd figured the local agent to be a cut-out, but Sidney Jamison wasn't even that. He was just a drunk with a P.O. Box number he'd front out to anyone for a fee. A dead end—just like my life, now that the FBI must have discovered me and Betty AWOL.

75

I looked up and down King's Highway, a lofty
description for the concrete and dirt strip road that circled the island, then walked
through the narrow concrete gates that led into the Bimini Big Game Club. The
guard by the entry ignored me. His job was to keep the locals away from the large
yachts and fishing boats in temporary residence here fifty miles east of Miami. At
the pool were a bevy of women beginning their day of sun tanning while their
men took to the sea. The marina seemed less than half full, but it was early. The
door to the hotel had a bell that announced my entry. A skinny woman with
braided hair and a yellow golf shirt that sported the Big Game Club's logo stood
up. CNN was on the TV behind her. The commentator stood before a map of
Cuba.

"Do you have any rooms?"

"Now you've gone and done it." She nodded toward the television.

Could my bolting in Betty already be on the news?

"Invading Cuba?"

I swallowed. "I'm not—"

"Says America's threatening to invade Cuba."

I explained that I didn't have a boat but wanted a room for a couple nights.

She checked her computer screen. "We got a couple rooms but only until
tomorrow afternoon. Might try the Angler?"

I thanked her and made my way down to the dock and walked along the broad wood planks. Sleek cigarette-style speedboats, trawlers set up for cruising, several fishing boats with Floridian ports of call, and a smattering of sailboats sat idle. As a neutral country, the Bahamas would be inundated with Cuban boats if CNN's speculation about an invasion caused an exodus. It was reminiscent of when President Carter stated that the U.S. would welcome Cuban refugees, and Castro emptied his jails and asylums onto rafts bound for Florida. Self-fulfilling prophecy, or the networks creating news? This was different from hyping summer squalls into hurricanes, this could lead to war. And the *Carnival* would vanish amidst miles of fiberglass.

The water was gin clear. Powder-coated bottles were visible on the bottom under the dock. Similar to the Keys in many ways, the water here was noticeably cleaner, the island far less polished. I imagined it to be how the Keys were fifty-years ago. Since I'd taken a vow of celibacy from the virtual life, all that electronic stimuli had been like a chain around my neck…cell phone, texting, instant messaging, email, personal web pages, television, news. Key West detoxed my dependence on technology, but when it came to the simple life, how far could I go? I had an idea and returned to the office.

"That was quick."

"I forgot to ask when my friends were supposed to arrive," I said. "They're aboard the *Carnival*."

She sighed and checked her screen. "They members here?"

"I think so."

"What's the name?"

"Hector Perez. She's a fifty-foot custom fishing boat registered here in Bimini."

"Why they stay here if they from here?"

"I just figured, since the Big Game Club's the best marina—"

"If they from here, they probably keep that boat up across from the Angler. This place is too expensive."

She found no reservation, and I realized the Big Game Club was too commercial for a boat on an illicit mission. If the *Carnival* was from Bimini, maybe they did have a more discreet location to dock. If I didn't find them by morning, I'd have to use what was left of Betty's hundred hours to scour the Florida straits.

"Is that the only other marina?"

"Only decent one, 'cept South Bimini. Where the condominiums are? But you got to own one of them."

Strike two. Bimini was starting to feel like a no-hitter.

76

I headed back to the pink store.

"Sidney help you?" the woman asked.

"Not exactly, but maybe you can." She shrugged. "I'm looking for Jackson Rolle, does he live around here?"

Her pleasant face took on an ugly scowl. "What you want the likes of him for?"

"Information. He's mixed-up in something—"

"Mixed-up's right. He's always mixed-up in trouble. Humph. *Jackson* Rolle." Her nose wrinkled as if she smelled rotten eggs. "Should still be in jail."

"*Still?* What for"

"Smuggling refugees into the States. Got busted good, the fool."

Refugees? "How long has he been out?"

"Too long, a year at least. He was here buying the booze a couple weeks ago, acting all Mr. Big Stuff. You could always tell when he up to no good, so full of hisself."

My surprise was held in check by her reaction. "Does he live here?"

"His mumma's place's just down the road, but I wouldn't be going there asking about what he's into now."

"Santeria?"

She pursed her lips. She waved her index finger at me. "If you talk that, his mumma might just club you. Jackson's one big embarrassment to Miss Lilly, he shouldn't show his dirty face round here at all."

"Shouldn't, or won't?"

"Shouldn't, but he likes chasing drunk girls at the Big Game Club and the Angler too much, so he'll be back."

She told me where the Rolle's family house was—as it turned out, I'd passed it on the road in from the airport. I thanked the woman. Jackson Rolle was from Bimini too. Smuggling? His *curriculum vitae* grew more impressive each day.

The noise of my grumbling stomach meshed with the crunch of gravel under my feet. A few cars were parked on the side of the road, rusted and battered. A golf cart, the vehicle of choice, buzzed past me carrying two women in business attire. Across from a small, bare-bones marina stood The Compleat Angler, a ramshackle combination bar and hotel that had been the island's primary watering hole since Zane Grey and Hemingway helped put the spot on the map. Grass and weeds grew between cracks in the concrete front yard where empty plastic cups flourished like flowers, mulched with cigarette butts.

A perfect place for a guy like Rolle to take advantage of vacationing women.

The Angler would be my base of operation. If Rolle was a local, there had to be people here who knew him. Maybe somebody would know the *Carnival*, otherwise my chips would be called and I'd be crapped out.

Stay off the ropes.

The bar was empty except for a threesome of sunburned men playing the ring game. The ring was attached to a long string connected to the ceiling, and each time someone missed landing it on the hook attached to the wall, he took a shot of rum. By the look and sound of them, they'd missed many more than they'd made. I had a beer and a burger, then paid two nights in advance for a corner room upstairs. Bare wood walls, a lumpy bed, a toilet and sink, a really small dresser. It wasn't the Ritz, hell, it wasn't even the La Concha, but it would have to do. And it had a clear view of the marina across the street.

77

With my amateur stakeout established, I rented a golf cart from the bartender, cruised past Rolle's house on the way to retrieve my gear from Betty, then collapsed on the warped mattress with the book on codes. Harry had said Julius Caesar was Cicero's muse. To my surprise there was a listing for Caesar in the codebook's index. He had his own cipher system, far simpler than Vigenère's—just a four-letter offset, where A became D, etc. I laid out the alphabet both ways.

A	B	C	D	E	F	G	H	I	J	K	L	M	N	O	P	Q	R	S	T	U	V	W	X	Y	Z
D	E	F	G	H	I	J	K	L	M	N	O	P	Q	R	S	T	U	V	W	X	Y	Z	A	B	C

Next I laid out the key word, and the ensuing blanks came to life.

O	R	Y	H	R	I	K	L	V	O	L	I	H
L	O	V	E	O	F	H	I	S	L	I	F	E

LOVE OF HIS LIFE?

It was the last clue. How could it be a Swiss bank account identification?

Another damn word puzzle. I dropped it on the floor, determined not to have to solve it. Unless Bimini turns out to be a dead end.

I studied the picture of Jackson Rolle on the *Carnival.* Had I gambled correctly? Had I made an irreconcilable mess out of my life? Would the hex in the clay figurine succeed? Had Ensign Frank Nardi figured out that I tricked him for information about the boat? Had the FBI issued a warrant for my arrest?

LOVE OF HIS LIFE? Thanks, Dad.

And finally, when I imagined that Karen was in the room with me, my dreams went where reality had not let me, and I fell into a deep sleep.

78

I jerked bolt upright in bed, sweat-soaked and disoriented. Loud music filled the dark room. Faint moonlight filtered through the tissue-thin curtain. How long had I slept? I checked my watch, surprised that it was 8:20.

Last night's near suicide flight and the weight of my fleeing Key West had turned what was to be a nap into a four-hour crash that left me groggy. A quick fifty push-ups and a splash of cold water on my face helped. The loud music shook the thin wood walls with a force that could only originate from a live band downstairs in the bar. I glanced out the window past the people loitering in the open courtyard, and my eyes followed the sidewalk to the street and across—

One, two… four large fishing boats were now docked at the marina.

Nervous anticipation had me off the bed and headed for the door. I stopped and pulled the envelope with Barrett's photographs from my backpack. I studied the faces of the three men known to have been on the boat. Rolle, Hector Perez, and the third man I called No-Name. Finally, Shaniqua Peebles's face smiled up and stirred the memory from the Dry Tortugas.

Are you still alive, and if so, how do you fit into this mess?

Having learned my lesson at the warehouse in Cuba, I didn't run over and burst onto the dock but instead slipped down the steps and out the back door. It took a few moments for my eyes to adjust to the blackness. The music blared, and light pulsed around the frame of a closed door on the back wall. The singer's deep voice resonated through the gap in the door.

"…Crisis time, I can't spare a dime," he sang.

A path through the dense foliage led me to the main street. I imitated the sway of the drunks who'd been playing the ring game at the bar, and nobody paid any attention to me as I sauntered toward the boats. The one closest had a dark hull, and the one in the adjacent slip was too small. The smell of seafood wafted from a portable deep-fat fryer ahead, where a man nearly as round as he was tall tended it on the dock behind the third boat. He looked up as I gave it a once-over.

"What time is it?" the man said. His eyes, like his cheeks, were red, set off by a shock of white hair.

I checked my watch. "Eight—"

"Eight what? Come on, this stuff's gonna burn!"

My eyes and brain were paralyzed, locked onto—

"Goddamnit. Darby!" The red man yelled toward his boat. "What time is it?"

"Eight-fifty," I said. "Sorry."

"You been hanging out across the street too long?"

The sight of the red bow flare on the last boat had me speechless. Light burned through a small porthole, but nobody was on deck. The tide was down, and the boat sat low in the water, but I could still see the transom. *Carnival.*

"You know those guys over there?" I said.

The man redirected his large frame with obvious effort, then turned back. "Nah. Seen the boat here a couple times, but never out fishing. Why, they friends of yours?"

"I was just curious what make she was and—"

"Hey, Darby, what kind of boat is—"

I grabbed the man's thick arm. "Never mind. What's that you're cooking?"

He didn't even flinch, just stared at me. His red eyes made him look like a komodo dragon. "Lobster." He tilted his round head toward the *Carnival.* "Couple of them boys headed down the road a few hours ago."

"Enjoy those lobsters," I said.

I walked back to the Angler, and could feel my pulse in my neck. If the *Carnival* were as wired here as they'd been in Cuba, my options would be severely limited. A direct approach would be suicidal.

The steady pounding of bass and treble resounded through the bar.

It was early, but the dance floor was packed at the foot of a five-piece local band hammering out original Bahamian music. The singer glistened in sweat, and drove the dancers into a hypnotic frenzy. The steady bass-beat reminded me of Salvo's studio in Cayo Hueso and Enrique's trailer on Stock Island. I scanned the room for a Santeria altar but found none.

The side room held a shrine to Hemingway filled with photographs, books, even quotes from *Islands in the Stream,* a novel partially written here on Bimini. One of the handwritten pages was framed on the wall.

> ""Jesus Christ," Eddy said. "There it comes!"
>
> Out across the blue water, showing like a brown dinghy sail and slicing through the water with heavy, tail propelled, lunging thrusts, the high triangular fin was coming in toward the hole at the edge of the reef where the boy with the mask on his face held his fish up out of the water.
>
> "Oh Jesus," Eddy said. "What a son of a bitching hammerhead. Jesus, Tom. Oh Jesus.""

At each stop in my Key West-Cuba-Bimini triangle I had found myself in Papa's footsteps. I was starting to feel that somehow, some way, my father was leading me toward a pre-ordained conclusion. Another thought hit me.

Was Fort Jefferson named after Thomas Jefferson? If so, were my father's ciphers connected to the map carved into the *Pilar's* gunwale, where Hemingway found the gold chain?

I pushed the thought aside. The *Carnival* was here, and more tangible results were within reach. The boat appeared to be settled for the night, so I sank into a worn red leather chair and tried to conjure up a plan. Macho images surrounded me, and from them I sought the clarity needed to make a one-man assault later tonight. The mere thought of it sounded foolhardy, even to me.

I stood to check out the crowd. The band had continued without a break, and the dance floor was now pressed tight with bodies, T-shirts, shorts, tank tops, and spaghetti-straps. The crowd was fearless and carefree. Nobody noticed the weight of the world on my shoulders.

Past the dance floor, the bar was filled with a blue haze of cigarette smoke. Spontaneous cheers erupted when a petite blond landed the ring on the hook. Shots of liquor were drunk in celebration, the price for victory matching that of defeat. When I finally squeezed myself up to the bar, I ordered a Kalik. The cold beer was refreshing, but it would be the only one tonight.

Laughter and shouting were everywhere, a good time being had by all except for one table in the back corner where two men sat talking. I spun back toward the bar and gagged on a mouthful of beer.

Scar and No-Name were here in the Angler.

I pretended to sip the beer and occasionally glanced over my shoulder. Their hand gestures led me to conclude they were arguing. A half-dozen empty highball glasses were pressed against the end of their table. The scars on Rolle's obsidian cheeks were ominous, made worse by his greasy hair and chain smoking.

The pair fell silent.

No-Name got up and came to the bar, three people down from me. Blue mono-color tattoos adorned his hands. His movements made it clear he was at least half in the bag. Rolle stared at a group of couples taking turns at the ring game, and you could almost see the raunchy thoughts turning inside his head.

No-Name pushed back through the crowd and placed two amber-colored drinks on the table. Rolle flung a wrist at him and they picked up where they left off, now refueled.

Were they arguing over the trip? Their share of the booty? Who was better with the ladies? All I could think of was where Shaniqua might be. The captain was nowhere to be seen, so hopefully they were still on the boat.

Could I get them to lead me to my stash? Not before bringing them to justice, whether here, in the States, or at the bottom of the ocean.

Four more drinks for them while I nursed my piss-warm Kalik. The bartender finally announced last call. No-Name suddenly stood, gave Rolle the finger, and turned away, knocking his chair over as he went. He shoved his way through the crowd, drawing several dirty looks before caroming out the door.

My stomach tightened. Show time. I had to do something, but what?

79

Rolle stood up and his torso moved in a slow circle.
I slid off my stool, still unsure what to do, but his and No-Name's condition was an opportunity I had to exploit. Rolle stopped in front of the exit, hesitated, then twisted on his heel toward the dance floor.

What!?

He bounced into swaying bodies like a pinball until he was by the band. The singer, who'd kept the crowd on their feet all evening, didn't seem to notice him. Was Rolle leaving through the back door, now open next to the drummer? He turned at the last second and disappeared into a hidden hallway.

I jumped onto the dance floor and negotiated my way through sweaty, bumping bodies, ignoring a beer-bombed brunette who grabbed my hand with an invitation to dance. As I entered the hallway I spotted the restroom sign, just as the door to the men's room opened. Jackson Rolle stared up at me. His mouth dropped open.

How could he recognize me?

Rolle's expression hardened. He dug his hand into the waist of his pants, and I stepped into him with a short uppercut to the chin that lifted him off the floor. His body went limp, dropped like a bag of concrete, and I caught him halfway down. I made a quick decision. I hoisted his left arm over my shoulder and held him up by the belt. The singer began a slow song.

"…Tell me why did you leave me, I think about you every morning, I think about you every day," he sang.

I lugged Rolle toward the drummer, who shot me a curious glance when I brushed his cymbal. "Drunk." I mouthed the word and the drummer nodded, never missing a beat.

Rolle remained limp, and my mind shot into overdrive. Did he remember me from the Dry Tortugas? I carried him to the hotel's back door, pulled it open, and dragged him up the flight of stairs. I fumbled in my pocket and jammed the key into the lock. Rolle was lighter than he looked. Evil fits snugly into small packages. Once inside, I let him slump to the floor, and his head hit with a coconut-off-the-tree thunk.

I tried to catch my breath while digging through my backpack for the duct tape. I used it to cover his mouth, then bound his hands behind his back. I found a six-inch knife stuffed into his waistband.

Rolle's stink was a combination of booze, cigarettes, brine, and perspiration. He stirred just as I used the last piece of tape around his ankles. I felt spent, running on fumes and adrenalin. Up close, Rolle's scars were crude, almost tribal in appearance, with no evidence of stitching or any other kind of care given to their healing. The red and white beaded necklace glowed on his slick black skin, and Enrique was right, the pendant was a horned ram's head.

He could try to summon Chango or Siete Rayos all he wanted, what he got was me.

80

Now awake, he narrowed his eyes until he was squinting. A brief struggle against his bonds was enough to make him realize he wasn't going anywhere.

"We can do this one of two ways," I said. "You tell me the truth, or you suffer the same fate as Jo Jo Jeffries and Rodney Claggett."

I couldn't read his look. Confused? Fearful? Or just wary?

"Not in the ocean, you don't deserve that much dignity."

I nodded toward the toilet in the corner of the room. All the anger and frustration over the past weeks fueled my determination, consuming me with a lust for answers.

"Don't test me, Rolle."

His eyes flickered.

"I know all about you. Your connections in Cuba, the whole stinking game. Doing time for smuggling refugees will be Boy Scout Camp compared to what you'll get in the States, if you make it that far."

The music soared again. The ballad was over and the band reignited the frenzy in the Angler for one last romp.

"I'm going to take the tape off your mouth and ask you some questions. You answer, you live. You get cute, you breathe toilet water. Got it?"

He gave a slight nod.

I cracked my knuckles, and pulled the tape free with a loud rip.

"HELP!"

I tried to slap the tape back over Rolle's mouth. His yellowed teeth gnashed at my fingers, piercing the side of my hand. I brought a crushing left jab down on his nose, shattering it in an explosion of blood and cartilage, before finally getting the tape back in place.

He squirmed uncontrollably, rolling on the floor, spraying blood all over my bare legs, unable to breathe through his flattened snout. I grabbed him and held him flat against the floor.

"You can drown in your own fucking blood for all I care! One more chance or the tape stays on."

His nostrils spewed blood as he fought to breathe. I yanked the tape free, and a putrid lungful of air hit me. I slapped him, then raised my hand again, and he hocked a bloody wad of spit into my face.

I flew to my feet, dragged him to the corner, grabbed his hair, then lifted and spun him over the toilet. The six inches of water turned red with his blood. I held his head down with all my strength while he kicked, squirmed, and swung himself from side to side.

"You think this is a game?"

After nearly a minute his struggling slowed, and I pulled him out of the abyss. He coughed uncontrollably and flopped to the floor. I pinned his shoulders with my knees. Blood streamed from his left nostril and washed over his face in a crimson mask. His eyes were finally free of resistance, now scintillating with fear.

Is that how Jo Jo looked before you killed him?

"Is Shaniqua Peebles on the boat?"

He pressed his lips tightly together. I jumped up and started to drag him back to the toilet.

"No! No, wait."

I threw him back down and again pinned my knees on his shoulders.

"Is she on board?"

He nodded.

Yes! "What about Ortega, the old Conch?" Now he *really* looked scared, and I intuitively knew the answer. I cocked my right arm, wanting to jam it through his skull but hesitated at the smell of urine through his filthy pants. "How many others are on the boat?"

"Just Hector and Pablo."

"Who's behind all this? The Cubans? Salvo?"

"I don't know, for true, I don't. Hector, he tells us what to do."

"Why'd you kill them?"

"It wasn't supposed to happen! They heard us, on the radio, the old Cuban—"

"Heard what?"

"We got a call saying the shipment was ready for the warehouse—the old Cuban figured it out."

"Figured *what* out?"

"That we had business. The missionaries were our cover, we started fighting—"

"Who told you to kill them?"

"The big one, he came at me—and Pablo, he hit him with the gun butt and wrecked his nose. Blood squirted everywhere and he went crazy, like a bull, and then the skinny one jumped Pablo and the shotgun went off...."

I envisioned the scene unfolding. "What about the girl?"

"We kept her as a hostage in case we got caught."

She's wasn't involved! "Why the Mayday?"

"A signal, to the man—"

"What about the boat, what's in the crates, weapons?"

"What? No, relics, Cuban junk."

My mind spun. *Relics? Junk?*

"From the warehouse..." Blood trailed into Rolle's mouth as he spoke, and he swallowed it between words. "Where you almost saw me."

I stopped breathing.

His growl of a laugh surprised me. A large pink bubble burst from his nose.

"I saw you at the Tata's, too, the night before."

Tata? Sanchez had used..."Salvo's studio? You were—" *Quasimodo!* Rolle was the man hiding in the shadows. "Did Salvo order the missionaries killed?"

"They weren't supposed to die! It was a mistake—they heard the call. They knew!" His eyelids fluttered. "Then, the man in Key West, he was so mad...he went crazy, threatened to kill us—"

"Who in Key West?" *My pouch!*

"The one Hector signaled, I don't know...He was crazy mad about them being killed. Until we told him about the treasure maps."

"Did Shaniqua tell you about the maps?"

"I heard her talking on the phone. Said you had a chart all marked up with search notes, that it must be for a sunken treasure ship."

"So how does that tie into all the shit in Key West? Hexes, candles, chickens, dogs? Who stole my—who's the man in Key West?"

Rolle's mouth snapped shut. He pulled hard against the bonds. I grabbed his arm and began to yank him toward the toilet again.

"I don't know, for true! We were never going to hurt them...just drop them off in Cuba. They were our cover."

"For Santeria or Palo Mayombe?" My heart raced. How had I been played?

"It's got nothing to do—"

"Then *who*?" I shouted in his face.

"I don't know, I swear! When Hector called in the Mayday, the man in Key West called him back on the cell phone. They talked in Spanish, I don't understand—"

"*Spanish?* Mingie Posada? Emilio? The CANC?"

"I told you—"

"What about Salvo, why were you at his studio?"

"I was picking up the relics, he's our contact—"

"The crates were in a government warehouse, Number One Obrapia, I saw—"

"I took them there. Salvo's cousins with the police…."

His cousin? "What's his last name?"

"Hector called him Señor Sanchez."

Sanchez! The Cuban connections crashed into place, but the tie back to the States was still—*Spanish?* Santeria and Cuba were one and the same, Ivan's and my daiquiri-debate was right…Ivan…but why? *Cuban junk?*

"What are you doing with the crates? Where are you taking them?"

"We always take them to a house in Miami."

"Always? A house?"

"On a canal. This is my third trip. There's been more. We usually start in the Bahamas, but this time, the missionaries gave us a story."

"What about Shaniqua, the girl? What's going to happen to her?"

Rolle turned his head to avert my eyes, and I slapped his face back toward me.

"Salvo told us to throw her in the ocean, like the others, but I…"

"You what?"

"I wanted to keep her."

"Is that what you were fighting about in the bar?"

He nodded.

With Rolle captured here, No-Name would have no deterrent to dumping Shaniqua overboard. Perfect. I glanced toward the window, surprised to see the glow of morning aflame on the cheesecloth curtain.

I flung it aside and checked across the road.

One, two, three…

"No!" I whirled toward Rolle. "They're gone!"

81

The second trip to the golf cart was more difficult
then the first. Rolle squirmed like a reluctant dog on the way to the vet. If he
didn't quit struggling, frontier justice would come long before the Florida border.

I dumped him in the back of the cart with the delicacy of a spent power lifter.
His eyes immediately darted around. I pressed my thumb down on his gelatinous
nose, sending an immediate convulsion through his erect body.

His scream was contained by the duct tape.

"Try anything stupid, your leg's next."

Rolle deflated against my duffle.

The problem with golf carts is they're slow, kind of like the game itself. King's
Highway was deserted. It was 5:45 now. The *Carnival* had left before sun-up. Had
Rolle's disappearance accelerated their timetable? Would it change their destina-
tion?

My prisoner's eyes skittered to each passing building, and the fact that he was
a Bimini native fueled my haste to reach Betty. Rolle's confession would take the
wind out of the media's zestful anticipation for a pre-emptive war, so getting him
home in one piece was imperative. A loud thud suddenly jarred the cart. I barely
avoided a grazing goat when I jammed on the brake.

Rolle was gone.

I found him lying in a heap on the concrete road. His elbow now oozed as much blood as his nose had in the room.

"Brilliant plan, Jacko."

His head bounced against the concrete as I dragged him by the feet back to the cart. His gaze was affixed on a dingy shack with corroded vehicles peppering its perimeter. The family estate. With an eye on the door, I reloaded him in the cart.

"No candles in the window, Bubba. One more stunt like that and I'll run your ass over."

With my duffle bag on top of him, we continued down the road. Security was nonexistent at the seaplane ramp, and Betty was majestically aglow in the warm-hued sunrise.

Okay, old girl, it's nut-cutting time.

After seat belting and taping Rolle into the back starboard passenger seat, I ran a quick circuit around Betty and determined her to be visibly free of candles, fish, and grenades. Back on board, I ducked under the suspended kayak and shimmied through the crowded fuselage. Rolle looked petrified.

"Get squirrelly, and you'll make a nice snack for a hammerhead."

The engines started clean, but then a loud backfire from the port side nearly sent me through the roof. What happened to the rest of the hundred hours? The RPM's spiked, then leveled off. I wheeled us down the ramp with my attention on the port engine indicators. Betty skipped across the water, hit takeoff speed, and I added flaps. Just as the hull let go of the waves, another backfire jolted us hard to the left.

The plane veered out of control, and swerved toward an anchored fishing smack and green channel marker. I hit the throttles with a force that threatened to bend their handles. The engine surged, and Betty cleared the boat by inches.

Goddamn hex!

Every one of my senses was redlined, and my ass was on the edge of the seat. I banked the Widgeon hard to the right, now fifty-feet over the water, pointed east and climbing fast.

The hunt was on.

Rolle's eyes were wide with terror. A smile bent my lips as I clicked on the microphone, poised to surface from oblivion, back on the offensive. My first call was a Mayday to the Coast Guard. I alerted them to the *Carnival's* anticipated course, which earned me the tentative confidence of the female dispatcher. She reluctantly patched me through a series of operators until a groggy voice whispered, "Hello?"

"Wake up, Killelea, it's Buck Reilly."

"Reilly?"

"I'm on the *Carnival's* ass heading out of Bimini, and have one of their crew in custody. The boat's making a run for Miami."

"What the hell?"

"Willy's daughter is still captive on board, and my prisoner tells me they plan to dump her on the crossing. Get your ass out of bed and rally the Cavalry!"

He gave me a number to call if I found the boat and promised to dispatch a ship out of Miami.

"There's a warrant out for your arrest," he said.

"This guy's testimony will prove the conspiracy theories are all bullshit."

"And you impersonated a federal agent—"

I changed frequencies. Nardi must be furious.

82

From a thousand feet a broad panorama spread
out below us. The sun hung above the water, and altocumulus clouds were
lined up in a domino formation along a weather front. I zigzagged Betty across
a twenty-degree heading and scanned for boats. A white hull appeared amidst
whitecaps, and I pushed Betty's nose forward, kamikaze-style. Rolle's eyes were
wide.

With no idea when the *Carnival* had left, it was impossible to estimate how
much water it had covered. The boat ahead grew rapidly in size, as the altimeter
spun backwards like the one in H.G. Wells' time machine. When we were at five
hundred feet above sea level, I estimated it to be a quarter-mile away. It turned
out to be a trawler.

We climbed again and I continued to work Rolle's information over in my
mind. One thing he said kept coming back. Hector Perez spoke Spanish with the
man in Key West. The few facts twisted in my head like a Rubik's cube: relics,
Salvo's and Sanchez's statements, the blackmailer's demands....

I kept coming up to the same conclusion, and reality hit like a Bruiser Lewis
uppercut. The answer had been in front of me all along.

Relics.

Betty's 180-mile-per-hour airspeed covered sixty-miles in twenty minutes.
Florida appeared as a black horizontal line in the distance. I had buzzed four

boats with no luck, and as the coast grew closer, concern over Shaniqua's safety consumed my thoughts.

Could Rolle be lying?

Another white hull appeared further north, and although it was outside the latitude I'd been searching, I changed course and began another descent. Rolle had become numb to the routine, his initial fear had changed to silent resignation.

The boat ahead was large and had the lines of a fishing craft. My fingers tightened on the wheel. She was the right size, pointed toward the coast, and running full out.

We closed the distance quickly. Our altitude was down to fifty feet, and Betty's nose was aimed dead at the white boat's ass. Figures emerged from the shadows. One pointed toward us, no doubt concerned that a lunatic was zeroing in for a colonoscopy.

My heart bounded into my throat as I saw a pile of wood crates on the deck, and *Carnival* on the transom above the roiling white water.

No-Name came into focus, holding a young woman by the arm.

Shaniqua!

We blew past them, just twenty feet over their tuna tower. I cut Betty into a sharp bank north, then turned back around in a tight radius. If I stayed on their tail it might disrupt No Name's plan to throw Shaniqua in, but if not, I'd land and pull her from the water.

I keyed the microphone to Killelea's frequency, and as the Coast Guard operator routed me to his cell, I dropped back down behind the *Carnival* for an intimidation run.

Shaniqua was nowhere to be seen. No, there! She was wrestling with someone on the captain's bridge.

A sudden burst of flame extended up from the tuna tower.

I caught a flash of No-Name crouched with a machine gun ablaze! My left foot nearly pressed the pedal through the floor to initiate an evasive course south.

Betty's engines were redlined as we hurtled at wave height, now perpendicular to the boat. I chanced a look back and didn't see any blood, but Rolle was frantically struggling against the tape. He pointed his chin to the floor. Sunlight peeked out of several holes through the teak deck.

We've been hit!

Holes in the floor meant holes through the roof. Each wing held seventy-five gallons of aviation fuel, which if hit would either ignite in a fireball or quickly leak out and leave Betty powerless. Holes at the waterline killed our ability to land on the water.

I strained to look out the starboard window and then the port. From what I could see, no smoke, fire, or stream of fuel trailed behind us. No-Name's bullets must have missed the fuel tanks.

"Reilly, you there?" I jumped at the sound of Killelea's voice. I'd forgotten all about the call to the Coast Guard.

"Shaniqua's struggling with the captain, and we've been hit by machine gun fire."

"What the *hell* are *you* doing?"

"Making sure she's on board." I relayed the GPS coordinates and was relieved to hear a Coast Guard interceptor was rapidly approaching.

"Break off contact before you get yourself killed," Killelea said.

"Not until your people show up. Can you conference in another number?"

After a brief delay, Harry Greenbaum answered his phone. "You're calling much too early for an explanation of the other day," he said.

"Can you do a quick search for me?"

"Are you in a hole, dear boy?"

"I'm in my airplane, some assholes are shooting at me, and I'm conferenced to your line via the cell phone of a Coast Guard investigator."

"Smashing! What can I do to help?"

"Check these names and look for connections to each other and in Cuba: Carnival, San Alejandro and Wilfredo Lam."

We circled the *Carnival* out of firing range while Harry did his thing.

I heard a click on the line. "Harry, you there?"

"I have a man at Data Source checking on this Wilfredo Lam. It sounds like a cigar brand."

Static from the cell phone hit my ears like an electronic shock. "What are you doing, Killelea?"

"Driving to my office, you mind?"

"All right, Buck," Harry said. "Wilfredo Lam was a Cuban painter who studied briefly at the San Alejandro Art School."

"What about Carnival?"

"According to my source, that was the hard part, but I think this must be it. There's a painting by another Cuban artist who also studied at San Alejandro, and one of his better known works is called Carnival."

"His name?"

"René Portocarrero."

"Bingo, Harry, that's got to be the answer."

"Your story's getting stranger by the minute. I do look forward to your filling in the blanks."

"Yeah, Reilly, what the hell's this all about?"

Killelea was speechless upon hearing my theory, but then he promised to find Booth and check it out. Booth's ambitions might skew his reason, but there was no choice, especially with the *Carnival* on the run.

83

With the throttles pulled back, I reduced airspeed, kept a wary eye on the fuel gauges, and fretted over the holes in the fuselage. Back at 1,000 feet, I circled high and wide over the *Carnival* as it continued in a broad splash of white wake toward the coast. Buildings grew rapidly in size, and I searched the horizon for the interceptor.

I looked back just in time to see Shaniqua jump off the bridge. She made a huge splash and then disappeared.

I swung Betty on her side as Shaniqua popped up and started waving frantically. I pushed the stick forward, and peered over my shoulder to check the holes in the fuselage. Rolle shook his head wildly as I counted six holes in a line through the floor. Betty spiraled downward, and I kept my eyes on Shaniqua.

Damn! The *Carnival* had turned back toward her.

A flame burst off the tuna tower aimed toward us, leaving me no choice but to veer off again. I screamed another Mayday to the dispatcher and explained that Shaniqua was in the water.

A long black knife of a boat appeared. It bounced at high speed toward the *Carnival*. It seemed too small. Was it an escape craft or would it rendezvous to off-load their cargo? I steered Betty toward it and realized it was a cigarette-type boat, hauling ass and jumping waves. My breathing eased at the sight of an American flag and an orange stripe on its hull.

When Killelea said they'd send an interceptor, he wasn't kidding. There were four men aboard the vessel, in full battle gear and loaded for bear. My tail numbers were announced by Miami Center, who directed me toward another frequency.

"So now you're Clint Eastwood?" Booth's voice grated.

"An interceptor's approaching the *Carnival,* what are you doing about—"

"Get your butt back to Key West, pronto."

"What about—"

"The offshore races started this morning. Gutierrez was last seen at Oceanside Marina."

"That's where he keeps his racing boat," I said.

"No shit, Sherlock. He hit the water a half-hour ago."

Damn!

"We'll get him, though. The Coasties have a Cutter equipped with helicopters due south of the island."

"Can they catch him?"

"They'd blow him out of the water except for one slight complication."

"I'm in no mood for riddles."

"He's got two people on board. One's a friend of yours, I think. That hot blond number from the La Concha."

My jaw landed on my chest. *No!*

A fast glance at the interceptor told me Shaniqua's fate was in their hands. I turned Betty on a dime, and instantly changed course over the mainland for Key West.

The hell with restricted airspace. I had to get home, and fast.

"You said two. Who's the other one?"

"His race navigator, Emilio Garcia, another hostage."

"Emilio? Check him out, if he's a waiter at El Aljibe, he's no—"

"Don't give me orders, Reilly, this is *my* investigation!"

I heaved a big sigh. "I'll be at Key West International in thirty minutes. Have someone there to collect the souvenir I brought you from the Bahamas."

"You get—"

I changed frequencies back to my trusty control tower at the southernmost airport. "Come in, Key West, this is Grumman-one-seven-four-one-November, do you read me?"

"Damn, Buck, thought we'd seen the last of you."

"Likewise, Donny. I'm on my way and in a hell of a hurry. The police will be there in a half-hour."

"Turning yourself in?"

"Hell no, dropping off some dirty laundry. Ray Floyd handy?"

A few moments passed and we were treetop flying over the everglades, no doubt setting off every radar installation in Southern Florida.

"I've been looking for you on television," Ray Floyd said.

"Lifestyles of the Formerly Rich and Famous?"

"America's Most Wanted."

Good old Ray. "Listen, can you to do me a favor?" I astonished him with the news about Manny Gutierrez, and that he and Blue Guayabara Boy had Karen hostage. Their connection still had my head spinning.

"Damn, son, you *do* know how to pick 'em."

"Call Lenny for me. Have him meet me at the airport in fifteen minutes. No excuses and no bullshit."

"You forming a posse?"

"You got it, partner."

A lone white egret took flight under my wings, thirty feet above its mangrove lair. My heart ached for Karen, and if Gutierrez hurt her, I'd close out his flea market myself. She'd been concerned about his interest in me, and I encouraged her to go aboard his racing boat.

And now Karen was his human shield, just as Shaniqua had been. If he sanctioned killing missionaries, Karen's fate would be no different. I had to dump Rolle, pick up Lenny, and get after Gutierrez before he hurt her. My heart was ablaze as we streaked to the southwest. To hell with my B/B ratio.

Redline
to Ruin

84

Webbed mangrove tufts spread out below like giant green hippopotami wading in the creamy green water. Intermittent dark clouds hung low over the Keys. I followed the islands toward their end, where uncertainty awaited. Small kitschy enclaves sporting odd names like Islamorada, Ramrod, Big Pine, Sugarloaf, and Saddle Bunch were flashes out my port window. Every one of the thirty minutes it took to reach Key West increased my heart rate.

As we leveled off on our approach, helicopters hovered above the island like buzzards circling road kill. Channel 4, CNN, Channel 56… Maybe the politicians had embraced the media's hype, and the pre-emptive doctrine had reached the point of no return.

Betty's wheels hit with a definitive thud, and we taxied toward a small group of uniforms at the end of the runway. Once there, I turned Betty around to face downwind. The moment the RPM's dropped, the group rushed toward the plane like a swarm of paparazzi. I left the engines running and climbed into the fuselage where I met eyes with Rolle. His nose was a swollen mess and there was dried blood on his cheeks, but he stared back defiantly.

"This is your stop."

The small hole in the duct tape that covered his mouth restricted his ability to reply, but his eyes said enough. I dragged him to the hatch, where tape still covered the window.

"Give my regards to Chango."

The door lifted and Booth was there with balled fists on his hips. Before he could say a word I thrust Rolle out the hatch like a bag of trash. He landed on the federal agent, who shrieked under his weight, and both collapsed to the ground.

"Sorry about your invasion," I said.

KWPD officers scrambled to grab their prize, and Lenny materialized from behind them. Ray Floyd gave me a nod and trotted around the starboard side of the plane, pulling a roll of duct tape from his pocket as he passed. He quickly put it to good use.

"You know how to make an entrance, man." Lenny had to scream to be heard over the roaring props. "Who the hell was that all tied up?"

"Get in and shut the hatch."

Booth struggled to get off the ground. His eyes were fixed on the closing door.

"That's your ass, Reilly, don't you—"

The snug fit of the hatch spared us the rest of his threats. "Buckle up in back. We've got no time to waste."

85

Betty gained momentum down the runway and
Booth kept pace alongside the first thirty-feet, shaking his fists and screaming.
We lifted off over the palm trees lining A1A as the wheels pulled into their wells.

"Damn, boy, you one fucking crazy cracker!" The volume of his voice nearly
burst my eardrums. "This shit better not ruin my political career."

"Hang on, we've got a lot of water to cover and damn little time."

"Where the hell we going?"

"Rat hunting." I switched frequencies back to the Coast Guard and asked the
operator to forward me to Killelea's cell.

"Who the hell's that?" Lenny asked.

"The plumber that's going to clear Booth's shit out of my life."

The faint ring in my headset was interrupted by Lenny's voice. "What's with
the duct tape on the windows?"

"Killelea here."

"I dumped Rolle in Key West. Where's Gutierrez?"

"Headed straight for Cuban waters."

Just what I was afraid of. "How far out is he?"

"Gutierrez, say what?" Lenny said.

"About twenty-five miles from the Cuban fourteen-mile limit, doing eighty
miles an hour and ignoring the Coast Guard's hail."

"How far away's the *Mohawk*?"

"Fifty miles, but they've got helicopters in pursuit."

"Can you patch me through to Frank Nardi?"

"What the hell for?"

"Franko, dude we play hoop with?" Lenny said.

"You don't need to be bothering—"

"I'm on my way and I want Gutierrez's twenty!"

"Absolutely not, Reilly. Get your butt back to—"

"A good friend of mine's the hostage on board, I'm not going to let her get hurt."

"Karen?" Lenny asked.

"There's a two-hundred-person Coast Guard cutter bearing down on them!"

"They'll never make it. Listen, Killelea, I will *not* sit back and watch this go down. If he gets away, I'll… I'll…."

"Hold on, goddamnit. You get yourself killed it's your own fool fault."

"What about the *Carnival*?"

"In custody after a brief battle."

"The girl?"

"We fished her out."

"And?"

"Tough as nails, prettier than—"

"Shaniqua?" Lenny said. "The hell you guys talking about—Gutierrez, Karen?"

"He's behind killing the missionaries and all the Santeria crap. Now he's snatched Karen and is headed for Cuba. All the bullshit bravado was just that, bullshit."

"You really CIA, man?"

"Gutierrez is a Cuban mole, a spy, burrowed in deep to keep Havana informed. And no, I'm just a pissed-off charter pilot."

"Kiss my Conch ass." Lenny pulled his lap belt tighter.

"If what their Director of State Security said is true, and the president leverages the media's coverage to do something stupid, Cuba's set to retaliate throughout the U.S."

"Who was that dude you dumped?"

"Scar."

A beep sounded in my ear and a Coast Guard communications officer aboard the *Mohawk* transferred me to the ship's bridge, no questions asked. Another officer answered and hesitated at my request to speak to Nardi.

"Tell him it's Buck Reilly and I'm halfway to Cuba in pursuit."

My compass reflected the same course I'd flown several bruises ago, it being the most direct line to Havana.

"This the asshole passing himself off as CIA?"

"The son of a bitch in that speedboat has my friend prisoner, Frank."

Lenny suddenly keyed in on the microphone. "More like his *girl*friend, man."

"Lenny Jackson? You fellas are a long way from Douglas Community Center."

"Give me a GPS mark, Frank, I'm closer to Gutierrez than you are."

"We've got helicopters armed with heat-seeking missiles, he won't get away."

"You can't shoot him, Karen's on board!"

"I've got orders, Reilly, he's a Cuban spy—"

"Worth a hell of a lot more alive."

The pause felt endless. Nardi had to be weighing the trouble he'd get into if he told me. I held my breath.

"He's only fifteen miles from their waters, you'll never—oh, screw it. They're at 23.7 degrees north by 82.2 degrees west on a heading of 186."

I punched in the coordinates into the GPS, and the machine mapped a course within seconds. We were already damn close to being on target.

"Keep the line open," I said.

86

Lenny rubbed his palms together, a broad grin on his face. The news about Shaniqua was manna from heaven.

"What's the plan, Commander?"

"I've got no idea." My eyes were fixed on the horizon, anxious to see Gutierrez's ocean racer in the distance.

"What the hell should I be doing, then?"

"Peel some duct tape off the windows and cover the bullet holes on the floor."

"*Bullet holes!* They been shooting at you?"

"Ray Floyd put tape on the outside."

"Tape? We ain't landing out here, right? Tape won't hold out shit, man."

Was that a faint trace of spent wake in the blue water? What appeared to be gnats inside my windshield was a pair of helicopters in the distance. The boat! With both of Betty's tachometers pressed to their red lines, we were gaining fast.

"You there, Reilly?" It was Frank Nardi.

"I'm closing in."

"We're running out of time, and there's another problem. Radar identified a Cuban Navy ship on their territorial line. Looks like they're waiting for him."

"How far out?"

"Seven miles and closing fast."

The throttles were pressed into the headliner, and the airspeed indicator quivered at 210 knots per hour. The engines were operating dangerously beyond capacity, and the airspeed was in excess of the airframe's rating. Betty's sixty-year-old body could break apart at any second.

"The choppers aren't doing shit, Frank. Tell them to get out of my way."

"What the hell can you do in that old bird?"

"Widgeons were torpedo planes in World War II."

"You have a *torpedo?*"

"*We* got a torpedo?"

I was locked in on the black speedboat, and my altimeter was dropping fast. Nardi must have warned the helicopters, because they parted in opposite directions as we bore down like a cruise missile. There were large spiders painted on the back of the boat along with some cursive writing that was illegible. It might as well have said murdering, thieving, kidnapping spy, but in my eyes it said *target*.

"Buck?" Lenny shouted.

"Five miles from Cuban waters," Nardi said. "The helicopters have orders to disable the boat before it reaches the line. That's less than five minutes from now."

Betty roared ten feet over top of the speedboat at two hundred miles an hour. The boat shifted suddenly to the left after we shot past them. Hopefully I'd given Gutierrez a heart attack.

"Lenny!" I shouted into the mike. "Open up the back locker and grab every loose item you see."

He jumped out of his seat without question, confirming my instinct about having him join me.

"Hold on!"

I banked hard to the left and did a sharp 180-degree chandelle turn that put me on a nose-to-nose course with the surging ocean racer. With Lenny in the back, Betty's turning was sluggish, the center of gravity thrown off just enough to impair performance.

"Hurry up!"

"Four miles!" Nardi's shout pierced my ears.

The distance closed fast. I counted three figures in the boat's enclosed cockpit. Maybe it was the black color, but the shape reminded me of the Batmobile. Perfect for a megalomaniac like Gutierrez. He swerved again as we blew past.

"I've got some shit, man, what do you want me to do?" Lenny said.

I stomped on the right pedal, and the rudder pulled us hard that way. Our airspeed dropped and I pulled back on the yoke. Lenny crashed into the wall.

"When I straighten out, open the hatch halfway. Remember, if you open it too far, I won't be able to use the flaps, and we'll yard-dart into the ocean. Use one of the bungee cords on the kayak to lock the hatch in place."

"Then what?"

"What have you got?"

"Your duffel bag, the magna-whatever-you-call-it, a basketball-sized wad of police-line tape, and an anchor."

I dropped Betty back down into position behind the boat.

"All right, open the hatch. When I say so, drop the duffel."

"Right!"

Twenty feet above the water's surface, Betty's nose was aimed up the rear of the boat like a dog sniffing out a bitch in heat. We closed the gap quickly, and at the last second I yelled, "Now!"

I couldn't see what happened but sensed the boat shift course again.

"Missed!" Lenny yelled.

We climbed and turned sharply. Gutierrez changed course, and his boat catapulted off the wave tips and flew through the air before tacking back toward the invisible line that meant freedom for him and death for Karen.

"Three miles!"

"Keep those helicopters out of here!"

"What next, Buck?"

"Get the anchor ready."

Betty dropped down and glided smoothly over the surface like a duck over a Canadian lake. Gutierrez's sneering face peered up through his windshield.

"Four...three...two... NOW!"

Lenny dropped the anchor twenty feet ahead of the boat.

"I hit him! I hit the son of a bitch!"

With the turnaround and drop procedure now perfected, we again came up behind him. There was a hole in one of the engine covers, but he hadn't slowed a bit.

"Two miles, Reilly! The Cuban Navy ship's radioing warnings of its intention to defend their frontier. They'll shoot you down if you get too close. Back off, we're running out of time, the helicopters need to finish the job."

Visions of my Cuban incarceration flashed through my head. I'd be damned if Sanchez would get the best of me again. If Gutierrez got away now, an invasion would be unstoppable.

"Get ready with the magnetometer, Lenny."

My treasure maps were gone, and my old man's puzzles were unsolvable, and Gutierrez and Emilio had to be Bush and Clinton, which meant I'd never see my pouch again. I bit down with a force that could powder my molars and felt a hot sensation on my cheeks. The taste of salt stung my lips.

"Three...two... NOW!"

We lifted off the boat and began to climb before Lenny could report if he'd scored a hit. The magnetometer didn't have enough weight to matter.

"I'm out of ammo, man, what are we going to do?"

I continued south and saw the Cuban Navy vessel looming large on the horizon. Gutierrez was ninety seconds from safety, destined to be greeted in Havana as a Hero of the Revolution. The thought twisted my gut, but not nearly as much as failing Karen. She had to be terrified, watching my feeble attempts to stop them, enduring Gutierrez's certain laughter at yet another Buck Reilly mishap.

"One mile! The helicopters are launching missiles in thirty seconds. Clear out, Reilly, or the heat seekers will nail your ass instead of the boat. That's an order!"

"Buck!" Lenny shouted. "I've got an idea. Try one more pass, make it slow."

"Right."

I didn't ask any questions, just dropped the nose and cut the rudder hard left, aiming for the water in front of the speedboat.

"All right, Lenny, he's closing in," I said.

I heard him struggling with something behind me, but we were too close to the water's surface for me to risk a glance back.

"The missiles will be launched in ten seconds, clear out now!"

"Ready, Lenny? Four...three...two...GO!"

"Bombs away, baby!"

The boat suddenly swerved.

"Got him! Oh, shit...Ohhh shit, ohhh—"

"What happened?"

"I skewered him with the kayak, man, right through the windshield."

"And?"

"They flipped, Buck, the boat flipped." Lenny's voice was a whisper.

87

The ocean racer was on its side. There was no sign
of movement. Our airspeed had dropped to eighty miles per hour, and as anxious
as I was to find Karen, it would be suicidal to repeat the same landing mistakes
that almost sank Betty in Bimini. We bounced hard onto the water's surface and
the props cut into the waves, which shot prop wash in all directions. The boat was
a quarter-mile ahead.

A deafening explosion, then a geyser of water erupted fifty feet away from the
foundering boat.

"Nardi! Call off the dogs, the boat's dead in the water. Cease fire, goddamnit!"

"Abort missiles!" Nardi's voice screamed in my headset.

"They're upside down." Lenny's voice was a whisper.

"If you hadn't scored with the kayak, they'd be on that Cuban Navy ship by
now."

Another cannon round landed seventy feet off our nose. I squeezed the microphone button so hard it nearly broke the stick in half.

"Nardi, cut the shit! That one almost hit us!"

"We're not firing, neither are the choppers."

"What the hell?" Lenny pulling the fuzz out of his chin.

"Got to be the Cubans," I said. The black hull of the ocean racer was starting
to sink into the purple water. "Nardi, you hear me?"

"Ten-four, Reilly, what's the boat's status?"

"Bow down and sinking fast. And the Cubans are shooting at us! Where the hell are the helicopters?"

"On their way."

"Do something about the damn Cubans!"

Another round landed off our starboard side. I glanced at Lenny, expecting terror, but saw fierce determination instead.

"Here's the deal," I said. "We'll be to the boat in thirty seconds, I'm going in after them."

"What about the plane?"

"You've got the helm."

"I can't—"

"The foot pedals steer your direction. Use the throttles to make a quick one-eighty turn back into the waves. By the time you get back, I'll have Karen."

"What throttles, where the hell—" He searched the cockpit, his eyes frantic.

"You've driven a boat, right?" He stared at me. "It's the same concept. Think of Betty as a twin-engine boat, and these are her throttles."

I tapped the twin metal handles extending down from the ceiling. His complexion had a sickly cast, but there was no other choice. I was going in after Karen. If Betty sank, she sank.

I got out of my seat just as another cannon round landed off our port side. The explosion and plume of water shot high above us. The Cubans were zeroing in, and if the *Mohawk* couldn't stop them, we'd soon be vaporized.

"Damn!" Lenny yelled. "You better hurry up!"

The hatch was still half open, and I sat on the edge. The fabric of the sky tore with the shriek of another round coming in. It hit just behind the plane. Water blasted inside the open hatch and drenched me.

"Nardi!" I screamed into the sky.

"Here it is, Buck, you better hurry, man, I ain't seen shit moving."

I dove into the water. The cold shocked me. The screaming engines launched water pellets at my face like shards of glass. I ducked under as Betty lumbered past. Another shell struck the water and ripped me back to the surface in a concussion of roiling wake. My arms pumped into the waves, and I dug hard toward the boat.

The black hull gleamed in the sunshine. The sudden taste of gasoline choked me, with vapors burning my eyes. I swam through a slick of fuel that if ignited would burn the boat and me to a crisp. The air filled with another wail of cannon fire, but in a different pitch. The shell screamed past and landed off the bow of the Cuban Navy ship a half-mile away.

I pulled myself on top of the capsized hull and shimmied toward the bow, which was almost completely under water. I dove down and found the door handle just below the surface. I swam into the cockpit, only to find it engulfed in a cloud of bloody water.

No!

The kayak was wedged through the windshield. It had impaled the person in the closest seat. I couldn't see who it was because of their helmet. Somebody else was moving in the middle—Karen!

Her helmet was off, her face pressed up into the corner of what had been the floor but was now the ceiling. Gutierrez was gone.

I swam to the other side, reached in and grabbed her leg. She swung toward me, her eyes bugged wide.

"Buck!"

"This way, let's go!"

"I can't move, my seat belt's crushed together."

The boat shifted in the water, and the door I'd entered was now completely immersed. The air bubble sustaining Karen was getting smaller by the second. I dug in my pocket for my knife—something grabbed my leg! An incredible tug dragged me out the door. We bobbed to the surface.

Gutierrez!

"You!"

He dove at me, and a blurred silver slash grazed my forehead. Blood squirted down into my eye. His arm swung back, and there was a huge knife in his hand. Instinct took over and I dove away from the next strike. Karen was sinking into oblivion, and this lunatic's thirst for revenge was now aimed at me.

"You ruined everything!" His voice was an angry shriek.

A cannon shell landed in the water near us, and its concussion rocked the speedboat over further. Gutierrez swung again, but this time I deflected the blow and counter-attacked with a right jab that caught him square on the nose. His eyes crossed for a second, and he must have inhaled water, because he started gagging. I attacked his wrist with a chop, and the knife fell from his grasp.

I dove back under and swam toward the open door. Just as I pulled my knife out of my pocket, Gutierrez caught my arm and knocked the knife away. The shining blade spiraled into the depths.

Bastard!

We crashed together in a death grip. I felt his fingernails dig into my neck, searching for my juggler. He landed a punch across my ear, but anger deflected the pain. I summoned an uppercut from twenty leagues beneath the sea that connected under his chin and lifted him out of the water. His body was limp before it splashed down.

A giant air bubble broke the water's surface. The boat was almost fully submerged. I kicked with all my strength back toward the boat's open door, now ten feet under water. Inside, Karen's face was pressed into the now Frisbee-sized air bubble. She was frozen with panic. I sucked in as little of the air as possible, pulled myself back down her seat belt, and pushed Emilio's limp leg aside to reach for the mangled—something caught my eye.

Under Emilio's leg was the edge of a yellow, plastic—*Yes!*

Karen's squirming pulled at the seat belt in my hand, but my attention was fixed on the yellow, waterproof—I let go of the seat belt and pulled the corner of... my pouch!

Something hit the side of my head. I lost half my air thinking Gutierrez had returned.

It was Karen, convulsing wildly. With my lungs burning, I dove back on the belt. My knife would have cut the webbing like butter, but now I had to improvise.

Only seconds of air remained. I willed every ounce of strength, determination, and rage to attack the handle. Twisted badly, the button hung from its spring, useless.

I pulled at the belt with both hands until my lungs felt ablaze.

The movement of light through the waves sent splintered shadows through the cockpit, or was it Gutierrez choosing the best angle for his next attack?

Back up to the bubble, there was one last breath for each of us. My eyes met Karen's. Her expression made it clear her life was in my hands. I launched a final assault on the handle, but this time instead of brute force, felt around the crumpled metal until I found a break in the seam that held it together.

Karen flailed next to me, her air spent.

The depleted oxygen in my chest felt like an acetylene torch. I dug my fingers into the broken gap and ripped it apart like an oyster. The handle crumbled in my hands, and the belt came free as the boat slowly rotated onto its side.

Karen struggled violently as I grabbed her around the waist and dragged her toward the door, now pointed toward the ocean floor. All I could see was deep blue. The boat was now entirely under water, and sinking fast. Instinct had Karen kicking upwards toward the light, but we had to first go down and out through the—my pouch!

It had floated to the top of the cabin and was pressed against the far door, ten feet away. My hand was wedged in Karen's belt. She fought me, now swimming down toward the open door.

Stretch! I couldn't hold her and reach the pouch. My maps…the key!

Regret filled my every cell, but there was no choice.

The light of the sun glistened through the seemingly endless distance to the surface. A wave broke above. Were those Gutierrez's kicking feet? He'd be waiting, but could I… Manic fear fueled the cauldron in my chest, afire with spent oxygen. As I rose upward with a few hard kicks, my senses faded to black.

89

Light hurt my eyes and the sound of coughing
jarred me. I was...in Karen's arms on the surface. I sprang from her grasp, and
searched wildly around us.

"Where is he?"

"What are you—are you all right?" she said.

Gutierrez had vanished.

The shriek of a cannon shell tore over our heads, followed by three others.
The explosions were nearly on top of us. The Cuban vessel was closing fast. I
shoved my head under water. Gutierrez's boat looked like a small toy sinking into
the darkness of a bottomless pool.

A loud buzz roared up behind us—Betty was bearing down fast. Lenny's
eyes were wide in the windshield. Beyond them, the horizon seemed filled by the
Coast Guard Cutter *Mohawk* at full steam. A naval battle was about to explode
all around us.

I yanked Karen's arm. "Come on!"

We swam hard toward Lenny, who to his credit held Betty straight and
pointed right at us. The props were perilously close to the water's surface, and in
order to reach the trailing rope ladder, we had to swim down the fuselage.

Karen followed me between the propellers that would carve us into mince-
meat if a wave pushed us inches off course. The sound of the twelve cylinders

roared, which combined with the sting of water from the props was disorienting, but I kept the hatch in sight and kicked for it with every remaining ounce of strength, clutching Karen around her waist.

Betty had slowed, but the hatch still shot past us. I dove for the trailing rope ladder, caught it with one finger, and clasped my hand around it. The pull from Karen on my other arm spread me to the point of splitting in half. A scream of determination gave me strength as I hauled her in. She kicked and grabbed hold.

She pulled herself up into the plane and disappeared head first inside the cabin. I crawled up and collapsed on top of her.

"We're gonna die!" Lenny screamed from the pilot's seat.

I crawled through the fuselage, which now contained several inches of water. The duct tape over the bullet holes had given out. Soon we'd be too heavy to take off.

"Close that hatch!"

Lenny slid over to the right seat. "Get us the hell out of here!"

I took quick stock of the situation. The Cuban Navy boat was bearing down at a speed that indicated their intent to ram us.

A splash caught my eye.

Gutierrez was swimming hard toward the Cuban ship, stopping every few strokes to wave his arms at them.

Bursts of flame detonated toward us, and a machine gun round blasted out my vent window.

I shoved the throttles down, and the RPM's leapt toward the red line. Betty jumped forward like a racehorse in response to an open gate. A hard stomp on the pedals turned us to the right, parallel with the waves, but there wasn't enough room to take off. The Cubans were blocking our path. Columns of water erupted in front of Betty's nose. Their deck guns were honing in.

The waves rocked us, and the props shot water in the blown-out vent window until Betty was turned into the waves, but the *Mohawk* threatened to block our runway.

"Hold on, this is going to be tight!"

With the throttles maxed, Betty shimmied in the surf, bounced, and heeled until we got up on the step. My eyes shifted from the *Mohawk* in front of us to the tachometers and airspeed indicator slowly edging clockwise.

"Reilly, what the hell are you doing?" Frank Nardi shouted in my headset.

What felt like the longest run-up since the Wright Brothers ran across the Kitty Hawk dunes finally ended when the airspeed indicators kissed 62-mph. I yanked the stick back, hit the flaps, and Betty jumped free of the ocean's pull.

The *Mohawk*'s superstructure filled my windshield. I pulled back on the yoke until our rate of climb threatened a stall.

Too close to bank, I held course. We cleared their tower by inches.

Lenny was a lump of nerves next to me, his eyes squeezed shut. Karen shot me a million-dollar smile. Her eyes sparkled in the sun pouring in between the strips of duct tape on the back windows.

It felt like an eternity since our kiss at Margaritaville. She pointed out the window at the red float hanging under the starboard wing, then mouthed the words: "Take me home, flyboy."

I pointed to the headset next to her and she pulled it onto her dripping blond head. Her laugh was like champagne bubbles after a freshly popped cork.

"I knew you'd show up, don't ask me why, but I knew in my heart knew you'd come."

The image of my pouch, floating trapped in Gutierrez's boat, tugged at me, but was eased by Karen's smile.

It no longer mattered.

Karen wasn't my beauty to rescue, it was she who'd rescued me.

90

The celebration upon our return was brief, cut short by Booth's intercepting me on the tarmac. His revenge-driven demeanor killed my excitement. Whether or not the facts behind what happened aboard the *Carnival* would reduce the pressure for action against Cuba remained to be seen, but Shaniqua and Karen were home safe, Jackson Rolle, Perez and No-Name were in custody, Emilio dead and Gutierrez vanished at sea.

Booth allowed me a brief hug from Karen before ordering me into the airport parking lot.

"Where's your Rover?"

No use in lying. "Back of the lot."

"Let's go."

As we passed glistening rental cars, the sound of my heart reverberated like fan blades in my ears.

"Keys?"

I dug into my backpack and held up the single key. My hand was shaking.

"I don't want it," he said. "Get in."

"What's going on?"

"Just drive. Go around the beach over there."

Booth rolled down his window, and loosened his tie. I bit my tongue. At least we weren't headed to the KWPD station. Yet.

"All right, let's hear it," he said.

"What?"

"The story. Your evidence on Gutierrez. You damn near started a war today, based on whatever crap you came up with."

"His running for Cuba only substantiated—"

"Oh, yeah, that'll look good in my report to the director of the FBI, the one the president of the United States is expecting any minute. 'The guy ran, so he must be guilty.' You better have more than that, Reilly."

Booth's expression was that of a tight-wire walker, confident overall, yet a discernible hint of fear. I enjoyed the pause, watching him—

"*Well?*"

"He was the rat behind killing the missionaries. My guess is that it was to fund a spy operation in Key West."

"Your *guess?* And what possible reason for killing—"

"The Cubans were smuggling him valuable art to ply the emotions of the Cuban- American community and raise hard currency. When the *Carnival's* mission went awry, Gutierrez kept attention off himself by using Palo Mayombe and diverted it to Santeria through his operative Emilio Garcia, the other guy on the boat."

His mouth curled into a sneer. "*Voodoo* is your evidence?"

"*Carnival,* the name of the boat, San Alejandro, the name of the limited liability corporation that owned the boat, and *The Jungle,* the name of the reproduction painting in the front window of Gutierrez's gallery that was painted by Wilfredo Lam, were all tied together in the Cuban art world."

"Fucking art? Everyone knows he was an art dealer."

I took my eye off the road long enough to look at Booth. "You came to Key West to investigate a smuggling ring, right? What was being smuggled?"

He bit his lip, holding back…what? A smile?

"Jackson Rolle confessed that they were smuggling relics, which is another word for paintings and sculpture," I said. "Just like the rare paintings mysteriously available ninety-miles north of Havana. The Cubans are too broke to send cash, so they fritter away their national treasures so they can be ready to start a terrorist war here if—"

"All right, Magnum, I've heard enough." He dug in his pocket and lit a smoke. "You know, Reilly, for a tomb raider and inside trader, you actually showed some decent investigative skills."

He spoke while looking out the window, blowing smoke at the girls on the beach. The statement was so far a field from the anticipated Miranda rights it was all I could do to shift the Rover's gears.

"I *was* down here investigating an art smuggling ring, but found you and cracked an espionage network to boot." He couldn't keep the smile off his face.

"Don't let that go to your head, though, you're still a bankrupt suspected criminal, as far as the laws concerned, but maybe, just maybe, I might have use for you every now and then."

I couldn't even manage a grunt.

"Getting to be an assistant director ain't easy. You need innovative thinking, you need to have developed assets. God knows I hate this wretched island anyway. You and that airplane proved pretty handy sticking your nose places I can't, as a federal officer, but under my direction...."

He was sounding more like Sanchez by the moment.

"Why would I—"

"I'll tell you why, Reilly." The smile slid into the familiar sneer. "Remember when I went to Washington after the bomb was found on your plane? That's when I met the director for the first time and received his personal commendation for discovering the *Carnival* in Havana. For that, we're even on your pissing away my life savings at e-Antiquity."

I swallowed hard. The tone in his voice indicated anything but gratitude.

"After that I had some time to kill before returning to this stink rock, so I paid a visit to a friend of yours."

The smile was back. My hands tightened on the wheel.

"Mrs. Jack Dodson."

Oh shit...

"When she heard you were on house arrest in Key West, she got indignant, Reilly, in fact she had some interesting things to say. She wanted to know who would pay her bills if you were in jail too. She said you and her husband had a deal." He reached into his pocket and pulled out a piece of paper. "She even gave me this."

It was a copy of a check from Fox Run Farm. "That's your brother's signature, Reilly, implicating him in your conspiracy to commit fraud against the Government."

"I...I...."

Booth laughed. "Then, someone left this at my hotel." It was the first page of my ledger, detailing a couple hundred thousand dollars of payments to the Dodson's. "Like I said, hot shot, I own your ass. It wouldn't take much to expose you and your brother's bankruptcy scam, or lean on Dodson, and then you could join him at Leavenworth."

"What do you want, Booth?"

"You stay down here, living the life of Reilly, pun intended, playing charter pilot and part-time treasure hunter, but when I call, you drop everything. I say 'roll over' you do it, I throw you a bone, you fetch. My private operative, *capiche*?"

My pride swelled with a dozen different retorts telling him what he could shove, swallow, eat, or do to himself, but an uncharacteristic restraint held me back as surely as if someone had their hand over my mouth.

"If you tell anyone about this, I'll deny it and throw your ass to the wolves. But if and when sufficient evidence turns up on your parent's case, I might let the judge know you'd been helpful, provided you were, but you'd still go down, this isn't any kind of pardon or anything. Consider it a *stay* of prosecution." He glanced over at me.

I dropped Booth off at the KWPD station, a smile on his lips as my parting gift. Still, a lot different from what I expected. A couple of turns later and I was smack in the middle of the parade launching the Old Island Days Festival. I half expected to see Karen, still soaking wet, hanging from a bungee chord from the top of the La Concha.

Some special event Gutierrez had turned out to be.

Numb from the past hours, days, and weeks, still wet, with dried blood caked on my forehead and wearing two-day old clothes, I must have looked like the Chain Saw murderer to the people in the hotel lobby.

The numbness wore off at the realization that the adventure wasn't over, only taking a new turn. There would be other battles to fight, but for now I just wanted a shower, a cold beer, and to start making a list of potential clues to crack the results of the last key word: CICEROSMUSE = LOVE OF HIS LIFE.

I scanned the lobby. But first, where was mine?

91

Laughter rang hollow in my ears as I studied the packed crowd inside Blue Heaven from the corner of the ring. My bout with Bruiser Lewis was a macabre form of dinner theater for them, for me a meal ticket. Bright lights shone down from the banyan tree, illuminating the ring and casting odd limb-shaped shadows over the tables where wild chickens foraged on crumbs. My opponent had yet to arrive. Maybe, just maybe, he wouldn't show.

The week since rescuing Karen felt like a month, and the twice postponed Saturday night had finally come. The *Carnival* had been packed to the gills with Cuban paintings, sculpture, and relics, but it was Shaniqua's wink and smile in the middle of the crowd below, where she was nestled closely to her father, that made the boat's capture more valuable than the gold-laden *Esmeralda*. She blew me a kiss, and I felt my cheeks flush.

I avoided Karen's emerald eyes. She was just a foot away, leaning onto the lower rope watching Ray Floyd rub liniment into my legs. Our return to Key West had synthesized into a spontaneous combustion that exceeded even my active imagination, interrupted only by her frenzied schedule of special events during the now concluded festival.

"The corner man's the hidden secret behind most successful boxers," Ray said. "Left to their own devices, most warriors of the ring dwindle into bloody lumps of scar tissue and—" Ray's jaw fell open.

Bruiser had arrived. His entourage encircled him, and his brother Truck brought up the rear. I hadn't seen Truck since our return from Cuba, and I'd never seen Bruiser through sober eyes. The Gargoyles, pressed into duty as ticket takers, stood up and started to clap. I swallowed hard. Karen followed Ray's rapture to my opponent. I tried to ignore her sharp intake of breath.

The cacophony escalated when the crowd realized all combatants were present and accounted for.

"Ladies and gentlemen…" Lenny was in the middle of the ring, wearing a Salvation Army rhinestone coat left over from a distant Fantasy Fest. He held his arms wide and exaggerated his expressions in his best imitation of a boxing promoter. I still hadn't forgiven him after he confessed having placed the white candle—for safety— under Betty's port wing before I took Truck and the boys to Cuba. He pranced around like Mick Jagger, he looked like a man whose aspirations to be Key West's mayor seemed bizarre, yet appropriate.

"Tonight's event is about to begin!"

I tuned out the hype and focused on the training I began at the YMCA as a teenager, honed to moderate success in Golden Gloves competition, and now hoped to dust off after a five-year hiatus. My game had once been multi-faceted; I'd been able to pummel inferior foes or dance around like a guerrilla warrior. Those days had been filled with miles of running, whereas tonight would depend upon cunning.

The crowd reverberated like a swarm of cicadas. Currito Salazar was at a back table with men huddled in close. I noted the exchange of currency. Frank Nardi sat next to Karen, drinking beer and laughing with Lieutenant Killelea at her persistent questions. A steady bongo beat led me to Enrique, the Stock Island Sancho, seated at a crowded table. I hoped he hadn't resented my refusal of a jock strap laced with beads in my old friend Chango's colors.

My visual circuit ended at the opposite end of the ring, where Bobby Barrett, the photographer from the *Key West Citizen,* was poised on a barstool. His camera hung from his neck, and his eyes shied away from mine. He'd gratefully accepted the invitation to meet next week for the overdue flight I'd bartered in exchange for the pictures that led to learning Jackson Rolle's and Emilio's identities.

The *Citizen's* story covering the case of the missing missionaries had been picked up by *USA TODAY.* It detailed Gutierrez's history of being funded by Cuba to create an art empire, the proceeds of which fueled covert cells around South Florida. Ironic that the Cuban Americans who detested the Cuban regime were inadvertently supporting their spying efforts here. The story also described the fiasco aboard the *Carnival* that blew the spy ring apart and noted the discovery of a prenda at Gutierrez's gallery, cementing him to Palo. Once all the facts were known, the "Cuban conspiracy" dwindled like a pierced balloon, leaving only Mingie Posada still crying for retribution, with

El Aljibe indefinitely closed down by the health department for cruelty to animals.

Booth wound up a hero, taking credit for busting up the smuggling ring, cracking a spy case, and defusing the rush to war. There was no mention of me at all, which suited me fine. Frank Nardi was quoted on the duel with the patrol boat that ended when the Cubans rescued Gutierrez and high-tailed it back to Havana. *Granma*, the Cuban State-owned newspaper, proclaimed Gutierrez a hero who'd single-handedly repelled a U.S. Coast Guard cutter and the inevitable invasion. He was decorated for bravery and installed as a senior officer within State Security. As for me, my fragile deal with Booth was quite the surprise, but my freedom was worth the occasional errand for him. It might even be interesting. My stash and GPS, however, along with the coordinates to the *Esmeralda*, were lost at sea.

Maybe I wouldn't tell the Park Service about the gold, just yet.

With Karen's help I had exhausted every thought on the last clue: LOVE OF HIS LIFE, with none hitting the mark. Nothing from Hemingway, Jefferson, Vigenère, Cicero, Caesar or any of the others resulted in a five-letter name or anything that came close to a clue that made sense.

Willy had stuck to his word, and the $10,000 reward went straight to Ray Floyd to commence the rebuild of Betty's port engine. I was now broke but hopeful at the prospect of earning a few thousand tonight.

The canvas sagged when Bruiser climbed in. I felt Ray's grip tighten on my bicep. "Make that ninety / ten, old buddy." Havana Club rum was on his breath.

I'd hit bottom of the brains end of the B/B Ratio in my trusty trainer's estimation. *Without brains to rein balls, overachievers hit walls.* Floyd's Law was indeed appropriate tonight, if not for my future epitaph in the Key West cemetery.

92

"And now, in the red corner..." Lenny began to whoop the crowd into a frenzy. "Key West's own Conch Cruncher... the Florida Hurricane... Brrooozzerr Lleewwiisssss!"

A strange sense of calm spread through my body. Having been here before, in many rings with other opponents boasting more impressive records, I'd walked away victorious more times then not. The restaurant's sound system suddenly burst to life, the theme to *Rocky* blaring at speaker-bursting capacity.

Lenny was sweating profusely and holding back a grin, clearly enjoying his own stage persona and musical grandiosity.

"And in the blue corner... Key West's newest action hero... the Virginia Vigilante... the Cantankerous Cracker. Wiiiilllldd Bbuuccckkk Rrryyyyllyyy!" He winked at me.

Karen tugged at my calf. She was leaning on the edge of her seat. I took a knee in what must have appeared to be a moment of prayer, because the boisterous crowd suddenly quieted down.

"You okay?" I asked.

She stood and pressed her lips hard against mine. Seconds passed and the crowd began cheering, whistling and clapping. When we finally pulled apart, I couldn't hear her voice over the noise. She repeated herself while pointing toward the Gargoyles, but the crowd's roar overpowered her voice.

"Are you ready to rock and roll?" Lenny I could hear. My attention shifted to Bruiser Lewis, standing in the center of the ring like a Cape buffalo poised to charge.

Ray slapped me on the back. I glanced around to catch his final advice.

"LET'S RUN!"

A bikini-clad transvestite circled the interior of the ring, lifting a large placard with a pink number "1" scribbled on the front. The crowd hooted and hollered at the apparition unique to this boxing community. She mooned the audience before slipping back through the ropes to a gaggle of friends who were holding signs "2" and "3." Hopefully they'd get to take their turns too.

Truck was in the far corner. He was mouthing something to me.

"Fool."

The referee, an elderly bearded man I'd never met before, pulled Bruiser and me together in the center of the ring and held up our gloves.

"Let's have a clean fight, boys. Remember, whether you win or lose, the sun will rise tomorrow." I felt a vague sense of recognition, but couldn't place where.

Lenny crashed a hammer against a bell that had Key West High School painted on it, and the crowd was on their feet. Bruiser lunged forward in a tight crouch, his dark eyes peering through his Everlast gloves. The electrical commands from my brain short-circuited. My feet were leaden on the canvas.

A red orb streaked toward my nose and I ducked in time for it to only graze my ear, a wakeup call that jump-started my dancing feet. I circled around him, standing a good six inches taller, but my 225 pounds fell 50 short of his stout, barrel-chested physique.

The opening seconds sped past with him in constant pursuit, and me trying to control my breathing so I wouldn't hyperventilate and collapse. For his size, he was deceptively fast. He bulled me into a corner and let loose a wicked barrage into my stomach. I connected with left then right crosses, knocking his mouthpiece askew. I skirted his bulk and found clear air, bolstered by the exchange but bent a couple inches lower from the punishment to my ribs.

Stay off the ropes.

Sounds from the crowd pulsed through my brain, then another sound surprised me—Lenny hammered on the bell. The old referee jumped between us and pointed to the corners. I'd survived Round One, now $1,000 richer.

Karen's seat was empty. Sitting on the stool in the corner, I put my head in my hands.

"Dear God, man, don't let that beast catch you!" Ray's advice bespoke his experience at fight management, this being his first round ever. I spit out the mouthpiece and between panting breaths guzzled water from a bottle bearing the name *Stolichnaya*.

"Trip him or something, maybe he'll fall and hit his head," Ray said.

Laughter rang out as the next Round Girl, or Guy, pranced around in the ring, dirty dancing with her placard. Lenny waved to Ray, rolling one hand and looking at a stopwatch in the other. A sudden commotion by the door caught my attention. Karen was running back in, waving her arms. She pushed through the packed crowd until she reached the ring, breathless.

"Buck, wait! I figured it out, I mean—listen, maybe your father wrote the clue referring to himself!"

The bell rang and Ray slapped me on the back. "Okay, champ, you've got clearance for takeoff."

I lumbered to my feet in a fog of surprise and confusion. Bruiser was on me instantaneously. My feet suddenly felt lighter than before, and I surprised him by launching myself toward him. He balled up behind blue tattoos on his broad ebony forearms. With my adrenalin coursing at a fevered pitch, I landed a half-dozen blows before he pressed his weight into me and shoved me back into the center of the ring.

Wasting no time, Bruiser switched back to offense, clearly his preferred mode. He mixed body blows with punishing hooks to my neck and shoulders. I protected my head by deflecting the assault with my body, but a growing numbness in my arms sounded an alarm in my besieged brain. My left eyebrow was impeding my sight, which I took to be a glob of Vaseline that had oozed off my forehead. After brushing at it to no effect, I realized I'd been wounded. It just made me more determined.

Fatigue sang a chorus in my body and summoned a tactical sea change. My circuit had been consistently clockwise around the ring with Bruiser in constant pursuit, herding me like a cutting horse toward an unsavory task. When I suddenly reversed direction, I coiled the weight of my body into an upper cut that started at my knee and arced through the halogen light, catching Bruiser dead on his exposed chin.

Surprise filled his eyes for a split second before they fluttered and he reeled backward, bounced off the ropes, spun into the center of the ring, and teetered again. His mouthpiece fell in slow motion toward the canvas.

Years ago I had the killer instinct down to a science, but life's experiences and the lack of ring time had softened my edge. Rather than closing in and hammering at my wounded foe, I watched him with hopeful expectation. A surreal whoosh from the crowd wafted through my ears. I dropped my arms and waited for the massive trunk of a man to fall.

Unfortunately, that proved to be a strategic error in judgment.

A veteran of dozens of battles, most occurring since I'd last donned the gloves, Bruiser had mastered his own technique of self-preservation and resurrection. On his third turn of the corkscrew toward the canvas, he inexplicably accelerated like a discus thrower, levitating up from the depths of defeat.

I was stunned by the sudden eclipse of light when the bright red leather crown of his left glove covered my face like a dinner plate.

The world turned upside down and somewhere in a disassociated cavity of my brain, Karen's epiphany that LOVE OF HIS LIFE might refer to my father struck a final spark. The spelling of my mother's name flickered in the fog: B-E-T-T-Y.

My world faded black to the sound of a steady drumbeat, and the sight of a rooster peering up from underneath the bottom rope a foot away.

He was wearing a smart blue ribbon.

THE END